BLAME THE DEAD

James Card, ex-Army Intelligence but now a professional bodyguard, is in France with Martin Fenwick, a Lloyd's underwriter who is being blackmailed. Fenwick is suddenly and inexplicably ambushed and shot dead. Card naturally feels that his reputation as a bodyguard is not enhanced; he takes the parcel that Fenwick had been carrying and returns to England determined to find out who had caused it all to happen—and why. He soon notices some strange things: Fenwick's widow is remarkably dry-eyed at the funeral but his secretary, Maggie Mackwood, is in tears; Fenwick's business associates are unusually secretive; and when Card opens the mysterious parcel, in which a number of people seem to be abnormally interested, he finds it contains only a copy of the *Bertie Bear Colouring Book*! His investigations lead him away from the maze of London's shipping insurance, via many violent encounters, to the lonely fjords of Norway and to a showdown in the mountains, where he finally learns the truth and also a reason for blaming those who can't answer back—the dead.

THE COMPANION BOOK CLUB

The Club is not a library; all books are the
property of members. There is no entrance
fee or any payment beyond the low Club
price of each book. Details of membership
will gladly be sent on request.
Write to:

The Companion Book Club,
Odhams Books, Rushden, Northants.

Made and printed in Great Britain
for the Companion Book Club
by Odhams (Watford) Ltd.
600871657
8·73/265

BLAME THE DEAD

★

GAVIN LYALL

THE
COMPANION BOOK CLUB
LONDON

BLAME THE DEAD

★

GAVIN LYALL

THE
COMPANION BOOK CLUB
LONDON

This edition, published in 1973 by
The Hamlyn Publishing Group Ltd,
is issued by arrangement with
Hodder and Stoughton Limited.

THE COMPANION BOOK CLUB

*Made and printed in Great Britain
for the Companion Book Club
by Odhams (Watford) Ltd.*
600871657
8·73/265

ONE

YOU COME INTO ARRAS just before six, the broad road shiny lonely in the Sunday twilight. Up the long straight hill of the avenue Michonneau, and because you've got the Guide Michelin open on your lap you warn him for the right turn just at the top. Just after that you're in the Grand Place.

At that time and day and season it looks like the crypt of a forgotten citadel, the rows of parked cars in the middle like stone coffins. Behind a hundred shuttered windows there must be light, warmth, people. There, or on a different planet.

'Where did they say?'

He nods to the right. 'The north-east corner. There.'

'Keep going. Around the far side.'

He keeps going. You make him park so we have a clear run for a fast take-off, because . . . well, just in case. The silence without the car engine and heater is just as you felt it would be. The crunch of the patches of frozen snow as you walk back zigzagging between the other cars is like broken glass. You reach the roadway just about twenty yards from the north-east corner, and still nobody waiting. . . .

I run it like that, over and over, instant slow-motion replay, a constant deliberate bad dream, trying to work out what else I could have done.

There was just the one shot, and maybe I heard the thud as it went into his body. Then I was on my face in the roadway, gun held straight in front, pointing at the last pillar of the arcade. Running footsteps—more than one person, away down the side street from the corner. I scrambled on to my feet, but Fenwick began to groan. And then a nasty gurgling noise.

He'd fallen back in a sitting position against a big Citroen. There was a bit of blood on the front of his overcoat, but my hand came out dripping when I felt around the back. Exit wounds are like that. Half a dozen windows lit up as people opened the shutters, and one brave soul actually leaned out. You don't always do that when you hear a gun-shot in France.

I yelled: 'Police! Telephone! Docteur!' What was the French for Ambulance? Hell, it was a French word already. 'Ombulonz!'

The figure ducked back in, so maybe he'd understood. Fenwick made another nasty noise and now blood was coming from his mouth. What the hell was I supposed to do? If he was bleeding that bad, he was bleeding a lot worse internally. In the end, I held a useless handkerchief to his back and tried to keep his head up until he died. By then I could hear the sirens.

There was a drain grating in the roadway just near by. Just before they got there, I shoved the gun and the belt holster down it. The holster I could buy again, but I'd be lucky to get another Walther PP chambered for ·380. I also had Fenwick's car keys, and when I stood up, I was holding his flat, square package.

Five minutes later, the place was a pool of light from car headlamps parked squintwise all round to block the area off. I was showing an inspecteur who spoke pretty good English just where I thought the shot had come from.

'Just only one?'

'Just one.' He didn't like that. Neither did I, but I wasn't going to offer any opinions.

He peered at the pavement, tapping my passport against his left hand.

'Ah!' He pounced on a tiny glint of brass, back against the wall under the arcade. Then he handed me back my passport and whistled up a sergeant. Between them, they picked up the cartridge case on the end of a pencil and marked the spot with a crayon.

'Neuf millimetres,' said the sergeant—just to show off. The inspecteur gave him a look and he scuttled away, carrying the pencil and cartridge case in front like a little Olympic torch.

The inspecteur said: 'You just met Monsieur Fenwick on the car ferry, then?'

'That's right. He found I was going to Arras, so he offered me a lift. He was going on to Paris, himself.' I don't often get that many lies into three sentences.

But he just nodded. They hadn't searched either me or Fenwick yet—that would come later—so they didn't know about the car keys.

'And why are you in Arras?'

'I was going to look at some First World War battlefields. My grandfather's buried near here.' The second half of that's true, actually.

'You liked him?' he asked innocently.

'Come off it. He was dead fifteen years before I was born.'

His mouth twitched a small smile. It had been a routine trick question. The real interrogation would also come later—and fairly soon, now.

I held up my left hand, still wet with Fenwick's blood. 'Look—can I get the doctor to clean this up?'

He looked around the busy circle of light. The ambulance was still waiting while they photographed Fenwick from every angle.

He nodded. 'Okay.'

So he didn't suspect me of anything—yet. I walked across and got the police doctor to swab off my hand with some spirit. Except for the cuff of my sheepskin jacket, there wasn't any blood on my clothes. Maybe there's some instinct that keeps you away from other people's blood; I don't think it's just a matter of your profession.

'C'était votre ami?' he asked. Was *that* your friend? To him, it was just another job.

I shrugged. 'Depuis quelques heures.'

He shook his head without meaning anything and checked my hands over for scratches, my fingernails for any interesting-looking dirt. Again, just routine.

Somebody by the body called: 'Docteur Delansorne!'

He called back, then glanced at me.

'No thanks, I've seen . . . je l'ai vu.'

He smiled a slightly superior smile and went. I leaned on the ambulance and looked around without moving my eyes.

7

Nobody seemed to be looking, and three big steps would get me back out of the light. I did it in a dozen small, casual ones.

Then I was moving fast, stooping low and zigzagging across the rows of parked cars, down the line of retreat—cover from view, cover from fire—that I'd planned for both of us. Just in case.

Maybe they didn't even hear the car start; maybe they heard it and it didn't mean anything to them; maybe they didn't immediately think of me taking the car—I don't know how many minutes' start I had. And when they searched Fenwick and found his green card insurance, they'd know it was a Rover 2000 and the number—but it doesn't say the colour.

For all that, I stayed off the autoroute. I cut across to Douai, and then hooked back again to come into Lille on the N25. I had to leave the car there: I couldn't get it across the Belgian frontier without the green card, and I wanted very much to be across the nearest frontier there was. Train to Brussels and a midnight flight back to London—just for the record. Off the record is the time just out of Douai when I got the shakes so hard I had to stop and get my duty-free bottle of Scotch out of my case in the boot.

Still, by then it had been a long day, even if I had been well paid for it.

TWO

MY NAME IS JAMES CARD, and if you're thinking of suing, then Oscar Underhill (of Randall, Tripp and Gilbert) will accept service on my behalf. Oscar would love you to sue; whenever I want advice, he insists on being taken to lunch at the Ritz—though not in the Grill, thank God. He says it's because the tables are wide-spaced and you can talk without being overheard. Unfortunately, that's true.

So we met at the Ritz—though I should have remembered that the arcaded front would remind me of another arcade . . .

I came in shivering even more than the mid-March weather called for.

'Morning, Jim. I see you got your name all over the papers.' He was already at the table, a small, thin man of about forty-five, with a cheery smile and a respectably untidy way of dressing. R.T. & G. are a big City firm of solicitors—mostly takeover bids and company law, but they keep on Oscar to handle the criminal stuff. The trouble is that too many clients who come for a few thousand pounds'-worth of advice on company law come back for another few thousands of how to get out from under a fraud charge. The one thing you know about a fraud charge is that your client can afford the best advice.

I nodded and sat down.

He said: 'I think I'll have the Parma ham and a grilled sole. Have you been home yet?'

'No, I stayed in a hotel near the airport.'

He smiled approvingly. 'Stick to hotels for a few days; the newspapers'll be sniffing around. You sounded a bit of a mystery man in those stories this morning—they'll want to know more.'

'*They* want to know?—hell, so do I.'

The waiter came, disapproved of Oscar's suit, and took our order. Oscar graciously permitted me to order a bottle of expensive hock.

Then he asked: 'Why *did* you run away? Or why didn't you run away earlier?'

'He didn't die until just before the cops got there—I had to stay that long. Then, sooner or later, they'd have searched me properly—and they'd have found my pistol licences. *That* would have interested them strangely. And soon they'll be poking down the drains in that area: standard procedure, looking for the murder gun. They'll find a Walther PP—unfired. After that, they've got to start asking nasty questions.'

'And you think you'd have cracked?'

'And told them what? *I* don't know anything. Now——'

Then I had to stop while the wine and our first courses

9

arrived. Oscar got in the first word afterwards: 'And you want to know if you can be extradited?'

I swallowed a mouthful of soup. 'My guess is not, but what d'you think?'

'What can they pin on you?'

'They'll be pretty sure I was carrying a gun without a French licence. They might try something about the car—stealing it, or messing up evidence or something. And there's plenty of French laws about hindering the police.'

He shook his head briskly. 'That doesn't mean anything to a British court. No—I think you're fireproof. They'll be hoping something comes up that proves you did it, but they won't do anything until then. Mind, you'd better not take a French holiday this year.'

'You want me to pay for *that* advice?'

'Well, I'll give you some that's really worth paying for: give up these bodyguard jobs. Stick to security advising—you're building up a nice little business there. You get your name in the papers on this sort of nonsense and you're going to lose your other clients.'

'You bloody hypocrite. Who got me this job?'

'I just put him in touch with you; nobody forced you to take it. You're a big boy now.'

I pushed away my soup and poured some more wine; if I was paying for it, I was going to get my share. 'Have you heard from the Arras police at all?'

He shook his head. 'Vice versa. We rang them this morning —after all, he was our client; one of us will be going over in a day or so. But all we want really is proof of his death and doing what we can about his possessions—getting that car back eventually. The criminal side's entirely a French matter.'

'So, officially, nobody over here's going to be concerned about who killed him or why.'

'I suppose that's true . . .' He cocked his head suspiciously. 'Are you getting a crusading spirit about this, Jim? You're not a trained detective: stay out of it.'

'Christ—the man pretty near died in my arms. You can't expect me to just walk away.'

'An unfortunate choice of phrase,' he said dryly, 'since what you did was run. Well——' Then he had to wait while they showed us the soles, grilled whole, just to prove they hadn't stolen any bits for the cat, took them aside and filleted them, finally let us get at them.

Oscar started: 'To be honest——'

'I love hearing lawyers say that.'

He looked sharp, then smiled. 'I honestly don't know what it was all about. Probably I didn't want to—solicitors sometimes don't. But I can tell you as much as the evening papers'll have about him.'

'It's a start.'

'He was a professional underwriter to a marine insurance syndicate at Lloyd's.'

'What exactly does that mean?'

'He sits in Lloyd's all day and insures ships. Or a few per cent of any one. On behalf of his syndicate.'

'He didn't act particularly rich.'

'The professionals in Lloyd's—underwriters and brokers—don't have to be. Usually aren't—it's a salaried job. The real money comes from the members, and some of them never go near the place. And he was married. One son.'

'Where did he live?'

'Stay away from his family, Jim.'

'Look, mate—I saw him *die*. Surely his wife——'

'I doubt it. She might even think you helped get him killed.'

I might even think so myself. Suddenly I wasn't so hungry. I sat back and watched his small, neat hands dissecting the fish with watchmaking precision.

After a time, I asked: 'Is that all?'

'What did he tell you himself?'

'Just that he had a package to deliver, that the other people might turn rough. So he might need guarding. I should have asked more—but hell, he came from you.'

He nodded. 'I don't really know any more than that.'

'But you know a lot more background. You must have known him fairly well for him to be able to ask you about a bodyguard. Particularly for you to recommend one.'

11

He bent his head gently, acknowledging this. But he didn't say anything.

So I said: 'You don't feel like hiring me yourself to find out what it was about?'

'On behalf of his estate? Thank you, we can plunder it without any of your help. And you're still not a detective; you couldn't find the ground with your feet. So don't try.'

'All right. But I'll tell you one thing you don't know: I've got the package he was going to deliver.'

He went very still, staring at me. After a while, he said: 'Then you know what it was all about.'

'Maybe.'

His voice was cold now. 'That would make a nice, simple charge—stealing.'

I grinned back. 'If anybody could prove it had existed, and that I took it. Anyway, you said the criminal side was a French affair.'

He stared at me a while longer, then laid down his knife and fork and beckoned up the water. And took out his wallet.

'I thought I was buying this.'

He shook his head. 'One day, we're going to make a lot of money out of you, Jim. You're going to be up on a charge—a big one. Murder, probably. And since we're going to lose it, we'll be able to stick you for every penny you've got. Meantime, I'll pay for the lunch.'

It was my turn to feel a little cold. I watched as he checked down the bill, calculated the exact tip, counted his change. He was a lawyer, all right.

He looked back at me. 'Do you want to turn that package over to me?'

'If you tell me the rest.'

'We might start proceedings about it. I'll have to consult my partners.'

'You'll have to specify what you're suing for.'

'I think,' he said slowly, 'that you might be bluffing.'

'Maybe.'

Maybe. I'd unwrapped the package. Of course—I wasn't carrying it through Customs without knowing what it was.

And maybe the estate of the late Martin Fenwick Esq. really would suffer for the lack of a brand-new copy of the *Bertie Bear Colouring Book.*

THREE

LLOYD'S IS A BIG PLACE, modern without much looking it, done in nursery-building block style: a curved bit and then a straight bit, a few arched windows and then some square ones, a little bit of everything plus little towers on top and maybe ketchup besides. I'd never been in it before—and it didn't look as if I was going to get in now. As I came up to the main entrance, a glassed-in lobby at the corner of Lime Street, I was pounced on by a tall type who'd wandered off an old huntin' print: black topper, red coat and all.

He said: 'Can I help you, sir?' with that particular politeness that suggests you'd better know the password—or else.

'I'm hoping to see somebody from Martin Fenwick's syndicate.'

That wasn't the password. He said: '*Hoping* to see *somebody*, sir?'

'That's right. How do I start?'

'There isn't anybody *expecting* you, sir?'

'No. It must have happened before. What d'you usually do?'

He considered—the idea and me both. Then he said crisply: 'If you'd see the waiter inside, sir.' I'd forgotten they called them 'waiters'—from the days when Lloyd's was a coffee-house where gents with money took on shipping insurance risks as an extra over their morning cuppa.

The lobby itself was tall, narrow, marble, with a bunch of flags on a war memorial at one end, and revolving glass doors at the other. Beyond them, was a big three-storey-high room which was obviously The Sanctum. A steady flow of men—no women at all—in sober dark suits flowed in and out and around the doors.

A waiter—this one in a blue coat—got up from a desk in the middle and said: 'Yes, sir?'

I told him what I wanted and my name, and he said doubt-fully: 'I'll ring the box, sir, but if there's nobody *expecting* you . . .' But he picked up the desk phone. Then, halfway through dialling, he remembered. 'But Mr Fenwick's dead, sir.'

I nodded. 'I wouldn't be here if he wasn't.'

He mumbled quickly and secretively into the receiver, then looked up. 'They say they don't know you, sir, and they're very busy just now.'

'Tell 'em I'm a nuclear submarine in disguise looking for life insurance.'

He told them something—but not that—and put the phone down. 'Perhaps if you wrote a letter, sir . . .' as soothing as cough syrup.

I turned away, then back. 'Just suppose I had been a ship-owner, asking about insurance . . .'

He shook his head without looking up. 'You wouldn't be, sir. It all has to be done through Lloyd's brokers.'

'Monopolist.'

'You could complain to the Monopolies Commission—sir.'

And I was out in the cold again.

After that, it was fairly easy. Lloyd's has three other entrances, and something over six thousand members, and by now I had some idea of the style: you just walked in, not saying good afternoon nor nothing to nobody. Luckily I'd been carrying around my dark blue pinstripe in the Arras luggage; it was definitely monopolist wear, that season.

Inside, I found myself opposite a row of lifts and rode one up three storeys just to get well behind their lines. Then found the stairs and started walking down; at the second floor I came out on to a wide gallery running all around the big room itself, and paused to regroup myself.

It was a vast, shapeless place full of the bustle and chatter of an Italian railway station. The floor was dotted with dozens of big double-sided old desks—the underwriters' 'boxes' I suppose—that looked tatty and third-hand against the hygienic cream marble walls and square green pillars. Hundreds, maybe thousands, of men were moving, standing, sitting and maybe even knowing what they were doing, but to me it looked as organized as the last minutes of the *Titanic*. Somewhere in that lot were Fenwick's business friends and neighbours, but where did I start?

I started by getting rid of my sheepskin coat; nobody else had outdoor clothes on. The gallery was also full of under-writing boxes, and a few had the odd hat or umbrella dumped around, so I quietly added mine. Then down to the main floor.

Once there, the only thing to do was look preoccupied and keep moving. I did a complete circuit of the perimeter, stop-ping to look at notice-boards—including one about thirty feet long with big pink and yellow sheets listing boats lost, damaged or missing in the last couple of days. I'd never have believed it; the damn things were going down like hailstones, the bottom of the sea was getting double-parked vertically, and nobody but me seemed to be caring. I moved on quickly.

But this wasn't getting me anywhere. I stopped, looked around, and latched on to a chubby-cheeked, fluffy-haired twenty-year-old. Putting the parade ground back in my voice, I growled: 'Remind me which the devil's Fenwick's box. Always get lost when I come in here, blast it.'

He should have called in the Mounties, but I'd guessed right about this place: the fact that I was in the right suit, twice his age and actually *here* outweighed any doubts about whether I *should* be here.

'I think it's three-eighty-something, sir—but I'll just check for you.' He scurried off and back. 'Yes, sir, it's three-eighty-seven. But you know he . . .'

'I wouldn't have had to come in if he hadn't, dammit. Thank you, boy.' And I stumped off.

Each box had a number on its side, so after that it was just a matter of reconnaissance and planning my approach. The box itself was one of the smallest I'd seen, not much longer than an ordinary desk and split lengthways by a bank of pigeonholes. A lad about the same age as the one who'd given me the number was taking down thick metal-bound book files from the pigeonholes and passing them to a large, worried-looking man next to him on the bench. A slim, elderly, elegant man was standing by, looking down.

The big man looked up as I arrived and said sharpish: 'Sorry, but we're not doing any business today.'

'My name's Card, James Card.'

Then the lad whispered to him and I caught '. . . one in France, sir, who . . .'

The man said: 'My God, you?' and got up at a remarkable speed for his size and age—he must have been about fifty and not much less around the tum.

For a time he just stared at me and I stared back and the world of marine insurance babbled busily on around us. He looked as if he'd grown from a chubby baby to a big fat man just by inflating: he still had the neat little features, the big blue eyes, the fat hands, the wispy hair—though it was white by now. But he was hard with it; he stood a clear three inches taller than me and if he punched his weight I hoped he'd pick on somebody his own size.

Then he pushed along the bench—the boy scuttling out of his way—until he towered over me face down to face. 'Well, I'm damned if I expected to see you here. Come to give your pay back?'

I didn't say anything.

He said: 'You didn't do much of a job last night, did you?'

I went on staring at the nice dark-blue silk suit, the tailored shirt, the obviously expensive silk tie, the gold watch-chain and cufflinks. All a bit richer, more individual, than the clothing I'd seen here so far.

'Not very talkative, are you?' he barked.

'We haven't been introduced.'

He snorted. 'I'm Paul Mockby'—as if he expected me to recognize it.

I just nodded; it didn't seem like an occasion for shaking hands. He swung back to the bench and grabbed handfuls of papers.

'Come upstairs and tell me about it.'

The elderly party at the far end of the box said vaguely: 'I'll leave it to you, then, Paul. You'll let me know?'

'I'll let everybody know.' Mockby jerked his head at me and steamed off across the floor at a Rifle Brigade pace.

I followed him back into a lift, up to the fourth floor and down a corridor that seemed very quiet after the big room. We turned in through a glass-panelled door labelled just M. J. FENWICK and there wasn't any nonsense about letting visitors go first or closing the door after them.

It was a surprisingly small, sparse room. Just one small desk, three simple hardbacked chairs, a glass-fronted bookcase and a couple of Canaletto prints on the walls. And another door, leading off to the side.

Behind the desk was a small mousy blonde girl who didn't look as if she'd been doing anything but stare into space. Mockby evicted her by throwing down a five-pound note and snapping: 'Hop out and get me five Bolivars. You know the size.' She hopped and he dumped himself behind the desk, lit a cigar the size of a copper's truncheon, and said: 'Well?'

'Funny. It doesn't seem the sort of place to handle hundreds of thousands in premiums.'

'Lloyd's doesn't need a front. Can undercut the big companies simply because we keep our overheads down. Under five per cent. Now—what happened?'

I sat down; I could have fossilized before he invited me to. 'He got shot from cover.'

'That's what you were there to stop!'

'Oh no. I was told we'd meet some people who might turn nasty *later*.'

He swatted the idea away with a big hand. 'What's the difference?'

'If he'd told me it could be an assassination job, I'd've wanted at least two more men and, even then, I wouldn't have let him near that place at that sort of time.'

While he was absorbing this, the inner door opened and a pretty, not-very-thin girl in her middle twenties came in carrying a bunch of papers. She had straight dark brown hair

17

pulled back in a mock-severe schoolmarm style, and she'd been crying behind her big round hornrims.

Mockby didn't get up. 'Here, Maggie—this is the bastard who got Martin killed.'

She looked at me quickly, didn't like me, swallowed and blinked back more tears, then hurried out again.

I said: 'And you count the day lost that you don't bring a little sunshine into somebody's life.'

He grunted. 'I still think you ballsed it up.'

I shrugged. 'Who was Mr Fenwick, anyway?'

'He didn't even tell you that? He was the underwriter to our syndicate. Christ!' He slammed his hand down on the papers he'd brought up. 'And his deputy's got the flu and the accountant doesn't come in on Mondays and we could have insured the whole Royal bloody Navy in the last month and I wouldn't know!'

'Maybe there won't be a war this week.'

He glared up at me. 'There was a packet Martin was going to hand over: what happened to it?'

'What was it?'

'Never mind what it bloody was! What happened to it?'

'Mr Mockby—I'd like to stay on this job; find out who killed Mr Fenwick. Can you . . .'

'You're trying to get into me for more money, are you?'

'No. I'm prepared to spend what I got paid on working on this. After that, well . . .'

'I don't imagine you could find your arse if you were sitting on it. You aren't a detective; you aren't even a decent body-guard. Just mind your own business, and *where's that packet?*'

'Maybe the police got it.'

'Hell.' He thought about this. 'You're sure nobody else did?'

'Not the people who shot him, anyway.'

'And you were too busy saving your own neck to bother with it.'

I stood up. 'You could have saved his life.'

He glared suspiciously. 'What d'you mean?'

'You know what it's all about.' He didn't say anything. 'And he worked for you.'

'Not me—the syndicate.'

'You're the rich man; he was the busy one. You could have gone in his place.'

He looked at me with a sort of glowering calm. Then he said quietly: 'Bugger off.'

And there wasn't much else to do.

FOUR

BUT NOT TOO FAR.

It was past three o'clock now, and I had a feeling Mockby wouldn't last much longer. The way he'd been throwing those papers around suggested he was either looking for something or trying to get a quick, rough overall impression. A real paper-worker—an auditor or intelligence operator—keeps his material neat and tidy.

In fact, he lasted about twenty more minutes, spending the last five down at the box—as I'd guessed he would. All I had to do was to stick to the gallery but not too long in one spot. And when he packed some papers into a briefcase and headed for the front door I repossessed my own coat and walked back up the stairs.

The little mousy blonde was back and she gave a little mousy squeak when she saw who it was. I soothed her quickly. 'It's all right—I forgot something. Wanted another quick word with Maggie.'

And I was knocking on Maggie's door before she could sort out the half-truths in that.

Maggie called: 'Who is it?' So I showed her.

It was the same size of room—small—but busier-looking. There was a serious desk and a typewriter with a balance-sheet sized carriage; a couple of old breakfront bookcases with some serious-looking books; a grey metal filing cabinet, a row of cactus pots on the windowsill, and a duplicating machine in the corner.

And Maggie. 'You? What on earth do *you* want?'

She had a comfortable figure like a slim cottage loaf wrapped in a simple short black dress that belonged to later in the day. No—she was in mourning, of course; that was the only black thing she owned. A sharp little nose, slightly over-large mouth, and still red-eyed from crying. But looked somehow more relaxed now.

I said: 'Just wanted a quick word about Mr Fenwick.'

'Haven't you done enough for him already?' she asked wearily. Since I'd half expected to get her fangs in my jugular, this was hopeful.

'I'd like to try and do a bit more.'

'Ha. I don't see how you could.'

'I'd like to know something about him.'

She shrugged. 'Like what?'

'Well, just give me a feel.'

'I *beg* your pardon?' She went rigid and her eyes opened wide.

'Fenwick—what sort of man he was.'

'Oh.' She relaxed and stared dreamily at nothing. 'He was a wonderful man.'

'I liked him myself,' I said encouragingly.

'You didn't know him.' She dreamed a bit more, blinked at some tears and fiddled with something in one of the desk drawers. 'He was a marvellous man to work for.'

'Did you know his family?'

'He's got a boy at Harrow. Nice boy.'

'What about his wife—did you meet her?'

She gave a slight snort and a little twisted smile. 'Just twice. She—doesn't come into London much.'

'Where does she live?'

'Why?'—and she fiddled in the drawer again.

'Well—I reckon the least I can do is go and see her.'

She shrugged. 'I don't suppose she'd care.'

Then the phone rang.

Maggie picked it up and spoke listlessly, saying that Mr Mockby and Mr Gale had been in . . . yes, there'd be a letter sent out in a day or two, just as soon as things had straightened out. . . .

I just stood and stared around the office.

Her desk had a clutter that didn't belong; not just papers, but bottles of nail varnish, a couple of paperbacks, a pair of evening shoes. She was still on the phone and looking bored with it. She glanced down and reached for that desk drawer again. It's a gesture that bothers me—somebody's hand reaching for something hidden. Professional training, I suppose. I took a couple of quick strides and leaned over to look.

I should have guessed; it was a glass, half full of some drink. She'd slipped it off the desk top as I came in. So she was saying farewell to her boss in something stronger than tears; she wasn't just relaxed, she was half cut.

She glared at me and I grinned back. When she finally put down the phone, I said: 'Go on—drink it in the open. It's not a normal day.'

She lifted the glass defiantly and took a healthy swig. 'I'm just clearing out his entertainment cupboard. It seems a pity to leave it for those rich creeps.'

'D'you need any help?'

'Serve yourself.' She waved a hand at the cupboard of one of the breakfronts. Inside, I found what had been a nice selection of drinking aids. I organized myself a Scotch and soda.

'Cheers.' I drank, then asked: 'Did you finish the vodka and sherry?'

'Why not?' Jesus—she wasn't just half cut, she was pretty near minced.

'You're quitting?' I nodded at the clutter on the desk.

'As soon as they let me. Or before.'

I smiled sympathetically and parked myself on the edge of the desk—visitors didn't seem to get asked to sit much in this office.

'Just what is Mr Mockby?'

'He's a Name.'

'He's about five that I can think of.'

She smiled briefly. 'That means a member; they call them Names. The rich bastards who are supposed to be risking their money here.'

21

'Well, you can't run an oil well without oil. And a bunch of Names is a syndicate, right? How many in a syndicate?'

'It can be over a hundred, it can be as small as we are: just nine. Though most of ours are pretty rich.'

'And they split the profits according to how much they've put up—is that right?' She nodded. 'The underwriter himself —does he put up anything? Get any of the profits?'

'Yes, but he doesn't have to be *rich*.' It was a dirty word. 'Big money doesn't make big minds. You don't own it; it owns you.'

'Sometimes.'

'D'you know any rich men?' Her tone suggested it was unlikely.

'It's only the rich men who can afford bodyguards. Or think they need it.'

'I wish Martin had afforded somebody better.'

Oh God, we were back to that.

But she was too far gone to stick to one subject, now. She finished her drink, heaved herself up and poured another— Scotch, this time.

'You're going to end up cronked.' Professionally, I didn't mind, but the residual officer-and-gentleman in me felt it had to say something.

'I'm a big girl now. And you said it wasn't a normal day.' She gulped.

'D'you know why Mr Fenwick was going to Arras?'

'It doesn't matter now. Nothing matters now.'

'But you know?'

'Ask Mockby.'

'Your Mr Fenwick hired me. Granted maybe I didn't do as good a job as I might have done. But I don't think he'd like me just to drop it now.' And I can sing Mother Macree hand-embroidered with roses and violets, too.

But if there was a psychological moment, I'd missed it. All she said was: 'Forget it. Just forget it all.' Then dumped herself back behind the desk and stared at the typewriter and went peck-peck-peck at one key.

Blast it.

22

I put on a more formal voice and said: 'You were going to give me Mrs Fenwick's address.'

'Was I?' She lifted her glass and stared through it. 'You wouldn't like her. She's a cow. You'd step in her cow-pats.' She giggled.

When she got over the top, she certainly went downhill fast.

'The address,' I said sternly.

'Kingscutt Manor, Kingscutt, Kent,' she droned.

I spaced it in my head. 'Thank you.'

'Any time. Anything for an old friend of Martin's.'

I stood up carefully. 'Thank you, Miss . . . ?'

'Mackwood. Miss Maggie Mackwood, at your service.'

Then she leaned her forehead on the typewriter and began to cry gently. I tiptoed out.

The little thing at the reception desk looked at me as severely as she could—like an angry mouse.

'I almost rang the box,' she said. 'I mean when you just walked in like that.'

I nodded. 'Next time, ring. You won't get anywhere unless you're ready to get tough with uninvited guests.'

She looked blank, then surprised, and then puzzled-but-friendly. The sound of sobbing came from the door behind her She cocked an ear and nodded. 'She was very fond of Mr Fenwick.'

'Make sure she gets a taxi home.'

'You think I ought to?'

'Just get one and then tell her when it's here. Be tough.'

She smiled uncertainly. 'All right. Did you really see him when he—got shot?'

I had my hand on the doorknob. 'Yes.'

'I wonder who ever did it.'

I turned and went back, meaning to pat her on the head. But suddenly she was a frightened mouse again, rearing back in her seat. So I just smiled, friendly like.

'Congratulations. It's about time somebody asked that.'

FIVE

AT A BIT BEFORE FOUR, the rush out of the City was thickening up (what hours do these people *work*?) but I still found a taxi inside five minutes. We only went as far as Fleet Street, where I knew a man who worked in a newspaper library.

A newspaper office is a lot easier than Lloyd's because it employs a much bigger variety of bods. You still have to look as if you know where you're going—but this time I did already. Most of the building has become the usual concrete-glass-fibreboard stuff in the last few years, but the library's in the old tribal country around the central light-well: the high dirty ceilings, long frayed light-flexes and dark mustiness of a real library. The boys there take a perverse pride about it. They say it's the heart of the organization and a face-lift on a heart never worked yet.

He stood up a bit quickly as I came up to his desk. 'Afternoon, Major.'

I said quietly: 'For Chrissake sit down, Pip.'

He slumped. 'Just instinct, I suppose.'

'I wasn't *that* bad.'

'You were still a major.' He picked up a packet of Gauloises and took one, then offered me. I shook my head. He nodded sadly. 'I don't like them myself, but they help me cut it down. I see you got your name in the papers at last. Have they caught you yet?'

'No. Just ring the newsroom and you'll have a scoop on your hands.'

He smiled gently. 'Let 'em do their own dirty work; they tell me how to do mine often enough.' He had a tall forehead that hid a remarkable private filing system, curly black hair and the pale skin of a man whose office never sees the sun. 'What can I do for you, Major?'

'Fenwick.' You don't tell a man like Pip what you want to see, you tell him what you want to know. He'll think of sources you couldn't dream of.

He shook his head slowly. 'We've been trying to get some-

24

thing on him all day. He's not in *Who's Who*, or the *Directory of Directors*, we've got no packets on him. Seems to be just a Lloyd's man. We don't keep any of their registers or stuff. You really don't know any more yourself?'

'Nope. I only knew him a few hours.'

'The *Standard*'s got everything we know.' He pushed across a fresh final edition. 'Anything else?'

'Mockby. Paul Mockby.'

He frowned thoughtfully. 'I think . . . Does he come into it?'

'He seems to be the bright light of Fenwick's syndicate, that's all. And while you're at it, I'd like some general stuff at Lloyd's—how it works and so on.'

'No can do. The packets are out.' He jerked his head at a young man sitting at a table about ten yards off, puffing at an oversized pipe and rumpling, alternately, his hair and a mass of newspaper clippings.

Pip said: 'He's working up some background on how an underwriter works. You ought to buy him a drink—he spent half last night waiting outside your pad for you to come home. I'll see what we've got on Mockby.'

I skimmed the *Evening Standard* while he was gone. The story was still front page—perhaps because the Arras police had announced finding a Walther PP down a drain; there's got to be a new fact to hang a new re-hash of old knowledge on, and the police know that as well as anybody. But they hadn't tied the gun to me, yet. Or else the *Standard* hadn't risked libel by saying so. The only new thing about me was that I'd once been a major in the Intelligence Corps. No picture. I didn't think they'd find one before the story ran dry, anyway.

Pip was leaning over my shoulder with the *Directory of Directors* open at Mockby's page. 'I've got a bit of personal stuff on him, too.' He sat down to sort through a handful of clippings while I went through the *Directory* entry.

It seemed he was a director of about twenty companies, none of which I'd heard of bar a small merchant bank and a shipping line. But there was perhaps something of a pattern to the rest of them. Most of the names—where the names told you anything—suggested electronics, chemicals and drugs or man-made fibres. Laboratory companies. Find a new cure for cancer or nylon and farm out your patents and then hold on to the rocket stick while your share values go through the ceiling.

Still, what did that tell me?—that Mockby was what the Irish call a 'chancer'. He liked to be where the action was, and I could have told the *Directory* that myself.

Pip said: 'He played polo against Prince Philip once.'

'Riding what?—a tank?'

He grinned and compared two cuttings. 'Yes, he's thickened up a bit. We all do. Divorced in 1962. It looks as if his first one was the polo piece—the Hon. Arabella. There isn't much about the new one. About fifteen years younger, that's all.'

'Roll on the revolution and the government'll give us all one fifteen years younger.'

He leaned back in his chair and sucked at a tooth. 'I'll swap my new one for a crate of beer, Major.'

'It's a deal.'

After a while he said: 'What happened to Mrs Card? I read a par; I didn't clip it.'

I shut the *Directory* with a snap. 'I didn't make lieutenant-colonel. It lasted four years.'

'Lieutenants might marry, captains may marry, majors should marry, colonels must marry,' he quoted. 'It doesn't say anything about corporals.'

'Corporals are less than the mud on an officer's boots.'

'They survive.' He smiled lazily and tuned a violin on his tooth again. 'The stories I read, it was just one shot. That isn't right, is it?'

I nodded.

His chair came back to earth with a bang. 'What calibre? What range was that?'

'Nine millimetre, about fifteen yards.'

He swung around to peer through the grimy window at the gloom gathering already in the well outside. 'At six o'clock? In that light? A *pistol*? Christ but he was lucky. Or you taught us wrong.'

26

'I was right.'

'Amateur, then. Just one shot. It must have been luck.'

'Or Hopalong Cassidy.'

'Yes.' He brooded on it.

The young reporter came across trailing smoke like a wounded Messerschmitt; he had to puff at that pipe every two seconds to keep it going. He dropped half a dozen fawn envelopes on Pip's desk.

'I've got all I need. I think the pieces are back in the right packets.'

'I bet they're not,' Pip said sourly. 'Are you out after the Card bloke again?'

'Yes.' He glanced gloomily at his watch. 'From six till the first edition closes. I bet he isn't even back in this country yet.'

'And you wouldn't even know him if you saw him.'

'Oh, I dunno. I got a pretty good description out of the French papers.' He consulted a notebook. 'About forty, six foot, thin face, receding brown hair, wears a dark blue-grey sheepskin jacket.'

My jacket was slung over the back of my chair, but he hadn't even glanced at me.

'Clever boy,' Pip commented.

'Well, I'd better write up the Lloyd's piece.' He puffed his way out through the door.

I asked: 'When's the first edition . . . ?'

'Half past eleven.' Pip picked up the *Standard* and fanned irritably at the smoke cloud hanging round his desk. 'But the agencies'll probably keep men there until about three in the morning.'

'Thanks.'

'Pray for a nice local sex murder and an airliner crash. D'you still want to look at these?'

He passed over the Lloyd's packets.

I was on the street just before six and the pubs were open—but some reporters might have sharper eyes than the boy wonder, so I walked along to the Strand and finally to the

Charing Cross Hotel. The bar there doesn't get crowded early, and anyway, my suitcase was parked in the station.

The sky was solid cloud, low enough to pick up a faint orange glow from the street lighting, and an east wind nibbled at the back of my neck all the way. Except there was no snow lying in London, it was the same weather it had been in Arras, just twenty-four hours ago. . . .

I took on one double Scotch and soda fast, just to improve the mood, and started a second one slowly as an aid to thought.

Our forces: well, just me so far. It looked as if nobody from Fenwick's syndicate was going to hire me, or even help me. Mockby and Maggie knew what it had been about—or some of it—and they weren't telling.

Enemy forces: at least two of them, with a nine-millimetre automatic—though maybe that was down a drain as well—and very willing to use it. Unless they'd panicked, of course, but what had we done to panic them? Just the sight of two men when they'd expected one? (But I'd thought of that and mentioned it to Fenwick; he'd said they wouldn't be surprised to see two . . . .)

Our intentions: that was a bit easier—just to find out what the hell it had all been about.

Method: just stagger blindly on asking the obvious questions of the obvious people.

Our secret weapons: one *Bertie Bear Colouring Book.* And a hell of a secret weapon it is when you don't know which button to press.

I looked into the bottom of my glass and made sign language for another.

Still, I must have advanced on some front today. If Mockby and Maggie knew something of what it was about, then it must touch on Fenwick's work—marine insurance. The newspaper clippings hadn't told me much, but they'd filled in some main features on the map. A full-time underwriter like Fenwick would have to put up no more than eight or ten thousand quid—in equities and gilt-edged shares—as a deposit with Lloyd's in order to become a member. Outside Names had to put up fifteen thousand and prove they actually had fifty thousand plus. So Fenwick could have been the beggar at the Princess's christening. Did that mean anything?

I also knew that our Maggie had been in love with Fenwick. Question: had he reciprocated? Don't be filthy. Maybe I'd find out when I met Mrs Fenwick. Meantime, it was another advance—although I couldn't tell in what direction.

Before I left I rang up and booked a room in a small tourist hotel up in Chalk Farm, not a quarter of a mile from my flat. It didn't have a proper bar and I'd heard the food wasn't much, so none of my resident reporters would be using it for a break.

The food *was* pretty foul, but I didn't want to risk eating out around my own neighbourhood. And I wasn't being entirely stupid in going there; I wanted to get hold of my car, and the safest time for that would be before seven in the morning. So I had to be close to start with. I went to bed about half past nine with my duty-free Scotch and Bertie Bear.

I read that damn book forwards, backwards and upside down for the best part of three hours. It was the usual sort of gump, except more of it: straightforward pictures to colour, three-letter word puzzles, mazes to trace ('Bertie Bear wants to get to the honey-pot. Can you draw the path for him?'), and pages where you link up the numbered dots and get a picture of you-know-who or his Best Chum, Dickie Donkey. Couple of right old security risks, if you ask me. I even drew in those pictures: they just might have turned into a map of where the *Lutine* sank with all her bullion. They didn't. And apart from my scribbling, there wasn't a mark on the book except the price. Unless it was in invisible ink.

Past midnight I threw the book across the room and tried to get to sleep. It took time and it wasn't helped by wondering if our Bertie wasn't just a bluff, a stand-in for another book or something that measured about fourteen inches by twelve and one inch thick. Getting Bertie instead might have been why Fenwick had thought the other side could turn rough.

It still hadn't been why they'd shot him.

SIX

I'D ASKED to be woken at six but forgotten that by International Standard Hotel Time that was twenty to seven. I swore a bit, jammed on a few clothes and decided I could shave when I came back for breakfast. I was outside my own block of flats just before seven.

It was just light—maybe too light for me, although that part of London doesn't get moving early. The sky had cleared to a pale cold blue and the windscreen of my blue Escort GT was solidly iced up. I got quickly into the driving seat and did my reconnaissance from there.

After a few minutes I was pretty sure nobody else was sitting and watching from a car, so it looked as if the day shift hadn't arrived. The only strange car I could spot—though that doesn't mean much in that area—was a maroon Jag XJ6. But it was iced up as badly as mine, and I didn't think reporters drove XJ6s. I was beginning to be tempted.

So far, I'd seen nothing moving except a lorry, one Post Office van, the newsboy who delivers to my block and an old boy in British Rail uniform. And yesterday's shirt was gritty on my back, and I could pick up another coat and stop being the man in blue-grey sheepskin and . . . It would take less than five minutes, wouldn't it?

It's a new block with no real entrance hall and certainly nowhere to sit down there, so nobody could be waiting. . . . I zipped through the glass doors and into a lift and up to the third floor. Again, no real corridor and nowhere to wait around. I was in through my door; dark, so I must have drawn the curtains before I left.

Then there was a creak and two dark figures stood up and one of them said: 'Come on in, Card. We've got things to talk about.'

A torch flashed on, straight in my eyes, and after that there just wasn't anything I could do. Hands came out of the darkness and explored my clothes carefully, but didn't take anything.

A second voice said quietly: 'He's safe.'

The torch flicked away and pointed at a deep, low chair. 'Sit in that one, Card. Nice and relaxed.'

I sat; in that chair, there was no way of doing anything sudden. But just in case I needed any further persuading, the torch shone briefly on the gun the first man had in his other hand. A Walther P38. A very nice automatic, that; supposed to be the standard German Army pistol in the last war, though they still used plenty of Lugers, too. Almost certainly nine-millimetre.

The torch came back on to me. 'So now you know,' the first voice said calmly. He was still just a dark shape to me, even when I wasn't being dazzled, but the voice sounded like a big man; not too young, and not too yobbovitch, but not a Cholmondleigh of Chatterley, neither.

'What can I do for you gentlemen?' I asked.

The second voice chuckled; the first said: 'That's nice. Co-operative. You brought something back from France. It doesn't belong to you. We'll take it.'

'Is it yours?'

'That isn't the point. It isn't *yours*.'

'Keep your voice down,' I warned. 'These new blocks are built of cardboard.' Which actually wasn't true for my block; I just wanted to get him to do something I told him to. Psychological, you know.

And his voice became a hoarse whisper. 'Just tell me where it is.'

'What are we talking about?' I whispered back.

'You know bloody well. Where is it?'

'You can search me.'

'Stop buggering about!' So he had some idea of the size of the thing he was after.

'Sorry, I haven't got any children's books to keep you happy.'

It was a chance. If he really was a Bertie Bear fan, then I couldn't play ignorant any longer. But if he wasn't . . .

He wasn't. The torch took three quick steps and something smashed on to my cheek. I couldn't even fall out of that chair, but it rocked with me.

31

'I said to stop buggering about. Now where is it?'

My eyeballs spun slowly to a stop. I touched my cheek, expecting to find it laid open; hell, I expected to find my head missing. Then I realized he'd used his hand, not the gun. It had still felt like Krupp steel.

The second voice whispered urgently: 'Keep it quiet!'

'The hell with that. Where is it?'

'I gave it back to the syndicate. Belongs to them.'

Clang. It was the other cheek this time, but his backhand was just as good as his forehand.

'For God's sake!' the second voice said. 'He's got it in a hotel or some bird's pad.'

The torch took a pace back. 'You're not tough,' the first voice said quietly. 'You're cheap. For a hundred quid you'll carry a gun without a licence. And come the first shot you're on the next boat home to mummy. You're just a mug.'

'I gave it to that big fat sod down at the office.'

'Mr Mockby? Mug.'

The torch moved in. I pressed back in my chair and kicked upwards. I must have got his thigh, though I wasn't aiming for quite that. He overbalanced and his hand swiped the back of the chair, his face fell on my knees. I banged both fists on the back of his neck, grabbed his hair and threw him aside and tried to spill over the other side of the chair. Then the second one jumped me.

The chair spilled then, all right. One of my feet caught a small table and lamp. Add the two of us hitting the floor at the same time, and you had a crash like the delivery of a year's coal in hell. The noise froze him for a moment, and I got my feet back from under him and kicked him a few times in the ribs. He made oofing noises and rolled away.

I grabbed the torch off the floor, got on my feet and flicked it across the two of them. The big one was down on his knees and forehead like a Muslim at prayer, rubbing the back of his neck. The other was just getting up. The light stopped him; the sound of the doorbell bloody well petrified him.

*   *   *

'Come in!' I yelled. Then I pulled back the window curtains and dumped the torch on the sofa.

A muffled voice called: 'It's locked!'

'Stay there! I'll be with you!' I got my first good look at the second voice: youngish, narrow-faced, long black hair, smart leather jacket.

I said: 'The rest we do with eye-witnesses. It's your decision.'

He just stayed crouched against the end of the sofa. I circled round the other man. He was big, all right, and about my own age or a bit more. He wore a rough tweed sports jacket with one pocket weighed down to the floor; I took the Walther out of it and began to feel more at home in my own home.

Then I backed off to the door and asked: 'Who is it?'

'It's Mr Norton. Is that Mr Card?'

'Yes.' The snoopy old bastard who lived one floor down.

'You're back, then?'

'Yes.'

'I heard a crash . . .'

'I'm sorry, Mr Norton. Knocked over a table in the dark. I'm not really awake.'

'It isn't good enough, Mr Card. At this time in the morning.'

'I know, Mr Norton. I'm sorry.'

'Some people are still trying to sleep.'

'I know. I'm sorry.'

Pause.

Then: 'I may have to speak to Miss O'Brien about it.'

'I hope not, Mr Norton.'

'And those stories about you in the papers, and the reporters coming round . . .'

'You don't want to believe everything you read in the papers, Mr Norton. Anyway, I'm going away again in a minute.'

Pause. You could just about hear the clockwork running down.

'Well, it isn't good enough.'

'I'm sorry, Mr Norton.'

Pause. 'Well . . .' Tick . . . tick . . . tick. He shuffled away.

I leaned back against the door. Even a punch-up is less exhausting than some things.

Back in the living-room, the young one was on his feet looking a bit uncertain, and the big one in a chair, still rubbing his neck and breathing in grunts. I showed him the gun.

'It isn't loaded,' he growled.

Keeping it pointed, I worked the slide a couple of times —and damn me, it wasn't. I went quickly through into the bedroom and took the commando knife from the bedside table drawer. The drawer was already open, and when I looked around, they'd really worked the place over. Well, of course they would have done. Blast. I checked my cufflinks box and the drawer of personal papers and they were all right. At least I don't keep any guns in the flat, except the antiques, and they were still on the living-room wall. And in my business you don't keep files at home.

I went back and showed them the knife. 'I'm good with these things, too. Now both of you get out.'

The big one stood up slowly and a bit shakily. 'What about the gun?'

'I'll keep it as a souvenir.'

He glowered at it in my hand. His face had a blunt, ruddy look, like a man who spends time out of doors. I'd have liked to know more about him; if the gun had been loaded, or if there'd been just him, I'd've gone through his wallet. But not with just a knife against the two of them.

He still seemed uncertain. I said: 'Breaking and entering with a firearm. Look, mate—I'm giving you the next five years of your life. I should take it.'

He took it—but still reluctantly. The other one wasn't so reluctant, though he remembered to pick up the torch as he went.

I watched them from the front window. They went to the big maroon Jag just down the road, and while they were scraping the windscreen clear of frost I remembered my binoculars. When they drove off—the big one at the wheel— I got the number.

And right then, I was ready to join Mr Norton in catching up on some rest. But I still had the power of the press to worry about. I spent five minutes picking my clothes off the bedroom floor and throwing some of them into a suitcase. As a second thought, I added the drawerful of personal papers, address book and so on. Then I went into the bathroom and splashed cold water around my face. Both cheeks had a red tinge that might need some explaining back at the hotel.

As I went out, I checked the door latch and told myself for the hundredth time to get a lock of my own put in. A hell of a security adviser I was who couldn't keep a couple of amateurs out of his own flat. Oh well. I know doctors who still smoke.

I'd half expected them to wait around the corner and try to tail me, but no maroon Jag followed. Maybe they felt too defeated, maybe they didn't realize I would be getting out again myself. Anyway, I picked up a bunch of morning papers in England's Lane and was back with my Genuine British Breakfast by eight.

On the whole, the news was better than the breakfast. The Arras cops had turned up traces of two other Britons who'd spent an hour in a café there just before Fenwick and I arrived, but hadn't stayed the night in town. In the meantime they still wanted a nice friendly chat with Monsieur Card, so would he please come forward, being assured he was not under suspicion . . .

Ho ho ho, yes mate, and up you, too. I'd come forward when and if I'd got a little bargaining power in my hand, and not until. The story of the two Britons was probably true, but for the moment it didn't matter if it wasn't: it still turned down the heat under me. And already the attitude to me in the papers was changing subtly: from being important because I was a Mystery Man, I was beginning to sound unimportant because, after twenty-four hours of looking, they hadn't found either me or much about me. We find out the news; if we can't find it out, it can't be news—right?

Right.

After breakfast, I started monopolizing one of the hotel's two telephone lines (they hadn't even asked about my cheek; anyhow, to them my name wasn't Card). First I rang my answering service; there was a mass of messages from newspapers that they insisted on reading to me; one saying ring Jack Morris at his Federal number; another from a Mr David Fenwick (brother? cousin?) leaving a number, please ring back; finally one from a client I'd been helping on office security saying, in effect, don't ring back. And he wouldn't be the last. The price of James Card slipped badly as first results of his Continental venture were released yesterday . . .

Would I have been better off in Arras jail?

I'd rather expected Mockby to live out of town and maybe he had a country place as well, but meanwhile there he was in the phone book occupying an obviously desirable residence in The Bishop's Avenue. There's nothing but desirable residences up there, as long as you can stand the street name being mentioned in half the fraud cases that come to trial.

I got a female voice, wife or housekeeper—they still have housekeepers in those parts—which suited me better than Mockby himself. I said quickly: 'Sergeant Harris, Kentish Town police. We've found an abandoned car. Are you the owners of a maroon Jaguar XJ6, licence number . . .' I read it off.

She sounded puzzled. 'Well . . . yes, that's one of Mr Mockby's cars, I think, but I'm sure it's back here. It was out most of the night, I know, but—would you like me to go and check?' Housekeeper, all right.

'Never mind, madam, it looks as if there's been an error.'

'Would you like to speak to Mr Mockby himself?'

What could I lose? He couldn't thump me by phone.

He came on, big, brawny and brave. 'Paul Mockby here. What is it?'

'Good morning, sir. Are you the owner of a Walther P38 automatic pistol, nine millimetre?'

'I . . . *what*? I thought it was about the car?'

'Just answer the question, please, sir.' Let the bastard sweat a bit; he could spare the weight.

36

'What? . . . I . . . why do you want . . . what's it to do with me?'

'Hello Mockers, old boy, James Card here—remember?'

There was a long pause while he climbed back into several layers of self-confidence. Then he said grimly: 'Impersonating a police officer now, boy? I could have you for that.'

'What about your boys? Impersonating burglars, KGB interrogators and carrying an unlicensed gun. War souvenir, was it?'

'You can't prove anything,' he said quickly.

'I might. My flat's still a mess, I can identify both them and the car, your housekeeper'll say it was out all night. And for my money, the young one'll talk. You're an accessory before the fact, old chum.'

After a while, he asked: 'I'd better talk to you.'

'You are already. This is close enough.'

'What are you going to do, then?'

'*You're* going to tell me what I got mixed up in.'

After another long time, he said just: 'No.'

That really shook me.

'Chum, you're taking a big risk.'

'Perhaps. But I don't think you're the sort that goes crying to the police. And I'm a pretty good judge of men—you have to be, to make money the way I do. Anyway, I call you. Play cards.'

It was my turn to add a little silence to the proceedings. Finally: 'That thing your little lads were after—it's in the bank. So don't try anything like that again. And if I'd been wearing a gun, we might not have been able to keep the police out of it.'

'I'll buy it off you. I'll do that. And a good price.'

'As far as I'm concerned, it's Fenwick's.'

'Fenwick's dead. That belongs to the syndicate.'

'I'll think about it.'

'And I still want to talk to you. We might be able to do a little business.'

'We'll talk—when I've got something more to say. And I'm choosey about whom I do business with.'

37

He chuckled—Mr Big again, riding tall in the saddle. 'That's no way to make a fortune.'

'No, but it helps keep you out of jail.' I hung up.

Hell. That had been a gold mine full of iron pyrites. The bastard *had* been right about me and the police—though my performance in Arras had given him a preview. Even so, he'd still been taking a risk. Or perhaps choosing between two risks.

I picked up *Bertie Bear* for the umpteenth time and stared at him. He was beginning to look like Paul Mockby except with fur.

'I don't see it, but somebody certainly loves you.'

SEVEN

I KNEW I'd have to wait until past ten before I could catch Oscar at his office, so I spent a little time field-stripping the P38. Jack Morris and Mr David Fenwick could wait; neither was likely to be good news. The gun wasn't new—I think they still make them—so it probably was a war souvenir. It didn't smell as if it had been fired recently, and when I pulled it through with a strip of torn handkerchief I got only dust, so it hadn't been cleaned recently, either. Still, I'm not a ballistics man.

I got through to Oscar at ten past.

'You're still out of prison?' he asked cheerfully.

'More or less. Have you sent a man to France yet?'

'No. Actually, I'm going myself at lunchtime.'

'Good. Find out from the police what sort of pistol fired the shot; they haven't said in the papers.'

'Will they know?'

'They've got a cartridge case. They can tell from the extractor and firing-pin marks.'

'Ummm . . .' He sounded doubtful. 'Well, I'll try and work the conversation around to it. But didn't I tell you to lay off the detective stuff?'

'Just curious. By the way—Paul Mockby isn't one of your clients, is he?'

'No.'

'But you know who I mean?'

'He's in Fenwick's syndicate. Probably the richest.'

'You wouldn't have been talking to him recently?'

'I haven't. I don't say he hasn't talked to somebody here. In fact——'

'He sent a couple of amateur tough guys around to convert me. He thought I had a little something belonging to somebody else.'

'I see. And you thought . . . You ought to read the French papers. *Le Monde* had a rather good description of you. Including a brown paper package you were carrying which you said was a present for a friend in Paris.' He paused to let me digest that, then added dryly. 'Oddly enough, I *am* doing my best to protect your interests. Somebody has to. And I told you to stay away from home.'

'Thanks, Oscar. Give my love to the inspecteur.'

Another angle folded up flat—though this time I was glad of it. It was about time for a drive down to Kingscutt—except for that call from a David Fenwick. It nagged me. He was probably offering to horsewhip me on the steps of my club if my club could afford steps and he could afford a horsewhip but still . . .

With these new all-figure telephone numbers, you don't have any idea of where in London you're ringing. You could work it out, I suppose, but life's too short.

A woman's voice said: 'Cundall's.'

'Could I spead to Mr David Fenwick?'

'Of course not, not at this time.'

'Oh.' What in hell was this? 'Look, I may sound stupid, but I just had a message to ring Mr Fenwick at this number and I don't know where I'm ringing . . .'

'Harrow School. Cundall's house.' Oh Gawd Blimey. 'He should have left more in the message. He can't take any calls until 4.15.'

'Sorry. I'll ring back then.'

'Just a moment—is this something to do with his father's death?'

'Probably, but I just don't know. I just got the message.'

'But you must know whether you had any connection with his father.'

'I did,' I said grimly. 'I was there when he died.'

'Oh!' Pause. 'You're that man.'

'I'm afraid so.'

'Hold on a moment, will you? My husband's just come in . . . I think he'd like to talk . . .'

Another pause, filled with distant mutterings.

Then a man's voice came on. 'John Hawthorn here. Is that Mr—er, James Card?' It was a slow, confident voice, but maybe a little strained. Probably just a man who didn't like the telephone much.

'I'm Card.'

'I know David Fenwick phoned you—he spoke to me about it.'

'Uh-huh.'

'I know he wants to see you. I'm not sure that I'd advise it, but he seems quite certain that he does . . .'

'Uh-huh.' Me, I have a great telephone manner.

'I wonder if you could come out here this afternoon and have a word with me first? Say half past three?'

'I suppose so.' Bang went my trip to Kent; I couldn't safely count on getting down to Kingscutt and back up to Harrow in time . . . Still, at least this was a positive step. It made a change for somebody actually to *want* to see me—apart from various authorities, of course.

Hawthorn said: 'I'm not prying, you understand, but in a situation like this . . .'

'I see your problem, Mr Hawthorn. You're the house-master, are you?'

'Yes.'

'Can I ask one question? I'm a bit surprised the boy isn't at home.'

Pause. Then: 'Ye-es. We did send him home yesterday—

but he came back in the evening. I suppose . . . well, here, at least we can keep him busy.'

'Sounds like the best thing. Half past three then?' We rang off.

Then I unpacked the fresh suitcase, changed my blue pinstripe for a slightly more swinging number in a chalky mud colour, with fresh shirt and tie to match, and after that there wasn't any reason not to call Jack Morris at the Ministry of Defence.

He wasn't in his room but he can't have been far off because his secretary said: 'Hold on, Mr Card,' in a cool voice and went away and came back and said: 'He wants to see you as soon as possible.'

'He can buy me lunch, then. Ask him where.'

She did another round trip. 'He says he's damned if he's going to be seen in public with a disreputable character like you. Be here at half past twelve and he may lend you half a cheese sandwich.'

'Tell him to stuff it up and blow it out.'

Still perfectly cool, she said: 'Half past twelve then, Mr Card.'

I was going to be there, and we both knew it.

I parked the car near the St John's Wood taxi rank and took a cab down to Chancery Lane—there's no hope of parking down there—and tucked Bertie Bear up in my safe deposit. On second thoughts, I took out one of my guns—a streamlined little Mauser HSC chambered for ·22. Mockby might get more subtle next time, but there would certainly be a next time. With him or somebody.

After that I prowled the bookshops until I found an identical copy of *Bertie Bear*. Well wrapped; I felt enough of a bloody fool just buying it. Then I dillied and dallied over to Morris's office.

At a conservative estimate, about half of London is Ministry of Defence buildings, ancient, modern and in-between. This one dated from the thirties and was probably taken over during the war; the oversized entrance hall and exaggeratedly solid stonework gave me the idea it had originally been built for an insurance company or the Masons.

I signed in at the box-office affair in the middle of the hall, was given a chit and an elderly uniformed guide, and we set off down the green-and-cream corridors of power or at any rate secrecy.

I'd first met Jack when I was a captain doing a stint of my own in the Ministry, though not the same building. His job was something rather vague on the civil counter-intelligence side—vague not because it was Above And Beyond Top Secret but because he was mostly supposed to be keeping a finger in whatever everybody else in CI was up to: the DI5 boys, Special Branch, Foreign Office and all the service intelligence and investigation outfits. He'd actually been on the streets for a time with what was then MI5, but you don't last long at that. Your face gets known and then you either get slung on the compost heap or transplanted into an office.

He was a shortish, chunky man of around sixty, with smooth grey hair, chubby bunched-up features, thin-rimmed glasses and a cheery manner. He waved a hand from behind his cluttered desk and said: 'Hullo, buster—pull up a chair.'

There were two other desks in the office, both the same round-edged green metal jobs, neither occupied. I found a spare chair dating from Ballista Mark I days, dragged it up and sat cautiously. Jack took a bite of a sandwich, waved the rest at me, and mumbled: 'Lemme see your licences.'

'Driving, dog or TV?'

He swallowed. 'You know which, buster.'

I passed them over. He skimmed through the Ministry one, took a little more time over the police one. Then looked up 'I'm cracking up, my eyes are going. I can't find any Walther PP in short nine-mil here.'

I shrugged. 'I don't have one.'

He chuckled. 'Now you mention it, you don't, do you? You must have been sorry to see that go down the drain.' And chuckled again, then took another bite of sandwich.

I said: 'If you know of one going, I'll apply to have it put on my licence.'

'Last one I heard of was in Arras. Our French chums have asked the Yard to try and trace it, with special reference to you. Now ain't that sweet?' He was a good contact man.

He added: 'No connection proven—so far.'

I was happy to hear it. I hadn't expected anything else, but you can never be dead sure.

He stood up and stretched his back and grunted. He was wearing indoor country clothes—houndstooth check suit, criss-cross pattern shirt, brown brogues, all in rather light-weight materials. Club tie, but I didn't know which club.

'Now—*I* know why you were carrying an unlicensed gun around France.' he said, aiming a ham sandwich at me. 'Because your own licences don't mean a thing over there, you couldn't get a French licence, and so you might as well take one that can't be traced back if you used it. I'm not even asking you where you got it and having you tell some bedtime story about it. But——'

'It wasn't in this country.'

He gave me a quick sharp look, then nodded. 'That's something, then. But the French papers have tied that gun to you and the ones here would have done if we didn't have a law of libel. So far as I know none of the newspaper boys has been clever enough to ask if you've got a pistol licence. *We* wouldn't tell them, and I've made sure the rozzers won't either, but there's plenty of other people who must know. Down at your pistol club and so on. Once that gets printed, there's going to be people asking why we give licences to people who then go running around France playing James Bond with unlicensed Walthers. Are you getting the picture, buster?'

I nodded.

'Why d'you keep calling me "buster"?'

He thought about it. 'Habit, I suppose. I usually only do it to people I like.' He sat down again and riffled through some papers. 'When's the last time we asked you to do a bodyguard job for us?'

'When those Libyans were over here for the oil treaty.'

'And that was last autumn. You've got a lot of guns on that

43

licence in return for not much work. How much d'you really need 'em? Or the licence?'

The windows were closed and the room was full of dry, warm dusty air faintly spiced with pipe-smoke. Civil Service air. They mix it up in a secret plant just south of the river and pipe it out to all the offices all over London. You can see the pipes running along the underground tunnels next time you're in a train. It's good for you. Breathe enough of it and you lose all anger, all pity, all concern. And you never die; you only fade away like the red ink on an old forgotten file.

I took a deep breath and it tasted familiar, almost reassuring, then let it go again slowly. There wasn't anything to be said. So I just shrugged.

He sipped coffee from a thick crock cup and leaned back in his chair. 'Why d'you go in for these outside jobs, buster? You're doing all right on the security consultancy, aren't you? Why not stick to it?'

'That's three questions and you don't expect me to answer any of them.' I got up and reached over and helped myself to one of his sandwiches. Cheese, just as he'd promised me, and the bread tasted of bread, so maybe his wife made it herself. 'You sound just like my solicitor.'

'I'm surprised you've got a solicitor. Why pay for advice if you don't take it?'

I sat down again. 'What's the overall situation?—about Fenwick?'

He sat forward and clasped his hands. 'The Yard's been asked to look up his background—and yours. Apart from that, Arras thinks it was probably a British murder that just happened to happen in France. They're rather niggled: seem to think it breaks some rule of exporting.'

'They could be right. So, what now?'

'Just keep your name out of the papers, buster. Think of yourself as on probation.'

'Thanks, Jack. Think of yourself as getting stuffed.'

'What are you up to, now?' he asked calmly.

'Asking a few questions here and there.'

'I should leave that to professionals.'

44

'It's a free country.'

'Thank God that at least isn't true,' he snorted. 'But if you wanted to find out what it was all about, why didn't you stick it out in Arras?'

'Because there wasn't anything I could tell them. And for Christ's sake, I'd've . . .'

'I know: you'd be in the freezer. Well, you deserve it, you knew you were breaking their laws, and you were being paid for it. But *if* you'd stayed, then we'd have some case for prodding them into action. You were in the business long enough to know how the Foreign Office works: it just needs to express concern that a British national got himself murdered over there and would they kindly get their fingers out? And we'd have done it, too.'

'For a Lloyd's underwriter, driving a Rover and with an address like Kingscutt Manor. I mean not a bus driver on a package tour.'

He looked at me in a growly sort of way. 'Are you getting class-conscious in your declining years? Never mind. But what happens if the FO expresses concern now?—the Arras rozzers express concern right back that the only witness has scarpered to Britain and what are we doing about *that*? HM Government really doesn't like its citizens getting bumped off abroad, underwriters *or* bus drivers, so don't bother to read the next Honours List too carefully, buster. You aren't on it.'

'You can't have been breathing the air in here too much recently.'

'I *what*?'

'Skip it.' I stood up. 'Was that the Order of the Day, then?'

'It was. Now get out and let a man have a working lunch in peace.'

'I can't until you've signed my pass. And I'm not supposed to walk these corridors unguarded.'

He scribbled a signature and threw the little green slip back at me. 'Find your own way out. Call it an initiative test.'

I looked back with my hand on the doorknob. He was hunched over his desk, munching savagely at another sandwich and sorting a bunch of loose papers with sharp flicks of a finger. Above him on the wall was a neat framed notice saying *Don't leave until tomorrow what you can get some other poor sod to do today.*

I said: 'Arras is right, you know. They're only where it happened. And I'll tell them when I know why.'

Without looking up, he took off his glasses, clenched his eyes and squeezed the bridge of his nose with forefinger and thumb. 'When we want to see you again, buster, you'll hear the sirens first.'

I closed the door behind me as gently as I could, but the click echoed like a gunshot in the tall corridor.

EIGHT

AT NEAR HALF PAST THREE I was winding up Harrow Hill in a convoy jammed behind a heavy truck. As far as I could remember, I'd never been up there before; I was sure I'd never visited the school, but just assumed I'd know it when I saw it. I didn't.

The road turned into a winding village street of cafés and shops that both seemed to sell only hunting horns, and then huge houses that looked as if they'd been built by Victorian and Edwardian tycoons. After that the slope started down the other side. Oh dammit!—the one thing everybody knows about Harrow School is it's on top of a hill. I squeezed over to the side and waved on a big white Vauxhall that immediately started hooting behind me.

There was a pure-looking young man in a shabby raincoat trudging along carrying a squash racket. I leaned across and called: 'Excuse me—can you tell me where the school is?'

He looked blank, then said: 'Well—here.'

I nodded at the tycoons' village. 'What, this?'

He glanced up and down the road. 'Yes, every building you can see is part of the School.' Then he grinned. 'It *is* a bit odd. What house did you want?'

'Cundall's.'

46

He pointed; it was only twenty yards away, a solid flat-faced red-brick affair, four storeys high. 'Thanks. Do you teach here?'

'For the last three years—I still get lost myself. And I teach geography.'

I parked in a tiny gravel forecourt that was already mostly full of a small estate car. Before I reached the door—a stone-framed item borrowed from a Robin Hood movie—it opened, and Hawthorn himself came out.

Well, it had to be; you'd've known him for a schoolmaster at half a mile in flat darkness. Tallish, thinnish, a bit stooped, with a close-cut fringe of white-grey hair, a moustache that was just a bristle patch of the same colour, and a camouflage-coloured tweed suit that looked as if he'd collided with it rather than put it on. Horn-rimmed bifocals and a pipe, of course.

We introduced ourselves and went through into a big room that was more or less furnished and overlooked a big garden at the back. There was a small coal fire burning in a big fireplace and it wasn't winning.

I chose a chair close to it.

Hawthorn spent a little time doing open-cast mining on his pipe, finally lit it and made a harrumphing sound.

'This is a rather odd sort of occasion. I thought I'd seen most things as a house-master but not this before. You must have a rather, ummm, interesting job.'

I understood: he was immigration control. But fair enough —that must be part of his job.

I made it friendly and chatty. 'I spent sixteen years in Army Intelligence. A lot of it was learning the latest interrogation procedures; you know the sort of thing—how to talk a man into talking, sizing him up, deciding what to believe and not. And a few years practising it.'

Now he got it. He gave me a resigned, but quite friendly, little smile.

I owed him more than that. 'Most of my work is advising on security: stopping industrial espionage and so on. All this electronic bugging gear—eavesdropping devices—were first

47

invented for the real espionage services, so I'm fairly well up in them. I don't do a bodyguard job very often.'

He said: 'Ummm,' and then: 'Quite so,' and then: 'You seem to have been rather an innocent bystander, on this occasion.'

'That's a fair summing up. I didn't know what was going on and I still don't.'

'You didn't, ummm, interrogate Mr Fenwick by the latest procedures?'

I grinned. 'No.'

He puffed smoke at the high ceiling and stared after it. 'I have a double problem here.' He looked down at me again. 'I'm talking about the boy, of course. In the first place, ummm, his father doesn't seem to have been quite such an innocent bystander—or am I wrong?'

I shrugged as delicately as I could. 'He knew more than he told me. He damn sure didn't know he was going to get shot at, just like that. But obviously he was involved in something.'

He nodded, jerking little puffs of smoke from his pipe. 'Quite so. The boy was rather close to his father. I'm wondering if this news would be, umm, helpful.'

'I might be the one who brings the bad news from Ghent to Aix; I couldn't be the one who stops it. There just ain't no way. The police in both countries are involved, now.'

He harrumphed again and looked sternly at the mouthpiece of his pipe. 'Quite so. But my second problem—you might well appear a rather glamorous figure to young Fenwick. The pistols and so forth, at his age. On the other hand——' he suddenly smiled at me, 'I don't think you do glamourize yourself.'

'Who knows? Why am I in this job?'

'Quite so.' He glanced at his watch. 'He'll be free from four-fifteen. You can either talk in his room—he shares it with another boy—or go out to one of the cafés on the Hill.'

'I'll leave it to him. How old is he?'

'Just fourteen. Rather a bright boy; he's in the Classical Remove now. That doesn't mean he's a classic, by the way. In fact, he's obviously going to be a historian.'

48

'You said he was close to his father. D'you mean he wasn't close to his mother?'

He cleared his throat and frowned at nothing. 'Ummm . . . I've only met the lady twice . . . Have you?'

'Not yet.'

'She gives him rather a lot of money. That's usually a sign that she isn't giving him much else.'

'You don't think Fenwick and his wife were breaking up?'

He said carefully: 'We usually learn about such things because they're reflected in the boy's behaviour. No, I can't say I've seen any of the, ummm, usual warning signs.'

There was a sound like distant thunder. Hawthorn smiled gently. 'The young lions have returned to their lairs. I'll have him shouted for.' He went through to the hall; I followed. He opened a door on the far side and the noise swept in over me. Hawthorn told a few people to shut up, then sent an older boy off down the corridors shouting: 'Fenwick! A visitor for Fenwick!'

'We appoint a few specific "shouters",' Hawthorn explained. 'If one makes it a privilege, they stop the rest of them shouting.' He smiled wryly. 'They'll probably entertain you rather more lavishly on the boys' side. Come back and see me on your way out—if you want to.'

A boy in the standard uniform of blue blazer, black tie and grey flannels came galloping up, then stopped dead when he saw me. He was thin, pale, tall for his age—maybe five-eight —and rather better-looking than I remembered his father. Delicate features, large brown eyes, dark hair that kept falling into his eyes and kept being swept back again.

'Mr Card?' he asked.

'James Card.'

'I'm David Fenwick, sir.' He held out his hand, long and slim, and I shook it. 'Would you like to come up to our room, sir?' His voice was very polite, very controlled.

I followed him along a tall, dim corridor, up two flights of stairs, along another corridor, and into a small square room that was surprisingly bright and well-furnished. Mrs Fenwick's

49

money, maybe? Anyway, you could see that the school cash had run out with a couple of iron bedsteads folded up against the wall, two small desks and chairs, and two elderly chests of drawers. Private enterprise had brought in two slim Scandinavian armchairs, elegantly shaded table lamps, a fan heater and some sprawling indoor plants. Probably the school hadn't provided the prints of armoured fighting vehicles, either, nor the big publicity picture of some Italian actress coming up out of the sea having lost almost everything except weight.

A second boy jumped up from a desk where he'd been working on a plastic model of a tank. A Russian T-34, I think. David introduced him as Harry Henderson: shorter, stocky, with a cheery red face and wild fair hair.

Harry said: 'I'll push off now,' and waited for David to say No. David did and Harry cheered up and turned back to me. 'Would you like a drink, sir? We've only got vodka and sherry at the moment, I'm afraid.'

He picked up a couple of dark bottles off the mantelpiece; one was labelled 'Liquid Plant Manure', the other 'Metal Polish'. 'We have to keep them in these to stop the monitors and old Hawthorn suspecting.'

Hawthorn had mentioned 'lavish entertainment', hadn't he? 'I'll take vodka, please.'

He poured me a healthy dose of plant manure. 'I'm afraid we're out of tonics, but half an Alka-Seltzer tablet makes——'

'I'll have it straight.'

We all sat down. Harry turned suddenly serious and stared at me, then at his feet; David just went on looking pale and controlled. I said: 'Cheers. Well, you rang me. Here I am.'

David said: 'Could you . . . well, would you mind sort of telling me what happened?'

So I told it again. When I'd finished, he nodded and asked: 'Do you think it hurt him?'

'Not much. A bad . . .' I looked at him, wondering if he could take it, decided he could. 'A bad bullet wound gives a tremendous amount of shock. You can't feel much through that.'

50

But it's pain that gives shock.

Harry asked: 'And you couldn't get a shot at them at all, sir?'

'Not a hope. They were behind a pillar and they took off just about the moment they'd fired. If I'd run after them, I might, but your father . . .' I looked back at David.

He nodded again. 'And you don't know who did it, or why?'

'No.'

'I spoke to the solicitor, Mr Underhill. He said you wanted to find out—is that right, sir?'

'Yes.'

'Why, sir?'

I stood up and walked around my chair. 'I don't know, really. Just inquisitiveness, maybe. A feeling of loose ends. Maybe no better reason than I hope I'll find out I couldn't have done anything more, anyway.'

David suddenly smiled for the first time. A nice, sympathetic smile. 'I think I understand, sir. Would you . . . would you find out for me, too? Can I hire you?'

I came to a dead stop, staring at him.

Harry said cheerfully: 'It was partly my idea, too, sir.'

'Look,' I said slowly. 'I'm not a proper private detective, I haven't got much experience in civilian investigations.'

David said: 'But you want to find out anyway.'

'Ye-es.' I sat down again. 'There's still another point. I don't know what I'm going to find—if anything. But it might turn out that your father was—well, mixed up in something.'

He was pale and serious again. After a while, he said quietly: 'I think I'd like to know, anyway. Will you do it, sir?'

'There's also the legal position . . .'

'You mean that I'm under age, sir? As I understand it, that means you can't enforce a contract against me. But if I paid you in advance, you'd be safe.'

'To quote your house-master—umm. If Oscar Underhill finds out, he'll want to have me pinched for stealing by trick, defrauding a minor and false pretences.'

David smiled politely. 'Then you needn't tell him, sir.'

51

'I needn't tell anybody—in fact, ethically I couldn't—without your permission.'

'He's going to do it!' Harry squeaked.

Hell, it did rather look that way. Certainly I needed a client. His father's fee hadn't run dry yet—I'd been paid in advance and cash, which is usual for bodyguard jobs—but pretty soon I'd have to be drumming up work on the security advice side and letting things slip on the Fenwick front. And he was supposed to have too much money from mother, wasn't he? I just hoped 'too much' was enough for me.

David reached into an inside pocket and took out a wad of crumpled fivers. 'There's fifty pounds here, sir—that's all you can get from the Post Office bank in one lump. I'll be able to get more from my real bank when I go through town again. Probably——' he paused and swallowed, 'for the funeral.'

The casual way he handled the notes cheered me up a bit. 'I don't know how much it'll take, but I'll give you a strict account weekly.'

'Probably quite a bit,' he said thoughtfully, 'if you have to follow where Daddy went.'

'Like where?'

'He's been in Norway recently; he sent me postcards from Bergen. But I don't know what he was doing—except that his syndicate rather specialized in Norwegian shipping.'

Harry added: 'It's the fifth biggest merchant fleet in the world. I think so, anyway.'

I nodded. 'Well, I won't start charging off to Norway until I've got a better excuse. Tell me one thing: did your father commute up from Kent every day?'

'Oh no. He had a flat in St John's Wood. He spent most of the week there.'

With or without the willing Miss Mackwood? I took out my notebook—in fact a last year's diary; I buy them by the dozen, cheap, at this time of the year—and wrote down the address. 'You wouldn't have a key to the flat, would you?'

'Yes.'

'D'you mind if I go along and burglarize it a bit?'

Instinctively, he did mind—but he saw the sense of it. He

took out a key ring and started working the key off it. Harry just sparkled: *this* was what private eyes were supposed to do —go busting into people's flats and turning them over.

David asked: 'Have you talked to any of the members in Daddy's syndicate, sir?'

I dodged. 'Who d'you recommend?'

'Well, there's Mr Winslow, he's rather cheerful, and of course Miss Mackwood. She ought to know what was happening.'

Her name didn't seem to have any particular echo, the way he said it. But I tried a little more, just in case: 'You've met her, then?'

'Oh yes. When I've visited Daddy at Lloyd's.'

He just might have said something about her turning up at a weekend, somewhere. So I just nodded and wrote down the name Winslow. I planned on trying just about everybody in the syndicate, if I needed to—but not until I knew more myself. The interrogator's biggest weapon isn't rubber truncheons or bright lights or electrodes on to the balls or anything—it's knowledge. Just that. The more you know, the more you can use as a lever to pry loose the rest.

I said carefully: 'How about your mother?'

He shrugged. 'I don't think she was very interested in Daddy's work.'

'I have to see her sooner or later. Do I mention that I'm working for you?'

'I'd rather you didn't.'

'Okay. You're the boss.'

He looked startled at the idea, then smiled.

'And now,' I said, bouncing a sideways look off Harry, 'I want you to talk generally about your father—if you feel like it.'

Harry got the look—or maybe he just had good manners. He got up sharpish. 'I'm off, now. I hope I'll see you again, sir.' We shook hands and he went out.

David smiled again, a little sadly. 'Well, sir . . . he was a rather quiet man. I think he worked hard. He loved Lloyd's— that was really his whole life. I mean he didn't have any hobbies; he just played golf most weekends, but I think that was for exercise. He didn't talk about his scores or anything.' He went off into a thoughtful dream.

I said gently: 'When he took you out at weekends or whatever—what did you do?'

'On our exeat Sundays . . . we went to a museum or to the pictures, or . . . whatever I wanted to do. He didn't have, sort of . . . many ideas of his own.' His eyes were slowly filling with tears; he blinked, annoyed. 'He was a very *honest* man. You know the Lloyd's motto is "Fidelity". Well, he really meant it, he really did. And I don't see why anybody should kill him!'

He put his head in his hands.

After a while I got up and touched his shoulder. 'All right, son—try a sip of liquid manure.'

He looked up and smiled through his tears and gulped at my glass, choked and sputtered, but looked a bit better.

'One last thing.' I began to unwrap my new *Bertie Bear* parcel. 'And I want you to take this seriously. Have you ever seen this book before? Does it mean anything to you?'

He stared at it, thumbed through it, finally looked up at me. 'What is it, sir?'

I sighed. I hadn't really expected, but I'd hoped. 'Your father was carrying it to Arras. Wrapped up. It was the parcel he was supposed to deliver.'

He looked back at it incredulously.

'Put it another way,' I said. 'Wrapped up, does it remind you of anything the same size? Anything to do with his work?'

He shook his head slowly.

'Most of his Lloyd's work was on little scraps of paper or big ledgers . . . You mean you think he was taking a dummy parcel?'

'That's one of the things you're paying me to find out. Well—is there anything else?'

He thought about it. 'I don't really *know*, but I *think* Daddy was hiring a private detective at one time.'

'You think?'

'Somebody rang up when I was staying at the flat at half-

54

term and I took a message for Daddy. It was just that he'd ring
again later and he said his name was James Bond and Daddy
said he was a sort of James Bond . . . well, that's all.'

I chewed it over and couldn't get any more taste from it
than he had. 'I'll see if I can track them down; there may be
some papers from them at the flat. And I'll keep in touch. If
you want me . . .' I explained about my problems with the
press, and gave him my hotel number—and my name there.

He showed me back down the stairs and to another front
door—the boy's entrance, I suppose. Did I want to see
Hawthorn again? No—I'd only end up telling him lies.

So I shook hands again, got quickly into my car and pushed
off.

By now the outbound traffic had built up into a snarling,
crawling stream, but I had a fairly clear run back to London.
I cruised past my flat and spotted what I had to assume was
the press Nachtwacht (so why couldn't a jumbo jet crash or
Princess Anne fall off her horse?). But at least the pubs were
just opening, so I parked at the hotel, then walked around to
the Washington.

Of course, I could have gone and burgled Fenwick's flat,
but maybe that should wait until the morrow. The building
would be emptier, and people are less suspicious of strangers
in daylight; they should read the crime statistics some time.
Then again, I could sit down with a big piece of paper and
write down everything I'd learned about Fenwick himself—
except I knew that would come out just a little bit south of
bugger-all. Or I could just have an early dinner and an early
bed. The day had got started rather early, and punch-ups
before breakfast take it out of me these days. Getting old.

NINE

I LET THE NEXT DAY get started at its own pace. When I
reckoned the working world had got into gear, I did a round
of telephoning: my answering service (nothing worthwhile),
Oscar (expected back this afternoon), and a couple of clients

just to reassure them that I was still around and in business (neither of them actually told me to get lost).

At about eleven o'clock I arrived at Fenwick's flat. It was on the second floor of one of those blocks built in the 1920s with rounded corners and metal-framed windows with lots of tiny panes; the best of German modernism and Elizabethan tradition combined. The flat door lock was a simple Yale without even a reinforcing strap, so I could have slipped it myself in a few seconds. But the key was my proof of respectability: an old family friend picking up some things for David in case anybody asked.

It was a simple two-bedroom, one living-room, kitchenette-off-the-tiny-hallway layout; the rooms weren't either big or small, but a bit higher than they'd build these days. I shut the outside door quietly and just sat down to try and absorb the feel of the place.

After a few minutes I gave that up; either I couldn't do it or it didn't work in this flat. The furniture was just furniture: not old or new, not cheap or pricey. Just comfortable. The only 'personality piece' was a small, round antique table, but you can't get a modern table that size and height anyway. There was a double bed in one room, a single in the other; built-in cupboards instead of wardrobes. No paintings on the walls—just a print of an old-style Admiralty chart and a couple of nice photographs of clippers under full sail.

So then I started to work the place over properly. Well, not properly: if you were on a real job—say an espionage case where you're up against professionals at hiding things—you'd take a team of men and spend a week on a flat that size. But I did what I could.

What interested me most was a smallish bureau-style desk, a reproduction of a style that had never existed outside Hollywood. It was locked, of course, but I thought that might be a problem that would solve itself if I left it long enough. It did: there was a duplicate key, along with one for a car and several for doors (at Kingscutt?) in an old tea caddy at the back of the kitchen cupboard. And people still wonder why burglars are traditionalists.

By then I'd learned that Fenwick hadn't been much of a cook, that he liked reasonably expensive, sober clothes, changed his shirts and pants a lot—anyway, he had twice as many as I owned, and presumably more down at Kingscutt—and kept everything neat and tidy. Using that description, pick this man out of a crowd.

There hadn't been any signs of Miss Mackwood—or any woman. And women usually manage to leave something around a place where they've got an emotional stake. Like a dog pissing up against lamp-posts and trees to mark out his territory. Not conclusive, of course (though it told me Mrs Fenwick never stayed there) but something.

Oh yes, and one other thing: somebody else had searched the flat recently.

There were only small signs, and maybe only somebody with a suspicious mind would have spotted them. A stack of clean sheets had been taken from the top shelf in the cupboard and put back too far, so that they were a bit crumpled; the trousers of a couple of suits hung slightly wrong; the bedside table lamp was moved so it didn't quite fit the dust pattern.

Mockby's boys? If so, he'd found himself new boys. This lot had been professionals, though not quite top class. The Yard? —no. They'd've done it properly, with a warrant and one of the family or Oscar in attendance, and they wouldn't have worried about leaving traces. Still, they'd do it sooner or later and *they* might spot traces; I put the sheets, trousers and lamp back in parade order.

So then I tried the bureau. I'd stopped being very hopeful about that; my predecessors would certainly have gone through it, and if Fenwick had been keeping a Dear Diary confessing All, then it wasn't likely to be there any more. The worst thing was I wouldn't *know* if there'd been a diary or anything; the place had stopped being a picture of Fenwick because somebody else might have taken, rearranged, even added, something. Hell's teeth—why hadn't I thought of him having a second place before, and come around and turned it over myself first?

57

Still, I did the bureau. It was as well-organized as I expected—household bills, bank statements, income tax returns and the jungle of paperwork that clings to any solid citizen like the ivy on the old garden wall. 'Dear Sir, with reference to your heating problems our engineering report suggests that the fault may lie in the ventilation system to the ultra-sub-dinglefoozit which indicates the need for a pre-frontal lobotomy and if you send us ten quid now we'll come round at the most inconvenient time and louse up your flat for twenty-four hours or infinitely whichever shall be the longer. . . .'

I grinned. At least Fenwick had had his small problems, too, like the rest of us. But those aren't the ones that get solved with a nine-millimetre pistol.

No strictly private stuff at all except a packet of photos of David taken maybe a year ago. And no letters or bills from private detectives, either. That didn't prove anything, of course, because you often don't want a detective to put anything in writing, and they often don't want to be paid by cheque; simplifies their tax problems.

So? So now it was one o'clock. I filed the bank statements and duplicate tax returns in the inside pocket of my raincoat and walked out into the rain with the brave, sad smile of any disappointed burglar.

First thing after lunch, I went around to a local woman who runs a small secretarial service. It took a little time to persuade her that I wanted to run her photo-copying machine by myself, and I may have given her the impression that I was protecting the private life of a cabinet minister, but I finally got it. By half past two the tax returns and bank statements were back in Fenwick's bureau and I was sitting on the hotel bed with the copies.

The bank statements might have sung like a sonnet to another computer, but to me they wouldn't mean a thing until I knew exactly what I was looking for. So I started on the tax returns. He'd given the Kingscutt address, allowances claim for wife, one Lois (how d'you pronounce that?) Linda

Fenwick . . . children: David James born such-and-such. I opened the form and got down to the meat.

It was thin on the bone. After a quarter of an hour I had a simple picture of Fenwick's financial life and times over the past three years. He'd had a basic salary of four thousand five hundred pounds plus a little less than five hundred in unearned income, which, at a guess, meant he'd got about ten or twelve thousand in shares. His wife had started off with about the same amount of share capital in her own name, but had sold maybe two or three thousand about a year ago.

Each year also had the note: 'Underwriting profits—to be agreed'. Well, I knew that Lloyd's doesn't let you take a profit until three years late: they keep it in the kitty in case of late claims. But I also knew that, for the years involved, he was as likely to have taken a loss as a profit. Lloyd's came a crunch with Hurricane Betsy in 1965 and stayed crunched for three years.

No mention of mortgage payments, but out of his total income of five thousand-odd, he was stumping up nearly a thousand a year in life insurance. I suppose that if you're in insurance you must believe in it, but this was ridiculous. His death would have cost the companies over thirty thousand quid—well over. Maybe it had been Mrs Lois Fenwick behind that pillar with a nine-millimetre.

That reminded me, and I rang Oscar. Yes, he'd just got back but he's very busy, no, even if it is about the trip, oh it's you is it? well, I suppose *all* right.

He came on.

'You again? There isn't much I can tell you.'

'You saw the cops over there?'

'Yes. Just between us, I don't think they're getting anywhere. They've asked Scotland Yard for help.'

'I heard about that. What about me?'

'Well, the inspecteur doesn't like you very much—he got his arse roasted for letting you run away—but they've come round to thinking you weren't very important. Just a small-time bodyguard who beat it at the first shot.' He enjoyed saying that.

Then he added: 'They'd still like to know what was in the parcel, mind.'

'I'll tell them some day. Did you ask about the gun?'

'Yes. A Browning pistol, I gather.'

'Which model?'

'Damn it all, I couldn't ask too many questions—they'd've had *me* in the small back room.'

'Sure. Thanks.' At least it hadn't been Mockby's Walther.

'In case you'd like to know, the body's being shipped back tomorrow. Funeral probably on Saturday. I wouldn't send any flowers, if I were you.'

'Bit quick, isn't it?'

He made a verbal shrugging noise. 'Why not? There's no question about identification, no problem about cause of death, there'll be no argument about the medical evidence—if they ever come to trial.'

'I suppose so. Well, at least he's left the missus pretty well fixed.'

His voice got suspicious. 'What d'you mean?'

'Just that. Nice dollop of insurance, hardly any death duties to pay, and nothing owing on the house.'

'Have you been playing nasty little private detective tricks?'

'Not really. I may not even have been illegal. Well?'

'Well what?'

'Was he shovelling the profits from the good years across to her, putting it in her name? And into the house?'

He sighed. 'You really don't know anything about Lloyd's, do you?'

'My word is my bond and my bonds are in my wife's name, you mean?'

'That's the Stock Exchange. Now stop being clever and start using your brains, unless you stuffed *them* down a drain in Arras. D'you know what Lloyd's is? The biggest betting shop in the world. And people like Martin Fenwick are just high-class bookmakers. D'you know how to make money as a bookie?'

'Set the right odds, I'd guess.'

'That's half of it, and it's what Fenwick did: insured only the right ships at the right premiums. But the other half is simply having as much money as possible so you can take as big bets as possible and make as much profit as possible. Lloyd's formalizes these things. The more capital you can show *in your own name* the more bets you can accept. I mean insurance you can write,' he added sourly.

'So you'd be a bloody fool to put it in your wife's name? It would just be cutting your own profit-making potential?'

'I'll say one thing for you, Jim: as long as it's written in letters of fire ten feet high you do get the message sooner or later.'

'All right, all right. So where did she get her money, then? And why did he buy that house outright?'

'Who says he owned it? Or that she did? No——' He repented hastily. 'Just forget that. And I told you *not* to go poking into these things.'

'Sorry, Oscar.'

'Now, I'm busy.' And he slapped the phone down.

I suppose I might have asked him about Fenwick hiring a private detective—he wouldn't have picked one from the yellow pages, he'd've asked his solicitor, same as he did about a bodyguard. But Oscar would never tell me, so why tell him I knew it had happened?

Slowly, reluctantly—and rather dazedly—I picked up the bank statements and started analysing them, as far as I could.

The standing orders were easy enough: they'd be payments to the life insurance companies and probably the rent on that flat. Then he seemed to take a regular twenty pounds a week, various odd amounts that were probably clothes or garage bills—and three times in the last year he'd drawn cheques for two hundred and fifty-nine pounds a time. Why? Why so precise a repetition of such an amount, and why three?

School fees, of course. Harrow would cost around seven hundred and fifty a year in these hard times.

But the real message was that the income and expenditure matched like a foot in a footprint. Yet it was only a one-legged trail I was following; half of Fenwick's life just wasn't there.

No cheque that could have covered a new Rover 2000 in the last year; nothing for running expenses on a house big enough to call itself a 'Manor'—and nothing for running expenses on a wife for that house, either.

Working just from those figures, it was as if Kingscutt didn't exist—neither did Mrs Fenwick. Except for paying a thousand pounds a year, more than a quarter of his net income, in life insurance for her.

Assuming it was for her, of course. I rang Hawthorn at Harrow.

We said a few polite things, then he asked: 'I suppose you, ummm, want to speak to David?'

'If he's available.'

'I'll have him shouted for. I rather get the impression that you're, ummm, working for him, now?'

His intelligence system was good—but that would be part of his job, too.

'You may be right.'

'I rather feel I stand—and particularly with this boy, now —*in loco parentis*. I can understand him wanting to know why his father got, ummm, killed, but I'm still a little apprehensive about the effect of him finding out anything detrimental to his father's image.'

'Yes. But I told you: the police in two countries are working on this, too. I can't stop them.'

'Quite so. It's, ummm, difficult.'

'They aren't interested in protecting anybody's good name. I just might be.'

'Yes. I'm sure you know your own business . . . Here's David now.'

He came on the line. 'Mr Card? Have you found out anything?'

'Nothing much. It takes time. But I wanted to ask you something. . . .'

'Yes, sir.'

'Have you heard from any insurance companies just now?'

'Well—yes, sir. There's been three of them.'

'Can you tell me what they said? I mean roughly?'

62

'Well, just that my father had taken out life insurance in my name. They said it's quite a lot.'

Ah!

'Fine,' I said. 'Good. Well, that's all I really wanted to know.'

'Is it?' He sounded disappointed.

'I'll be in touch.'

'I hope you'll be coming to the funeral, sir. It's on Saturday, at twelve o'clock.'

'Well, I . . .' I hadn't expected this.

'You'd have a chance to meet my mother, sir. And the other members of the syndicate.'

'Fine,' I said. 'It's at Kingscutt, is it?'

'At the village church; you can't miss it. Will you come up to the house afterwards?'

'I'll be there.'

You bet I would. By now I was very curious to meet Mrs Lois Linda Fenwick. There has to be a reason why a man spends a quarter of his income, money he must be hungry to use to build up his career at Lloyd's, just to make sure that, if anything happens to him, his son will be financially independent of his own mother.

TEN

I MOVED BACK into my flat that night. The story had dropped out of the day's papers, and I scouted the place three times and found nobody watching, so by half past nine I was home, unpacked and drinking at a price I could afford.

The phone rang. Oh hell—that could be tricky. I thought about letting it ring, then decided not. I was going to have to come back to life some time.

But just in case, I tried to disguise my voice. Scots; it comes easiest. Well, at least I could say: 'Aye?'

The other voice was distant, female and also stage Scots. 'Would it be posseeble to speak to Meester Card?'

'Who is it wanting him?'

A moment of confused mumbling, then: 'It is Mrs Card.'

'Mother? What the hell are you doing with that accent?'

'It's Jamie? Are you at the flat? I thought you were on the run. I didn't want to give myself away in case the police were there.'

'Ah, it isn't as bad as that. I . . .'

'It's exciting, isn't it? I'm so glad your job isn't turning out too dull. Security advice sounds so *dreary*. Your father would have loved this.'

Ummm. Maybe.

She rushed on: 'I just wanted to make sure you didn't want anything, dear. Like money or a place to hide out.'

'No, it's fine. I just——'

'Well, I mustn't keep you. I expect you're after the men who did it, aren't you? And I won't say any more because they're sure to be tapping this line.'

'No, I don't think——'

'Look after yourself, dear, and don't put anything in writing. Tell me all about it some day. Goodbye, now."

I put the phone down and slumped. Mother's phone calls always took it out of me. Had I really joined 'I' Corps of my own free will? Had father really chosen to spend the 1930s playing Lawrence of Arabia when he could have stuck to straight regimental soldiering? Or had we both been pushed just a bit?

I spent the rest of the evening tidying up the mess the Mockby boys had left, poured myself a final Scotch and was ready for bed at about eleven.

So then the doorbell rang. I grabbed up the little Mauser and called: 'Who is it?'

A calm voice said: 'Police, sir. Will you open the door, please?'

Just like those bastards to come around and start their just-a-few-simple-questions when you've had a long day. Intentional, of course.

I looked around for a place to park the gun, but finally just

64

shoved it in a pocket. No reason for them to have search warrants. I opened the door.

They came in quickly and the first one hit me in the stomach. As I folded over I just had time to see there were at least two, with the flattened faces of men with stocking masks on. Then my hands were grabbed and wrenched behind me and fingers started working on my neck—exploring, then pressing skilfully. The room seemed to fill with mist.

A voice said: 'He's going.'

I tried to choke, but darkness beat me to it.

'My name is James Card. My rank is Major. My number is 2530510.'

I knew him, didn't I? Must have been in the Army with me.

'Come on, now, old friend—where have you got it?'

'My name is James Card. My rank is Major. My number is 2530510.'

I knew that voice, too.

'Give him a bit more.'

'You've got to be careful with this stuff.'

'Give him more.'

Part of me was floating, gently, drowsily. But there was pain, stiffness, only felt distantly, as if telepathically from another body. It surged and then fell away in the drowsiness. . . .

'Now come on, old friend . . . where do you keep the book?'

'My name is James Card . . . my rank is Major . . . my number is 2530510.'

'Where is it? Just tell me, then you can sleep.'

'My name is James . . . Card . . . m'rank is . . . Major . . . number . . .'

'A bit more . . . Now where is it? Where did you put it?'

'My name . . . Bertie Bear . . . Major Bertie . . . Bear . . .'

'What the hell's he babbling about? . . . Now where's the book?'

'Bertie Bear . . . is in the . . . bank.'

'Jesus Christ—have you sent him crazy?'

'You can't be sure about how this works.'

'Well, give him some more.'

'He may have too much already . . . maybe he'll get better.'

'Bertie Bear . . . in the bank . . .'

'Great galloping Jesus . . .'

The drowsiness ebbed, the pain rushed in, giving me a moment of vicious clarity. I knew who I was; I knew I was tied up and blindfolded; there was a steady pain in my left arm . . .

'Give him more.'

'I told you——'

'And I'm telling you!'

A little movement of the pain. I suddenly clenched every muscle and jerked and twisted as hard as I could. I felt a needle grate on my elbow bones and a wild extra stab of agony . . .

'God, he's broken the needle.'

'You clumsy bastard.'

'He did it!'

'Get another one in, then.'

'I haven't got another . . .'

'Jesus, I've got a right moron here.'

'We can't go on. What do we do with him?'

'Leave him. Just cut him loose.'

'I haven't got a knife . . .'

'You haven't got a future, mate!'

Hands jerked me, sending more pains through my stomach and neck. Then I felt my body loosen.

'He'll do for a while. Come on.'

Noises, feet on thin boards. A voice fading away, plaintively: 'I just don't understand why it didn't . . .'

Then just silence, darkness, loneliness and time not passing. Am I dying? Not alone, not in the dark! I want voices! I want that lovely drowsiness, the non-pain, the sleep . . . No. The drowsiness is dying. The pain is living. And God, am I living.

I moved carefully, then reached and pulled loose the rag around my eyes. It made no difference; the darkness around me was close and solid and windless. The inside of my left elbow was a steady ache laced with sudden pain. I sent my right hand exploring.

66

I was lying on a metal camp bed, just that, on the raw thin springs. Useful frame for lashing a man out on, when you come to think of it. But where was here? I reached around and touched canvas. Below it, a low wooden wall. And along it, an upright metal pole. So?

Very carefully, I pulled myself upright, clinging to the pole. The invisible world spun around me, the floor shifted slightly under me, creaking. Then I knew I was in the back of a lorry.

It took me time, I don't know how much time, to feel my way to the tailgate and slide, carefully carefully, down to the ground. Rough concrete below. And no sky above.

But a faint dim square in the darkness far off. I shuffled towards it. Hit something. A car. Another. Then I was trudging up a slope into the air and the cold blue streetlights. So then I had to be sick.

Maybe it cleared my head a bit. I sat on a low wall and stared around at the empty bright street, the parked cars, the trees at the corner, black and bright green in the lamplight. I'd been in an underground car park beneath a new block of flats over near Primrose Hill. Less than half a mile from home. And no further to a doctor's house, or maybe even the Moon. I started to get started.

ELEVEN

HE SAT on the foot of my bed—his spare bed, to be accurate —and said: 'Do you remember much of last night?'

'It hurt like hell, you butcher.'

'Aye.' He'd been twenty-five years south of Scotland but a flavour of the accent remained. 'You've told me yourself you'd been shot full of Pentathol. I couldn't risk giving you anything else while I dug out that needle. Did they teach you to break off needles in your own arm in Intelligence?'

'They suggested it. You didn't give me a whisky either, you old Scrooge.'

'Same reason,' he said calmly. He leaned forward and looked into my eyes professionally. 'Aye—you're clear by now.' He handed me a glass of brownish stuff. 'I don't doubt you breakfast off it usually, though it's lunchtime for the law-abiding classes.'

I sniffed the drink suspiciously, but it was real Scotch. 'Thanks, Alec. Cheers.'

I swallowed and nearly unswallowed immediately. It hurt.

He nodded. 'Yes, you've had a bomp in the stomach; it'll hurt for a while and there's nothing I can do about it. And your neck, too.'

I sipped cautiously.

'And now,' he said, 'we'll talk about the police.'

'Did you report me?'

'No, not yet. There's no law against breaking off a needle in your own arm, though it's quite a trick. And there's nothing to stop a man falling against something and bruising his stomach. But it's the neck, man, the neck. Anybody who could put that much pressure on his own carotid with his own hands could likely bugger himself as well and we'd have fewer problems with roving queers.'

I grinned—and even that reminded me of the neck. 'Alec— I'd report it myself if it would do any good. But these lads were professionals; nobody would know where to start looking.' Then a thought struck me. 'The one using the needle —did he know his stuff?'

He considered. 'There's nothing to finding the vein in your arm—it sticks out at you. But knowing how to use Pentathol, drip-feeding it in and keeping you just on the edge of consciousness—well, maybe that took some training.' He stood up. 'If it was a doctor I'd want to see him struck off.'

'If he was a doctor I'll bet he has been.'

He nodded. 'Well, come back tomorrow and I'll change the dressing. It'll ache for a while, but you can buy yourself a fancy black sling and collect a lot of misplaced sympathy.'

He turned to go, then turned back and gave me the Scotch bottle. 'One more—just one, mind, and Laura'll bring you up some soup. I've got patients who don't look for trouble.'

68

I walked around to my flat, feeling naked and vulnerable without a gun. Outside my own front door, I suddenly wished I'd had somebody walk with me: there was no reason why the Pentathol squad shouldn't be waiting for a second crack. The thumbscrews this time, maybe.

But they weren't.

They'd turned the place over again, of course. Hastily, but just efficiently enough to make sure I wasn't hiding anything of Bertie Bear size. And they'd left Bertie himself—the second copy—lying there only half hidden in a pile of books. Well, that settled that, anyway: nobody loved Bertie for himself alone, which was a relief.

I searched only well enough to make sure they hadn't left my Mauser HSC lying around and they hadn't, of course. All this was getting a bit awkward: I was running out of small, easily-concealed guns. All the stuff in my deposit box was long-barrelled target ·22s or serious ·38 revolvers and nine-millimetre automatics—including Mockby's Walther. I did a little telephoning around among friends more or less in the gun business, and by the time I was back home watching a frozen pizza defrost, I'd done a trade. If Mockby had ever thought he'd get his gun back again it was too late now.

What I'd got wasn't ideal, but it was a help: a four-inch-long Italian copy of the old Remington derringer, which itself had been a near-copy of the gamblers' sleeve gun designed by Derringer. This had two superposed barrels in ·38 Special calibre, which gave it the punch of the normal American police revolver but was small and flat enough to hide on a spring clip up my left sleeve. The nameless friend threw in the clip holster as well; he should never have had the gun—even the Ministry won't license that sort of weapon, let alone the cops—and I think he was getting tired of the risk. There was at least a chance of getting the Walther on his licence (you pretend a relative died and left it to you: they don't believe you, but it saves face all round).

When I'd finished the pizza I spent an hour watching TV and practising a fast draw whenever a bad guy appeared. In fact, you can't really be fast with a sleeve gun unless your hands are close together already, as when praying or shaking hands with yourself, both of which look a bit odd in a tense situation. But you're as fast sitting down as standing up, so it's a good gun to watch TV with, at any rate.

TWELVE

FRIDAY MORNING WAS MISTY, with a touch of frost underneath. I got up slowly, feeling stiff just about everywhere, started the electric percolator, then busted my last egg trying to boil it. The only letter was a formal invitation to the Kingscutt funeral—posted in Harrow. I still didn't like the idea, but I was still going to have to do it.

I spent most of the morning typing up a report I was doing for a chemicals firm:

'Dear Sirs, I have examined your offices, laboratories and manufacturing plant with regard to the security aspects, and must say that I am impressed by the measures you have taken to render them espionage-proof (*always flatter the bastards first; they'll tell others that you're a bright, observant type*). However, there are a few areas in which I feel security might be improved . . .' And you end up: 'I suggest you keep this letter in a safe place and do NOT have it copied since it would be a useful guide to any industrial spy trying to penetrate your organization . . .' That always impresses them.

Actually, the worst danger they had was the managing director, the sort who wouldn't tell you his first name during the working day and boasts about his new inventions in the golf club. How the hell d'you put *that* in a formal letter?

About the same time I was wondering if I'd got a stamp, and if so, where, the phone rang. I skipped the Scots accent this time, but still I only said: 'Yes?'

'Major?' A familiar voice. 'Dave Tanner.'

A private detective I'd first met when he was a Military Police officer. A tough one, though if you're not breeding a tough army you may as well give up wars and where's the fun in that?

Anyway, Dave had got out earlier than me and gone further; he now ran quite a sizeable agency, and I'd worked for him for nearly the first year after I got out—though my guess was still that some of his boys specialized in the sort of thing I was busy guarding against.

I asked: 'What can I do for you? You've got a case that's baffling the keenest brains in your mighty organization?'

He chuckled. 'Could be, could be. How're you keeping?'

'Don't you read the papers?'

'Thought you'd done a pretty good job of staying out of them. Feel like a pint of lunch?'

'Maybe. Where?'

'The Lamb in Lamb's Conduit Street?'

'Okay. What's it all about, Dave?'

'Half past twelve. I'll tell you then.'

So that was that. I decided to take the car—I probably wouldn't have too much trouble parking there, and I wanted to know how my left arm would stand up to it. So I stopped off at the Regent's Park Road post office to send my report, and then it seemed easier to keep on that road and cross Camden Town through Parkway.

I got suspicious at the lights just before Parkway itself: a dark green Morris 1300 didn't pull up beside me where there was room for him. Instead, he slowed and dawdled up behind me. And he stayed there for the next mile. Mind, so did several others: this was a main route towards King's Cross and the City. But there was something in his pattern of driving that looked as if it was based on what I did.

Any other time, I'd have been happy to make his acquaintance; we could have run up a quiet dead end and had a nice cosy chat about who and why and related topics. But right now I had a date, so he'd have to go in the deep freeze. Lose him but make it look pure chance.

For that, you can't do anything fancy—no doubling back or suchlike. Just stick on a logical route and use the traffic opportunities. I put a big Ford in between us at the turn into St Pancras Road, added a Post Office van at the Euston Road lights, and a couple of taxis at Guilford Street. After that, it was just a matter of time before he got chopped off by a red light. It happened at the Gray's Inn Road, and I was clear to circle back.

I hadn't given anybody a lesson in road manners, but it hadn't been any worse than you expect from people who drive small, slightly hotted-up cars. Nothing to make him suspicious; he'd be back.

Dave was waiting for me well back in the bar and getting started on a plate of sandwiches and a pint of bitter. I bought myself the same—so much for an invitation to lunch—and sat down.

With the blue suit, the neat short grey hair and the well-fed build, you'd have placed him in the Stock Exchange or maybe on the floor of Lloyd's. Except for the face. The face had that shapeless, slightly lop-sided look of a small-time pro boxer. Dave had never boxed and I'd never asked him what else had happened: with a military cop you don't need to ask. Some soldier with a grudge had gone for a route march on that face one dark, lonely night. It's never the same after they use the boot.

He grinned at me, then saw the marks on my neck. 'You been having fun and games, Major?'

'No, somebody else was. How's business?'

He took a vast bite of cheese and tomato sandwich, showing a bunch of teeth that hadn't been improved by that dark night, and spoke around it. 'Full house; we're up to our ears. And that bastard Laurie's leaving me to work from an office again.'

Laurie was his security specialist; it wasn't good news for me, either, because he'd been reaching for work in my field. Still, I liked being on my own. 'No thanks, Dave. But I'll lend you a good book about security.'

'Get knotted, Major. D'you feel like doing a little sub-contract work, then?'

That was more like it. It might even be like picking up a new client or two. Firms that go security conscious usually stay that way and come back to you when they're making some

72

change. I might persuade them to come back to me, not Tanner. I waved a friendly sandwich. 'Any time.'

'I'll let you know—could be soon. Keep in touch, hey?'

'Will do.' I took a mouthful of beer and wondered why I hadn't ordered Scotch on that cold morning. 'You might do something for me, Dave. D'you know what inquiry firms Randall, Tripp and Gilbert usually use?'

'Never worked for them myself. . . . I think they've used MacGill. And Herb Harris. Why?'

'I think they recommended somebody to a client some weeks back. Name of Martin Fenwick.'

He cocked his head and squinted at me curiously. 'Fenwick? Is that the bloke that got killed in France?'

'That's the bloke.'

'Are you still mixed up in that, then?'

'Sort of.'

He munched thoughtfully, then shrugged. 'Well, it's your business. I'll ask around.'

'Thanks. And one more thing.' I gave him the number of the green Morris.

'Hell,' he said disgustedly, 'you can pretend to be a copper on the phone as easy as I can.'

'It isn't always that easy.' And I knew Dave didn't work that way anyhow; he had his own private contact with the Central Vehicle Index.

'All right.' He stuck the piece of paper in his wallet. After that we just chatted about the Army until the place jammed up with fashionable young things from the *Sunday Times* having double-spread four-colour ideas in each other's Cinzanos.

I bought enough food to last me through the weekend and got home soon after two. My faithful green Morris wasn't around, but he turned up half an hour later and parked almost out of sight beside the church. Did I want to go and talk things over with him? No, it was too public and too cold and my left arm was stiffening up again. Let the bastard freeze alone.

Dave rang back in the middle of the afternoon. 'Hope you

73

weren't expecting too much, Major. Hired car.' He named a small firm in West Kensington. 'D'you want us to try and shake something out of them?'

I thought it over. 'No, leave it lay. Thanks anyway.'

'Pleasure. I'm hoping to hear something about a job on Monday, but it's likely to be out of town. Could you make it?'

'What company is that?'

'Come off it, Major; they're *my* clients. No poaching. Will you be free?'

I could probably fit it in; Fenwick's affairs weren't exactly developing at a rush. 'Likely enough.'

'See you, then.'

I walked to the window and the Morris was still down there. A hired car probably meant a professional. A newspaperman wouldn't need to hire a car in London, and anyway, he wouldn't get a story just by following me around. It looked as if somebody had put a private eye on me. Mockby? He was the obvious thought, but he'd probably have done it on a bigger scale; one man to watch one man was bloody nonsense. In a city, a proper inconspicuous tail job takes thirty men and several vehicles; no kidding, that's what it takes.

When the pubs opened I strolled up to the Washington for a jar and a hope of getting a look at my new friend. But he wasn't that sort of fool. The Morris followed me, all right, but he didn't rush into the pub right behind me. Probably he came in some time in the next ten minutes, just to see if I was meeting somebody, but a whole lot of people came in around that time. And when I went out, the Morris had gone.

He was back by the church when I reached the flat. I don't know what time he went to bed, but I made it by half past ten.

THIRTEEN

SATURDAY was a crisp, clear day; so far we'd had every sort of March weather except the traditional winds. Now it was blue and bright, but still with snow lying in the Kent fields and the farmers indoors swearing the hop harvest was fruz to hell and they'd have to sell the Rolls if the Government didn't increase the subsidy.

I had company heading down through South London, but he didn't really stand a chance in that Saturday shopping traffic; I lost him by real accident before we reached Bromley. And once I was on clear roads, I let the Escort go. Nothing too chancy, but just holding her on a chosen line through the bends a couple of m.p.h. before her back end would start hedge-climbing, the grass brushing the sides. It made me feel . . . well, maybe in control of something, for once.

A quarter of an hour before Kingscutt I slowed down; my left arm was starting to ache again anyway. I drove in like any sober City gent—apart from the car, my suit and various purple marks on my neck; I put on my black sling once I'd parked, too.

It was a small village of varying styles up to and including advertising agency weekend restoration, but the church was genuine Norman and The Volunteer pub, just across a triangular village green, was genuinely open. I took a large Scotch and soda.

A man in a black suit and a gin-and-tonic asked politely if I was there for the funeral. I said I was, then pinned him down before he could pin me: 'Did you know him in the City?'

'I'm in Lloyd's, yes. On the brokerage side. And you?'

I chose the opposite alibi. 'Just a friend of the family. Terrible business.'

'Yes. And that other chap with him, running away like that. Englishman, as well.'

I shrugged hopelessly. 'I suppose every country has its share of them.'

'Very true, very true. Well, I don't know about you, but we're certainly going to miss old Martin.'

'Popular chap, was he?'

He chuckled briefly. 'Oh, everybody knew Martin and his little tricks.'

'He . . . *what*?'

'The last of the old-style underwriters. In the old building

75

where we were really crammed together, there was a great tradition of practical joking, you know. Real clubroom atmosphere. Just about all gone since we moved to the new place—but Martin did his best.'

'Well, I'm damned.' I stared into my glass, but the dizzy feeling wasn't coming from there.

He smiled knowingly. 'Seemed a bit of a dull dog to you, did he?'

'Well, you know . . . nice bloke, straightforward . . . no real hobbies or anything. . . .'

'I suppose that was his way of relaxing—just switching off the power. Rest is as good as a change, eh? But Lloyd's certainly won't be the same without him, and damned if you can say that for most of them. I mean us.' A church bell began to toll and he emptied his glass quickly. 'Sounds like action stations. You had a bit of an accident?'

I went with him to the door. 'Yes. Just met a ditch that was driving dangerously.'

He laughed cheerfully and we marched out towards the church. A convoy of big black cars was just closing up beside it, with a sizeable and well-dressed crowd spilling out and around. There was money in that mob; almost all the men had real black suits, like my brokerage friend, not just 'something darkish' like mine.

'See what I mean?' he said. 'They wouldn't turn out like that for most of us.'

I put on an impressed expression and managed to lose him on the fringes of the crowd. I took my time going in, which was a mistake: I'd forgotten the old English tradition of rushing for the darkest back pew, so I got a nice conspicuous seat in the middle. Paul Mockby spotted me coming past and said: 'Jesus Christ,' but not the way it usually gets said in church.

The service was the full works, and we sang, not muttered, the 23rd Psalm. Somebody with a voice so inbred that it could hardly climb out of his mouth read the lesson, and the vicar —a pleasant-looking fluffy old boy—gave an address.

He did his best, but he was carrying too much handicap for that course. Partly because it was soon clear that Fenwick had never been inside the church before, so we had the bit about pressures of honourable toil in the ancient market places of the City; and partly he was obviously scared that the Sunday papers might prove the corpse to have been the biggest fraudsman since the Swedish Match King. Overall, he ran steadiest on the midst-of-life-we-are-in-death and cut-down-in-his-prime stretches.

I spent most of my time talent-spotting, but all I got was Hawthorn near me, David and young Harry Henderson up front beside a tall, slim woman. No Maggie Mackwood that I could find.

Then we back on our feet and the coffin was processing past on top of six of the tallest, smoothest-dressed men I'd ever seen. *They* didn't come out of any Kent hopfield. You know, there *is* something about the rich being bigger than the rest of us; maybe their mother's milk comes pasteurized.

I caught David's eye as he passed and got a quick, nervous smile. I tried to get a proper look at the tall woman—who must be Mrs Lois Fenwick—but she was wearing a proper veil, and all I did was confirm that tallness and slimness. And she moved well. A black, prim-looking governess dress that fitted the occasion nicely.

I hung back again, and was just about last out. We didn't have far to go: they'd found a plot in the churchyard itself. And, if you care, there's worse places than an old Kentish churchyard to go down for the last time.

'Can't stand this sort of thing. Harping on death and all that. Turns me over, rather. Sorry, old boy.'

He was standing deliberately well back, just as I was, and stirring a little heap of damp confetti with an elegant black shoe. The rest of him was tall, thin—and also mostly black, of course. Except the tangled fair hair, the blue eyes, the face with its mid-thirties boyish good looks.

'Three quick volleys, shoulder arms, right turn and run for the canteen?' I suggested. It was a guess, but he was old enough to have done National Service.

'That's more like it,' he admitted, then grinned suddenly. 'What were you in?'

'"I" Corps.'

'Ah.' He nodded, like when you say you clean out dustbins. 'I was only National Service, of course.' He named a Lancer regiment where you have to prove your father was a colonel and your mother a horse, and one of them rich besides.

'Willie Winslow,' he added.

That struck a bell louder than the verger had done so far. 'You're in Fenwick's syndicate? I'm James Card.'

Automatically, he started to hold out a hand—then froze it halfway. His face got wary.

'You weren't the chap who . . . ?'

'That's right.'

'Oh, I say.' He thought about it, frowning. 'It's all right for you to be here, is it?'

'I've got a better reason for feeling sorry than most here today.' I *needed* somebody in the syndicate, and if the Army Pals act wasn't going to work, then maybe the self-pity bit would.

He looked at me sharply, then relaxed into an uncertain smile. 'Well, I suppose that's right. . . .'

In the middle of the black crowd the vicar's voice started buzzing.

I whispered loudly: 'Met a broker chap in the pub just now —he was telling me Fenwick had been the life and soul of the party at Lloyd's.'

Willie looked firmly front but sounded quite friendly out of the side of his mouth. 'Oh rather. You should have been there the day they launched the new Cunarder. He kidded one old boy the thing had capsized, and the damned fool believed him for quite five minutes. Nearly went through the roof. Terribly funny.'

'Odd . . . he didn't seem like that to me.'

'Well, you hardly really knew him, did you, old boy?' He was letting me down lightly. Kindly.

Then there was the hollow sound of earth on the coffin lid, and that was the loudest bell of the day. Willie winced, but stiffened himself. 'Suppose I'd better . . .'

'Not me.' He looked rather relieved, then strode into the

crowd with that loose-jointed action of a Lancer walking
away from a dead horse.

The crowd began to break up, slowly but speeding up as they
got away from the smell of mortality.

Mockby was one of the first going past me. 'What the hell
are you doing here?'

'I didn't see Miss Mackwood,' I said pleasantly.

'At least *she* had the decency to stay away.' Thank you,
chum—every little helps, even if it's only somebody else's
conclusions. 'What happened to you?'

'Some mob tried the same thing that your boys did, only
more so.'

He considered this, then nodded. 'Good.'

'Real pros—including the truth drug bit.'

'My God,' he hissed. 'Did you talk?'

'Some. They didn't seem to think it was enough—so maybe
they'll be back.'

'Look, boy, you're too small for this business.' He was
talking fast and low. 'Come and see me back in London.
Right?'

'Can I bring a bodyguard?'

He gave me a quick sneer. 'D'you know a good one?' and
went away.

David Fenwick appeared at my elbow.

'You don't seem to get on with Mr Mockby, sir. Did you
have an accident?'

'Nope. It was entirely intentional.'

His eyes opened wide. 'You mean it was to do with . . . ?'

'Yes.'

'Oh. I didn't want you to get involved in——' And just
then, Mrs Fenwick appeared behind him. She'd pushed back
her veil and it was entirely an improvement; it isn't always,
even at weddings. An oval face, almost little-girlish, with a
small nose, large brown eyes and sculptured Cupid's-bow lips.
She looked pale, but pale looked like her colour, and calm and
dry-eyed.

She smiled gently in my direction and murmured: 'I don't

79

think we've . . .' and let it fade away so I could ignore it if I wanted to. Her voice had a faint American accent.

David stood forward. 'He's Mr Card, Mother. He was with Daddy when . . .'

For the moment her face went blank. Just zero. 'Oh . . . you're the . . . How nice of you to come.' She managed to look pleased.

'I invited him,' David said firmly, not letting me take any of the blame.

Mrs Fenwick nodded without looking away from me. 'Quite right, darling. I do hope you'll come up to the Manor now. I'm sure Willie will give you a lift. . . .' She glanced over her shoulder and Willie appeared there.

'Willie, dear, have you met Mr Card?'

Willie said Yes, and went on looking at me as if I was something new at the zoo whose habits might not be suitable for children.

Mrs Fenwick smiled again and passed on. David gave me a glance and followed.

The crowd flowed around us. After a moment Willie took out a gold cigarette case, offered it to me, took one for himself. 'I suppose it's permitted on Holy Ground. . . . I see you know young David.'

'Yes.'

He thought of asking me how, then didn't. 'Brave young fellow. What a business, what a business.' He puffed for a moment. 'I suppose there wasn't anything else you could do, really.'

'Except get stuck in Arras jail.'

'Oh yes, just so. Quite frightful. D'you think they'll catch the chap that did it?'

'Not unless somebody tells them what it was all about.'

We started to walk towards the gate. He said thoughtfully: 'I say—it couldn't have been anything to do with the syndicate, could it?'

'I'm bloody sure it was.'

He looked at me. 'Did Martin tell you, then, before he . . . ?'

'No, but Mockby's as good as told me since.'

'Really?'

'Well, he's really been threatening me and sending his chauffeur round to sort me out and search my pad. To me, that's telling.'

He went thoughtful. I'd been piling it on a bit, of course. Our Willie seemed a little limp to use as a lever, but when you're trying to prise information out of men like Mockby you take whatever you can get.

He went on being thoughtful about it until we reached the cars. There he waved a hand. 'This is my bus. Be a bit of a squeeze, but . . .'

The 'bus' was a long black-and-silver streak of pre-war Mercedes, all bonnet and exhaust pipes and huge headlights and twin horns and a sort of miniature engine-driver's cab stuck on the back as an afterthought. It was as old as I was, but lasting a hell of a sight better. I've never seen a car in more beautiful nick.

'Not really the thing for these occasions,' he said, vaguely apologetic, 'but it's the only black job I've got right now.'

I clambered in and he twiddled a few knobs and the engine went off like a peal of thunder, first time, just as you knew it would. We prowled gently round two sides of the green, then blasted off up a short hill. But he never got a chance to get really moving: we were part of a long queue of expensive transportation winding up to the top, turning right, then in through a pillared gateway.

The Manor turned out to be a square Victorian pile, built long after real manorial times. But solid under its gothic trimmings, with well-kept sloping lawns and rose-beds and low garden walls. He parked on the gravel driveway—the forecourt was jammed already—and we walked round and up half a dozen wide stone steps and in.

The serious drinkers were already scraping the bottoms of their first glasses and the chatter was beginning to warm up. I caught Harry Henderson carting a tray around and latched on to a Scotch, then stood on the fringe of the crowd and looked around. We were in a tall, rather shapeless hallway, with a log fire burning in a grate at one side and a wide stair-case on the other. A couple of pictures on the walls looked genuine, if a little pale, and were well lit. The furniture was thin on the ground, but real antique stuff. It hadn't been the same taste that had furnished the St John's Wood flat. And it hadn't been the income declared on those tax returns that had furnished here, either. What had Oscar implied about this house?

Behind me, a man's voice said: 'She makes a damn pretty widow, anyway.'

Another said: 'Don't suppose she'll make one for long.'

'Hardly. Wouldn't mind a nibble myself, if it comes to that.'

'Not quite the thing to say when you're standing here drink-ing poor old Martin's gin.'

'Hers, old boy, hers.'

The voices faded into the general babble and I drifted on through to a big, light corner room. It was sparsely furnished —even the concert grand didn't crowd you in that room—but all good. I stared at a picture on the wall and decided it must be late Turner. And nobody got later than Turner.

David came up with a tray of drinks and I reloaded.

'Can I have a talk with you, sir?'

'Sure. I'll hang around until you're clear.'

He pushed off; I collected a couple of classy canapés off a housekeeper-shaped woman and went on wandering gently. So far, I hadn't seen Mockby, and since he was difficult to miss I assumed he'd headed back to London to weed his money patch.

Then I came on a collision course with Willie, wandering lonely as an upper-class cloud with a fixed half-smile on his face.

He looked at me. 'I say—you've had an accident.'

It was only the third time we'd met that day. I tell you, you could bleed to death in this country until somebody decides he knows you well enough to call an ambulance.

'Nothing too bad.' I reckoned he'd had enough horror stories for one day. 'Tell me—was Fenwick a good under-writer?'

'Oh, marvellous, old boy—quite the best. We're clear up the creek and grounded on a falling tide without him. He actually knew something about shipping, you see. Most of them don't know a bosun from a binnacle.'

'The underwriters? How the hell do they insure them, then?'

'Oh, experience, statistics, averages, you know. I mean, you don't have to know anything about life to write life insurance, do you, old boy?' He grinned in his mild way; you couldn't quite imagine Willie giving a real rollicking grin. Might frighten the horses; even the tanks. 'But Martin was really interested, particularly in the Norwegian companies. Made us a leader, far as Norway went.'

'Leader?'

'Yes. You know what I mean? Well, it means the syndicates that traditionally set the rates with the brokers, they're the leaders—what? Another underwriter sees a broker hawking around a slip for a Norwegian ship and he looks to see if Fenwick's taken a line on it and if they have, well, he knows the premium's right—you know? Other syndicates are leaders in tankers or oil rigs or towing risks . . . but most just follow the lead of the leaders, what?'

I nodded. 'You sound as if you know something about shipping yourself.'

'The family used to be in it, old boy. But we got taken over in the fifties, so I just have to play with it at one remove instead of going for nice long cruises in the owner's cabin, what?'

He smiled and I smiled back. The politely vacant expression might be genuine, but I had a feeling there was something behind it. A man who knew himself, perhaps.

'How did the syndicate do, then?'

'I say, you're asking rather a lot of questions, aren't you, old boy?' But he was still perfectly pleasant with it.

'Guilt feeling, maybe. Wanting to know something about Fenwick, after what happened. . . .' I dangled the bait.

'Oh, mustn't be hard on yourself, old boy. Sure you did everything . . .' He let his voice drift away.

'It just bothers me.'

'Well, it's no secret we were doing all right. At least Martin kept us afloat in the bad years—and some syndicates broke up then, you know—and we were just about to get going again . . . and well, you know?'

'How did Fenwick himself manage in the bad years—without profits?'

His eyes went cool and distant, but a fragment of smile remained. 'Just haven't the foggiest notion, old boy. Know I had to sell a few hunters, though. Do you hunt?'

It was a bloody silly question, but it made it politely clear he wanted a quick change of topic.

'Only fleas on cats.'

'I . . . don't think I got that?'

'Fleas on cats. Great sport when I was in Cyprus. Get a light-coloured, short-haired cat—white or ginger's the best. And a pair of eyebrow tweezers, and track them through the undergrowth and—click!'

'Sounds rather sporting. But by rights there should be an element of risk in a blood sport.'

I shrugged. 'You could always try it on an unfriendly cat.'

He put on his vague smile and his eyes focused somewhere else. 'Just so, just so,' he murmured, then sort of faded away.

The party had thinned out a bit, but the remainder were settling in for the duration. David wandered past me, made a conspiratorial face, and led the way upstairs.

He had a big room—well, I suppose there weren't any small rooms in that house, except for the servants—nicely cluttered with the fallout of childhood. A worn old teddy-bear sat on the deep window-sill, a fancy electric train set was collecting dust in one corner, a battered control-line model Spitfire hung on the wall. And books; he had books the way Cyprus cats have fleas.

I picked up a fat volume from beside the bed: Barbara Tuchman's *The Guns of August*. 'Have you read this?'

'Only once so far, sir. Do you know it?'

'Marvellous book. I think she treads a bit gentle on the original Schlieffen Plan, though.'

He concentrated. 'I thought it only went wrong because . . . von Kluck came down east of Paris instead of west—and exposed his flank.'

'Maybe. But nobody seems to have asked what would have happened if he'd followed the Plan and gone west. He'd've been out of touch with Second Army—or stretched pretty thin —and he'd still have been marching for a month and moving further than anybody else. Either way, he'd got a damned tired Army. And that was the Plan's fault.'

'I suppose so.' He smiled. 'Can I quote you in my essay, sir? —as an ex-Major of Intelligence?'

'If you like. Now—d'you want to hear how I've been getting on?'

'I'd like to know why you were attacked like that.'

'They were after whatever Bertie Bear was supposed to be. They found the new copy in my flat, and I babbled about him when they hit me with the truth drug technique, and they didn't want to know. So we know he was a blind, and there's something that size and shape around.'

'Not in Daddy's flat?'

'No. Somebody searched there before me, mind—' his eyes opened wide; '—but I got jumped *after* that, so if it was the same mob they didn't find it at the flat, either. And it can't be at Lloyd's or Mockby would have nicked it. He knows what it is, by the way.'

He thought about this. 'It might be in this house, then.'

'Yes. Can you go through his stuff here?'

He looked doubtful, but nodded slowly and fumbled at his inside pocket. 'I don't know if I should have done this, but— it's a letter my mother threw away.'

I suppose the code of the greater public schools doesn't encourage snooping through parents' wastebaskets, so I uncrumpled it—it had been screwed into a ball—and said quickly: 'Oh yes, you were right,' long before I'd found out he certainly *was* right.

It was on the office notepaper of Jonas Steen, Marine Surveyor (it actually said that in English), of Bergen, Norway. Handwritten, in a mature but slightly inaccurate style of a man who usually gets his thoughts typed out for him. And it said:

Dear Madam,

May I express my great sorrow at the terrible death of your husband, whom I also knew? It must be a very great shock.

I would not trouble you more at this dreadful time but there was a certain book I think he was carrying to France when he died. If it was not taken by Mr Card who was with him, do you please know where it is?

Yours with great sorrow,
Jonas Steen.

I read it twice, then said: 'A book. Just "a book". He's playing it pretty canny, isn't he? Not much help to your mother in finding it. You don't happen to know if she wrote back?'

He made a rueful face. 'I can't very well ask her.'

'No, I see that. Well, at least I can talk to this bloke Steen.'

'I'm not sure you really ought to go on, sir. I didn't know it would get as rough as . . . well, as beating you up.'

'Didn't know myself. But I can't stop as long as anybody thinks I've got this book.'

'You could say it was just a colouring book.'

'Yes? And you think they'd believe me?'

'I see, sir. I suppose they couldn't *risk* believing you.'

'Anyway, as long as they think I've got it they'll keep coming to me—and they won't be looking too hard in other places. It's made Mockby commit himself. And the party of the third part.'

'Do you think it could have been Mr Mockby who sent those gangsters to beat you up?'

'Very much doubt it. It's more the style of the Arras boys.'

He went pale, blinked, and turned away quickly.

I said: 'So I'll ring this bloke Steen and—well, we'll see. One other thing: would you consider bringing Willie Winslow in on this? Tell him you've hired me and so on?'

He fiddled at the train layout, switched a couple of points, joined a couple of carriages. 'If you like, sir. Why, though?'

'We might need somebody to put pressure on Mockby. Winslow's one of the syndicate, and he seems a sympathetic enough bloke, so . . .'

He still hadn't turned around and wasn't going to until he'd found a way of wiping his eyes without me noticing. 'All right, sir. Will you talk to him or shall I?'

'Better be you. Get him to take you for a ride in that ruddy great Panzerkampfwagen of his. But ask him if he'd ring me.'

He managed to get his sleeve into his eyes fairly unobtrusively, then wandered on and twiddled the model Spitfire. 'Did you find out anything at the flat?'

Had I? Had I honestly found out anything except a lot of figures that barely added up even into guesses?

'Not really. Just a general picture of your father's pattern of life. . . . I hadn't known your mother was American until today. Do you know her side of the family well?'

'I've met some of them. They're rather rich, I think. Mummy goes over to see them every year but . . . but I don't think Daddy got on with them very well. I don't think he wanted me to go. I haven't been since I was . . . nine, I think.'

Mummy flies over every year, does she? Which would mop up half her investment income for the year in itself—unless somebody over there sent her a ticket. And if they're rather rich, why shouldn't they? Why shouldn't they send her more than airline tickets? Like late Turners for the wall of the house. Like the house itself. And money to run it.

How would a proud man like Fenwick have taken that?

I said: 'Here—you'd better have the key of the flat back. The solicitors'll want it sooner or later.'

He turned and took it, looking no more than a little red-eyed.

As gently as I could, I said: 'I've seen soldiers cry in action. The best ones, too. I'll keep in touch.'

Downstairs, the party had dwindled to a handful who were sitting down by now and looking as if they'd move when the liquor ran out. Mrs Fenwick caught us at the bottom of the

87

stairs and looked at David with a slightly reproachful smile.

'You've been monopolizing Mr Card, dear. Now run along and see if anybody wants a drink.'

David said dutifully: 'Yes, Mummy,' and pushed off. Around her, he seemed to drop a couple of years. But maybe most children do around most mothers.

Mrs F sat firmly but elegantly on a long bench sofa and patted the space beside her. 'Do you want to tell me what happened that day?'

And that was as much choice as I got about speaking to her or not. So I told her—most of it, anyway. I left out Bertie B and some of the colourful bits when Fenwick died, but she got the rest pretty straight.

She sipped her gin-and-tonic and listened carefully, nodding occasionally. When I'd finished she just said: 'I'm sure you did everything you could.'

It was nice to hear, but a bit unexpected. 'He obviously wasn't expecting anything like that,' I said defensively.

'I'm sure he wasn't,' she smiled reassuringly. It was a nice, easy, little-girl smile, and she looked as if she could laugh out loud without spoiling anything. Most women look either as if they're acting or trying to call the fire brigade.

I asked: 'Have you any idea of who could be involved?'

'I'm afraid not.' A rather sad smile this time. 'He didn't talk about his work much. If it was anything to do with the syndicate, Willie might know. Mr Mockby certainly would.'

'Yes, and what he'd tell me you could write on a pinhead and leave room for all those angels, too.'

'You don't like Mr Mockby?' She looked almost mischievous.

'Only on first and second impressions.'

She nodded. 'I sometimes wish he hadn't joined the syndicate. Of course, he did bring in a lot of money. . . .'

That was as good a cue as I was ever likely to get. I ahem-ed and asked, as politely as I could: 'Are you . . . going to have any problems that way?'

For a moment her face went blank again, like when she'd first found out who I was. But then she smiled again. 'Oh, I think I'll manage. David's schooling will be covered by insurance. . . . I may leave this house; it seems a bit of a waste to keep on such a big place . . . and Martin's deposit in Lloyd's will come back to me, of course.'

'Of course.' Then I realized what she'd said. 'Come "back", was that?'

The smile got a little wistful. 'Oh yes. It was always mine to start with. You have to be born with money these days, and Martin wasn't.'

I picked my words like a man pulling thorns out of a lion's paw. 'You helped start Mr Fenwick up in Lloyd's then?'

'He was already a broker there when we married, but he wanted to become an underwriter and they have to have capital, you see. So of course he had to have mine.'

I'd've liked to know what that *of course* meant, but maybe I'd gone far enough in the thorn country. 'How long have you been living in England, Mrs Fenwick?'

'About sixteen years now. Are you going on trying to find out what happened to Martin?'

'Well, sort of. You haven't heard anything about why he was going to France? What he was taking, or anything like that?'

She looked at me for a moment, then said: 'No. I haven't heard a thing, I'm afraid.'

I just nodded, letting the lie sink in. It had been beautifully done; if I hadn't known it was there I'd never have felt it hit.

'I'm not really being much help, am I?' she asked kindly.

'Oh, I don't know. . . .'

'Had you thought he could have been being blackmailed?'

I paused and just looked at her sweet smile. She sipped her gin calmly.

'No,' I said slowly. 'I hadn't really thought that. Why should I?'

'Well, it does sound so much like it. He's taking something to a secret rendezvous to hand over to strangers . . . that was right, wasn't it?'

'Blackmailers aren't killers. The golden goose and all that.'

'I suppose not.' She sighed, as if sorry to see a good theory go down.

'Anyway—blackmailed for what?'

'How would I know? What do men with a flat in town get up to?'

'I don't know,' I said carefully.

'Have you met Miss Mackwood?'

I suppose if she'd painted it on a board and then hit me over the head with it, I might have got the message stronger. Just might.

I nodded.

'Pretty little thing, isn't she?'

I nodded again.

'Have you got a cigarette?'

'Sorry. Don't smoke.'

'Clever you.' She stood up with an easy flowing movement. 'I'll just . . . Would you like Willie to run you back down the hill?'

Upon the command 'Dismiss!' you execute a right turn, a normal salute, then break off and proceed in an orderly fashion back to your quarters.

I said: 'That would be very kind.'

FOURTEEN

I HADN'T HAD ANY LUNCH and it was too late for any pub to have anything edible left, so I'd just have to live on the canapés I'd lifted. For the first half hour I drove fast—not because of the Scotch, or at least I didn't think so—but because if I went slow I'd have time to think and that would muddle me even more.

But past Sevenoaks the traffic slowed me anyway. And maybe it was time I really tried to remember the Fenwick I'd known. No, not 'known'; just met.

He'd picked me up at the put-down place for Euston station. My idea: it's a one-way underground street so you can easily spot if somebody's being followed by a car that doesn't stop or doesn't let anybody off. But nobody was.

My first impression was of a man near fifty who'd probably stand up at just under six feet. Neatly dressed in a checked country suit (abroad counts as country to some people), with shortish greying hair and trim slight sideboards as his one concession to fashion. Generally fit-looking and tidy: you'd think he was Something In The City and you'd be right. And seemed a nice bloke. Had I ever learned anything more?

Driving south he'd told me as much as he ever did about the job: just that I was to be there at a rendezvous in Arras in case somebody or bodies unknown turned nasty. I should have asked more, of course, and a couple of times I'd probed gently, but . . . had he headed me off? Would he have told me if I'd asked him head on?

Then we'd chatted about the weather, the Common Market, a bit about cars—neither of us knew or cared much, but it's standard masculine manners—and rugger. He'd said he was married and I'd said I wasn't, not any more, and we'd left it at that. Maybe he'd seemed a little concerned—pre-occupied—but most clients in this work are ready to climb the walls.

We went to Folkestone-Bologne instead of Dover-Calais—just because it seemed less likely—and I bailed out before we reached the boat. Then we 'met' in the bar after I was pretty sure nobody had picked him up. He took water with it, I took soda. Significant?

The drive to Arras was quiet; I suppose both of us were thinking ahead. One thing, though: halfway along, he'd asked: 'Are you carrying a gun?'

Most people wouldn't say 'carrying'; it's more or less of a professional word. I said: 'Yes.'

'What type?'

'Are you interested in pistols?'

'Not all that much, but I met a lot in the Army: Control Commission in Germany in '45. Even had to carry one, at times.'

'Walther PP chambered for short nine-mil.'

'The old ·380 round? Not too common, are they?'

'They are now. Standard gun in a lot of British police

91

forces. Small enough to hide, doesn't shoot into the next county, makes a nice big bang. For me, the idea's to scare them, throw them off their aim. I don't usually get a chance for a really careful shot; the assassin gets that.'

I'd picked the word carefully; my last attempt to probe. But he just gave a grunt of laughter. 'Oh, there won't be anything like that.'

Well, so I now knew something he hadn't known.

But not much more. Because, in a way, I still agreed with him. There *shouldn't* have been 'anything like that'. Fenwick just wasn't the type to get shot, and believe me, I know the type. Most of my bodyguard clients just can't count the number of people anxious to get a shot at them, nor the good reasons for each shooter. That's why I like payment in advance. But Fenwick? No. It just doesn't happen to people like him. Except when it does, I mean.

Back home, I reheated the last of the breakfast coffee and washed up the breakfast bits and pieces and turned on the television and turned it off again when it was just football scores and finally settled down to ring Jonas Steen in Bergen. Now, there are several things you need to know about ringing a total stranger whose number you don't know—the office number on the notepaper was no use for a Saturday—in a foreign country, but the first is the most important: you shift the Scotch and the soda across to the telephone table before you even start. It saves a lot of dashing to and from the cupboard in the next hour or so.

So finally I got through. The line wasn't all that clear, so I couldn't guess much about him bar that he wasn't senile and his English was very good.

'My name is James Card. You knew Martin Fenwick, I think.'

'Ye-es.' Rather reluctantly.

'Well, I was with him when he died . . .'

'Why didn't you stop it?' Sharply.

'I would if I could, believe me. Now, you wrote to Mrs Fenwick about a book—right?'

92

'Why? Why do you ask?'

'I might be able to help you. What book were you talking about?'

'I didn't send him any book.'

I laid off to consider that. It sounded like a lie, though four hundred miles of telephone wire don't make these things easy. But if he *had* sent the book, what did that mean?

I asked: 'Well, where did he get if from, then?'

'I don't know. I don't think I want to talk to you any more.'

'Now hold on. I may have the book. What one were you asking Mrs Fenwick about?'

'It doesn't matter.'

I had the problem that must sometimes occur to people who ride alligators for a living: who's in charge around here? Steen sounded scared, but what of? Did I have some hold over him or was I begging from him? It helps to know these things.

I said: 'Who does it legally belong to, then?'

'The owners, of course.' And *that* was a power of help, too.

'Do you want it back, then?'

'It doesn't matter. I am stopping now.' And stop he did. Suddenly I was just sitting there staring at a humming phone and my left hand actually hurting, I was clutching so hard.

So I said: 'Damn, damn, damn.' Then I said: 'But don't think that you have seen the last of James Card. There is no mountain high enough, no sea deep enough, to hide you from my relentless pursuit. Unless it costs too much, of course.'

I put the phone down and immediately it started to ring, which always startles me. I had a brief wild idea it might be Steen ringing to Tell Me All, but it wasn't, of course.

'I say,' the voice said. 'It's Willie Winslow—you know? I've been trying to ring you for ages.'

'Sorry.'

'I had a chat with young David after you'd left. I see now why you were asking all those questions. I rather apologize you know.'

'That's okay—I knew I was sounding snoopy. Well, are you joining the Classical Remove Hell's Angels?'

93

'Am I . . . ? Oh, I see. Yes, rather. I mean, I think you're doing just the right thing. Anything I can do to help?—I'd like to pay my share, you know.'

'Well, if you feel like helping finance a trip to Norway. Bergen. Did David tell you about this bloke Jonas Steen?'

'He sort of mentioned it.' Of course, Willie wouldn't be the sort to approve of grubbing through Mummy's wastebasket, either. The Lancers almost never do.

'I just rang him. He sounds shifty as hell and scared with it.' That was putting it a bit strong, but it might help justify David's snoopery. 'He wouldn't tell me anything on the phone, but I'd rather like to go over and sort of lean on him, face to face.'

'Oh yes, of course.' Then his feet suddenly cooled. 'I say, you won't do any of that "I" Corps stuff, will you? It might look bad if you landed in jail.'

'I'll try and control myself. By the way, you haven't heard of him before, have you? He's a marine surveyor, whatever that is.'

'David told me. No, I don't think I know him . . . surveyors sort of value ships, you know—and tell you what needs doing or what damage has been done. Very important in insurance, of course.'

'That would be how Fenwick knew him?'

'I suppose, probably. I say, what was that about a book?'

'I was going to ask you. I *think* he sent Fenwick some book. I *think* it was what Fenwick was taking to Arras. So I *think* it was what got him killed. Now—have you got any ideas what it might be?'

There was a sort of silence with Willie making er and um noises, probably wondering how in hell you answered *that*. But he might just have had some inspiration; who was it said the only truly silly question is the one you don't ask?

What he actually came up with was: 'Just can't imagine, old boy. I suppose that's what you'll be asking him?'

'Among other things. Meantime, you might check up and see if there's anything in the syndicate's files that mentions Steen.'

94

'I'll do that on Monday.'

'And you might try leaning on Mockby and asking him what it's all about. He knows a lot more than we do.'

That was different; Willie found a whole new stock of ers and ums, then said: 'Yes, of course, I'll . . . The trouble is, he always looks at you as if you were a bloody fool and then explains things so that you don't understand them any better anyway.'

'Well, he won't tell *me* and I don't suppose we can get David to ask him, can we?' A slightly dirty crack, but I wanted results.

'Oh no, of course. Well, I'll see what I can do—you know?'

Getting determination into Willie was like fitting shoes on to a snake. And you can only try for so long.

I sighed and said: 'I'll keep in touch. Any ideas about boats to Bergen at this time of year?'

He tried to explain about aeroplanes and I tried to explain about aspects of aeroplanes I didn't like, such as getting searched and having a pistol found on you, particularly since some goon had hijacked a plane on Scandinavian flight only last week and they'd still be hopping, skipping and jumping about it. Perhaps he didn't get the exact point, but at least he recalled that the Bergen Line ran an overnight service from Newcastle on various days including possibly Monday. 'Do you know Norway?' he added.

'Never been there,' though it was about the one NATO country I hadn't managed to visit in the Army.

'Try the Norge Hotel. And their buffet lunches.'

Then he gave me his number—out in Berkshire—and assured me his mother would take any messages if he wasn't around (somehow I'd already decided Willie wasn't married, although he'd never quite said so) and we rang off.

I mixed one last Scotch and soda before taking the mind-bursting decision about what to eat for dinner, and drifted over to the window. The faithful green Morris 1300 was still there, glinting faintly in the street lighting. I wondered if he liked ocean travel.

FIFTEEN

AS IT TURNED OUT, HE DID.

Probably I could have shaken him on the way to King's Cross that Monday morning, but now I was curious about how far he'd go. So I just called a taxi and he stuck behind it all the way to the station. I couldn't be sure he'd caught the train because I still didn't know what he looked like. I'd know soon enough, though. I settled down with a small guidebook on Norwegian mountains, morals and prices. All seemed high.

Sunday I'd spent drip-drying my shirt collection, writing to David to tell him when I expected to have some news, and leaving a message at Dave Tanner's—they were big enough to keep a twenty-four-hour phone watch—saying Sorry but have to go to Norway. The Norway bit was pure swank: I just didn't want him thinking of me as small-time and priced to match.

At about noon I went along to the buffet car and drank a beer that came at blood temperature, and gnawed on a sausage roll that looked as if it was travelling on a season ticket. Then I just leant against the counter and stared at the steamed-up window, which was an improvement on what you can see without the steam on that line. Peterborough, Grantham, Retford, Darlington—that's no Golden Road, and Newcastle itself isn't Samarkand when you get there.

I took my time getting off and into the taxi queue, which was the one place where my shadow—if he'd caught the train —just *had* to be the bloke right behind me. What I got was smallish, middle-aged, with a blunt reddish face, thin hair and no interest in me at all. His clothes were just clothes: a thin overcoat in grey check, a mud-coloured suit, a solid old briefcase.

I didn't give him any help by shouting out: 'Bergen Line Terminal' to my driver or anything like that: I waited and saw. And the next taxi stayed right behind us all the way out of town—I hadn't realized how far the docks were—so he must have had more luck with the driver than I ever do. The few times I've had to say: 'Follow that car,' they always tell me I've been watching too much TV.

But we were alone by the time we reached the terminal—though that was likely on purpose, by then.

I got a first-class cabin without any trouble, but boarding didn't start until three o'clock. So I roosted in the terminal bar and caught up with the day's newspapers. At half past two my new-found friend came in, carrying a second-hand (I guessed) suitcase. So he'd been doing a little telephoning and shopping; he couldn't have been authorized in advance to catch boats to anywhere, even if he had the sense always to carry his passport.

The ship was the *Jupiter*, a nice enough modern job a bit bigger than the cross-Channel steamers. My cabin was on the inside—no porthole—and that apart, it was just a cabin with a bed and dressing-table and tiny bathroom, exactly what was needed and as memorable as a slice of bread and butter when you happen to need that.

I did a little unpacking and then went for a general snoop —carrying *Bertie Bear* in a big envelope. I'd brought it along just to see if it was the size of thing Steen meant, but now it might have a second use.

We sailed at five o'clock and when we were ten feet from the shore they opened the bar. The ship was far from full, and about half the other passengers seemed to be a ballet company: all tight trousers and thick sweaters and heavy makeup and voices that could strip paint at fifteen paces.

After half an hour my new friend came in and bought a beer and I started my Bertie Bear act. It involved just leaving the envelope where somebody like the barman would need to move it, then snatching it away before he could lay a finger on it. I did this twice, then felt I was risking overplaying the scene, so I just hugged it to me like an autographed copy of the Bible.

I played the same game at dinner, but after that the timing got tricky. On the boat, he didn't have to follow me around; in fact, he could have stayed in his cabin the whole voyage

and not lost me—if that was all he wanted. I hoped he wanted
a little more by now, but I couldn't always tell just where he
was. Anyhow, I spent half an hour in my cabin, then went
along to another, smaller, bar by the swimming pool just at
the end of my corridor. Bertie stayed under my pillow.

I nibbled my way through two Scotches and was ordering
the third when he caught up with me again. He paused,
smiled at the barman, gave the place a careful look—just as
if he was merely exploring—and headed down my corridor.

I let him have a minute and a half.

The cabin doors don't lock except from the inside. I tried
mine—gently, gently—and it was locked. I waited; he daren't
stay long. And I prayed the corridor would be empty when
he came up for air.

It was. He was back inside against the far wall and with the
door locked again before he could say a word, though maybe
that was because he had the derringer's two barrels up
against his teeth.

I held him pinned there for a moment, then counted: 'And
one, and two, and three . . .' and pulled back the hammer.
His face went dead white and he started to shiver. I reached
into his inside pocket and started tossing stuff down on to the
bed.

'Who are you working for?' I asked pleasantly.

'I got to sit down,' he croaked.

'Who are you working for?'

'I shall be sick.'

'Be sick. Who are you working for?'

By now I had all the paperwork from all his pockets. He
wasn't armed unless you count a small penknife, and he wasn't
going to kick or swing at me. His arms and legs were quite
busy enough just trembling.

'Who are you working for?'

'Herb Harris.'

'Ah. And who's *he* working for?'

He just folded up. On the way down he grabbed a chair
and got most of himself into it, then hung there, panting.

I backed off and sorted through his belongings. His name was Arthur Draper and his passport just said 'salesman', but he had calling cards and a phone credit card for the Harris Inquiry Agency. He hadn't stolen anything of mine, not that I could find.

Me and the gun sat and watched him. Gradually his breathing slowed down, he got a bit of colour back, and his trembling faded into nervous fiddling movements with his hands. The moment had gone, now—the loss of identity and will that goes with capture and makes it the best time for interrogation. If I reached him now, it would have to be another way.

'Where did you park the green 1300?' I asked.

He looked at me emptily, his hands plucking at his jacket.

'Should take more care of a hire car,' I told him. 'Herb won't like it. Who are you working for, by the way?'

'Get stuffed.'

'You're in no position to say things like that, mate. It's a big jungle and you took a wrong turning. Now . . . ?'

'You think I'm going to tell you?' He was getting back a bit of confidence; his hands were almost still.

'Oh yes.' I stood up.

'You won't use that gun.'

'Probably not.' I went over to my suitcase and kicked open the lid and scooped some clothes out on to the floor.

'You can't exactly torture me.' But he sounded puzzled.

'Nope.' I opened the drawers in the little dressing-table.

'So why should I tell you?'

I ripped open my bed and tossed the *Bertie Bear* book over to the suitcase. 'Because if you don't you're going slam into a Norwegian jail for robbery on the high seas and carrying a gun.'

He went flat pale again. 'I haven't got a gun.'

'You will have, friend. It isn't licensed to me, and you *are* in my cabin, and you *did* search it, and you're a private eye who might have romantic ideas about carting a gun around. It just fits—it sounds right. *And* it gets you off my back. What do I lose?'

I propped myself on the wall by the steward's call button and held up my wristwatch and stared at it. He lasted fourteen more seconds.

'Miss Mackwood.'

I met him again next morning, in the cafeteria. I'd got up too late for the real breakfast, but I obviously hadn't missed much else: that particular piece of North Sea was cold, misty and wet. Above the surface as well, I mean.

I was sitting over my third cup of coffee and trying not to hear the ballet troupe telling itself how much it had drunk last night and who'd spent how long in whose cabin when Draper dumped himself down opposite. He looked pink and cheery, although he hadn't changed his shirt, and was smoking a long thin cigar that smelt like diesel fumes. Unless it was his shirt.

'I've been thinking,' he told me. 'Right now you can't do a thing to me. I'm not in your cabin, you can't plant a gun on me—I'm fireproof. But you're not.'

'You've been thinking,' I said sourly. 'You want to lay off that stuff. Stunts your growth.'

'All right, Mister Big Time. All I have to do is call an officer and tell him you're wearing a gun. Him or the Customs when we get ashore. So why don't I do it?'

He looked as if he really wanted to know. I said: 'Because it's outside your brief and because all I have to do is tell Herb Harris how much you've told me and you're an unemployment statistic by return of post.'

He took a bite of smoke the wrong way and choked privately for a little while. When he'd finished, I said: 'I'll be staying at the Norge, if I can get a room, so there's no reason to tread on my heels. I'll spend the afternoon talking to people or perhaps something else. Come see me this evening and I'll tell you what I've done, or perhaps I won't.'

He glowered at me, his eyes thick with tears. But he was screwed and he knew it; there was no way in the world for him to follow me if I didn't want to be followed, so he might as well save his time and money.

'And give my love to Miss Mackwood,' I added.

SIXTEEN

WE ARRIVED IN BERGEN by the servants' entrance. Probably I'd expected to come up some great sheer-sided fjord out of a Daumier engraving, but I must have been thinking of a different season or place or something. What I got was twenty miles of low, humpy green islands on one side and low humpy green land on the other, dotted with houses and oil tanks, then a right turn and into Bergen harbour itself.

Also, it was raining. Not just casually, as if it was something it did every second day there—which is what the guidebook says—but as if this was the first and last time in years and it was going to get it right.

We docked just after midday, and I hung back, hoping the rain would get tired. It didn't. So at about half past I was out through the terminal and last in line for a taxi. But at least there wasn't any trouble getting a room at the Norge when I finally arrived. It was a modern block, seven or eight storeys high, with the town's air terminal occupying one corner at street level and a vast lobby occupying most of the rest—in contradiction to Hilton's First Law: keep the lobby small so anybody waiting gets squeezed out into the nice big cocktail bar and has to spend money.

It was also pricey, but a good hotel's an investment, I always tell my clients. They don't lose your mail or forget telephone messages, they fix your tickets in a hurry, they don't care what hours you keep.

Upstairs, I changed most of my clothes, hung my sheepskin on the radiator, took a duty-free swig from the bottle I'd bought on the *Jupiter* and rang Jonas Steen. I wasn't worried about him being out to lunch: according to the guidebook, Norwegians eat sandwiches at their desks but then knock off for the day at four or earlier. Anyhow, whatever he was or wasn't eating, Steen was still at his desk.

'James Card again,' I said cheerily. 'I rang you on Saturday, remember? Now I've come over to see you; just got off the boat. How're you keeping?'

'I do not want to see you. I told you that.'

'I know, but I didn't think you sounded totally sincere. Can I come round now?'

'No, of course you cannot. You cannot come ever.'

'Ah, I bet you say that to everybody. Snap out of it, get sociable. Just think of the trouble I've taken merely to get here: d'you really think I'm going to turn around and go home, just like that? No, of course not. I'm going to stick around and stir up a fuss. Talk to people about Fenwick, and books you sent him and things . . .'

'I did not.'

'No?'

I waited. Then, suddenly sounding weary about it, he said: 'Oh, so all right.'

'When?—now?'

'No—do not come to the office. I will finish at half past three today. There is a café, the Fontenen, by the office. I will see you there.'

'Half past three, Fontenen—right.' He rang off.

Nice hours they work; wonder if I could get Britain to take them up? Though, come to think of it, most places in the City already have.

By then I reckoned it was a bit late for my own lunch— though I found out later I was wrong—and tried the sand-wiches-at-the-desk routine by having Room Service send up one of their specials: smoked salmon and scrambled egg, which was a new experience. After that I felt dry enough to go exploring; it was still raining outside, so I just changed some more money, pinpointed various restaurants and bars—'I'm sorry, sir, but nobody in Norway is permitted to serve spirits before three in the afternoon' (which may account for the size of that lobby)—and got hold of a town map.

Still no sign of Draper, not since breakfast.

When it came time to go, the rain had eased up, fooling me into trying to walk it: according to the map, Steen's office and the Fontenen were only about eight blocks away. The centre of the town, the business area, seemed to be built over a short steep peninsula—and I mean steep—that separated two harbours. By now a lot of it had been rebuilt in that glass-and-concrete style that doesn't tell if you're in Tallahasee or Tashkent, but the dockside of the north harbour was a row of solid, high-peaked old warehouses, somehow bare-looking without the forest of sailing-ship masts in front of them. And behind, a steep wooded slope with crooked shelves of modern houses stepped up and up into the cloud that spilled over the mountain top.

A clean-looking, fresh-painted town, even in that weather, or maybe because of it. All the cars seemed to be white or pastel colours, every building—offices included—had the windows jammed with indoor plants. So then it had to start raining again and I made the last quarter mile to the Fontenen dodging the citizens playing at overhead fencing-matches with umbrellas across the narrow pavements.

The café was low-ceilinged, smoky, dark-panelled, as clearly Men Only as a nudie magazine. And they didn't serve whisky at all, ever or any time. I ordered beer and waited.

He was late. After half past three the place started gradually filling up, but not with Jonas Steen. When he was ten minutes late I found a phone and rang him and got no reply.

And so? So, being a master of disguise, he'd transformed his features with a couple of smears of greasepaint and shipped out as a Chinese cook on a guano boat bound for Chile. Or, realizing that he could never match his puny wits against the mighty brain of James Card, he'd taken a long step out of a tenth-floor window. . . .

I found myself swallowing hard. That last idea wasn't too impossible, not remembering how jittery he'd sounded on the phone. I gobbled my beer, and hurried out to see for myself.

The building was one of the new jobs, slim, glassy, five storeys high, with a small lobby of veined cat-grey marble, now jammed with typists waiting for the rain to stop or the boy-friends to start or just swapping gossip. I picked the name Steen off the board—third floor—pushed through the mob and piloted myself up in a lift.

SEVENTEEN

UP THERE, it was quiet and empty under cold neon lighting, just a straight bare corridor with offices at either side. I prowled the names—most of them seemed to be connected with shipping in some way—until I found Steen's. There was a light on behind the glass panel, so I knocked. And waited. And waited.

So? So because the door didn't seem to be locked and I'd come all the bloody way from bloody London via bloody Newcastle, I went in.

And I was just too late. By maybe a few minutes and certainly a lifetime. He didn't look anything but dead—sprawled back in his chair, arms and legs outflung, two neat, slightly bloody holes in his temple. When I took a deep breath I could smell the sweet-sour scent of powder-smoke.

I shut the door quietly and just stood for a while. Then I remembered he might not be Steen at all, so I wrapped a handkerchief round my hand and explored the pockets of the natty golden-brown suit. And it was him, all right. Alive, I'd guess he'd been in his late thirties, with fair hair left a bit long for Norwegian standards, no sideboards or moustache, a handsome fleshy face whose eyes probably hadn't bulged like that until a couple of small bullets burst his brain.

I moved away and something crunched under my foot: a little copper-coloured cartridge case. A .22, which I'd guessed already. And what else did I want to know?—apart from the way home to Mummy. But not this time; this time I had to stay I reached for the phone, then remembered the cops would prefer me to use another one, and then noticed the gun beside it. A .22, of course—Mauser HSC model, just like the one I'd had and had pinched a few evenings back.

It even had the same number.

'Now that,' I said out loud, 'really *is* cheating.' Then I just stood and looked carefully around the office. Time was running out and I was following it—but I'd still come all the way from London to see this bloke and—well, here he was.

104

It wasn't a particularly big room, and the only desk was Steen's own oiled-teak job, so he didn't have a full-time secretary. The rest of the room matched the desk: teak arms on the slim black-leather chairs, low teak bookcase, teak filing cabinets. Even the indoor plants on the window-sill were in a long teak trough. Maybe he knew somebody in a teak jungle.

All of which was fine if I was writing him up in *Homes and Gardens* but no help when it came to explaining things to the boys with big feet and disbelieving eyes. And I was going to have to explain—some, anyhow.

Top priority was that second cartridge case; that wasted me another half-minute. There were also a small cushion and a pen down on the floor—the sort of pen you stick in a desk-top holder. Probably he'd been writing when he got shot. I left it lying there, then started on the filing cabinet. D, E, F for Fenwick . . . Fenwick . . . no Fenwick. Not a whisper of one. Odd? How could I tell? Try Lloyd's—and there was more than a drawerful of that, but subdivided by what looked like ship names.

Anyway, still no Fenwick.

Try the desk diary—a nice big affair bound in black leather. Appointments for today: a shipping line in the morning, Larsen at two-fifteen, Fontenen at three-thirty but no mention of my name. And whoever Larsen had been, he wouldn't have left that diary if he was the killer. The rest of the desk was pretty clear: a small card index—names of ships and shipping lines—a brass pot full of pencils, the empty penholder.

But what had he been writing on? Well, whatever it was, my guess was the killer had lifted it. Probably a telephone notepad. So why pinch a whole pad when you can just tear off a page?

I'm writing something. Important. Secret. Somebody knocks on the door. I'm not expecting anybody, it's late in the day, I'm surprised. I call 'Come in,' but at the same time I open the central desk drawer and just slide the notepad in and out of sight, and he comes in before I've had time to put away the pen and—bang. And bang again.

I opened the drawer and took out the pad and tore off the

top half-dozen pages. And five seconds after, I was starting down the stairs.

There was still a small crowd in the lobby, so I strolled through listening to the thunder of my heartbeat, and just getting outside was the first day of spring. Even if I knew winter was on its way back.

By then the Fontenen was really filling up with prosperous-looking types steaming out the rain over the first beer of the day.

I ordered one for myself, then went to explore the gents' lavatory. It had a modern cistern, but the lid still lifted off, and the Mauser and the derringer—plus the clip holster—went down into the water, well clear of the ball-and-cock gear. The two cartridge cases and five blank sheets of note-paper just got flushed away; I was prepared to chance the sheet with writing on it—even if it did start off with the word CARD. Five minutes later, I was back in the lobby of Steen's building.

The crowd had thinned to three girls getting the word from two young men. I marched up to the janitor at his marble-topped counter and asked for Jonas Steen.

He looked curious at me, significantly at the wall clock.

'Does he expect you?'

'He said he'd meet me at the Fontenen café, but he's twenty minutes late and I just wondered . . .'

He shrugged, dialled on the house phone. No reply. He shrugged. 'He has gone.'

'But he *can't* have. He arranged to meet me. I've come all the way from London to see him.'

He shrugged again, but called something to the group and one of the girls considered and called something back. I don't know what, but enough to get him puzzled. And I'd done my part. Steen wouldn't rest lonely all night.

Even then, it took time. Janitors don't make fast, purposeful decisions. They stand there and think, or at least stand there. Then they pick up the phone and make two other calls and get two other no replies. Then they think, or stand there, some more. And finally they haul out a big bunch of keys and lead you over to the lift.

I watched, trying to look bored, as he went through the inevitable, useless ritual of knocking, knocking again louder, and then pasting an apologetic smile on his face and opening the door and leaning in to have a look.

'——!' he said. I mean, I don't know what he said but I know what he meant. And even from the back of his head I could tell there wasn't any more smile on the front. He lunged into the room, and I followed.

Just for the record, I said something like 'Good Christ!' but it was wasted. He'd rushed straight across to the body but was just standing there, not touching it, not really looking at it, not doing anything.

'Is it Mr Steen?' I asked.

'Yes, yes,' he said impatiently—and went on doing nothing.

After a while, I suggested: 'What about the police?'

'Yes, yes.'

And at last he picked up the phone.

They were fast and, as far as I could tell, good. There were a couple of uniformed cops on the spot inside two minutes, two motor-cyclists a half-minute later, and after that a car-load of plainclothes jacks. One of these took me back downstairs and parked me in the janitor's room behind the marble counter and leant against the door to stop the draught coming in or something.

And we waited.

For a long time voices and feet went hither and yon outside. Then at last somebody stuck his head around the door and called me out.

They'd turned the marble-topped counter into a sort of interrogation desk and communications centre. One of the plainclothes men was on the phone to somewhere, a uniformed cop was using a small walkie-talkie and accepting lousy transmission rather than go outside in the wet. Another jack was sitting and writing in a notebook. He looked up as I came in behind him.

He must have been about forty-five, with a rumpled brown suit, a bush of white-grey hair brushed back from a bony, triangular face with a big nose. And a cold. The nose was red and had a permanent drip on the end, the sunken grey eyes were damp and bleary. He looked at me with about as much interest as he'd've given to a lost umbrella and asked: 'You are English?'

'Yes.'

'Your name, please.'

I gave him my passport and he started copying.

'You are at a hotel?'

'The Norge.'

Calmly, without any embarrassment, he reached out for the phone and asked for the hotel, and checked.

When he'd finished, he said: 'You came only today?'

'Yes.'

'When did you come here, to this office?'

'Oh—ten to four maybe.'

The time struck him as odd, so we had to have the story about me waiting in the café and then going out to look if I'd made a mistake and there was another café nearby (just in case he checked and some waiter remembered my in-and-out bit) and coming back finally, then coming to the office and . . .

Halfway through this there was a shiver in the crowd and everybody seemed to be standing to attention—except my boy. A new man, tall and solid in a smooth black overcoat, black hair except for neat silver wings over the ears, a well-fed face, was suddenly among those present. If we'd been a regiment he'd have been the colonel; as everybody except me was a copper, he had to be the Superintendent.

He reviewed the troops with a cold bright eye until he reached me; then came over and asked a couple of brisk questions of my questioner. He answered them without looking up from his notebook and I knew just how he felt about senior officers who think they're helping The Chaps by barging into the middle of an interrogation.

Finally he'd helped enough and went away. My man dug in his pockets and found a handful of used Kleenex to wipe his nose on, a benzedrine sniffer to inhale from and a couple of yellow pills for dessert.

Then he looked up at me. 'That was the Superintendent.'

I nodded. 'I didn't catch your name.'

'Vik. Inspector (First Class) Vik.' He sighed and put away the notebook. 'I will perhaps call on you tonight. You will be at the hotel?'

'Sure. I came over just to see Steen. Now . . .' I shrugged.

EIGHTEEN

IT WAS GETTING DARK by the time I reached the Norge again, and well into legal whisky time so I found out why they don't serve the stuff until the end of the working day: because you need a whole day's pay to buy a single shot, that's why. I sat in the lounge bar on the balcony above the lobby and stretched a single Scotch into a slow-drinking record.

Maybe I chose that seat by instinct: at a low table right up against the glass front of the hotel, so that by looking down through the balcony railings and past a modern sunburst chandelier I had a perfect view of the lobby desk and the three lifts. I might have been thinking of getting early warning of Vik; as it was, I got early warning of Draper and Maggie Mackwood.

She was wearing a thick green-blue tartan cloak and carrying a brown vanity case; he was lugging a soft tapestry bag that looked more hers than his. When they reached the desk, she was obviously the only one checking in. When she and a porter headed for the lift (she actually got her bags carried; my researches had suggested that only happened in Norway for the King, and then only when he'd got a bad back), Draper wandered off and sat down in one of the chairs scattered over the middle of the big lobby.

Well, well. There wasn't any problem to how she'd got here —given a bit of luck in the air schedules she could have been here this morning to meet me—but that didn't tell me *why*. Unless she was thinking of taking up tailing me where Draper had left off.

Then one of the lobby porters started calling my name. It took a few moments for it to sink into Draper and for him to start wriggling to peer all around him, so I had time to duck. But now he knew I was still around the hotel.

A couple of minutes later the message reached my bar and a waiter with a nice balletic style curvetted over with a folded message slip. It said just:

> With reference to HSC will you take a telephone call at 7 this night exactly?

No signature.

Nijinsky was still hanging around because I was still clinking coins in my pocket. I asked: 'Who took this?'

'The telephone lady, sir.'

Was it worth chasing her up?—asking what accent the caller had had? But they never remember. I nodded and dumped some coins—too much, by his expression and fast take-off.

I suppose it was as good a way to do it as any. They'd be calling from a public phone so it didn't much matter if I had the cops listening in—and they knew I wouldn't have. But it didn't exactly help the naked feeling of wandering around without a gun. A quick trip back to the Fontenen?—but that area would still be under two thick coatings of coppers, and Vik would likely want to search me and mine if he came in tonight. The pistols would just have to stay there overnight and I hoped they would.

I had most of an hour before the phone call that would tell me something to my disadvantage, but the next drink was coming out of my own bottle. So I went upstairs, poured one, and tried putting a call through to Willie. I dug out Steen's last words and studied them while I was waiting. They went:

CARD

Gulbrandsens??

H & Thornton????

And a power of good that was to man, beast or female.

The operator couldn't raise anybody on the syndicate's number at Lloyd's, which wasn't so surprising at that hour, so I told her to switch to Willie's Berkshire one. Then I copied out Steen's message and threw the original down the lavatory. At least, I suppose it was a message: a note of what he *might*— as those question marks implied—have been going to tell me. H & Thornton didn't mean a thing except sounding English; Gulbrandsens just sounded like a name . . . well, that was easily settled: the telephone directory gave a choice of a dozen. Apart from anything else, it was a Bergen street name: Gulbrandsens Gate. But Steen hadn't lived there—that was the next thing I checked.

Then an elderly, well-bred female voice came through from darkest Berkshire to say Willie was expected back around nine and would I like to leave a message? I just gave my name and said I'd call back.

After that, I sat and stared at Steen's message until the phone rang—a couple of minutes after seven, by my watch.

A voice asked: 'James Card?'

'That's me. Who's that?'

'Never mind. Are you alone?'

'Yes.' I was trying to place the voice; it just might have been Norwegian—I'd learnt that the time they spend not carrying your bags they use practising perfect English—but I didn't quite think so.

I said: 'So what d'you want?'

'I'm glad you asked that question. A certain book you have with you, I believe. It doesn't belong to you, so . . .'

'What book are you talking about?'

'*Oh, for Chrissake!*' A spurt of involuntary anger that just couldn't have been Norwegian. 'You know what I'm talking about. Now I'll tell you how to get it to us.'

I had to remember to sound unworried, not knowing he had anything on me. So, in a merry insouciant voice: 'Up you, mate, and double up *your* mate. I'm not a travelling library service. Any time you——'

He overrode me: '*Or* we'll tell the local coppers to check

with London on who owns that Mauser HSC they found in Steen's office.'

I counted a silent one-two-three to show implications sinking in, then said cautiously: 'I knew he was dead. I didn't know about the gun.'

He chuckled. 'That's right—yours. Remember the number?' He told me the number.

Another one-two-three to be appalled in. Then, quick and hopeful: 'They'd never believe I did it.'

'You may even be right. I'd say it was six-to-five on. But either way, you'll spend a nice long time here while they make up their minds. Now d'you feel any different about that book?'

Had I heard the voice before? I thought it was the one down in the underground car park while I was getting pumped full of Pentathol, but I could be just assuming the probable. Certainly that lot had latched on to my Mauser.

I asked: 'What guarantee do I get that you won't tell the cops about the Mauser anyway?'

He sighed. I think. 'Now, Major—you've been out of the Army long enough to know no blackmailer ever gives a real guarantee. He can't, can he? Whatever it is he knows, he can't just stop knowing it.'

'I'll give it you back in London,' I said.

'*You'll give it tonight!*'

Thank God he'd insisted.

He calmed down. 'Now, I'll tell you where. Are you listening?'

'I'm listening.'

NINETEEN

I'D HARDLY GOT AWAY from the phone when it went again. A voice that was soggy but sharp, like wet salt: 'Mr Card? I am Inspector (First Class) Vik. We met this afternoon.'

'Of course. Are you coming round?'

'If you please. Will you wait there?—I will be only a few minutes.'

He was less than one minute, so the bastard must have been ringing from the lobby. Maybe he'd hoped to catch me still swallowing the plans of the fort.

He was wearing the same creased brown suit, and carrying an old overcoat in some loose-woven pale green stuff with several loose strands sticking out and the lining hanging loose at the bottom. If you'd met that coat on the street you'd have given it five pence for a cup of coffee and kept upwind while doing so.

I held up the bottle of Teacher's. 'Does the Superintendent let you drink on duty?'

He sniffed loudly. 'I can say it was medicine. No water, please.'

I passed him a good medicinal dose.

'Skol.'

'Skol.' He gulped. 'To be a Superintendent in Norway you must have a degree in Law. I will never be a Superintendent. I had a war instead of a university course. Then . . .' He shrugged and looked at me with bleary thoughtfulness. It hadn't been self-pity: it was just a gentle, roundabout warning that he didn't believe in legal niceties.

Then he said: 'I have talked to your Scotland Yard. . . .'

I nodded. That would be pure routine, of course; but their answer hadn't been.

He asked: 'Do you have a gun with you?'

'No.'

He emptied his glass, stood up. 'Do you object if I search? I have no . . . you call it a warrant.'

I shrugged and held my arms out ready.

He sat down again, satisfied. If I was ready to let him search then there wasn't anything to be found. It told me something about what the Yard had told him, but maybe even more about him.

He held up his glass and I poured him another and looked at the level in the bottle. 'I'll have to start travelling again soon.'

'Skol. But not too soon, please. Do you have a .22 of an inch pistol?'

'I've got four—at home. Was that what shot him?'

He just nodded, then got out a handful of Kleenex and started excavations on his nose. 'Now—why did you come to see Steen?'

And so I gave him the story. About being with Fenwick when he got shot, about wanting to know why, about getting hired to find out, about Fenwick having visited Bergen before, about Steen's letter to Mrs Fenwick. All I left out was various guns, Mockby, *Bertie Bear*, truth drugs and Miss Mackwood having me tailed. Maybe it made it all a bit duller, but at least it came out shorter.

Of course, the Yard might have told him I'd been carrying a gun when Fenwick got killed, but he wouldn't expect me to admit that sort of thing anyhow.

'What did you believe Steen would tell you?'

I thought about that. 'What it was all about, I suppose.'

'You truly do not know?'

'Something to do with ships—I'd guess. Steen surveyed them and Fenwick insured them; that's the obvious connection. There could be others.'

'Such as getting murdered, perhaps?'

'That, too. By the way—Fenwick was shot with a nine-millimetre Browning, I was told. I don't know what model.'

He nodded appreciatively, shaking a small cloud of moisture from his nose. 'Thank you.' He made a note about it.

I said: 'D'you know *when* Steen got shot, yet?'

'Doctors never know. He was alive until at least three o'clock. He telephoned to an agency that does secretary work for him. Why do you ask that?'

'A .22 isn't a cannon, but it isn't a typewriter, either.'

He nodded again. 'He—they—held up a cushion against the head and fired through it. The doctors found threads in the . . . the wounds. I believe it makes a good silencer.'

I'd heard the same myself, though never tried it. And you can't fit a proper silencer on a gun like the Mauser, where the slide comes right to the muzzle.

I asked: 'Did you find the gun?'

'No. And he even took away the empty shells—unless it was a revolver and that I do not expect. He was most careful.'

Friend, you have no idea of just how careful he was. I wanted to ask about the condition of the bullets—could they be matched to the gun? (I doubted it: a lead bullet going through bone isn't going to show many clear rifling marks afterwards.) But I'd pushed the talk of guns far enough, even for somebody with my built-in interest.

He asked: 'Have you telephoned to your friends in England, yet?'

'I tried. Couldn't get through.'

'How long will you stay in Bergen, now?'

'It's getting a little difficult to justify, isn't it? Anyhow, how much work are you going to let me do?'

He considered this and then, knowing exactly what I'd meant, asked: 'What do you mean?'

'Talk to people. Like that secretarial service. And his wife and friends. Parents.'

'There is no wife. And only his father is alive. He lives near Oslo.'

'You haven't answered me. Can I ask questions without you jumping all over me?'

He swilled the last of the whisky around the glass and gulped it down in a rather formal gesture. 'Perhaps, if the family permits.' Then he stood up. 'But perhaps tomorrow, it will all become very simple. Something will appear from his papers, his private letters—and we need not worry about your strange mysteries.'

'Do you really think so?'

'I do not know. With this murder, there was a very great hatred—or none at all. That careful cushion, the picking up of the shells. I think perhaps you know of the world where one does not need hatred to kill. We will see.'

I shrugged—and shivered a bit, inside.

He picked up his overcoat, gave me one serious but damp look, and went his way.

TWENTY

I LOOKED AT THE BOTTLE, then decided not. The evening wasn't over yet. So I drifted down to the ground-floor Grill, which turned out to be one of those places with candle-light and wooden pews and all the old chop-house atmospherics. And I'd honestly—or stupidly—forgotten about Draper and Maggie Mackwood until they sat down on the other side of my table.

Draper grinned, yellowish in the candle-light. 'Mind if we share this with you?'

I half got up, awkward against the high-backed wooden bench. 'Go ahead. Nice flight?'—to Maggie.

She sat stiff and upright, breasts jutting towards me, but not as if she was asking me to make her an offer; just the prim attitude of somebody with a good posture or a bad back. That apart, she had on a dark suede skirt and a blouse of what looked like raw sail canvas: all pockets and heavy stitching. Her dark brown hair was pulled back into a neat bun, her face arranged in a wary but neutral expression like a good secretary awaiting dictation.

'Very pleasant, thank you.'

An elderly waiter with clipped iron-grey hair arrived and handed out menus.

'And something to drink,' Draper said.

'I'll send the wine waiter, sir.'

'Just send a Scotch and a gin-and-tonic.' Draper looked at me. 'How about you?'

'Are you buying?'

He snorted with laughter. 'All goes on expenses.'

Maggie put on a forced smile. I shook my head: no drink.

The old waiter said patiently: 'I'll send the wine waiter, sir.' He went away.

Draper snorted again. 'Poncey sort of pub, this. Cost you a packet, does it?'

I shrugged and the wine waiter arrived and took the order. Draper pulled out a long thin cigar and the waiter did a fast draw with a book of matches.

But Draper shook his head. 'I'll just chew it awhile. Don't last so long if you light 'em—ha-ha!'

The waiter looked at him, puzzled but getting the message that Draper wasn't directly related to Royalty.

Maggie said formally: 'I suppose I ought to apologize for asking Mr Draper to follow you.'

'That's all right. You can send as many as you like if they're no better than he is.'

'Thanks, chum,' he said bitterly. 'Maybe someday I can do *you* a good turn.'

I said: 'But what did you expect him to tell you anyway?'

'Oh . . .' she fiddled with the silverware, 'just what you were doing.'

'You knew bloody well what I was doing. Trying to find out who killed Martin Fenwick.'

She looked up at me quickly. 'Well, that's what you *said*, but . . .'

'You were worried about what else I might find out?'

Maybe she blushed, maybe not. Damn interrogations by candle-light. 'Well, I don't know. . . . And Mr Mockby said you'd taken the parcel Mart—— Mr Fenwick was carrying . . .'

'That's something I meant to ask you: *why* was he taking it to France?'

Draper said quickly: 'You don't have to tell. Not a thing, you don't.'

I said: 'I'll get around to you in a moment. Behave yourself until then.'

'Stuff it up.'

But just as his employer was giving him a prim look, the wine waiter arrived with their drinks. Both grabbed and gulped, but then Maggie caught my eye and looked briefly shamefaced about it. Probably remembering the last—and first—time we'd met, when she was getting smashed out of her little pointed mind.

'Now let's get back to why Fenwick was going to France.' But then the table waiter arrived to take our orders. Damn interrogations over dinner tables. I took prawn cocktail and half a grilled lobster—after all, we weren't much more than a quarter of a mile from the fish market on the edge of the quay. And I *was* on expenses.

When the waiter had gone, I said to Maggie: 'Well?'

But she'd had too long to work out her reply: it was just a half-shrug, half-shake of her head.

I turned to Draper.

'Fenwick hired some inquiry firm—that was Herb Harris, wasn't it?'

'No.'

'Too fast.' I tried to look reproving. 'The right answer should be "Don't know". You wouldn't know every job Herb took on, would you? And why should *she* go to him? She doesn't know about private detectives; natch, she'd use the one her boss had used. So now, what were you trying to find out for Fenwick?'

This time it was Maggie looking at him apprehensively. But he just took the chewed-up cigar out of his face, spat a bit off his lip, and said: 'Stuff it up again.'

I shook my head sadly. 'I really am going to have to have a word with Herb about you.'

'I've met some slimy creeping bastards in my time——'

'And now you've met another. Come on.'

He rammed the cigar back in his mouth, glanced at Maggie, and growled: 'He was being blackmailed. Wanted us to find out who.'

'Blackmailed about what?'

He shrugged, and his voice seemed lighter and more confident now. 'He never told us. Something personal, he said. Not business.'

'What about notes and so on?'

'No notes. All done by telephone.'

'You didn't have much to go on.'

'You're bloody right, there. Didn't bloody get anywhere, either.'

Then our first course arrived, and I found I'd been right about being close to the fish market. Those prawns actually tasted of something beside the sauce. Can you imagine that?

So for a time, I just ate.

When I'd finished, I asked Maggie: 'What was he being blackmailed about?'

She stiffened. So she knew. That was the important step.

I said: 'Well?'

Draper was leaning on one elbow and looking at her curiously.

I said it again.

She put on the voice she would have used for getting rid of beggars and life insurance salesmen. 'You really don't think I'm going to discuss Mr Fenwick's private life with a . . . a mere bodyguard, do you?'

I pulled the pin out of my temper, counted three, and let it blow. 'Just tell me what in hell gives you the exclusive rights to the late Martin Fenwick, underwriter, will you? He had a wife, a son, he had partners and friends—as well as a silly little secretary with a schoolgirl crush on the boss. And maybe some of *them* want to know why he got his guts blown in even if you don't care a damn!'

I was projecting fine, just fine. Maybe La Scala in Milan had heard better, but never the Grill at the Norge. Several groups at nearby tables were giving me snowbound looks, and the wine waiter was teetering on his toes, praying I'd stop before he had to stop me.

Even Draper was looking a bit shook, making shushing movements with his hands.

'Here, cool it off, chummie——'

I snapped at him. '*And* you, unless you want your tits kicked through your trapezium!'

And probably that about covered the situation. The trouble with all those years of interrogation procedures is that by now I can't tell how honest my anger really is. But for the moment, it seemed good enough.

Maggie had a definite flush now, and tears sparkling in her eyes. She finished her gin at a gulp.

'All right, all right. It was . . . I was . . . having an affair with him.' And she glanced at me quickly, then back to her plate.

Draper was looking at her speculatively, probably wondering what *his* chances were. About one in infinity squared, I'd say.

I said: 'All right, so now we know. It happens all the time.' Though it doesn't, you know, not as much as everybody seems to think. In most firms, the one person you *don't* start ring-a-dinging is your own secretary. It changes an important business relationship into something else, and the boardroom doesn't like it. It's a good way to find yourself promoted manager of the North Greenland branch.

Which makes it a better blackmailing point than you might otherwise think, of course.

'And that leaves us,' I said, 'with the question of what he was being blackmailed *for*. What they wanted from him.'

I knew it was a bloody stupid remark the moment I'd finished it. She stared at me, tears spilling from suddenly widened eyes. 'Well, you ought to know. You've got it.'

Fast, now. 'What did he tell you?'

'Just that it was evidence about a claim.'

'Well—could you identify it again?' Oh, a crafty one, that. But: 'No—I never saw it. It was sent to his home, I think. His flat.'

Yet without leaving any traces around the flat, like covering letters. Unless the party of the other part had nicked them before I'd got there.

'Did he tell you what claim?—what ship?'

'No, I never knew that.' Not true, darling. I can tell.

'You didn't have to write any letters about it?'

'No.'

'He didn't talk in bed much, did he, your Fenwick?'

Her eyes filled with fresh tears, and Draper looked at me and said: 'You know, you're a bit of a right sod.'

At the time, I almost agreed with him.

The old waiter wheeled up a trolley with the next course, giving me a couple of suspicious looks free and with the compliments of the management. He'd long ago formed a private view about Draper, but after my concerto for unaccompanied bad temper he was getting a second opinion on me, too.

Still, whatever he felt hadn't transferred itself to the lobster.

It was just firm and white, with little golden trickles of melted butter, as simple as a million dollars. Usually when I feel up to affording lobster I overdo it and ask for it à la everything on the menu and curried cheese besides. Under that, what I get for lobster is left over from last summer's staff tennis dance.

I must have looked the way I was feeling, because Draper asked: 'D'you usually eat lobster in these pads?'

'Only when there's an expense account in the month.' I looked back to Maggie, nibbling her filleted sole. 'I forgot to ask—how did Fenwick get this . . . evidence? Who did you say sent it?'

'I didn't . . . ' but she was trying to remember what she *had* said, and Draper was glaring sideways at her. 'From Norway, anyway. Bergen, I think.'

'You mean Steen?'

'I . . . er . . .' And both Draper and I knew she meant Steen. Suddenly she realized this. 'Well, you *know*, don't you? Isn't he the man you came to see? What did he tell you?'

'Him?—nothing. Somebody shot him just before I got there.'

Her surprise was real. The piece of fish on her fork went slowly on into her mouth and got chewed up and swallowed and her eyes were looking at me but they were listening to something over the hills and gone.

I looked back at Draper. He put his knife and fork gently back together on the plate and asked, slow and careful: 'Dead? —why?'

'Basically because of a couple of .22 bullets. After that I'm guessing. I guess it was because of something he was going to tell me, but that could be just pure conceit.'

Draper picked up the worn cigar from the ashtray and took out a lighter and—finally—tried to light it. It took time, since it was mostly Havana Saliva by now, but he wasn't in any hurry. At last he said: 'You've told the police and done all the unsporting things like that, eh, Major?'

'Oh yes. I imagine it's in the evening paper and radio and so on. You could ask the waiter.' Was I really going to scrape the inside of the lobster's tail completely clean? No—let it rest in peace. 'What I was thinking was—I think I've got a date with the blokes that did it, later on this evening. Could be the same ones that killed Fenwick, as well. I just wondered if you'd like to come along and help out?'

TWENTY-ONE

I REACHED WILLIE soon after ten, and I didn't waste any of his money on idle chat. 'Steen was murdered before I reached him.'

'Good God! How did it——'

'Never mind. I'll tell you all about it tomorrow—if the police let me leave.'

'I say—you haven't got yourself——'

'No, I haven't. Just routine. Now: have you found out anything about him?'

'Oh yes. Well, something. He's a sort of Lloyd's sub-agent, done quite a lot of survey work on claims for us when the usual chap there isn't available.'

'Specifically for your syndicate?'

'It doesn't work quite that way . . . but I did a list of the ships he surveyed where we were involved. Over the last three years that was the *Gefjon*, *Bergen Wayfarer*, *Skadi*, *Runic Queen*, *Idun*. Those five.'

'Is any of them special? I've found out that Steen sent Fenwick some sort of evidence about a shipping claim—that's the book-thing he was supposed to be taking to France.'

The line hummed and crackled to itself for a time. Then Willie said slowly: 'Well, each one's special in its own way. Insurance deals with the exceptional—that's what it's all about, what?'

'I suppose so.' I wanted to tell him about Maggie Mackwood and Draper, and about my appointment for later on—but if I was Inspector (First Class) Vik I'd have a copper with a tape recorder down in the switchboard keeping an ear on James Card.

But at least I could ask: 'Does the name Gulbrandsen or Gulbrandsens mean anything to you?'

He automatically corrected my pronunciation, but he couldn't do any more.

'H and Thornton—does *that* mean anything?'

'What is it?'

'Don't know. Could be two blokes or a firm or what.'

'I haven't heard of it. Sorry, old boy.'

'Never mind. Just keep the great brain bent on it and ring me if anything occurs to you. But with a bit of luck I'll learn a bit more tonight. I'll probably be home tomorrow—okay?'

And now it was time to go and meet Draper.

He'd been a pretty reluctant conscript—but wars are won by them. Probably it was only a feeling of guilt about the cock-up he'd made of following me plus the promise of a gun that had recruited him. Either way, it was far safer for him to go snooping in the Fontenen's cistern; it could still have a blight of policemen who might know me by sight.

We met in the Norge's basement lavatory—just in case. He took a careful look over my shoulder, just to make sure, and hissed: 'You bleeding git! The bleeding place shut a bleeding hour ago!'

No guns.

'Hold on.' I grabbed his arm as he started around me for the door.

'Get away,' he snarled. 'I'm not going out to play funny-buggers in the park without some protection, and you can tell Herb and the ABD and the House of bleeding Lords, too.'

'Stop panicking, you're making yourself conspicuous.' That hushed him—although there wasn't anybody else there to be conspicuous to. 'Look—you don't have to be involved, you can be an innocent bystander as long as you like. I just want you there as a witness . . . for if I don't get back.'

'Sing it again—I only cried out of one eye that time.'

I took a deep breath. 'So screw you, Draper. You're only hired; I really want to know about these people. For once they've stuck their necks out, made a date. *I'm* keeping it.'

'Oh my God,' he said slowly. 'How did the First World War ever get on without you?' Long pause. 'All right, then.'

But that didn't solve the weapons problem; Draper might be mug enough to walk into trouble stark naked, but I certainly wasn't. Room service had just closed down and the Grill was shut—so I couldn't get myself issued with a steak knife. There wouldn't be any shops open at this time—or would there?

I asked at the desk. The clerk looked politely surprised, thought about it, shrugged. 'I think only the tourist shop, sir.'

'Where's that?'

He pointed at the corner. 'By the air terminal, sir.'

'What do they sell there?'

'Souvenirs, sir. Sweaters for ski-ing, beer mugs, little figures of trolls, paper-knives——'

'*Thank* you.'

I was round there three seconds later. The shop-girl was just closing up, but didn't mind waiting an extra couple of minutes. I pretended to take my time, but there was really only a choice between a longish stiletto-shaped paper-knife and a short, sharp reindeer-horn-handle 'hunting' knife in a twee little fur sheath. In the end I took the sheath job; for all its fancy looks, it was four inches of real sharp steel—and lungs aren't four inches behind your ribs.

I was ready for a stroll in the Park.

TWENTY-TWO

OUTSIDE, the night was full of thick, soggy snowflakes that drifted prettily in the lamplight and splattered into ice water the moment they touched you. I turned up my fur collar, shoved my chin down into it, and headed for the Park.

According to the map, it was at the end of the street, the street itself being the Ole Bull's Plass, and Ole himself—to judge from the statue—had been a violinist or maybe composer. I mean, how do you do a statue of a composer anyway? Have him looking soulfully upwards and he could have been the man who discovered meteorology or the eighth deadly sin, and we all know they composed on pianos anyhow. But show me a town council that can afford a statue of *that*.

It was a good, wide street lined with big student cafés that looked warm and safe behind the steamed-up windows, and only me outside. A couple of motorcycle cops, with little green lamps besides their headlights, paused to give me suspicious glances, and then zoomed away ahead. I slowed down so as not to lose Draper. He was supposed to be following me to make sure nobody else did.

The Park—again according to the map—was a square job mostly filled with an artificial lake, but touching on main roads at every corner. That would be why they'd chosen it, of course: a selection of getaways if I happened to bring the Riot Squad with me. Though if the snow got any thicker that wouldn't mean much. And it was thickening, all right.

I waited at the main road before the Park itself, and Draper wandered up, shook his head without looking at me, and went across into the billowing curtains of snow ahead. I followed slower. The lights of the town faded behind me and the snow-flakes went from silver-white to a vague grey to invisible wet fingerprints in the darkness.

The timing was tricky. I wanted Draper arriving at the rendezvous about a minute after I did, and from the opposite direction; they might expect somebody to be following me, but I hoped they wouldn't think of a collision course. To get there, he'd have to walk all around the lake, but the exercise would do him good.

I found the lake myself by almost tripping over a low iron railing; beyond it was a slope of snow-speckled grass and then the glint of black water. I turned right and slowly followed the path around. Now I was really alone, just me and the whirling snow like dead kisses on my face and dribbling icily down my neck. I'd done ten paces . . . and twenty . . . and thirty . . .

A figure, waiting, loomed up ahead; just a dark shape with

an odd blurriness to the face. I stopped and something poked into my back.

A voice behind said: 'Hands high, please.' Then, over my shoulder to the first shape: 'He's clear; nobody following.'

I held the *Bertie Bear* envelope high in my right hand and stared at the vague figure in front while other hands explored my clothes.

'Do you bring your nylon stockings all the way from London, or do you find the Norwegian ones do just as well?'

'Shut up, Card.' Then, more relaxed: 'No gun, friend? Are you slipping or learning?'

'I'm just running out of them.'

He chuckled into the back of my neck. 'All right, I'll take it now.'

'Hold on. I want some sort of guarantee that I'm in the clear with the police.'

'I told you that's bloody nonsense. Hand it over.' Yes, I was sure I knew that voice.

'You'll get me into trouble, losing this.'

'Don't worry, chummie. You'll never hear of it again. Now —*give*!'

I'd stalled as long as I could; wherever Draper was, I had to act now or for ever hold my peace. I lowered my right hand slowly; the knife was already in my palm, the blade hidden inside the envelope. I twitched it, the envelope fell off and he instinctively ducked to catch it.

I whipped around.

There was a stocking-masked face and a gun—but it had wandered off its aim. I slashed for it; the knife bounced off metal, sliced flesh and stopped on bone.

He screamed and threw himself away from me—but didn't drop the gun. Instead, the torn envelope finally ripped wide open and Bertie Bear came bouncing free.

I jumped, trying to smother that gun hand, and he kicked as he fell and got me on the knee.

Behind me, another pistol exploded, close enough to light the snowflakes in the air around me. The man on the ground yelled: 'Don't kill him!'

I turned as fast as I could, but when I saw the gun it was already swinging. I did the only thing left—tried to throw my head in the direction it was about to be thrown anyhow. But it caught me just above the right ear and I tripped on the railing and did half a cartwheel down the snowy grass bank and ended spread on my face just short of the lake.

And there I let things rest for a bit.

My vision seemed shattered, actually busted like a mirror so that I saw several versions of anything I looked at. Dimly, I knew the man who'd thumped me was staring at me. Then helped up the one with the cut hand. Then picking up something. And then both of them watching me for a while, and finally vanishing behind the snow.

They must have said something, too, but something inside my head was screaming far too loud for any outside noise to get in.

I stared at my hand, flat on the grass ahead of me, and gradually all the versions of it faded into one. The sounds inside my head localized themselves to just above my right ear, and when I touched it, there was already a solid lump. But no stickiness, thank God.

About then, Draper appeared above me. 'Are you all right?'

'Of course I'm not bloody all right!' I said through clenched teeth. 'And where were you when the world ended?'

'Watching it. You did all right, Major.' He helped me on to my feet, or thereabouts.

I brushed off some of the snow on my jacket, looked around and found the knife. It had blood on the tip, which was about all we seemed to have achieved; at a guess, that hand would hurt a lot longer than my head would. Should I tell Vik to watch the hospitals for a man with a cut right hand? And have Vik ask why I was carrying the knife on his patch, and why I hadn't told him about the meeting and why I could be blackmailed into it. . . . Hell, a professional like that would never go near a hospital.

'Well, *that* wasn't really worth staying up late for, was it?'

I said bitterly. 'I hope you didn't get too cold or wet or anything frightful like that?'

'Don't say such things, Major. He had a gun, that's why I didn't come out. He'd've recognized me.'

It took a long time for the message to find an unoccupied brain cell. 'You mean you recognized one of *them*? In that mask?'

'I'd know that voice anywhere. He worked for Herb for a couple of years. Pat Kavanagh, that was.'

TWENTY-THREE

THE PHONE WOKE ME.

I'd put myself and my headache to bed with a sleeping pill washed down by Scotch, and now I had that dispersed feeling a drugged hangover gives; it took a long time to find and fit together, more or less, my body, soul and, more or less, mind. Then I dropped the receiver on the floor and had to grope for it head down, which wasn't a good idea.

'I told you not to wake me,' I gurgled.

'*I* told them to wake you,' Inspector Vik said.

'What time is it?'

'Nearly ten o'clock. If you want to be a good detective you must first learn to get up in the morning. I am coming to see you, so please stay there.'

'Hell.'

'Did you know there is a town in Norway called Hell? All tourists go to it to send postcards home.'

'Thanks. Now get off the line so I can ring for some coffee.'

'Two cups, if you please.'

He rang off and I got Room Service and ordered coffee for two and a couple of eggs done any way they pleased, I just wasn't up to such mind-bending decisions yet. Oh—and any morning papers in Norwegian, too.

The eggs arrived rather hard-boiled which wasn't anybody's fault but mine, along with a couple of papers. I didn't understand a word, but I found the Steen story in both. My name included.

Then I had to get out of bed and let Vik in. He was wearing a different suit—dark blue, this time—but which still looked as if he'd slept in it and a restless night besides. Plus the same overcoat.

I waved my hand at the coffee and left him to it. Halfway through pouring, he caught sight of the papers. 'Do you understand Norwegian?'

'No. It's so's you can read the story to me. Or pay for your own coffee.'

He smiled bleakly and a bit gummily—the cold was still with him—then leaned against the radiator, sipped his coffee and started reading: 'Er . . . last night there was . . . er . . . shot to death Jonas Steen, aged thirty-seven . . . er, a ship surveyor . . .'

And so it went on, simple and factual but, even in translation, sounding a little uncertain, like a man unwrapping an unexpected parcel. It obviously wasn't the sort of crime Bergen was used to.

I drank coffee and nibbled various sorts of bread and only listened properly when he said: 'The police are searching for a . . . er, ·22 pistol . . .'

So the boys would now know the Mauser had got away and there wasn't any point in trying to lean on me about it any more. That's all I'd been trying to find out, but I had to look interested right to the end.

When he'd finished he half-folded the paper and tossed it on to the bed. 'And now the other one, perhaps?'

'No thanks.' Then I added quickly: 'Not unless it tells me more about Steen.'

He shrugged and reached for the coffee-pot. 'Nothing much.'

'So—how's it going?'

'It is over.'

I spilled coffee into the saucer and the cup wasn't even half full. 'It's *what*? Have you caught somebody?'

He shrugged again. 'You might say.'

He stared damply at me for a good long time before saying: 'Henrick Lie. We know him. Not a nice person. He knew Steen already, it seems.'

'How d'you know it was him?'

'He has confessed.'

'Do you believe him?'

'The superintendent believes him.'

'He could change his mind.'

'Which?—but it does not matter. Neither of them ever will.'

I suppose I was still a bit dozy from the alcohol and pill and too much of my thinking was concentrated just above my right ear, but it finally sank in. 'You mean Lie's dead?'

'With a nine-millimetre, through the mouth.'

And on through the back of the head, taking a lot of the head and brain with it and the gun often recoiling clear out of the fast-dying hand and ending up several feet away. The classic pistol suicide, as simple and formal as a cheque. And faked about as often.

After a while I asked: 'And when did all this happen?'

'He was found at perhaps six o'clock this morning in a car near the Nordnesparken.'

'And I suppose all the fingerprints and powder-stains are in the right places and the handwriting on the confession's the real thing?'

He nodded gently. 'The writing we do not know about yet. But I think it will be right.'

'I bet it will.'

'You know a lot about gunshot suicide.'

'I was sixteen years in the Army.'

'Ah yes.'

'And so?—what did he say? What about Steen?'

He took out a fistful of soggy Kleenex, selected the driest corner, and blew his nose powerfully. 'It is a secret document until the *likskue*—the inquest.'

'For Christ's sake.'

'It is not my decision. But have you told *me* everything?'

I didn't have an answer to that, so I said: 'But you aren't going to let it lay, are you? He wasn't in it alone.'

'We have a confession. The superintendent has decided. So, now we need not trouble with your mysteries. You are free, you can go at any time, anywhere. You could even go to Hell.'

I got up slowly and stiffly—I'd pulled a few muscles taking the count last night—and took a shower, a shave and a look in the mirror. My face looked slack and my eyes bloodshot, but at least the bump above my ear didn't show unless you were looking for it. I'd rather have that than Kavanagh's hand.

Not that it had stopped him doing some fast thinking and ruthless improvisation, if Lie's 'suicide' had been his idea. That certainly couldn't have been planned ahead, not if they originally counted on implicating me in Steen's death. But once that had fallen through, the suicide had done the next best thing: stopped the police investigation cold in the simplest possible way. Ideas *that* simply scare the hell out of me and I don't mean the town.

Draper rang at half past ten, mostly to say goodbye; he was catching the afternoon plane. I told him I expected to catch it myself and his lack of enthusiasm was almost tangible. I think he regarded me as a bad influence. So I asked about Maggie and he said she was probably staying on a while, but he didn't know why. Neither did I.

I was out on the street just before eleven. Last night's snow hadn't settled, and for the moment it wasn't even raining, so the town was just damp, not really wet. I drifted towards the north harbour, looking in shop windows until I was certain I was alone.

Then straight to the Fontenen.

The guns were still safe in the cistern. I dried them as much as I could on the toilet paper but I wasn't going to risk wearing one—or, by implication, firing it—until I'd had a chance to strip them properly. So I just finished my beer and headed back to the Norge. And there was a telephone message waiting: please ring Mrs Smith-Bang at a given number.

'Smith-Bang?'

The desk clerk smiled briefly and nodded. 'Bang is a usual

Norwegian name, sir. Some time a Bang married a Smith, I think.'

'Ah, but did Smith bang Bang or Bang bang Smith?' After a single beer? 'I'm sorry. You wouldn't happen to have heard of the lady, would you?'

He'd gone a little stiff and puzzled. But he reached for the message and looked at it—at the telephone number, I suppose, then said: 'Excuse me,' and went away and came back with a telephone directory. 'Yes, it is the Mrs Smith-Bang who is a—you say "widow" I think, who owns the ship line.'

'Which one?' Not that I'd know it anyway.

'The ADP Line, sir.'

'Thanks. I'll call her back.'

But the first thing I did upstairs was to field-strip the Mauser and derringer, wipe them down with more toilet paper and spread the bits over the radiator to dry. The ammunition should be all right—modern stuff should survive a few hours in water—but how d'you know until you're wrong? So I planned to wear the derringer: if the first one didn't go bang, thumb-cocking was easier than working the slide of the Mauser. And that reminded me.

A man's voice answered the phone—in Norwegian.

I said carefully: 'My name's James Card: I think Mrs Smith-Bang wanted me to call her.'

'Oh yes, sir. She is out, I am afraid, but I have a message. She asks if you will please go to have a drink at the *Hringhorni*.'

'The what?'

'The ship, sir, *Hringhorni*.'

'Ummm . . .' How d'you explain that you've learnt to be cagey about accepting invitations in this town and will the lady please swear her intentions are honourable or at least non-violent? '. . . Well, where is it?'

He told me the berth number. 'Near to the Bergen Line.'

Oh well, it was a fairly public invitation. 'Okay, but I don't want to make it a long one—I want to catch the half-past-two plane.'

So I accepted for twelve noon.

By then I'd packed up, paid my bill, been told insincerely that the Norge could hardly wait to see me back again (you could read in the clerk's eyes what he thought of guests who get called on by police Inspectors (First Class)), carried my own luggage out of the door as usual and got myself taxied down to the docks.

TWENTY-FOUR

THE HRINGHORNI was a smallish, old-fashioned cargo boat with her superstructure stuck in the middle instead of right aft like a lot of modern jobs you see nowadays. The hull was a light grey-green where it wasn't long smears of rust, and the funnel was painted black with a white band that broadened into a stylized snowflake with the letters ADP in red.

The derricks around the foremast (or whatever) were hauling crates into the hold, but when I'd climbed the shaky metal-and-rope gangway there wasn't anybody around. Still that was normal; every time I've gone aboard a ship in harbour I could have stolen the propellers, the skipper's pyjamas and half the cargo before anybody noticed I was there. I chose the nearest doorway and ducked in out of the wind.

There wasn't anybody there, either, only a faint buzz of chat from a stairway leading upwards. I followed it up, along a stretch of metal corridor, through an open door and a heavy green curtain—and I was home. Maybe it had been an initiative test.

The inhabitants were a middle-aged square man with four stripes on his uniform sleeve and a big briar pipe—and Mrs Smith-Bang, I presume. She took a couple of long strides and held out a bony brown hand.

'You're Jim Card, are you? Well, hi there. What're you drinking? Scotch suit you? Great. Meet Captain Jensen. Now siddown, siddown. How d'you like this Bergen weather? This is the only place in the world they talk about the climate more than you English. Now you know why, ha?'

133

I shook hands, a little dazed, and sat in an armchair with a very loose cover in a coarse floral fabric. The captain went over to a large enamel kitchen bucket in the corner, full of bottles and ice, and started organizing my drink.

Mrs Smith-Bang waved her own glass—it looked like a dry martini—and said: 'Cheers. Nice of you to drop around. Sorry it couldn't be my house, but this tub's supposed to be sailing at four o'clock and I have to make sure everybody's aboard and half sober. Maybe you're wondering who in hell I am?'

'You're the boss of the ADP Line.' Just as if I'd always known.

The boss of the ADP Line nodded and looked pleased. She must have been at least sixty-plus, but she had the long-lasting sharp lines of a Boston clipper along with the genuine Yankee accent. Her hair was a frizzy cloud of tobacco-stained grey, her face long and grained like seaworn wood, her eyes very bright grey pebbles. She wore a raw silk blouse, a soft tabby-coloured tweed skirt and a matching coat slung around her shoulders.

'That's righty,' she said. 'I've run the thing since my last husband went to glory or wherever they put my husbands. He was Bang. I was Smith and damn if I wanted to see a good New England name like that get lost just because I needed a third husband in a hurry.' And she cackled like a slatting mainsail.

I sipped—no, gulped—and looked carefully around. With the cheap wood panelling and the worn red carpet the cabin could have been a small-time city office—except that it all hummed and trembled faintly from some power source. That and the rust bubbles in the white-gloss ceiling and the rows of thick, round-cornered windows looking out into the wavering tree of derricks.

Mrs Smith-Bang was watching me. 'Who're you working for, son? Lloyd's or Lois?'

Lois? Lois?—oh, Mrs Fenwick, of course. I just shrugged and looked inscrutable.

She sighed. 'Yeah, I heard you'd been in the spy business. You'd be good at it, with that face. Okay, son, I'll level with you. I think you've got something from Martin Fenwick that belongs to me. I'll buy it off you if you like, but I'm betting you're more interested in finding out why he got himself killed—right?'

'Could be. You knew Fenwick?'

'Martin?—sure. He's been taking a first line on my fleet for years now. Hell, he's had more hot dinners in my house than I've had nights with my knees up, and I wasn't a late starter, son.' And she laughed again. Captain Jensen stiffened, blushed, and made burbling noises through his pipe.

I nodded—meaninglessly—and said: 'What d'you think I've got, then?'

'The log of the *Skadi*.'

So now I knew. It was as easy as that.

So now I knew *what*? I kept the last dregs of inscrutability on my face and asked: 'It belongs to you, does it?'

'The *Skadi* did, the log must. Any log belongs to the owners.'

Wasn't that what Steen had said: 'It belongs to the owners?' And I hadn't had the nous to see that he meant 'ship-owners'.

Captain Jensen gave me a severe red-faced look and nodded ponderously, backing her up.

I tried the casual touch: 'Why d'you think I've got it?'

'You think I don't keep in touch with my insurance on a thing like this?' Well, it was no secret around Lloyd's that I'd got away with a certain package Fenwick had been carrying.'

'How did you know Fenwick had got it?'

'He told me, of course.'

'Then why didn't he give it back to you?'

'It didn't matter which one of us had it, not when he was alive, as long as it was our side. Now he's dead—well, thank the Lord you got it instead of them.'

'Who's them?'

She cocked her head on one side like a scraggy bright-eyed bird and looked at me suspiciously. Jensen suddenly hauled his weight on to his feet, and my right hand got close to my left sleeve. But he only wanted to find a new bottle of beer in the corner bucket.

Mrs Smith-Bang asked: 'Son—you do know what all this *Skadi* business is about?'

'Well . . . I didn't understand the log itself and I've had a fair bit of other stuff to do since then, and——'

'You mean No,' she said.

'Give or take a bit—that's what I mean.'

'Okay, son. It's about time you found out. Want anything to eat while it happens?'

We ate where we sat. Captain Jensen issued some fast orders through a squawk-box fixed to the wall above the bottle bucket and then ducked out. His pipe had made more comments than he had since we'd met, so I wasn't going to miss his flow of ready wit.

A man wearing the classic high-necked white jacket of a ship's steward came in carrying a big tray loaded with small dishes. Mrs Smith-Bang waved a hand and said: 'Guess you haven't been in Norway long enough to get sick of herring yet. Help yourself.'

So I had to: the dishes had herring fillets in vinegar sauce, in tomato sauce, with peppers, with mushrooms, with sliced onions, with shrimps . . . It was a lot of choice or none at all, depending on your point of view. Until then, mine had been that herrings were something God made just to fill up empty bits of sea and they could go on doing it forever as far as I was concerned. I found I was wrong—in about eight different ways.

When we'd got organized, she said: 'So where do I begin?'

'A bit before the beginning.'

She cackled. 'Okay, that sounds honest enough. So—the *Skadi* was one of my ships, around two thousand five hundred tons, dry cargo same as this. That time, last September, she was carrying rolls of newsprint and a deck cargo of wood from the Gulf of Finland. For Tilbury. Then there's the *Prometheus Sahara*, one of these new liquid gas tankers, around twelve thousand tons, she was one of the earliest ones, bringing methane from Algeria to Stockholm. British registration—Sahara Line. Say, are you sure you don't recall this?'

Perhaps I did. 'They bumped, didn't they?'

'Bumped and blew to buggery. Like the Fourth of July. You just think of that gas suddenly spilling and igniting—over a cargo of wood.'

I certainly remembered something in the papers and TV news—the usual aerial view with the plane's wingtip in the foreground and a ship lying on her side pouring out smoke from end to end. But it didn't have to be the right disaster: they all look the same to me.

'Remind me—where did this happen?'

'Down in the Skagerrak. In fog, of course.'

'Of course?'

She snorted and spat out a peppercorn. 'You get some dumb buggers on ships these days, but they don't usually run each other down if they can *see*.'

'It sounds as if somebody got killed in all this.'

'You're damn right. We lost four out of five officers and seven out of ten crewmen. The *Prometheus* wasn't quite so bad, she managed to launch a boat, but she still lost more than half.'

'Both of them sank?'

'The *Prometheus* did. You know what those methane ships are like?—just a row of special tanks like damn great cauldrons. One gets busted and starts a fire and it heats up the ones on either side and when *they* blow . . . It must be like taking a coupla torpedoes.

'But in a way, the *Skadi* wasn't quite so bad off. She got swamped with one rush of fire—that's when our boys got killed, mostly—then drifted clear before the *Prometheus* really blew. But she was still burning and you can't fight that with four men and two of them badly burned anyhow. So in the end they had to jump. She grounded on a small island near Mandal. Constructive total loss.'

'Eh?'

'A write-off, for insurance purposes. Like some more?'

I shook my head. She let out a hoot like a fog-horn and the steward zipped in and reorganized our plates.

Mrs Smith-Bang gave me a sort of leer and said: 'Don't know if you know the Norwegians only have sandwiches for lunch?'

'I read the guidebook.'

'Fine, so that's what you're getting.'

Well, I suppose it had a couple of pieces of bread to hold it by, but the middle was a juicy great rumpsteak the size of a bedside Bible.

The steward looked down on it with that lean sad face of people who spend their time handing good things to other people. And only occasionally spit on them first.

'Have you eaten meat in Norway yet?' Mrs S-B asked.

Come to think of it: 'No.'

'So don't unless you're eating with me. Norwegian cows are half mountain goat and they've got short legs on one side from feeding on a slope. I get these steaks shipped from Scotland. Hope you like it medium rare.'

Luckily I did. She took a massive crunch at her own, dribbling watery blood on and around her plate.

I got my first mouthful down, and asked: 'How big's the ADP Line?'

'Nothing so much. This is the biggest, *Skadi* was the next, and the rest's just a couple of five-hundred-ton coasters. We're one of the few Norwegian lines that ever dock in Norway.'

'D'you come of a shipping family in America?'

'Sure. Our Smiths have been shipping out of New Bedford since you could bring Moby Dick home in a jelly jar.' She guzzled a lump of steak and you could watch the bulge go right down that long thin throat. She looked up and caught me watching. 'You want to hear any more about the *Skadi* business? Don't you like steak?'

'It's fine.' I took another bite and mumbled out past it: 'Who was to blame for all this?'

'We haven't got to court yet. Everybody's suing and counter-suing everybody else, but that's routine. You should have been a lawyer, Jim. That's where the money goes.'

'Too many ethics involved.'

'Hell, you really think so?'

'Mine, I mean.' She gave a bark of laughter and a few shreds of meat almost reached my side of the room. I went on: 'But it'll be another year or two before they come to trial on a case like this. Don't they have some sort of inquiry as well?'

'Sure. They had the Norwegian one in December, soon's my chief engineer was fit again. The British one'll be in a month or two.'

'What did they prove?'

'They didn't *prove* a damn thing. But their report said we were just about totally to blame. If the captain and watch officer hadn't been dead, I guess they'd've been prosecuted. It can happen, under Norwegian law. Bugger it.'

'Will the British one make any difference?'

'Doesn't work quite the same way. Your boys are only interested if your officers have behaved like British officers, what ho?' She munched for a few moments. 'I guess if your Department of Trade and whatnot pulled the licence from under the *Prometheus*'s captain it wouldn't sound too good in court . . . but they won't.'

'It's beginning to sound as if your ship *was* to blame. Was it?'

She put her half-sandwich down on the plate and just gazed at me. 'Now how in hell would I know? Without seeing the log?'

Somewhere below us, somebody knocked over a few tons of cargo and the whole boat shuddered. She didn't notice. I put down my own sandwich—I'd had enough anyway; I was only trying to get one meal out of it—and said very carefully: 'But the log wouldn't show what happened at a collision. You don't stand on a burning bridge writing up the thing.'

'Oh sure, it's likely twenty-four hours out of date. And I'm not saying it'll prove my boys were sugar-candy saints, God rest and rot 'em. It usually takes two fools to make one collision. But everybody on our bridge was killed: captain, watch officer, helmsman and we don't even know who else. Just swept off with the first blast of fire. So we can't put up any witnesses to say what the *Skadi* was doing or their ship either.'

I thought I was getting the idea, now. 'So the court of inquiry had to believe what the *Prometheus*'s officers said?'

'You're right, son. They put up the captain, another officer and a helmsman to swear we were doing ten knots—full speed—through fog, when we hit her.'

She looked around, found her glass and drained the last few drops.

'Son, the *Skadi* couldn't have been doing more than five knots if the whole crew had been facing forward and eating beans. Half our power had cracked up the day before and *that log'll prove it.*'

She leant back and stared at me, chewing on thin old lips that looked permanently dry. 'But d'you see what *else* that proves? It proves three damn liars on the bridge of the *Prometheus Sahara*, *that's* what it proves. Collusion. Conspiracy —what you damn like. Prove that, and the case busts wide open.'

After a while I cleared my throat of something that wasn't there and said: 'But didn't you argue this at the inquiry?'

'Oh sure: one old tramp-ship chief engineer up against three smooth young Limeys off—sorry, Jim, I was forgetting where you come from.'

'Scotland, mostly.'

'Well, then . . . Anyhow, that log'll prove it.'

Without really meaning to, I got up and walked over to the bucket and organized another Scotch for myself. The bump on the side of my head was throbbing gently but insistently. I sat down again.

'That means,' I said, 'that the other people interested in the log are the other line. Sahara Line, you said—right?'

'The way I see it, there's only two sides to this one.'

Plus Paul Mockby, of course, who'd be ready to make up a third on anybody's wedding night. But thinking about him had never helped my digestion yet.

I said: 'And they'd be happy to see it buried at sea again. Where it was supposed to be. You think they were after Fenwick, then?'

'That's your end of the business, son. I want that log out in open court, that's all. You want some coffee?'

I nodded and she went across to the intercom and pushed

various switches and yelled something about *kaffe* each time. The artillery calls it a 'barrage'.

She came back, looked at the rags of her steak sandwich—she'd eaten far more than I had, though where she put it in a figure shaped like a mainmast I couldn't tell—and pushed it aside. Then: 'Well, what d'you say?'

'This could make a big difference—financially—to you, the ADP Line, if you could fight this case seriously?'

She shrugged. 'Not much, no.'

'No?'

'We were insured, we've been paid, they're building a new *Skadi* right now. Our next premiums'll cost more, of course, but that's all. The case is really between two lots of insurers; it's *their* money.'

It usually is, these days. I glanced at my watch: I could still catch the two-thirty plane. 'By the way, how did you know I was in Bergen?'

She cackled again. 'You didn't exactly make the society column, son, but you sure got your name in the paper.'

I winced. Jack Morris wasn't likely to read Norwegian papers, but some Reuters man might pick it up and . . . I'd know soon enough. 'Did you know this chap Steen?'

'The one who got himself murdered? Sure—I know everybody in the shipping biz here. Good surveyor.'

'Do you have any idea why he was killed?'

'There was a piece on the radio this morning: it said they'd got a confession from some local lad. Personal squabble.'

'I don't believe it. He was killed to stop him telling me something.'

She raised her eyebrows. 'Have you told the police?'

'Oh yes. But as you say—they've got a confession and a suicide. You don't argue with a jigsaw when all the pieces fit. I still don't believe it.' And neither did Vik, and he didn't even know about my Mauser being involved. Just then, the steward trundled in with a tray and two thick crock cups of coffee.

When he'd gone, I said: 'It still doesn't change the fact that Steen *was* going to talk to me. But what was he going to tell me—about the log or the *Skadi* or something?'

She blew delicately across her coffee. 'Haven't a damn notion. Maybe how he found the log. He *did* find it, didn't he?'

'I imagine so. Though I don't see how, in a burnt-out wreck.'

'It could happen. These guys are *supposed* to keep the thing in a fireproof box. But I never thought any of them did. God damn. If I'd known, I'd've had the thing in time for the inquiry.

'When did Steen survey the wreck, then?'

'Just last month.'

'*What*? And the collision was last September?'

'Oh, she was surveyed before, all right—but it doesn't take ten minutes to see if a burnt-out hulk's irrepairable. Steen was surveying her for scrap value: see if it's worth cutting her up, now they'll be getting some good weather. But that's Lloyd's business. It's their wreck now.'

'Was that why he sent the log to Fenwick and not you?'

She looked at me a little warily, then shrugged. 'Could be. You didn't ever meet this Steen?'

'Not alive.'

'Of course. Well . . . good surveyor.'

Time was running out. I gulped my coffee and stood up.

She bounced to her own feet, held out her hand. 'Thanks for dropping in, son. Hope you'll get in touch with our London solicitors with that log.'

I made non-committal agreeing noises, turned for the door, and then turned back. 'But if it's really just an insurance case now, why are you so concerned?'

Her eyes were bright and level. 'Most of my crew died, son. Nothing I can do for them now except pay up on their pensions—*and* see they don't get more blame than they're entitled to. It's always the easiest way out, to blame the dead.'

I nodded, didn't say anything, and went on out.

The gangway was blocked by a line of dockers or somebody carrying up cardboard boxes and crates of beer. Captain Jensen was leaning over the rail with a clip-board checking

142

each box aboard. I waited beside him; he looked at me, grunted and nodded.

'Did you know the crew of the *Skadi*?' I asked sociably.

'I know. Small line, you know everybody. Good men.'

'The chief engineer still with the Line?'

'Nygaard? He retire. Much worried. Very bad. Hurt the hands.' He held up his own hands in stiff, claw-like positions—and nearly dropped the clip-board. 'I go see him sometimes. At the—how you say? *sjomannshjem*—home of seamen. Take little whisky.' He broke off to yell something at the foreman on the dockside below.

The gangway was clear. I nodded goodbye, hurried down and started hunting for a taxi.

I was in good time; it wasn't half past one when we picked up my luggage. (I was going to chance the guns; with the Mauser still in pieces and planted all over my big case it wouldn't look sinister to any metal detector. And the derringer was going to be tucked into my crutch: they're wary about shovelling radiation at you down there, in these gene-conscious days.) We zoomed across a high bridge over the south harbour, then through a long tunnel through the mountainside, heading for the airport.

So that had been Bergen, the economy twenty-four-hour tour. In that you only get one murder, a single beating-up and just a touch of blackmail; what did you expect, you cheapskate—the St Valentine's Day Massacre?

I studied the back of the driver's neck—wide and thick and red—and didn't know whether to feel a louse or a small-time gambler trying to ride out a high-stakes game on a small pair. I could tell David that at least I knew what we were looking for, now—but not that we were closer to finding it. But what more could I have done? I'd talked to everybody involved, hadn't I? Well, hadn't I?

I leant forward. 'Do you know any retired seamen's homes? I think you call it *sjomannshjem*.'

The question surprised him; he wriggled his wide shoulders and said: 'I know one, and I think two more.'

'What are they called? Their names?'

He told me one name and it didn't mean a thing. Then: 'The one in Gulbrandsens Gaten.'

'Thanks.'

I went back to staring out through the steady drizzle. The big suburban houses were thinning out, getting wider spaced. With a sudden blare a twin-engined jet charged overhead and vanished down behind a hill. I was a couple of hours from home.

Oh hell.

'Turn around,' I said wearily. 'Back to the railway station. I forgot something.'

TWENTY-FIVE

GULBRANDSENS SEAMEN'S HOME was over by the south harbour, by the shipbuilding yards, as it turned out. You climbed a street borrowed from San Francisco—so steep that a big house could lose a whole floor in its own length, over through the mixed old and new buildings of the university at the top, and started down the other side—and suddenly you were on the wrong side of town.

Every town has it. The dull, shabby streets walled with drab apartments and windows like rheumy old eyes. Quiet and still, because noise and movement cost money, and without laughter or anger because those cost something, too. The part that now can't even remember when it did anything but wait in front of a cold stove for it to be time to climb into bed and lie without real sleep, waiting for it to be time to be not really awake again. Every town has it; even Bergen.

The Home itself was on the corner of Gulbrandsens Gaten; a four-storey Victorian building in faded yellow stucco and small tight-lipped windows, barred on the ground floor. I leant my thumb on the old saucer-shaped bellpush and waited.

After a long time, footsteps shuffled up inside and the door groaned open a crack and a face looked out at me. It must have been in its late fifties, a sandpaper skin stretched tight over the sharp bones but bunching under the faded blue eyes and hanging loose at the throat. He didn't say anything.

'I'd like to see Chief Engineer Nygaard, please,' I said cheerily. The door started to swing shut, but my foot got there first. 'Hold on, now. At least we could ask the gent if he wants to see me, couldn't we?'

'He does not want you.' And he leant all of his weight on the door. I leant back.

'You don't even know who I am! I've brought him a present!' And I waved the half-bottle of Scotch I'd picked up at the Vinmonopolet—the state booze shop—on the way over. If Captain Jensen had been right, that should be the passport.

The faded blue eyes just looked impassive. 'He does not want visitors.'

'Just ask him!' I gave the door an exasperated shove and it ripped out of his hands, throwing him off against the wall, scrabbling for support.

I looked down and he had on one carpet slipper, one stiff shiny boot. So he'd lost a leg sometime. Well . . . he ought to have enough sense not to get into fights, then.

He looked at me with pure, patient hatred.

I said: 'Is Nygaard at home?'

'Room 14.' A dull, flat tone.

'Thank you, Herr . . . ?'

'Ruud. Superintendent Ruud.'

I shut the door and walked down the gloomy hallway, over lino that was uneven and gritty under my feet. And up the uncarpeted stairs. At the turn, I looked back, Ruud was still leaning against the wall, still staring after me. I went on up.

Room 14 was on the second floor, down a narrow corridor that was dark and had that indefinable but unmistakable smell of old people. Small private noises leaked out around me; somebody coughed rackingly, a lavatory flushed at the third pull, a plate clattered. I knocked on the door.

At the second knock, a bed creaked and a bleared voice mumbled something, and footsteps moved reluctantly towards the door.

Maybe he was sixty, maybe more, but it wasn't his age you saw first, it was his defeat. He'd quit, switched off, surrendered. His face was puffy, making his red-rimmed eyes look too small, his stomach bulged out over trousers unbuttoned at the top— but for a big man, the way he peered out was small and furtive. And his breath was a meal in itself, only a week late.

'Ja? Hva onsker De?'

I held my ground and tried not to breathe in. 'Chief Engineer Nygaard? I'm James Card from London. I brought you a . . .' and I showed him the bottle.

'Oh, ja!' He took it, held it up to stare at it closely—and then I saw his hands. The backs, from where they stuck out of the frayed old sweater, were a mass of crumpled blue-white scar tissues right to the ends of his fingers. The fingernails, the three or four still there, were thick dirty little wedges. But from the way he handled the bottle the fingers weren't locked: they could move from about half clenched to almost wide open.

Fire. Only fire does that.

Then he tried to square his shoulders against the pull of his gut, threw the door wide and said cheerfully: 'Come in, my friend, come in. I was having a little—you say, snooze.'

I went in. I could guess what the room would be like—but I was wrong. It was surprisingly clean, bright and almost tidy. Not that there was much to get in a mess, but the bed was made, if rumpled, and the table, chest of drawers and shelves had been freshly painted white. There were even a couple of flowers in the glass on the narrow tiled window-sill.

Nygaard half opened a drawer, changed his mind, and left the bottle in plain view. Then he picked up an electric kettle and shook it. 'Would you want some coffee, ja?'

'If you're making it anyway.' I perched myself on the arm of a middle-aged armchair that was wearing an old but recently cleaned cover.

He got the kettle switched on, found a jar of instant coffee and a couple of mugs and a bag of sugar, and even that effort made him wheeze a bit. 'Are you a sailor man, Mr—er——?'

'Card. No.'

'So why do you visit an old man like me, hey?'

'I'm doing some work for somebody in Lloyd's of London.' Well, there was a reasonable percentage of truth in that. 'I understand you were on the *Skadi* when she . . .'

He turned his back and the big shoulders trembled. 'No. I do not talk about that.'

'Sorry.' I suppose I shouldn't be surprised. 'But you're going to have to talk about it to the court if the case ever comes to trial. Why not to me?'

'Always lawyers, questions, why this and that, all the time. No. Why cannot an old man die by himself, with his own people?' He still had his back to me.

'You're not dying, come off it.' He didn't answer. 'All right, don't talk about the collision, then. Did you ever meet a man called Steen?'

He turned around again and seemed calmer. 'Ja, I meet him. Once, twice.'

'Recently?'

'A month, I think. Ja.'

'What did he ask you about?'

He flapped his arms like stiff wings. 'Always the same, *Skadi*, *Skadi*, *Skadi*.' Then the kettle hissed and he turned away to make the coffee.

I asked: 'Did you read this morning's papers?'

'I don't read newspapers. Only the shipping magazine.'

'Steen got himself killed yesterday. Murdered.'

He shook his head. 'I did not like him.'

'Why not?' Though I could see why a neat, fastidious man like Steen—to judge from his clothes and office—wouldn't get on too well with Nygaard.

He turned round with a couple of steaming mugs. 'Just always questions. *Skadi*, *Skadi*, *Skadi*.'

His hand trembled as he held out the mug, and just the touch of warmth from it reminded me how cold the room was; I still had my sheepskin coat on. There was a serious-looking electric fan heater in the corner, but Nygaard obviously preferred to use his spare cash for other things.

For a while we just sipped, and probably he was wondering why I was there as much as I was myself. Then I managed to slop some coffee down my coat collar, and reached for my handkerchief.

He jerked like a shot puppet. 'No, no! You must not smoke! No light, no!' One crumpled, shivering hand was stretched out towards me.

Very carefully, I took out the handkerchief and mopped myself. He slumped and half turned away. I said: 'You don't like naked flame? Well, that sounds reasonable, after what you went through.'

His hand reached for the whisky, then pulled back and patted the thin white strands on his scalp. And then tried to reach the bottle again. He gave me a quick sideways glance that was both sly and hopeful and I wanted to tell him to go ahead and have one. But you can't; not even when you know you can't stop it, you can't be the one to start it.

Then he picked the bottle up as if he'd never seen it before and studied the label carefully. 'I do not know this type before. It is good, ja?'

I shrugged. 'Don't know it myself.' Though at more than three quid for a half-bottle it had ruddy well better be good.

He waved the bottle at me. 'You like some in the coffee?'

'Well . . .' What do you say? The small eyes looked at me yearningly.

He said quickly. 'I don't drink in the afternoon. But just once, to try it, ja?'

He had the cap unscrewed. Silently, I held out my mug and he shook, rather than poured, a tot in. Then turned his back to me so that, maybe by accident, I couldn't see how much he gave himself.

'Skol.' He lifted the mug and took a gulp, and smiled easily. 'Is good, ja?'

'Yes, sure.' A car stopped somewhere outside—a rare enough noise in that street for him to hear it and pause. But he didn't go to look. I sipped on; he gulped.

Then: 'You ever heard of something called H and Thornton?'

He had. He gave another jerk, then buried his face in the mug, and came up with a carefully thoughtful expression. 'You say what?'

148

'H and Thornton. I think they're a firm of solicitors, or maybe ship surveyors or something.'

Now he was looking genuinely puzzled. He shook his head. 'No, I do not know them. No.'

Hell. I'd had him and I'd lost him, but I didn't know how or where.

Then feet came galloping down the corridor—young feet. There was the briefest of knocks on the door, it slammed open, and she came straight in—and not to wish me a Merry Christmas.

She was young, tall, blonde and then at least she might have quite a figure under the dark blue anarak and black ski pants. Right now, she just stood and stared fiercely at me, flushed and panting slightly and with the funny little white student cap on her head knocked sideways.

'What are you doing here?'

'Having a quiet cup of coffee with Herr Nygaard.'

She glared suspiciously around, then spotted the whisky. 'Did you bring this?'

I nodded.

'It is not good for him!' For a moment I thought she was going to heave it through the window—and so did he. I've never seen anybody look so simply horrified.

But she controlled herself. 'Who are you?'

I told her but it didn't mean anything.

'Why do you want to see him?'

'Hold on a minute. Who are *you*?—his daughter?'

'No, I am only a student. But I help look after him.' That accounted for the fresh-painted furniture, then, and the flowers and general tidiness.

'Very charitable of you,' I said approvingly. 'Nice to know there are still some students who don't spend all their time smashing up the campus and sleeping three in a bed. But I'm not doing him any harm.'

Ruud's face appeared over her shoulder and he gave me a triumphant leer. A quick man with a telephone, Herr Ruud.

The girl said: 'You will go, now.'

I looked at Nygaard. 'It's your room, chum.'

But he wasn't looking back. So I nodded and said: 'Thanks for the coffee, anyhow.'

'I thank you for the whisky,' he mumbled back.

'Any time.' The girl stepped aside and let me through the door, then followed. Ruud stayed in, and shut the door.

She followed me clear down the stairs and out into the street —and then we just stood there in the drizzle and looked at each other.

She said firmly: 'You are going home, now.'

'Nope. I'm just standing here admiring the view.'

That made her blink thoughtfully. Then she had a bright idea. 'I know some students, very rough ones. They will make you go.'

'Dare say you do know them—every university's got some and they like being known—but they don't know you. Not some pansy do-gooding Christian piece like you. So forget the goon squad; they wouldn't do anything for you.'

She flushed. 'Then I get the police.'

'Try for Inspector Vik.' I was standing by a ramshackle old Volkswagen—so old it had the twin rear windows, and so beat up that it looked as if it had been dumped. I patted a wing and then had to stop it going on shaking. 'Yours?'

'I own one half of it.'

'Give me a lift back into town and I'll buy the beer at the other end.'

'I do not drink.' But the rest of the idea suited her; at least it got me clear of Gulbrandsens Gaten. As she climbed in, she said: 'I am Kari Skagen.' So now I knew her name, it was all right for us to be alone in a car.

TWENTY-SIX

AS WE CHUGGED down the patched-up street, I asked: 'How long have you known Nygaard?'

'Since before Christmas.'

'From about when he came to the Home? How did you get to know him?'

'There is a . . . sort of club. Called Student Christian. We help old people and like that.'

'So it was pure chance you drew him?'

'Ja. . . .' She stirred the gear lever around until she found a noise that suited her. 'But why did you——'

But I was determined to keep *this* interrogation in my hands for a while longer. 'Hasn't he got any family?'

'His wife is dead for ten years. They have no children. His sister lives in Denmark but she is also very old. So . . .'

We turned a corner and I got slung against the door—which tried to open. I scrambled back into my seat. 'But can't his old employers at ADP do anything? Like get him out of that dump? Have you seen Mrs Smith-Bang?'

'You know her? Yes, I have seen her. But she says she cannot pay more than his pension—and he says he does not want to leave the Home. He likes being with sailors.'

Come to think of it, why *should* Mrs S-B pay any more? She hardly owed a bonus to a crew that had done at least its fair share of running the *Skadi* into legal history, at whatever speed. And over-paying a star witness can look bad in court.

Then we turned on to the main road and she bollicksed the clutch work and we crossed two lines of fast traffic hoppity-hoppity-hop like a storybook bunny. A white Mercedes swerved around us and vanished ahead in a dying scream of its horn and my nerves.

Kari said seriously: 'I am a better driver with boats.'

I nodded breathlessly and she finally got a question in. 'Why did you come to see him—and bring the whisky?'

'Just as a present. Is that bastard Ruud going to steal it?'

'No. I asked him to, many times. If he did, he could stop Engineer Nygaard drinking very soon.'

'And clap hands if you believe in fairies,' I murmured.

'Pardon?'

'Never mind. Just believe I wouldn't have brought the Scotch if I'd known he was an alcoholic.' Wouldn't I, though? Well, it was a moral problem I didn't have to solve right now. 'But you know Nygaard's an important witness in a legal affair?'

'Ja. He was on a boat that burned up.'

'So I'm hardly the first person to come asking questions, right?'

'Ja,' she admitted.

'And did you ever hear of a man called Jonas Steen?'

'Engineer Nygaard said about him. He did not like him.'

'Maybe, but that wasn't why he got murdered.'

'*Hva?*' she said incredulously.

'D'you want to know why women will never rule the world? Because they can't be bothered to read a newspaper to find out if they've taken over the world, that's why. Spread all over the front page, that story had been—*and* the radio.

I tried to explain. When I'd finished, she asked carefully: 'But you do not think it was this man Lie who killed him?'

'Well . . .' Come to that, Lie might easily have done it; certainly he was an accessory. 'It's more a question of why it was done. Did Nygaard ever tell you what he told Steen?'

She tried to remember, her forehead crinkling into a small frown. With that fine long hair, firm profile and fair skin, she was quite a looker. Just too much character behind the blue eyes for me. 'I think he talked about the accident . . . and the rescue.'

Great. Bloody marvellous. They wouldn't have mentioned the weather, as well? Or pollution or politics or the traffic problem?

'Well,' I growled, 'if you can ever get him to tell you more about what Steen knew, it could help.'

'Why should I help you?'

I kept my temper for about the next five yards. 'Because Steen was murdered because of it! And another man was murdered because of it ten days ago—a man Steen had been talking to! And Lie himself—oh hell's feathers, never mind, just go on being Christian charitable.'

She was staring at me. Left to itself, the Volkswagen jumped like a terrier and snapped at a passing van. Both of us grabbed at the steering wheel.

When we'd got it back on the leash again, she said: 'Do you mean that Engineer Nygaard may be killed also?'

'I don't know. I really don't.' And I really didn't. 'Maybe

they're counting on him doing it to himself. Drop me off at the railway station; I want to pick up my bags.'

In the end, she offered to drive me to the airport as well and I accepted out of sheer devotion to duty. If anybody could get through to Nygaard, she seemed the likeliest—*if* she wanted to try. And on her side, I think she was feeling a bit guilty about giving me the heave-ho from his room so promptly.

At intervals when it didn't seem likely to distract her from keeping us alive, I learnt that she was studying history and English, that her parents lived somewhere further south, that she wasn't engaged. She didn't learn as much from me; I tried to give the impression that I worked for a big legal firm in London.

At the airport, it turned out that the only way I could get home that night was to fly a local to Oslo, change for Gothenburg in Sweden, then pick up the eleven thirty-five p.m. for London. The ticket desk thought I was crazy and maybe insulting their country besides, the trouble I was going to to get out of it, but they wrote me out a whole pack of tickets.

Then we had half an hour to wait for the Oslo plane, so she took a coffee while I had a beer—despite her disapproving frown. I honestly don't think the girl could help it any more than Nygaard could, by now, help the opposite approach.

I asked casually: 'Did Nygaard ever talk to you about the collision?'

'No—not truly. I asked him, but he said he cannot remember much.'

'How was he rescued?'

'He was on a . . . a raft, you call it. For all the night and in the day also. Then a fishing-boat found him. I think it, with the burns. . . .' She tapped her forehead. 'Made him forget, you understand?'

'Yes.' I could also understand what impression he'd make in court. But you aren't supposed to pick your witnesses like casting a movie, though I've known it happen. Kari added: 'That is why he drinks so much now, of course.'

'Uh-huh? And who buys him his booze? You?'

I'd've got less reaction from suggesting we stretched out on the cafeteria table and became just good friends. I said hastily: 'All right, all right—you just keep him clean and tidy. But who *does* buy his whisky and aquavit and so forth?'

Now she was just puzzled. 'Himself, of course. He goes out.'

'I mean who pays for it? I know Norwegian pensions are good, but to stay in his condition he's drinking nearly a bottle a day. Over a hundred kroner; maybe thirty quid a week before he's paid a penny for bed and breakfast.'

'Oh no.'

'Oh yes. That's what it costs.'

She looked puzzled. Like most teetotallers, she'd assumed that all it took to become an alcoholic was a couple of secretive gulps before noon. But you have to work at it, although it doesn't seem like work at the time.

She said slowly: 'Perhaps Herr Ruud would know. . . .'

'You could ask. But he seems pretty protective about the old boy.'

'Ja. They were friends on the ship—how do you say that?'

'Shipmates.'

'In the war. When Herr Ruud lost the leg. And after that he could not be an officer, so . . .'

The loudspeaker crackled something that could be my flight. I stood up and held out my hand. It got a genuine warm shake, and I got a real smile. She said: 'I am sorry I was—too quick, hasty.'

'Never mind.' I gave her one of my cards—the one with my address and phone but not profession on. 'If he tells you anything about Steen—give me a ring, would you? I'll pay you back.'

She nodded.

I hurried out across the wet tarmac and when I looked back from the top of the plane's steps she was standing out in the drizzle herself, waving rather formally.

The best you could say of the trip home was that nobody found my pistols. I had a three-hour break for dinner in Oslo, than an hour's drinking at Gothenburg. I reached Heathrow just before two in the morning, and bed just after three. And stayed there until eleven the next morning.

TWENTY-SEVEN

I RANG HARROW FIRST, then tried for Willie. He rang me back before lunch. I asked: 'Can you make a board meeting before the end of the afternoon?'

'Er, I think so—d'you mean with young David, too?'

'That's the idea. He's free to go out to local cafés after four-fifteen. I fixed a date for four-thirty.'

'Rather. Jolly good. Would you like me to pick you up?'

'That's not a bad idea.' Then we could leave my car—which just might get recognized—out of it. 'But have you got anything less conspicuous than the Tiger Royal?'

He chuckled. 'What about a red Mini-Cooper?'

It would have to do. So I arranged to meet him outside the Swiss Cottage pub at four o'clock. Getting over there would give me space to lose any extra shadow I happened to be throwing.

But meantime, there was one extra piece of insurance I wanted to take out. I drove over to my rifle-and-pistol club and conned the resident watchdog into letting me use the pistol range; in winter, it doesn't usually open on weekdays. Then I put fifty rounds through the Mauser HSC and after *that* the rifling marks would be distinctly different from those on any bullet they dug out of Steen's head.

While I was there I also fired the derringer for the first time. The kick and bang were something very extra special—with a barrel that length the cartridge was practically exploding in the open air—but both the waterlogged rounds went off, although God knows where they went off to. I fired another six shots and it wasn't until I'd closed in to ten yards that I could even see where I was putting them: way high to the right. Don't shoot till you can smell the garlic on their breath.

I got in just as the telephone started ringing.

'Major. Where the bloody hell have *you* been?'

Dave Tanner, of course. 'Sorry about that, Dave. Something came up. I'm back now.'

'Yes?' he asked sourly. 'And for how long?'

'Can't see anything else coming up. Have you got anything for me?'

'I had it last Monday. I don't know if we've still got it. But I'll check and let you know.'

He rang off. I stood there with the phone in my hand, remembering I hadn't asked about Pat Kavanagh; Dave could likely have heard of him. But he didn't exactly owe me any favours and you don't want to build up too much of a debit. It could wait.

Willie was right on time. I folded myself up into the Mini-Cooper's front seat—why a man of *his* height and income chose that even as a second or third (or ninth, for all I knew) car, I just couldn't guess. We scuttled away up the Finchley Road.

Today he was the country squire: cavalry twill trousers, flared hacking jacket, thick soft shirt with a faint check—just like the last three generations of Winslows except that he wore the silk neck-scarf flapping loose and theirs would have been tied like a riding stock. Wherever Willie put his immortal gift of originality, it wasn't in his wardrobe.

'Any news of H and Thornton?' I asked.

'Sorry, old boy. They're not solicitors—I checked.'

'Something in shipping? A line?'

'Not a shipping line. But——'

'Marine surveyors? Or any other sort of subsidiary firm?'

'You mean chartering brokers or forwarding agents or ship-brokers or warehousing agents or a bunkering firm or perhaps just the two chaps who have the barnacle-scraping concession on Ilfracombe lifeboat?' He gave me a quick, dry sideways glance.

'All right,' I growled. 'So shipping's still bigger business than most people think. But——'

'*But*,' he said firmly, 'one chap I mentioned it to at Lloyd's said he thought he'd heard it before only it didn't sound quite right somehow, you know?'

'What sort of chap?'

'A solicitor.'

That didn't tell me anything, though. I gave up. 'How's the syndicate getting on?'

'Hardly at all, what? We'll probably merge with one of the bigger ones—best thing, I dare say. We only kept going as a small affair because of Martin.'

'Tell me: am I right in thinking he only had about the minimum deposit in Lloyd's?—even for an underwriter?'

He took his time answering; hell, he took his time deciding whether or not to answer at all. He was driving a wide but busy road with a precise opportunism, keeping in a lower gear than most drivers would have done, and letting the engine work for its living. It didn't create any great hush, but it made for some natty wrong-side overtaking.

But finally we got caught at a traffic light. Willie took a long cigarette from a magnetic-based box clinging to the dashboard, lit it with a rolled-gold Dunhill and said: 'You were almost asking that at the funeral, weren't you, old boy?'

'Almost.'

'You're sure it's really relevant?'

I hauled my head back from the rear seat and said: 'It could be. But I'm not planning to put it in my best-selling memoirs.'

He grinned quickly. 'Sorry, old boy. Yes—Martin only had about ten or eleven thousand in the kitty and you can't go much below that. I suppose with a place in the country and a flat in London and David going to Harrow . . . and then the bad years at Lloyd's, well—he just couldn't build it up.'

I could have told him a little more detail about Fenwick's income and outgo, but I didn't think he'd like the way I'd got it. The point was that he'd confirmed my basic thesis. Well, almost.

We swung left down Hendon Way and speeded up. After a time, Willie asked: 'Is there anything more you want to check on before you see David?'

'Why?—are you worried I might have found out something about his father that you think he shouldn't know?'

'Yes.' For Willie, that was good bluff stuff. For a moment, it threw me. Then I managed to ask: 'Such as what?'

'God knows, old boy. But there must have been something —what? People don't get shot for nothing.'

'Tell that to the next innocent bystander at a bank raid.' I stared at the road and wondered. But David had hired me first. 'No, I'll tell you both everything at the same time.'

He nodded, seeming quite contented. After that, we hardly said a word until we'd parked at the top of the Hill itself. By then, both pavements were crawling with groups of schoolboys hurrying here and there and all wearing straw boaters that made them look like actors in costume against that gloomy, dank afternoon. The style seemed to be for the hat tipped right forward and the elastic chinstrap bunching up the hair at the back of the neck. Anyway, that's how David was wearing it when we met outside a small café. We shook hands formally all round then went on in.

Long ago, the proprietor must have realized that his main clients were interested in quantity of food for money and nothing else. Apart from a jukebox, the only overhead in the place was the ceiling and that looked a fairly written-down value. Willie looked cautiously around the grimy, rough-plastered walls speckled with notices and shuddered delicately.

David said politely: 'What would you like?—I'll get it. The hamburger and onions is rather nice.'

'Just tea,' I said quickly.

'Coffee, please,' said Willie and then caught my hard stare and realized what the coffee would be like in there and said: 'No, sorry—tea.'

When David had gone, we sat down at one of half a dozen simple riot-proof tables. Only one other was occupied, by a group of fifteen-year-old Harrovians who glanced at us and forgot us.

'Good God,' Willie muttered. 'You forget how . . . *primitive* schoolboys are.'

'I'm sure you never were.'

'I wasn't at Harrow, of course, but . . .' He stared at the group. 'Just look at that lot, what? They look as if they've run an assault course through pig-food in those clothes. And yet I'll bet I know half their families.'

'Willie, you're a snob.'

'Oh yes, rather.'

David came back with our teas, a Coke and a meat pasty for himself. 'Well, sir,' he started. 'Mr Winslow told me about the chap Steen getting killed, of course. But did you find out any more?'

I said pompously: 'We now know what we're looking for is the log of the *Skadi*.'

Willie said: 'Oh, *that* ship? Well, sorry, old boy, but we aren't looking for *the* log. Do you mean the deck log or the engine log or the rough drafts of either, or the official log? Not to mention the movements book—what?'

'So don't mention it, then,' I growled. 'Mrs Smith-Bang didn't tell me.'

'Oh, you saw her?'

'You know her?'

'Everybody in shipping knows her. And the ADP Line was one of our regulars.'

'So I gathered. Well—' And I started to tell my story.

They listened quietly, Willie sipping his tea and looking equally pained at each sip, David just ploughing through his pasty and watching me carefully.

When I finished, Willie said: 'You do live, don't you?'

'Barely.'

David said: 'You were jolly lucky about your Mauser and finding it first.'

'Not entirely. The other side was counting on luck as well. Somebody else might have found the body before I could possibly have got there—I could have had a perfect alibi, like boozing in a bar with the King, or something.'

'It was still your pistol,' he pointed out.

'Oh yes, but I'd only have been in trouble with the Min of Def for not having reported it lost. That's not murder. No, they had the luck that theoretically I could have done the killing and the bad luck that I was snoopy enough to get there first and start fiddling the evidence. Or unfiddle it.'

Willie said slowly: 'So it mattered more to them to kill Steen before you saw him than to get you blamed for it?'

'I'm sure of that.'

'But all he was going to do—from his notes—was tell you about the Chief Engineer, Nygaard, and where he lived.'

'*And* H and Thornton. And anything else he thought of before he saw me.'

'Ye-es.' He scratched his cheekbone.

David asked: 'But why was Daddy having to take this log to Arras?'

Willie watched me carefully. I shrugged. 'Being black-mailed, I think.'

'Was he? What about?'

'I don't really know; it doesn't matter. The important thing is that they tried the same trick with me and I ended up doing exactly the same thing: playing along to see if I could find out who was behind it, and taking some protection. I took Draper, like your father had taken me.'

David was only half listening. 'But how could they black-mail him? Do you think he was having an affair?'

Willie made a strangled coughing-gulping noise. I tried to look uninterested.

David said, as much to himself as anybody: 'I suppose he might have done . . . but with whom? Anybody we know? It could be Miss Mackwood, couldn't it, and that was why she was involved?' He glanced at Willie, who did a good job of not having heard of Fenwick, Maggie or fornication, either.

I said firmly: 'But at least we got a firm identification out of it. According to Draper, this Kavanagh's a bit of a hard case. Herb apparently fired him for trying to bribe a juryman, and before that he'd left the police in something of a hurry. Sounds like one of those times when they say 'Oh he's a terribly nice chap, he'd never do a thing like that,' and privately tell him to resign in six months, or else.'

David's eyes opened a little wider. 'Do they do that?'

'Every organization does it, what?' said Willie, glad to find something new to talk about. 'Including the public schools. But what are you proposing to do about Kavanagh?—tell the police?'

'Whose? The Steen case is closed; I never reported the truth-drug business over here, and as for Arras——'

I stopped. David had gone very white and his clenched fists were bouncing nervously on the edge of the table. His eyes glittered at me. 'Do you think,' he said in a thick voice, 'that he killed my father?'

I wished I'd seen where I'd been leading. Smearing as much calm consideration on my voice as possible, I said: 'We know there were *two* men in Arras; from what we now know of Kavanagh he could have been one of them, and I'm going to get the word to Arras—indirectly—to check his name in hotels and any cross-Channel passenger lists they can find. Not that such things exist much nowadays.'

I wasn't looking directly at him, but from the edge of my eye I could see he was cooling down. I went on with my lecture: 'Meanwhile, Draper's doing some quiet work trying to find out what Kavanagh's been doing recently—remember, we've got an advantage that he doesn't know we know him. But also, he's not working for himself and we don't know who he *is* working for.'

David was staring down at his plate, nodding gently to himself. In the corner, one fifteen-year-old voice said: 'And don't tell me that was a director's film. Two directors walked off it before he got there.'

Another voice asked: 'Have you *seen* the film?'

'No, of course not. What are film reviews for?'

'I've often wondered that.'

Closer to home, Willie lit a cigarette carefully and said: 'But it does rather bring up the question of who the other side is in all this.'

I said: 'First, does Mrs Smith-Bang's story hold up? About engine trouble and the log proving it?'

'Yes, it sounds pretty possible, you know. Could be an important point, all right. Though to my mind, it doesn't so much prove the *Prometheus Sahara* officers are liars as that their radar set must have had a screw loose. And that's rather a worse offence, in fog. The courts expect the odd tall story, you know; most collisions take place between two stationary ships ten miles apart both hooting and firing off rocket signals, if you know what I mean? But trusting a duff radar set—that's serious.'

I grinned. 'Fine. So the Sahara Line's got a good case for wanting that log suppressed.'

He sighed. 'Yes, but . . . they're a big, solid company, you know. They don't do the sort of thing like . . . like Arras.'

But David took it calmly, this time.

I said: 'That's bunk, Willie. As you said yourself, all organizations do, and the bigger the oftener. Were you and your Lancers ever in the Middle East?'

He shook his head.

'Well, half *our* work in Intelligence out there was finding out if the oil companies were going to start a revolution, never mind the Russians and Egyptians and our friends in the CIA. It's never the chairman of the board who does it, of course, and he may not even know, but somewhere down the line somebody else gets the idea that the boss is interested in results and not methods, and a few more steps down somebody picks up a gun and goes bang. *Somebody* hired Kavanagh and others to get that log; he wasn't working on spec.'

Willie nodded sadly and we sat silent for a while. Then he said: 'Of course, I don't suppose it would do any good, but you could always ask Paul.'

David said: 'D'you mean Mr Mockby, sir?'

'Yes. He's a director of the Sahara Line, you know.'

TWENTY-EIGHT

THE PUBS WERE JUST OPEN by the time Willie and I started back, so we stopped at one halfway down the Hill and he phoned around to find Mockby while I washed away the taste of that tea. He didn't tell me what Mockby had said, apart from come and see me at home at half past six, but his expression showed the fat man hadn't undergone any injections of Christian charity on my behalf. Well, I could live with or without that from Mr Paul Mockby.

It was getting dark and the outbound traffic was the usual bad-tempered, many-eyed snake plus a few kamikaze pilots —as usual. Willie drove thoughtfully and quietly, his slightly melted Greek god profile outlined against the passing headlights.

After a time, he asked: 'Do you really think Paul could be . . . ah . . . well, you know?'

'I don't know, but if there's a profit in it and he wouldn't be caught, I'm sure the answer's Yes. Am I right?'

'Probably, I'm afraid.' He said nothing for a distance, and then: 'I didn't want to mention it with David there, you know —but do you have a real idea why Martin was being blackmailed?'

'Well, he *was* having it off with Maggie Mackwood. Didn't *you* know?'

'Er . . . but how did you find out?'

'She told me herself.'

'Good God Almighty.' But he said it gently, mostly to himself. 'I suppose you *did* have to mention blackmail to David?'

'I think so. It's the keystone of the whole thing, as far as I can see—Fenwick's vulnerability to a divorce.'

'Oh, I don't know. . . . They aren't too old-fashioned about these things at Lloyd's.'

'I'll bet they're pretty old-fashioned about an underwriter suddenly losing most of his deposit.

'And that's what would have happened. Give a divorce judge a nice clear-cut case where the man's been set up in business on what was his wife's money and then the break-up's all his fault . . . Christ, Fenwick would have come out of court with his bus fare home and a sixpence for the meter to gas himself with.'

'Yes—I suppose a judge's decision would override everything else,' he mused.

'The prisons are full of people who disagree.'

'But of course, you *are* assuming Lois would have divorced him. She might not.'

'Yes. . . .' After all, Mrs F herself had as near as dammit told me she believed Fenwick was taking a horizontal opinion of Maggie. 'Probably it was that he couldn't afford *any* risk of divorce, it would have been so final for him. So he was vulnerable to any threat at all.'

'I suppose you must be right. . . .' He did a neat piece of light-jumping that brought us out ahead of a Rolls-Royce. Headlamps flashed angrily behind us. 'What do you make of this business of Maggie having you followed to Norway and so on?'

'That she was damn fond of him—didn't want me raking up anything to discredit him. And maybe her as well.'

'But she then went and told you about it.'

'Yes—when I was bound to find out anyhow. And I'd suspected it before.'

'Ah. I say, how much would it cost her to hire him?'

I calculated. The Rolls's headlights were still throwing broadsides after us, making Willie's rear-view mirror flash like a warning lamp. 'In case you hadn't noticed,' I said nervously, 'you're about to be rammed by a Cunarder abaft the starboard lug-hole.'

He grunted. 'Some damn silly little East-European ambassador.' But he pulled over and we rocked in the wake of the big car whooshing past.

I said: 'With sea and air fares, she must have spent at least two hundred pounds on that jaunt.'

'Probably more than we've spent on you, so far, what?'

'Certainly.'

'Impressive, rather.'

'Maybe it just proves she was in love with him. Sex hardly proves that, these days.'

'Bit cynical, what, old boy?'

I just shrugged again.

The houses in The Bishop's Avenue have just two things in common: they're all set back from the road, giving room for nice big lawns and a good piece of driveway, and people like you and me couldn't afford them in a million years. These aspects apart, each house is different—and intended to be. Not just Stockbroker's Tudor and Banker's Georgian, but everything from the Third Gothic Age to North London Chateau of the Loire via green-tiled Hacienda à la Rudolph Valentino and Plantation Scarlett O'Hara.

This last was Mockby's: a square-cut block of the Deep South in red brick with a white Grecian portico and a flood of wide steps sweeping down to the green tarmac drive. Willie found a bellpush in among the brasswork of the double front doors, but the house was too big and solid for you to hear it ring inside.

After a cold wait, one side of the doors opened and the big chauffeur I'd met at my flat looked stonily out.

Willie said pleasantly: 'Mr Mockby's expecting us.'

The big one nodded at me. '*And* him?'

I gave him a friendly smile.

'Passed your finals in robbery with violence yet? Or d'you want some more lessons?'

He bunched his fist. Willie looked at me reprovingly. Then, from somewhere inside, Mockby bellowed: 'Don't fart about, Charles! Let 'em in!'

We went through an inner set of french doors, along a big hallway with enough furniture to start a chain store, and into the lounge.

It was a big room but with an odd confined feeling. There must have been windows somewhere behind the gold silk drapes, but you wouldn't bother with them: there was too much to look at inside. The place was jammed with furniture; usable stuff like fat wing chairs and sofas and couches, unusable bits like tiny tables covered in silver photo frames, carved benches, embroidered footstools.

Even the flock wallpaper was put up in panels, and each panel with a gold-framed still-life of dead pheasants and careful beads of moisture on every grape.

Willie must have seen it all before, but I thought I heard him give a little sad sigh.

Mockby was standing in the middle, wrapped in a vast red velvet smoking jacket with green lapels.

'Hullo, Willie,' he called, 'what are you doing with that blackmailing bastard?'

Willie twitched like a nervous horse. His faith in me wasn't even skin deep, after all: he'd taken me more or less on David's trust.

'Blackmailing?' he asked warily.

'Of course,' said Mockby. 'Trying to sell us something that belongs to us already.'

I said: 'You mean the *Skadi*'s log?'

'That's what I mean, sonny.'

Willie said: 'Oh, that,' and looked vaguely relieved. Even he couldn't believe I was fool enough to try and sell Mockby something I hadn't got.

Mockby seemed puzzled, but recovered fast. 'Well, have you come to do business now?'

I shrugged. 'Anything could happen.'

'I suppose you want a drink first.' He strode over to a book-case that turned out, of course, of course, to be a cocktail cabinet lined in rose-tinted mirror glass (one of these days I'm going to market a cocktail cabinet that turns out to be a book-case; there must be *some* secret readers in The Bishop's Avenue).

'Scotch? And you, Willie?'

'Ah—pink gin, if you could.'

'Oh Christ,' Mockby said impatiently. 'Mix your own.' He strode back with two big cut-glass tumblers and shoved one into my hand. Willie went and started necromancing with the little bottle of bitters.

Mockby and I drank, then he said: 'Well, now are you going to hand it over?'

Willie called: 'I've never seen this thing. Which log are we talking about?'

Mockby swung round. 'Deck log—chief officer's log. The fair copy.'

'Ah yes.' He went on blending.

'Well?' Mockby asked me.

'What does it prove?—the log, I mean.'

'You've had it long enough, haven't you?'

Willie was zigzagging elegantly along the furniture towards us. 'I don't suppose Mr Card reads Norwegian sea-going terms frightfully well, what?'

You know, it's damn silly, but maybe it was hearing all those Norwegians talking perfect English that had made me forget they'd write up their logs in Norwegian. I'd somehow imagined Fenwick skimming through the book and saying: 'Aha!—the Captain's butler did it!'

'Did Martin Fenwick read Norwegian?' I asked quickly.

Mockby and Willie looked at each other; Willie sipped his pale pink mixture and shrugged delicately. Mockby said: 'Bit, I think. Not much.'

So Fenwick must have got an explanatory letter with the log. Or phone call. But if you're parcelling up the log, you'd add a letter as well anyway. Would Fenwick have kept that? Say, in the bureau at his flat? And would an interested party have swiped it before I got there?

Mockby was staring down into his glass, baby features crowded into a slight frown.

I said: 'So, what did he tell you the log showed?'

He stretched his big chest with a deep breath. 'Oh, something about whether it invalidated the policy or not.'

Willie stared at him. '*Invalidated* it? Did he really say that?'

Mockby got angry. 'Of course he did. I just said so.'

I said: 'If you do pay out in full on the collision, how much? —it'll be pretty big, won't it?'

Mockby heaved his shoulders in a shrug. 'The whole claim'll come to about half a million—plus bloody great fees to every lawyer that can get his greedy great gob into the honeypot. *We* had a line of seven-and-a-half per cent. It'll cost us nearly forty thousand.'

'But the *Prometheus Sahara* must have been worth a hell of a lot more than any of that?'

Willie said: 'About ten million, I'd imagine. These liquid-gas jobs come costly. All the stainless steel and what-not, you know?'

'Well, if it's your side's fault, aren't you liable for that?'

'Limitation,' Mockby barked. 'You don't know bugger-all about insurance, do you? Owner applies to the courts to limit his liability; the figures get a bit fancy, but it works out that, even if he's totally to blame, he can't owe the other side more than about the value of his *own* vessel.'

'Who pays the other nine and something million, then?'

'The other side's insurers, of course. Most likely Lloyd's again but probably not the same syndicates. Anyway, not us. Thank God Martin kept us out of tankers.'

'I think,' said Willie, 'that it was all worked out originally to encourage the small ship-owner, make it so he couldn't go bust on one accident. They didn't want the big boys to create a monopoly situation, like you've got with the airlines now, you know?'

'So whatever happens,' I said, 'you can't be liable, as a syndicate, for more than forty thousand pounds?'

'S'right,' said Mockby briskly. 'Just because we're all gentlemen at Lloyd's doesn't mean we've got heads full of horse-shit.'

Willie winced.

I asked: 'Could that be the difference between a profit and a loss on the year?'

'Oh Christ, no. It's only two percent of turnover.'

'But still worth saving?'

He frowned at me, shrugged. 'Of course. That's the first sensible thing you've said this evening.'

'And you knew Fenwick was being blackmailed for this log?'

Pause. He looked at me, his Scotch, then nothing, but realized he couldn't lie on that one. 'He told me.'

'And you agreed on his going to Arras?'

'Christ, I didn't think he was going to get killed, boy! And how could I stop him!—it was his cock on the block.'

So then Willie had to help. 'Maggie told Mr Card about . . . about her and Martin having an affair.'

Mockby stared at him, his face melting from surprise into vague disbelief. 'Christ. Gabby little bit, ain't she?' Then he turned to me and became the prison camp commandant again. 'And how many people have *you* told?'

I just sipped my drink and for a while nobody said anything. Then I asked politely: 'And your interest has nothing to do with being in the Sahara Line as well.'

'No, of course not!' But I wasn't sure if I believed his eyes.

'I had to ask. It could represent a conflict of interests.'

'Get them every day in the City, if you're on enough boards.' Then he swung on Willie and exploded: 'Is *that* why you brought him along? Little bloody ray of sunshine, ain't you?'

Willie looked genuinely embarrassed. 'Well, old chap . . . I mean, Mr Card rather insisted, you know?'

I could have done with something stronger than that. Mockby turned sourly back to me. 'Oh, he's a bloody marvellous insister, he is. Pity he's such a lousy bodyguard. Well?'

I said calmly: 'Did Fenwick mention the log proving engine trouble in the *Skadi*?'

'Er—he said something. I thought you couldn't read it?'

'Happened to run into a Mrs Smith-Bang the other day. In Bergen.'

'That crooked old bag?'

I smiled and shrugged. 'You know her, obviously.'

'Everybody knows her.' He guffawed heartily, then remembered my character weaknesses again. 'You're not giving her that log. What were you doing in Bergen?'

Willie blushed but Mockby didn't notice.

'Went to see a surveyor called Steen. But he got himself shot before we could talk.'

Now his expression was plain bewilderment, but with a growing unease behind the eyes. 'So, then?'

I finished my drink and put the glass down. 'So I don't know any more. Thanks for the drink.'

'Hey, wait a minute! You didn't give that log to her, did you?'

'No.'

'That's something, then. So—hand it over.'

'I'll think about it.'

'I'll pay you a thousand.'

'I'll think about it.'

'Fifteen hundred and that's it. In cash. No tax.'

'I'll think about it.'

Willie said uncomfortable: 'Oh, do we really need this, Paul?'

'We need that bloody log!' Back to me. 'Two thousand.'

'I'll think——'

'*Stop saying that!*'

'Can I help it if I'm a great thinker?'

'I don't believe you've got the bloody thing at all!' he shouted.

I knew how to react: a negligent shrug of believe-what-you-like-old-mate. But Willie looked as if he'd been caught bringing a female into his club.

And Mockby saw it. He swung round. '*Has* he got it?'

Willie made a sort of neighing noise.

'Great God on a gondola,' Modkby whispered hoarsely. 'You never had it.' His voice lifted to roaring-forties levels. 'Charles! *Charles!*'

The door crashed open and the big chauffeur stood there, looking surprised.

'Throw this cheap swindling sod out. I mean *throw* him.'

The ruddy face creased into a happy grin. 'Right away, Mr Mockby.' He moved forward.

I took the Mauser out of the holster inside the waistband on my hip and just held it, pointing at the floor.

I knew what Mockby would say and he did: 'You won't use that thing.'

I reached out and fired, and after the bang there was a lovely long clattering clanking tinkling noise from inside the cocktail cabinet. One side of the mirror lining was totally gone, and a couple of glasses gone with it.

'Not too serious,' I soothed him. 'At least I didn't hit a bottle. And you can always tell your wife you were practising for the polo season. Come on, Willie.'

He looked only faintly surprised; the other two were petrified. He finished his drink, smiled politely at Mockby and walked around him to the door. I followed; Charles stepped out of our way.

'I'll get you for——' he began.

'Don't trouble yourself. We'll find our own way out.'

The Bishop's Avenue was wide and bright and still, every light in every house blazing and nothing moving at all. Nobody running to see what the small sound of a .22 exploding had meant, even if they'd heard. You could stand and scream in the middle of the street there and if you did it long enough, somebody would ring the cops to come and take you away and abate the nuisance. But they wouldn't want to know why you screamed. Innocence is something you can buy for yourself, just as you can buy deafness for others.

As he swung out of the driveway, Willie said: 'I've always wanted *something* frightful to happen to that cabinet, but did you have to drag me away as well?'

'The less you say to Mockby right now, the better. And I needed a lift.'

His profile looked pained for a moment. 'Yes, I'm frightfully sorry about that. But does it really matter if Paul knows you haven't got the log?'

'It'll start him looking again, and I don't like his methods.'

'Of course.' Then: 'D'you think he was telling the truth?'

'No.'

'Oh, I *say*!' He glanced at me and the car slowed and a part-time Homo Sapiens who'd been doing forty m.p.h. eighteen inches behind us braked and hooted wildly. Willie took no notice at all. 'But why not?'

'For one thing it's too neat. If it's really only about the validity of the policy then the argument's only between your syndicate—or Lloyd's—and the ADP Line. So Sahara doesn't come into it at all; they're covered by their own insurance, whatever happens. Right?'

'Er . . . yes, just about.'

'So the only people trying to get that log off Fenwick—and who killed him—are the ADP Line, right?'

He nodded slowly. 'I think I see, now. But when you mentioned her, he was only normally rude, what? He doesn't really think she got Martin killed.'

'Something like that. Assuming he really cared about Fenwick, that is.'

'Oh, I think he did, all right. If nothing else, he thought Martin was a jolly valuable asset. Or he wouldn't have joined our syndicate—you know?' And after a while, he added: 'But what does it all add up to?'

'It doesn't. Not until we've got that log—if it still exists.'

'Well—what are you going to do next?'

'Just don't know.' But I knew what I was going to try.

It didn't seem too unrespectable an hour when I got home, so I rang Kingscutt straight off. Of course, she might have turned it in and come to stay in London somewhere, or even gone back to America—no, hardly likely, with David still in school.

Then she answered. Her voice was cool, polite, composed.

I said: 'I'm sorry to trouble you, Mrs Fenwick; it's James Card.'

'Oh? How nice to hear from you. How are you getting on?'

'Well . . . I'm not sure. Would you be in if I popped down to see you tomorrow?'

After only a moment's pause, she said calmly: 'Yes, of course. Please come for lunch.'

'Thanks very much, I'll do that. About twelve, then.'

After that I mixed myself another Scotch and went back to Vegetius on *Preparations for a General Engagement* until it was past time to go out for dinner, so I opened a tin of chilli.

TWENTY-NINE

I WAS THERE at twelve precisely.

The Manor looked a little cold and lonely without the shiny mass of parked cars that had been there last time. Now there was just a scruffy old Morris Minor—so old it had the V-shaped windscreen—parked on the gravel beside the front door. I climbed the steps and pulled an old bellknob and heard it jangle.

The housekeeper-shaped woman who'd been shovelling round the food at the funeral opened the door, nodded a little dourly at me, and led the way in. Lois Fenwick was in the big drawing-room, now looking even bigger and emptier, sitting on the rug in front of a big log fire.

She smiled pleasantly and just reached up a long arm and I shook her hand. 'It's very nice of you to come all this way. We don't see many people these days, do we Mrs Benson?'

The housekeeper made a noncommittal grunting noise. Mrs Fenwick looked at a neat little gold wristwatch and said: 'Time for our medicine, Mrs Benson.' Then, to me; 'What would you like to drink?'

'D'you have any beer?' I'd still got the drive back. But no beer, so I had to have a Scotch and soda anyway. Mrs Benson mixed them from a tray in the corner. It was obviously a daily ritual. She brought Mrs Fenwick a gin-and-tonic, me my Scotch, herself a glass of what looked like sweet sherry.

Lois said: 'Well, cheers.'

Mrs Benson gave another strangled grunt, sank her sherry in one lump, and went away. Far away, I heard a vacuum cleaner start up.

Lois laughed gaily. 'Dear Mrs Benson. I don't know what I'd do without her, but she doesn't really approve of me having men to visit. Now sit down and tell me what you've been doing.'

She was wearing a high-necked Victorian cream silk blouse and slim black trousers that really were slim, and leaning against a big brass and leather club fender. The nearest chair was a good six feet away so I perched on one corner of the fender.

'I've been sort of trying to find out who killed your husband.' And she took that without blinking. 'But not getting very far. There's one thing, a ship's logbook, that was sent him from Norway. You wouldn't have any idea what happened to it, would you?'

She smiled prettily. 'It's probably at Lloyd's.'

'No. I'm quite sure it isn't. The only place I can think of is here.'

She sipped her gin and smiled. 'So now you want to search this house, do you? Won't that be a pretty long job?'

'It's a fairly big book, Mrs Fenwick. And I'm a fairly experienced searcher.'

'Are you really? How exciting. Where did you learn that?'

'Army Intelligence Corps. Mrs Fenwick——'

'Why don't you call me Lois? The Fenwick part's rather gone out of my life.'

'All right—Lois: I'm not the only one looking for this log. They haven't been here because they thought I had it. Now one lot know I haven't. And believe me, they aren't the sort to *ask* if they can have a look around. That might make it risky for you.'

If I was worrying her, I couldn't see any sign of it. She just sipped, raised her almost invisible eyebrows, and said: 'D'you mean Mr Mockby?'

'He's one of them.'

'Then you're wrong about him. He did ask, this morning.'

I got cold inside.

'And you told him . . . ?'

'Oh, just that now Martin's dead and buried I don't even have to *pretend* to like Paul Mockby.'

I grinned and relaxed. Everybody seemed to be picking on poor old Mockers, these days. Then I unrelaxed. 'I'm still only half wrong. Sometimes he might ask first, but after that he takes.'

She uncoiled herself and stood up in one perfectly balanced movement like a well-bred cat, and with the same sense of natural self-importance. 'Well, I don't imagine he'll try it until after lunch. Let's go see what Mrs Benson's found in the larder.'

Either Mrs Benson was very lucky or she'd looked very hard, because what she'd found was a smoked trout, and a home-made *quiche lorraine* with green salad to follow. But nothing to drink except water; maybe that was the residual American influence—though she ate European-style, fork always in her left hand.

I hardly said a word until I was most of the way through my *quiche*, and then asked: 'Did you make this yourself?'

She nodded.

'Lovely light pastry.'

'Thank you, kind sir.' But she seemed really pleased. 'I don't often get the chance to do much cooking.'

I'd guessed something like that. The table we were eating off—a round Georgian affair—was too small for the big dining-room, and only had six chairs with it. But that made it all of a piece with the rest of the house—good furniture, but rather sparse and with the formality of a house that is more arranged than lived in. Well, with Fenwick up in London and David away at school. . . .

'Have you lived here long?'

'Since we were married. My family sort of gave it us as a wedding present.'

Hadn't Oscar Underhill hinted at that? I nodded and asked: 'D'you know many people around here?'

'Well enough not to let most of them in the house,' she said calmly.

'They're a bit County, are they?'

'It's not them. The few real ones are rather sweet. It's the ones who pretend they've always lived in the country and buy damn great dogs they can't control and won't go out to post a letter except on horse-back, even if they're facing the wrong end.' She helped herself to salad. 'Occasionally we got one of Martin's friends in for Sunday lunch, or David brings somebody to stay. . . . But not those phoney country women.' Then, abruptly: 'Are you married? You don't somehow sound it.'

'I was for a time.'

She didn't quite ask what had happened. Not directly. 'Did you have any children?'

'No.'

'I suppose that's lucky. You didn't want them?'

I shrugged. 'We never got round to deciding we *wanted* them, anyway. I was moving around a fair bit in the Army . . . we never got a chance to dig in anywhere. . . .'

175

She went on looking at me with a bland but interested smile. 'And you don't feel dynastic about it—that the name of Card shall not vanish from this earth?'

'Good God, no.'

'What happened to your wife?'

'Oh, she married again. A nice solid foundry executive.'

'Family?'

'Yes. Two, by now.'

And that seemed to satisfy her for the moment. I asked: 'What are you planning to do now? Going back to the States?'

'I haven't figured it out. I don't fancy I'd too much like to live over there, now, and David's very happy at school here, so . . . I guess I need a little time to see.' She got up and poured us coffee from a pot sitting on a sideboard hotplate.

'Did David go with you to the States when you visited?'

She glanced at me quickly, but I was stirring my cup. 'No, not for a few years.' She sat down again. 'Martin and my father didn't get on too well. So—I guess I didn't want David to hear my father sounding off about *his* father. Dad doesn't exactly watch his language. But it's a shame David can't see America as well. Harrow's . . . well, it is rather English.'

'Just rather.'

She smiled suddenly. 'Now I'll bet I've said the wrong thing: were you at Harrow?'

'Like hell I was. I was at grammar school in Glasgow during the war, then we moved down to Worcester. Nowhere anybody heard of.'

There was a knock on the door and Mrs Benson waddled in. 'If you've finished, madam, I'll clear up and then be off.' And I got a look that suggested I was badly overdue, as well.

Mrs Fenwick answered in a slightly nervous sing-song voice. 'Thank you very much, Mrs Benson. We'll go through.' She led the way back across the hall.

When the door was closed, I said: 'Mrs Fenwick—I mean Lois—could I ask if you're going to let me search this house?'

She made an elegant little shivery movement. 'How very blunt. Well, of course you can. I'm going into the village to do some shopping, so you'll be all alone for at least an hour.'

'Fine,' I said. She lit a cigarette and leaned gracefully on the end of the mantelpiece, and smiled at me. I said: 'Fine,' again, but still wondering why it was that easy.

Mrs Benson and the old Morris Minor had gone by the time I went out to see Mrs Fenwick off. I helped her drag open the rather rickety doors of the wooden two-car garage—and hadn't expected to feel the gut punch like a suddenly remembered shame. Just at the sight of a car.

She noticed. 'The AA brought it home on Wednesday.'

'Yes.' I went on staring at it. They hadn't even cleaned it— why should they? It still had the stains of Calais and Arras and Lille, and his fingerprints and mine. . . .

She said: 'The other one's mine. Little Trotsky.'

The other one was a red Morgan Plus 4, the last of the handmade small sports cars, built with deliberately old-fashioned lines: cutaway doors, running-board, spare wheel out in the open and all.

'Trotsky?' I asked, coming out of my daze.

'He's red and a bit wild but with great integrity.'

'And he hasn't been to Mexico yet.'

She laughed, a cheery silver-bells sound. 'What a lovely idea. When he's on his last legs, I'll maybe take him over there to die.' She slipped a ready-knotted silk headscarf over her hair, climbed in and started up.

I stood aside as she backed out. She swung neatly around, called: 'It's all yours,' then waved and roared off around the house. I swung the doors closed and walked slowly back up the steps.

For a time I stood inside the front door and did the old trick of trying to feel the house that sat around me. It didn't help, of course, because it wasn't *his* house. But in another way, that might make things easier; if he'd been just the Occupying Power it limited the places he'd think of hiding something. So, just to start with, I fell back on the standard rules and began looking.

A man doesn't hide something in a kitchen; not his territory.

Nor, for much the same reason, in a dining-room. Nor in a bedroom, even if he has his own one, as Fenwick had there. It doesn't feel private to a man, the way it does to a woman. Just look at the suicide statistics; women usually kill themselves in bedrooms, men almost never.

That cut out a fair bit of territory, and I could add David's room and probably a few larders and cloakrooms and coalhouses where Mrs Benson had the grazing rights. Which didn't leave us much positive information except that men hide things high rather than low, unless they're young or short-arsed, and Fenwick had been neither.

All those rules are taught in the best CI schools and are both beautiful and true, but they miss out one thing: there has to be something there to be found. And here, there wasn't. After nearly two hours, I was absolutely damn certain of that. It wasn't in the cellar and it wasn't in the attic and it wasn't anywhere in between. It wasn't in the gardening shed and it wasn't in the garage.

Of course, it might be locked in a treasure chest and buried anywhere in the acre or so of ground—but that didn't make sense. Fenwick hadn't been laying it down for the future like port or savings bonds. This was a live piece of evidence; if he'd bothered to hide it at all, it had to be somewhere simple, where he could get it back quickly.

Like his bank or his solicitor's office?

I drifted gloomily back to Fenwick's study and sat down at his desk and helped myself to a mouthful of Norwegian aquavit from a bottle in the corner. It was a nice, small, crowded, very masculine room; all tobacco browns and rich dark greens. A couple of comfortable deep leather chairs, rows of Folio Society books, one of those bone galleons that French prisoners on Dartmoor used to carve in Napoleonic times. Or a good fake of one, of course.

A handsome room, although maybe a bit like The Master's Study layout in a furniture exhibition, and a bit wasted, seeing how little time Fenwick can have spent here. Unless somebody else had built it for him, as bait.

THIRTY

LOIS—I was beginning to think of her by her Christian name, now—got back soon after four. I heard the Morgan grinding across the gravel and went out to open the garage doors for her.

'Any luck?' she asked cheerfully.

I shook my head. She drove past me and parked beside the Rover. I picked some of the food boxes out of the back; there was enough there to feed an army for a campaign.

'David'll be home on Tuesday,' she explained, then looked a little bleak. 'At least I hope so.' She perked up again, and turned to my problem. 'Never mind, I expect it'll turn up. Perhaps he left it at his apartment in town.'

'He didn't.'

She turned quickly. 'How d'you know?'

I shrugged. 'I managed to get in there.'

She looked at me carefully, then smiled. 'I suppose you have to do things like that. And you didn't find anything?'

'Nothing.' We went up into the house, me wondering why she had looked shocked at my turning over the flat when she hadn't even blinked at the idea of me doing it to her own house. But not wondering very hard.

We dumped the boxes in the kitchen and she looked around and said: 'It's very tidy. You don't seem to have moved anything. But I suppose you were trained to leave it like that.'

'Something like it. Well—thank you for letting me try.'

'Must you hurry back to London? Would you like a cup of tea?'

Some silences are louder than a scream, some things unsaid are clearer than a parade-ground order. I hesitated, looking at her and seeing only a gentle, guileless, baby-faced smile. But thinking suddenly of her as a woman, not Fenwick's widow or David's mother or a style or an accent . . . but as small neat breasts that looked sharp and would feel very soft, and pale skin like silk and long, agile legs and a clutching warm welcome. . . .

'Yes,' I said carefully. 'A cup of tea would be very nice.'

We sat on opposite sides of the big kitchen table and sipped politely.

'What are you thinking?' she asked innocently.

'Oh . . . about the weather.'

'Of course.' Her smile got a little mischievous. 'Warm for the time of year, what?'

'Something to do with a region of high pressure.'

'No cold fronts, then.'

'Strictly warm ones. Or occluded, of course.'

'I never understood what an occluded front was.'

'A mixture of warm and cold fronts.'

She nodded. 'How very wicked it does sound.'

'No, that's just the way it looks on the weather map.'

'Does somebody have to draw you a map?'

She smiled innocently, again.

And the phone rang.

We stared at each other, eyes steady with false calm. Then she slowly got up and went out to the hall to answer it.

I collected the cups and saucers and teapot and jug and sugar and put them away or stacked them neatly. I don't know why. Instinct, from living alone. Or for something to do.

Then I went out to the hall. She was standing with the phone, listening and nodding. She reached out a hand to me and I held it. Her strong slim fingers twined round mine.

She said into the phone: 'That's all right, Mr Baker, but you don't have to worry about that side of it.'

She lifted my hand and rubbed it gently against her cheek. I moved closer and smelt just the lightest touch of scent; something fragile and fresh, like a broken petal.

'No, Mr Baker, my father's lawyers'll handle all that. I only——'

Baker muttered on. I leaned and started nibbling her ear; she lifted her head towards me.

'Yes, Mr Baker, but the house is still in his name so I couldn't decide that anyway.'

She moved my hand slowly and drifted it across her breasts,

caressing herself with me. Her bra under the blouse was very thin; I could feel her nipples hardening slowly.

'Well, Mr Baker, if the tax people really want an answer then they'd better write to the States. I can't tell them.'

I moved my other hand across and down her body.

'All right, Mr Baker. Any time. Goodbye.'

She turned towards me and let the receiver clatter loose on the table and her mouth reached for mine.

It happened there, on the hall rug, a fast frantic rape—except I don't know who raped who. In a few minutes we were lying side by side in a tangle of rugs and clothes—not even naked ourselves.

'Do you think of me as a loose woman now?' she asked dreamily.

'Well, not exactly as a tight one.'

She laughed quietly, then shivered and wrapped herself in a corner of the long-haired white rug. 'Does this all go in your reports?'

'I'm not writing reports for anybody.'

'Ah. You must be a very private detective to employ your-self.'

'I'm not a detective. Can I have a drink?'

I found my trousers and carried them through into the drawing-room. It was suddenly bright in there, although the day beyond the windows wasn't. Just that the hall had a permanent twilight.

I heard her going upstairs.

A quarter of an hour later she came in, looking bright and fresh and now wearing a light blue cashmere sweater and rather worn blue jeans. She'd tidied her hair a bit, as well.

I had a glass of weak Scotch-and-water in my hand. 'Can I get you one?'

'No thanks, Jim. Or is it Jimmie, or what? I really ought to have asked before.' She actually blushed.

I laughed aloud. 'Jamie, mostly. The Scottish thing.'

'Let's go out and have a drink. I haven't been to a pub in— oh, I don't know. . . .'

'What about the neighbours?'

'We'll find a small village place where nobody'll possibly recognize me.'

So we went. On the way out, at the top of the steps, she stopped suddenly and said: 'Kiss me.'

I did. She was suddenly shaking all over.

We sat in the corner of a small boozer, too small for the brewery ever to bother tarting up, just across the Sussex border, and talked in near-whispers. We were the first there and the barmaid's ear was waggling like a radar aerial only eight feet away.

Lois almost giggled into her cider. 'If we *were* committing adultery this would be a great place to get remembered in. The first customers of the evening, my accent and clothes, your city suit—I bet that woman could describe us exactly in a court a year from now.'

'Dare say she's done it before. Adulterers probably come from three counties to find somewhere as out-of-the-way and genuinely folksy as this.' It was the true English village pub, all right, with its hard wooden benches, a mean little iron fireplace that was empty anyway, the walls decorated with a bus timetable and the bar with a vase of plastic flowers.

Lois lit a cigarette. 'Where do you live, Jamie?'

'Flat in London. Chalk Farm. Not far from . . .'

She nodded. 'Why did you leave the Army—you were a career officer, weren't you?'

'Sixteen years, yes. I'd just served my time and I didn't get to be a lieutenant-colonel. I could have hung on, but . . . promotion gets a bit rare in the Intelligence Corps, after that level.'

'Why?'

'We were specialists, most of our work didn't involve much in the way of command. And the Army wants itself run by people who can command troops. I believe the Air Force has the same bias towards people who can fly aeroplanes—pilots. It makes a sort of sense.'

'What did your wife think of you leaving?'

'That's when we busted up.'

'She wanted you to stay?'

'She wanted me to be colonel.' Then, after a long mouthful of beer-flavoured water: 'I don't know if that's quite fair. I don't think she was all that rank-conscious. Maybe she wanted me to be the sort of person colonels are. Maybe she just married the wrong person.'

'It can happen.'

'To you?'

'Oh no. Martin was quite right for me—and I hope I was for him.'

'Your father didn't think so.'

'Oh, Dad . . .'

'What had he got against Martin?'

'I think he thought he was a bit of a stuffed shirt. Too English. He wanted me to marry some hot-shot lawyer.' She swigged her cider and changed the subject. 'What else do you do—out of working hours?'

'I visit lovely ladies.'

She laughed her cheery bell-toned laugh. 'I thought that was in the line of duty.'

'Strictly above and beyond. And one day I'll finish a commentary on Vegetius.'

'On what?'

So I had to explain about him.

'What makes him so interesting?' she asked.

'He wrote the most complete description of the Roman armies, and that was everybody's ideal army for better than a thousand years after. They all read him: Charlemagne, Richard Coeur de Lion, all the Renaissance princes.'

'Was he a great general himself?'

'No, probably not even a soldier. He was pretty much of a historian in his own day; the Roman army had gone to pieces by his time. Rome itself got sacked a few years later. Prophet without honour and all that.'

'Will you publish this when you've finished it?'

'Oh yes. I've got a publisher who wants it for a specialist military series. But it'll be a time yet.'

'Will you ever finish it?'

'Course I will.' Maybe I sounded a bit annoyed, because she smiled kindly and put a hand on mine.

'I'm sorry,' she said. 'I wonder if they've got anything to eat here?'

'A bag of crisps, a pickled egg and an aspirin, if you're lucky, I should think.'

She laughed again. I said: 'We could find somewhere else to eat.'

'No, let's try here. Are you going back to London tonight?'

The baby-faced innocence with which she could say things like that. I said slowly: 'I suppose not.'

The loving was slower, gentler, calmer. A careful exploration, a memorizing of each other's bodies. But at first she was nervous, dodging from shy stiffness to clutching hunger . . . almost inexperienced, though that couldn't have been it.

And afterwards we lay side by side in her bed, not quite touching each other. The house, and the countryside beyond it, were very quiet.

Funny how I missed the constant noises of the city that you never notice until they're gone, like a forest without birds.

Lois lit a cigarette and the light glowed from her pale soft body. 'Jamie . . . ?'

'Yes?'

'Do you always have a gun with you?' She'd seen me take the derringer off my wrist; she hadn't seen the Mauser in my jacket pocket.

'No—but recently, yes. Things have been getting a bit rough since . . . Arras.'

'Why was Martin going to Arras?—have you found out?'

'He was being blackmailed, I think. To give up the log-book.'

'What about? Was it little Maggie Mackwood?'

'I think so.'

'Ah.' She sounded quite calm. 'Martin was rather highly sexed. He was a very good lover.'

There's a time and place for comments like that, like some other time and place. But I didn't say anything.

Suddenly, but quite gently, she began to cry. I put an arm around her but she didn't come any closer. She was weeping for memories I would never know, never share.

After a while she got up, leaned over me and kissed me gently. A few tears touched my cheek. 'I'll sleep in Martin's room,' she whispered. 'Sleep well, Jamie.'

When she'd gone, I pulled the bed apart and remade it and then lay down again. Sleep well. Why not?—I was alone, as usual.

After a time, I remembered the half-finished drink I'd brought upstairs and found and finished it. And some time after that, I slept.

THIRTY-ONE

IT WAS STILL DARK, still silent. I didn't know what had woken me but it must have been something positive because I'd come awake with a rush. I lay and listened.

Far away, a lorry made a painful gear-change on a hill and wheezed out of hearing. Nothing else. I lifted my wrist to look at my watch. And a door clicked.

It could be Lois. It could be the wind. In a strange house it could be a dozen things I wouldn't know about. But I wanted to know. I reached for my trousers, my shoes, then the Mauser.

Outside the room I stopped, trying to remember the layout. Stairs to my right. I paused again at the head of them, and a cold draught breathed on my chest. The front door was open.

Down there, the dining-room was ahead on the right, the drawing-room back on the right, the study ahead on the left. And that was where a faint line of light glowed and vanished. Somebody was working by torchlight in there. It was the obvious place to begin, just as I had.

I kept right over against the wall where the stairs were least likely to creak and mousied my way down.

Halfway down, the door opened and a pool of torchlight wavered across the hall floor. Two figures, barely more than shadows, followed it. I leaned against the wall and held my breath.

The light shifted around indecisively, the figures blended and an indecipherable whisper floated up towards me.

Then the torch flashed up the stairs, across me, away, and back, pinning me down like a butterfly in a case.

An incredulous voice said: 'Christ, it's Card!'

A younger voice yelped: 'He's got a gun!'

Something long glinted at the base of the light, the older voice shouted: 'Don't shoot!' and I threw myself against the banister.

A gigantic double explosion slammed through the house and the air swirled around me. A red-hot fingernail scored across my back.

I got my hand out from under me and fired blindly down into the dazzle of the torch. The little Mauser snapped feebly in the ringing deafness after those bangs.

I'd fired three before I realized what I was doing, and stopped. The double bang meant a shotgun, of course, and now an empty one. The torch tilted towards the floor, fell and went out.

I shouted: 'Hold it! You're a lovely target in that doorway!' Then I stood up carefully and winced at the pain in my back. I could feel a trickle of hot blood slide down it. Behind me, a light went on, and Lois said: 'Jamie, what are you——' Then she screamed.

I didn't look round. I kept the gun pointed and moved slowly, carefully, down towards the two figures in the hall. I was beginning to tremble, and not just from the cold blast coming through the front door.

It was Mockby's chauffeur, Charles. It had to be, of course. And his young friend, still clutching the twelve-bore. Charles was holding his right arm out in almost a hand-shaking position, but as I watched, it began to drip blood.

'I got you,' I said. My voice sounded high and strained. 'You got me, too. That makes it all square, doesn't it? Perfectly fair, what? I was aiming at the torch, so it wasn't a bad shot, was it? Only a few inches off. I suppose none of the others got you, did they? Not like through the stomach? I'd like you to have got one through the stomach. It takes about five minutes to come on really strong, they say, but then it apparently feels like rather bad peritonitis. Rather jolly, that. I could stand watching you have peritonitis. You aren't saying much, are you?'

Both of them were standing rigid as ice statues, staring at the Mauser. It was shaking in my hand like the last leaf of summer, but it couldn't miss at that range, And a part of me, a part beyond legality and morality and common sense and probably humanity itself, wanted to squeeze the trigger and go on squeezing until the slide locked open. And they knew it.

I said: 'I think I'd better sit down,' and sat on the stairs. My voice must have sounded more natural because they both took deep breaths and relaxed. The younger one let the shotgun droop.

'You want to be careful with that thing,' I said cheerfully. 'You never know how being mistaken for a partridge is going to affect people. Some people take it one way, some another. You just can't tell, can you? I'm sorry about your arm, Charles, but I think we'd better both stay here bleeding until the U.S. Cavalry arrives.'

At the top of the stairs, a phone bell gave a single ting.

Charles said evenly: 'We're having the coppers in, are we?'

'It sounds like it, doesn't it? I suppose it had to happen eventually. Not my decision, but it's probably all for the best. You know how frightfully jealous the fuzz gets when you try to keep gunshot wounds to yourself.'

He lifted his forearm until it was vertical; from wrist to elbow, his thin suede jacket was black with blood. He looked at it unemotionally and then at the young man with the shotgun.

'You stupid little sod,' he said wearily.

It took time; it always does. These things start fast but finish very slowly—if ever. A bullet leaves a gun at around a thousand feet a second, and it starts a file that they keep going until long after you're dead, just in case somebody wants to check back to that night when . . .

By five o'clock things had settled down a bit. Charles and I had been to the hospital and I'd come back; the other lad was down at the local nick talking over his past and future with a chief inspector. All I had on the far side of the dining-room table was a detective sergeant, name of Keating.

He had my statement—two long, laborious pages of police prose that make every action sound so mundane and planned. Even mine, almost.

'"Mrs Fenwick seemed worried at the news I told her and asked me to spend the night at Kingscutt Manor to protect her,"' he quoted. Then looked up. 'Is that correct, sir?'

I nodded dully; I felt tired and stiff and the casualty ward had smeared my back with something that itched like a forest fire.

'You do realize that the defence will get a big laugh from this in court, sir?'

I shrugged again. 'I doubt it. They'll dodge the whole issue of why I was here.'

He was a stocky, broad-shouldered type with the sort of gut detectives get in their forties through too much 'observing' in pubs. Normally, his face would have been stolid and impassive; at this hour, expressions kept slipping on or off and he had to pull the pieces together again.

He said: 'Why do you think that, sir?'

'Because any argument about why I was here keeps bringing us back to Paul Mockby. I say it was because I expected his goons to come around, and sure enough around comes his chauffeur, at least. He doesn't want that argument, and who d'you think's paying for the defence—Father Christmas?'

'Who pays for a defence isn't something we can bring out n court.'

'Sure. That'll be why he does it. Have you got hold of Mockby yet?'

The new expression went on like a slide in a projector: I'm-only-a-sergeant-and-I-only-work-here. 'I just wouldn't know about that, sir. Coming back to your statement. . . . The question of why you had a gun with you, the Mauser—that could come up.'

'Same answer—for Mockby. I brought a gun because I thought Mockby would etcetera and etcetera and so on. It's licensed, anyway.'

He nodded; he'd seen the licence. He'd still got the gun, if it came to that, him or one of his mates. All neatly labelled and tied up in a polythene bag and the spent cases in the other bags and the three bullets being dug patiently out of the woodwork of the hallway outside.

He sighed. 'These Ministry licences are tricky things.'

'I wasn't carrying it in public. This is a private house, even if it isn't my home.'

'It didn't walk from London to Kingscutt, did it? Sir?'

Just then Lois came in. Carrying a tray with an elegant enamel-ware coffee-pot, two blue-striped mugs, cream and sugar.

'I thought you might like something by now,' she said brightly. 'You haven't finished yet? How these things do stretch on.'

Keating was torn between annoyance and politeness to his hostess; he half got his backside out of the chair, decided that was polite enough and flopped back.

Me, I was glad to see the coffee and her both. She was wearing a long housecoat in royal blue with gold trimmings, although there'd been plenty of time to change into anything else by now. Certainly she'd had time to put on exactly the right amount of make-up—very little—for entertaining early-morning gangbusters.

Or maybe I'm being bitchy. Some women retreat into choosing exactly the right clothes and make-up and coffee-pot for an emergency the way others go into hysterics or the brandy bottle. I preferred it this way. Certainly the coffee part.

Lois looked at me with her cheery baby-faced expression, but perhaps a hint of anxiety behind the eyes. 'Is everything all right, Mr Card?'

'Fine. Fine, thanks, Mrs Fenwick.'

That was the password. She smiled and swept out.

Keating shovelled sugar into his coffee in a way that suggested his tummy wasn't built on beer alone. 'I admire an old hand like you, sir,' he murmured. 'Taking your shirt and vest off before you got shot. Saves all that danger of infection from dirty fibres. Brilliant, I call that.'

I murmured back: 'Screw you, Sergeant.'

'No thank you, sir, you're not my type. But her—I might take my shirt off to defend her, if anybody asked me.' He took a sip of coffee, blinked, and slid back into the present time continuum. 'Now, sir, are you prepared to sign this statement?'

'Sure.'

He looked momentarily surprised, then pushed it across to me. I signed. 'Will you need me in the magistrates' court this morning?'

'Ah, we're not charg——' Then his expression snapped into midday form. 'We don't need witnesses when we're asking for a remand in custody on this sort of charge—sir. You should know that.'

'Silly of me.' I inhaled coffee fumes and he watched me. 'Tell me one thing, Sergeant—am *I* going to be charged?'

His face went blank and meaningless as an official form. 'I really couldn't say, sir.'

'You must know this Chief pretty well. What d'you guess?'

'It isn't my business to go guessing, sir.' He slipped my report into a thin black plastic-leather briefcase and zipped it shut. 'But you did have a shooter and somebody did get shot.'

'How very true. Are you trying to get Mockby on conspiracy or accessory before?'

'I still couldn't say, sir.'

'How would the Chief like a plea of guilty from the two goons and no other people or charges involved at all?'

After a time, he said slowly: 'Do you think you could arrange that, sir?'

'I think it might sort of arrange itself.'

He sat very still, working out the implications of this. Then he got up. 'I'll see what he says. That's all I can do.'

I poured another cup and waited. The phone pinged in the

distance and slow footsteps came in behind me. 'No luck, huh?'

'He says to mind your own bloody business and he's not making any promises to anybody.'

'Okay. There comes a time when you have to guard your own back.'

'The police guard people—sir. If the lady felt she was in danger she could have asked us.'

'And would you have come?'

'Nobody'll ever know, will they, sir?'

I nodded and stood up and walked with him to the front door. Away to the east there was a dirty yellow smear in the sky, right down on the horizon.

He stood on the steps in the cold nibbling wind and buttoned his coat. 'Are you really going to bugger things up?' he asked politely.

'I really couldn't say.'

'I'd've thought a man in your business would need friends in the police.'

'My business is what I've just been told to mind.'

He just nodded and walked down to his car.

Back inside the house, it was suddenly quiet again. The last bright-eyed young detective constables had finished their measurements and sketched out their plans and gone while we were in the dining-room. The study door was locked and guarded by a chair for when the fingerprint boys came around (it wouldn't do any good: both of them had worn gloves). I leant against the wall by the downstairs phone and waited for the energy to go ahead and bugger things up, just like the sergeant had said.

Lois came out from the kitchen door behind the stairs. 'Have they all gone, Jamie?'

'All gone.'

She came and put one arm round my neck and leant her head on my shoulder. 'I wonder whatever they thought—about you being here.'

'Just jealous.'

She looked up and smiled, then went serious again. 'I suppose—will it all come out in court? I'm thinking of David.'

'I don't know. Maybe not. I want to make a phone call that could help.'

She stood back briskly. 'Go ahead. Like me to put on bacon and eggs now?'

'That'd be fine.' She went away and I sat down and started dialling.

It rang only twice and the voice answering was remarkably wide-awake for that time of day. 'Yes? Who is it?'

'Hello, Mockers. Card here.'

'Don't you know what time——'

'I'm calling on behalf of Charles. And his friend. They're sorry they can't do it themselves, but they're in the nick. Well, actually Charles is in hospital right now, but he'll be in the nick when he comes out.'

Pause. Then: 'I don't know what you're talking about.'

'That's the spirit. Just keep that up and you may get away with it. Now, here's what you do: you get a solicitor and you get him *fast*. They've got the boy in the back room and they're working on him and they can do that for seventy-two hours unless somebody comes up with a habeas corpus writ. Then they'll have to charge him and stop questioning him. Same for Charles, of course, but it's not so urgent.'

Another pause. 'What the hell's all this to do with you?'

'Oh, I just happened to be staying at Kingscutt when your boys dropped in. It was me they fired that shotgun at.'

'*They did what?*' That squawk was genuine, all right. Probably he'd told them not repeat not to take a gun and they'd known better.

'Afraid so. But most of it missed. Anyway, the point is they got them cold, on the premises, gun in hand, all the rest of it. So you spend a bit of time and a lot of money and you can get them to plead guilty.'

'What good's that to anybody?'

'You're not too bright at this time in the morning, are you? A guilty plea and there's no real trial: no jury, no witnesses, no cross-examination, no awkward questions about who sent them or Mrs Fenwick's saying you'd rung up about that logbook—remember? But don't take it from me, ask your solicitor.'

'I will, boy. But when did you get elected Jesus Christ?—you're getting something out of this.'

'I damn well hope so. I'd like to keep out of it as much as possible, but if I'm in then you're in and *I'm* standing on your shoulders. Ask your solicitor about *that*, too.'

He worried at this for a while, then said carefully: 'You lousy stinking rotten little son-of-a-bitch. Get off the line; I've got calls to make.'

'Now you're sounding more reasonable.'

We ate in the kitchen and I tried to explain what I'd been up to. Lois listened thoughtfully, then asked: 'But I don't see why those characters should plead guilty—what have they got to lose?'

'Depends what they're charged with. In a case like this the police like to have a real banquet, and the menu starts with attempted murder. After that, it comes down to wounding with intent to do grievous bodily harm and then unlawful wounding. They'd probably accept a plea of unlawful wounding plus a side dish from the Firearms Act. Possession with intent or carrying with criminal intent. They shouldn't get more than three years or so for that. But make a fight of it and it won't cost the cops any more to try for attempted murder and a life sentence. *I* think they'll plead.'

She mused on it, scooping delicately at a boiled egg. 'So Paul Mockby will get off scot free?'

'I'd think so.'

'You don't sound as if you mind.'

'Maybe not. . . . I *know* what he did. In a sort of way, knowing's enough. But it would never have been easy to involve him anyway. You can show Charles was his chauffeur, but it's a big long step to prove Mockby sent him down here. Even if Charles claimed it, no judge would let a jury convict on his word. And since Charles's pay has at least doubled since I talked to Mockby, I somehow doubt he'll do any implicating.'

'We implicated Paul, though, in those statements we made.'
She pushed aside her egg and lit a cigarette.

'Witnesses' statements aren't evidence, not unless you try
to deny them. Anyway, if they plead guilty there's no witnesses,
no statements, nothing in court.'

'So—David won't have to know?'

I shrugged. 'You and I'll get mentioned at the trial; have
to be. But maybe . . .'

'Well, I think you handled it all with great delicacy.'

'Don't sound so surprised.' I was wondering what a certain
chief inspector would think of my handling when Mockby's
solicitor suddenly landed on him waving a writ. I'd done more
influencing people than making friends in the last night.

I looked at my watch—nearly seven, by now—and Lois
caught the gesture. 'Are you off back to London now?' she
asked, a little wanly.

I smiled as cheerfully as I could, and shrugged. 'I've got to
go some time, but . . .' I didn't really know what the hell I *was*
going to do next. I hadn't found the log, and it was a Saturday
besides. 'What are you going to do?'

'I've got to take the Rover down to the garage in the village;
they're going to clean it and maybe make me an offer for it.'

'You're not keeping it?'

'No. I can't think of it except as Martin's.' She shuddered
at an abrupt memory. 'That means I've got to unpack it first.
So I'd better get dressed.'

'Unpack it?'

'There's Martin's suitcase still in the trunk. I just kept
putting off having to . . .'

'I'll do that.'

'You won't hurt your back?'

'No. I'll be okay.'

The garage was as cold as Caesar's nose, and I didn't waste
time there. I hauled the solid black-leather suitcase out of the
boot and slammed the lid. Actually it did make my back
twinge a bit, but I'd promised.

Back in the house I humped it up the stairs and into his

bedroom and on to the bed. Then wondered if I shouldn't unpack it as well. Anyway, I opened it. The log of the *Skadi* was the first thing I saw.

THIRTY-TWO

'JUST AS SIMPLE AS THAT?' Willie asked.

'You could say so.'

'So Martin was ready to hand over the real thing if it came to it, what? If they called his bluff?'

'Well—he was keeping that option open, anyway. The blackmail was working that well, at least.'

'M'yessss.' And he went back to staring at the log.

I'd rung him from Kingscutt and we'd met at my flat. I'd given him a rough, rather simplified, outline of the night's events and then handed over the log. For the moment he was happy, but I had a feeling he was going to come back to last night.

The book itself was the size I'd expected—about fourteen inches by twelve, and bound in stiff fawn cardboard, like a big but not too expensive desk diary. What I hadn't expected was the mess it was in, which was silly of me when I remembered it had spent at least four wintery months in a burnt-out hulk. The covers were soaked in oil and stained with rust and rubbed away at the corners; the pages themselves were buckled and wavy with damp, and some torn besides—but not stuck together (unless Steen had separated them, of course). But luckily the entries were all in ball-point and hadn't run. . . . What did I mean 'luckily'? Damp must be a problem sailors have met before.

Willie held it like a First Folio and leafed slowly through it without seeming to breathe.

'D'you make anything of it?' I asked.

'Not a lot yet. I know some Norwegian but . . . I think I can see what most of the figures are. And I know what a British log looks like; this is just about the same, you know.'

Each page was laid out like some crazy ledger, with sixteen thin vertical columns and one wide one. Horizontally, it was divided into two batches of twelve, subdivided into fours, with some extra bits and pieces at the end of each twelve.

Even I could work out that each page was a day, each line an hour and each four a 'watch', but the headings and the figures written into each column didn't mean a dicky-bird.

Willie explained: 'Oh, they're things like course steered, compass error, wind force and direction, that one's obviously the barometer reading, air and sea temperatures—you know?'

'Is it the right log?'

He turned hastily to the last filled-in page. 'September 16th. Yes, that was the day before the accident. That'd be right.'

'Who fills in this sort of log—the captain?'

'Oh no, the chief officer. He does this. The master does the official log, but that's mostly about personnel, you know? Smith was sentenced to twenty lashes, Brown lost a sock overboard, the cat had kittens, that sort of thing.'

I nodded, then yawned. I couldn't help it. 'Sorry. So, what now?—d'you want to take it round to somebody who reads Norwegian?'

'I don't think so, not yet. I mean, we don't want to make a song-and-dance about having it, do we?'

'Everybody else has been singing and dancing, and mostly on me, when they *thought* I had it. . . . No, you're quite right. So . . . ?'

'I'd just like to see what I can make of it, from the figures and so on, you know?'

'You're happy just sitting here?'

'Oh, yes, old boy. You want to get a bit of a snooze, what? How's the back?'

'Not so bad, but—it was a long night.'

'Rather eventful, too.' But his face was sweet innocence. 'You don't expect any frightful comebacks, do you? After shooting that chap and all that?'

'I just hope it keeps Mockby quiet for a day or two.'

He nodded and frowned down at the table. 'I suppose he

did send those chaps down because . . . because of what I said back at his place when——'

'And because of what I'd said before that and Fenwick before me and probably Steen before him.' I was too tired even to listen to regrets. 'There's some beer in the fridge and some eggs—no, I'm out of eggs—and a lock on the door, and I'm in bed.'

And half a minute later, that was true.

It was three o'clock when I woke up, soaked in sweat and completely lost, the way you get after a deep daytime sleep. But gradually I began to remember who I was, where and why. After a time I put on a fresh shirt and staggered through into the main room.

Willie was still at the table, which was littered with full ashtrays, a plate with a few crumbs on it, a coffee mug, an empty beer can, papers, atlas—and the log. He didn't look any tidier himself, with his hair rumpled and his shirt sleeves rolled up.

'How are you doing?' I asked.

'I don't think I can do much more, you know. You had a good sleep.'

'Yes.' I went through into the kitchenette, found another can of beer in the fridge and took it back to the table.

Willie stood up and stretched and lit another cigarette. 'I've just about translated the whole last voyage. I used your phone to get on to a chap who reads Norwegian properly and got him to do some of the phrases for me, you know?

It seemed safer than letting anybody see the whole thing.'

I nodded approvingly. 'Well, what does it all show?'

'Well . . .' He shuffled some papers. 'She went from Bergen to Leith. From there back to Gothenburg in Sweden. On to Stockholm. Then to Helsinki, then to Tallinn.'

'Where?'

'Tallinn, in Estonia. Russia, really. Just across from Helsinki. I must say I'd like to know what cargoes she was heaving on and off in these places.'

'She ended up with rolls of paper—newsprint—and timber on deck, didn't she?'

'I believe so. Anyway, she was in Tallinn about two days.' He turned the stiffened, wavery pages. 'Then sailed on the morning of the fourteenth.'

'Fine, but *did* she have engine trouble?'

'Oh yes.' He turned another page. 'That started late on the fifteenth. As far as I can make out, something packed up and they had to shut down one engine. You did know she was diesel-engined?'

'She could have been run by faith, hope and clockwork for all I knew.'

He frowned briefly. 'Well, she was—that's why she could run with an engine-room staff of one chief and three men. Two Burmeister and Wain thousand-horsepower jobs driving a single shaft. Shut one down and you naturally halve your power and speed.' He tracked his finger across the page, column by column. 'It all fits, you know. Speed comes down to five knots, that checks with the distance covered, and that with the noon position. I worked it out on the atlas, what? And that engine's off the line right through the sixteenth— and that's the last entry we've got. The collision was next day.' He turned a page and it was bleared and grimy—but blank.

'The chief officer would copy this up daily?' I picked up the log and riffled through it.

'Most likely. It'd be part of his daily routine.'

'So the ADP Line's got its case, has it?'

'It looks like it—provided they've got somebody to swear that the other engine hadn't been restarted some time on the seventeenth, before the crunch.'

'They've got Nygaard, unless the drink's got him first.' Then something else occurred to me. 'There were three other survivors. Were any of them from the engine-room?'

'No. They were all deck-hands who'd been off watch at the time. So their evidence about the state of the engines wouldn't be worth a thing, what? And they weren't on the bridge either —everybody up there got killed—so they can't give more than guesses about the speed.'

'They're going to need Nygaard then.' I tossed the logbook on to the table and it blew ash from the overloaded ashtray. 'Was this the sort of damage you can repair at sea?'

'Just can't say, old boy, and this sort of log doesn't give enough detail. It only says things like—' he picked up a piece of paper '—"still at half speed, engineers working on injection pump" at the end of each watch. Mind you, they'd had pump trouble a few weeks before. Once it took a couple of watches to fix it—about eight hours—once around twelve hours. Sounds as if they needed a new one, you know? This time it could have broken forever—but Nygaard should be able to say. Pity the engine log wasn't the one to survive, really.'

'What about invalidation?'

'Eh? What? Oh—what Paul was going on about.'

'What Fenwick was *supposed* to have told him.'

'Yes.' He peered at his fingernails and looked as if he was deciding whether to Tell Tales about the school bully. Finally he cleared his throat and said formally: 'There's nothing in here that suggests it might invalidate the policy at all. And it takes an awful lot to invalidate a Lloyd's policy, you know. That's one reason people insure with us—what?'

I nodded moodily. 'Well—now what, then?'

He began unrolling his shirt sleeves, slow and thoughtful. 'Legally, it must belong to the owners. ADP, I mean. The whole point of a log's to allow the owners to check up on what actually happened on a voyage—you know? So I suppose——'

Then the phone rang. I picked it up. 'Yes?'

Either it was an electric storm calling or one was bugging the line. A tinny, distant shout came through: 'Mister Card?'

'That's me,' I shouted back.

'It is Kari Skagen.'

'Hello. How're things?'

'Chief Engineer Nygaard is gone.'

'Gone? You mean dead?' Behind me, I heard Willie jerk to Action Stations.

'No, I think. He has gone away. From the Home. I do not know where.'

'Well . . . what about Ruud?'

'He does not know where.'

'Christ Almighty.'

'Pardon?' she shouted.

'Never mind. But . . . Can you ask anybody else? At the Home and so on? And ring me again?'

'Very well.'

'Is there a number where I can get you?'

She gave one. 'It is a university lodging house, so please leave a message if I am not there.'

'I'll do that. See you—probably soon.'

When I turned around, Willie was still standing tensed, wound up, and if I'd said 'Fly' he'd have grown feathers.

He asked: 'Did somebody else get killed?'

'No—well, I don't really know. But ADP's lost their witness.'

A little while later I was nibbling on a Scotch—and the hell with it being just after four in the afternoon—and sitting in the one comfortable chair. Willie was still at the table, sipping coffee.

'But when you come right down to it,' I said, 'there's no reason why he shouldn't have gone walkies just by himself. He's past the age of consent, and that place wasn't a prison or a mental bin. He can walk out any time he likes and go anywhere he chooses.'

'Didn't you say he was short of money?' Willie asked.

'I thought he probably was, but he could have a few quid hidden away—enough to go out on a private honk and now he's lying under some bush in the park dead of pneumonia.'

He nodded. 'I suppose that *is* more likely than anything sinister. So you're not going to rush back across there?'

'Not yet, anyway. Kari can do more than I could. I'll wait to hear from her.' I splashed more Scotch into my glass.

Willie raised an eyebrow, and bounced the book in his hand with a weighing motion. 'You know, old boy, we're the only two people alive who've actually read this thing. The last few pages, anyway. Steen and Martin are dead and so are all the people who'd see it on the ship itself. The deck-hands certainly wouldn't and there's no reason why the chief engineer should see a deck log—you know what I mean?'

'Are you thinking it's the idol's eye or the moonstone and we're all doomed?'

'Well, you seem to have been, rather.' He smiled wryly. 'But no—I mean nobody else actually *knows* what's written here. They're just guessing or assuming.'

I eased my back and winced. 'They assume bloody hard, then.'

'Oh, quite so. But the chief officer could have left these pages blank or filled them with rude rhymes—and you'd've had exactly the same troubles you've had these past couple of weeks. Funny.'

'Hilarious.' I reached for the Scotch again.

This time, Willie said: 'I say, old boy, isn't that stuff supposed to inflame a wound, you know?'

'Let it try.'

'I say, are you planning on getting smashed, old boy?'

'Something along those lines. It's a Saturday night and the upper and lower classes traditionally get spiffled on Saturdays. The middle class just look on with jealous disapproval.'

'That isn't the reason.'

'No, that isn't the reason, Willie.'

'Ah. That rather answers a question I was going to . . .'

'No you weren't, Willie. Not you. You're far too much of a gentleman to ask it. Now get out and leave me to it.'

THIRTY-THREE

I WOKE SLOWLY and immediately tried to get back to sleep again. Awake hurt too much. And for a time I just lay there, trying to dream of the calm, innocent golden days of childhood, with the gentle warm breezes through the tall summer pines, and—

Christ, my childhood hadn't been anything like *that*! I

201

slammed my feet on the floor and got myself mostly on top of them and worked my way towards the kitchenette. My head felt soft and bloated and my hands were waving like flags; give me a gun and I couldn't have hit William Tell Junior, let alone the apple on top.

But the water in the tap ran hot and there was some instant coffee in a jar and I could just remember how to put the two together. After that, I propped my bottom against the sink and stared at the message I'd pencilled on the opposite wall: *buy eggs*. It must have seemed like a good idea at the time.

After twenty minutes, give or take half an hour, I could remember the secret formula for making the coffee percolator work. While it did, I washed and shaved fairly close to my face, and put on some clothes. The suitcase I'd taken to Bergen was still sitting there only half unpacked. Today I'd really have to do something about it, or at any rate maybe. By then it was past eleven.

I'd just finished my second cup of real coffee and was thinking of re-applying for associate membership of mankind when the phone went. It was Jack Morris, from the Ministry. On a Sunday?

'How're you doing, buster?'

'Staggering along. What are you doing awake on a Sunday?'

'Just keeping in touch. Hold on. . . .' The phone went quiet. I rammed it against my ear, trying to pick out barking dogs, squawling children, birdsongs. Very faintly, in the distance, I heard another phone buzz.

Jack came back on. 'We had a little talk about getting your name in the papers, remember?'

'I remember.'

'I unders and you've been making guest appearances in the Norwegian press.'

I carried the phone across to the window. The sky beyond the church was the colour of a coal-miner's bathwater and not much drier. The street shone dully, empty except for parked cars.

'Didn't know you read Norwegian,' I said. 'Anyway, I only found a dead man over there. Could happen to anybody.'

202

A blue Triumph 1500 turned in from Haverstock Hill and drifted casually towards my block.

'I've had a busy twenty-four hours, buster. The Kent bobbies were on to me about this time yesterday and they do *not* love you. They have the wild idea that you don't only carry guns and take shots at people but then you tip other people off about what's happened and get them sending sharp solicitors down to play habeas corpus. They wanted to know if that counts the same as raping the royal family and burning a naval dockyard. I said yes.'

The Triumph hesitated by the forecourt to my block, decided there wasn't room, and crawled along a bit further.

I said: 'They'd never have got Mockby and they'd always have taken a plea on unlawful wounding. I just cooled things down and speeded them up. And anyway, my gun was licensed.'

Two large men in short dark car-coats climbed out of the Triumph and moved slowly but purposefully towards the block.

Jack said heavily: 'Your gun was licensed. Jesus, you'd better think of something more interesting than that. You remember I said when we wanted you you'd hear sirens? You can hear sirens, buster.'

'Thanks, Jack.' I slammed the phone down and ran.

The bastard: trying to pin me down on the end of the phone like that. Or maybe he'd been warning me—if I was bright enough to take a hint. He might feel he owed me that much.

I yanked open my front door, reached the lift and pressed the button. As I ran back I could hear it start whining upwards, and that might give me an extra minute. Whatever sort of cops they were, they'd be the sort whose feet prefer riding lifts to climbing stairs.

Back inside my own door, I threw an unopened laundry parcel into the Bergen suitcase, added the log, the derringer and clip, my wallet and passport, thanked God I'd put on real shoes and not slippers, remembered the pigskin hip flask, then grabbed up a sports jacket and my sheepskin and started travelling.

The lift was still whining back down, so I tiptoed down the first flight of stairs—noise carried in that stairwell—then heard it open, shut and start back up. Now I could afford to run. I ran.

The Escort was on the far side of the road but that didn't matter because the landings in our block don't have windows. Nobody could see me—unless they'd left a third man in the car, but they'd looked a bit casual for that. And they hadn't. I shoved the case into the back seat, started up and drove soberly away.

For the moment, I was fireproof. I hadn't shot any coppers or raped any children, so I wasn't worth a real hunt. Just a description on the teletypes with a please-keep-a-lookout-for, and not even that for maybe an hour. But knowing Jack and Jack knowing me, the airports and docks would be specially notified; I could have trouble there. Still, for the moment I was fireproof.

I drove into the big car park at the bottom of Hampstead Heath and finished dressing out of sight of the road or houses. With fawn trousers, a green shirt, black-and-grey tweed jacket and a brown silk tie I thought I'd lost in Brussels six months ago but found in a pocket of the suitcase, I was liable to lose my place in the Ten Best Dressed Men List. But as long as I looked complete I didn't mind looking terrible.

The derringer and clip went on my left forearm again, spare rounds in my pocket, and then I started taking the pigskin flask apart.

I'd found it in Cyprus when the original owner had departed for Russia in—obviously—rather more of a hurry than I'd just left home. It was a lovely piece of work, but the KGB have always been the Asprey's of the espionage business. It poured whisky, of course, but when you wound the cap hard the wrong way the whole short neck came off and you could lift the shoulders of the flask right out of the leather, leaving a long inner neck down to the booze compartment at the bottom. That was the master touch; who'd think of what is, essentially, a bottle having a false *top*? Certainly not me; I'd only been suspicious enough to get the thing X-rayed by an industrial unit.

As there'd been nothing in it and we hadn't caught the bloke anyway, I hadn't suppressed evidence by latching on to it. Now, it was my private savings bank: the teetotal end held two hundred quid in sterling and nearly another hundred in Swiss francs. I took out seventy-five quid in fivers, smoothed them as much as I could, and shoved them in my wallet. Then reassembled the flask and drove across to Paddington station. No particular reason except that I wanted to park the suitcase and Paddington's about the one station that doesn't point to the Continent or Scandinavia.

Then I got on the phone to Willie.

'You're still with us, are you?' he asked cheerfully.

'More or less.'

'Have you heard any more from Bergen?'

'No—but I'm sort of heading in that direction myself anyway. Could you ring this number—' I read across the one Kari had given me '—and tell her I'm on my way?'

'Of course, but—why the rush?'

'I'm sort of on the run. The Ministry decided to pull the chain on me. I don't know what the charges are, and I think it's just general stroppiness about the shooting at Kingscutt, but I don't want to be tied down right now. All right?'

'Well—are you going to be able to make it?'

'I think so. I've got an idea or two. I'll try and keep in touch.'

After that, there didn't seem much more to say.

Then I rang Dave Tanner's office; I knew he checked in around noon, so I hoped he'd get my message in a few minutes.

I tried to make it simple but obscure—the man on the other end might be law-abiding or stupid or something. 'Tell Tanner that Jamie rang and it's urgent. Ask him to leave a number and I'll ring back to get it in a quarter of an hour. Okay?'

205

He started to argue, then realized he'd understood me, and just said: 'All right, Mr Jamie.'

I had a coffee and skimmed a couple of Sunday papers and then the buffet opened and I had a beer as well. And then it was time to try Tanner's office again. He'd left a London number for me; I rang it straight away.

'Morning, Major. What's the hurry?'

'I need to get abroad, and I don't want to put the passport boys to any bother.'

After a moment, he asked: 'Are you hot?'

'Barely warm. I don't suppose it'll even be in the papers.'

Another thoughtful hush. 'Well, if you're really not in bad trouble. . . . I'll see what we can do. Anywhere special or just out?'

'Just across the Channel will do me. I'd prefer not France, but I'll risk it if I have to.'

'O-okay, Major. Where are you now?'

I instinctively paused, and he felt it, chuckled, and said: 'Doesn't matter. Ring me here at half past three and maybe I'll have something. But these things work better on Fridays and Saturdays.'

After that I had another beer, found an Indian restaurant a couple of streets away and loaded up on curried beef and rice. Eating might become rare in the next twenty-four hours. Then I spent a couple of hours in a cinema learning the Real Truth about the Old West. It seems they didn't only spend all their time shooting each other, but—this was the big news —they bled a lot, too. Some day somebody's going to do the Real Truth about the chances of hitting anybody with a .44 or .45 without five minutes' aiming time first.

Or then again, maybe they won't.

I got through to Tanner again at the right time.

'You're travelling, Major. I'll meet you at the office—long as you make sure you come alone. Right?'

'Right.'

'Hate to mention it, but how are you for money—real cash?'

'I can do you fifty as a down payment,' I said carefully.

'Yes, all right. Seeing as you're an old and trusted client. See you.'

I got my suitcase out of the left-luggage and strolled across towards the taxi-rank in the middle of the station. Nearly there, I noticed one of those copying machines they stick in railway stations nowadays for no good reason I can think of except they must make a profit. I changed some money into five-pence pieces, got out the log, and copied off the last four pages. The copies went in my pocket, the log back in the case.

My car could just stay where it was; it was too complicated to start organizing anybody to collect it. It was in a quiet street with the steering lock on, so . . . I shrugged to myself and lined up for a taxi.

Dave's office was in a converted Georgian terrace literally on the fringes of the law north of Gray's Inn and the Theobald's Road police station. All around were the small-time solicitors who could remember the name of the Duke but not where they'd put your file, the income tax advisors who were careful not to call themselves accountants, the doctors who could get your friend into a good nursing home cheap. Dave's organization didn't belong with them, but he'd move if they did; he knew his place and it wasn't behind a big glass front in Leadenhall Street. If you had a problem that was a teensy-weensy bit disgusting or just slightly illegal, he might or might not take your case, but he didn't want a classy décor to put you off telling him about it.

I was let in by a lad who couldn't have been more than twenty-five—which was probably why he found himself hand-ling the Sunday business—but already had the hard, prove-it eyes of his trade. I said I was Jamie to see Dave and he led me upstairs without a word.

Dave nodded to him, waited till he'd closed the door, then waved me to a seat. 'Evening, Major. Sorry to hear about all this.'

I shrugged and sat. His office, and the others in his organiza-tion, had the atmosphere of an old-established newspaper: big battered desks, solid filing cabinets, a general air of inexpensive efficiency. In the corner was a big grey safe, a really serious job where Dave told his clients he kept their files and actually did keep a few.

'Does Dunkirk suit you?—sorry I can't do Belgium direct, but you'll be over the frontier in half an hour or so.'

'It's fine. When?'

'You're on the eight o'clock boat from Dover. Coach trip— five capitals in four days, lucky you. Denniston's Tours, here's your ticket. Have you got any luggage, or want to borrow some?'

'I'm okay. It wasn't that much of a hurry.'

He lifted his eyebrows but let it pass. Then he opened a drawer and took out a British passport, almost handed it over, then remembered to scrub it clean of fingerprints first. Just in case.

'Victoria coach station, five o'clock. See the tour guide, give him your ticket and that passport.'

I'd been looking at my new identity. Apart from the fact that it was about a man of roughly my age, it fitted me as well as a halo did. He was two inches shorter, with different coloured eyes and hair, and the photograph showed glasses.

'I hate to quibble, Dave, but somehow this just isn't *me*, if you know what I mean.'

'Doesn't matter, Major. Could be for a performing bear and nobody would know. The courier hands it up with twenty-four others, they count twenty-five heads, twenty-five passports, bingo, you're through. On these tours half the old berks would lose their passports if you let 'em keep them for themselves.'

'Is that how you came by this one?'

'Not quite. This one lost his life, too. There's always some, every year. Run a coach over a cliff, caught in an avalanche, hotel burns down or they just freeze to death waiting for it to be built. The Army's got nothing on these tours, Major. And if the passport's still with the courier or hotel, well, who can prove it?'

And there's always somebody to remember there's a market

208

for these things. In some countries, of course, it's a state monopoly: the KGB could take them, all right, but an agent's too valuable to risk with a forged passport that needs only a single check to show its number was never issued, or to a different name. It takes longer to pin down a real one, even if the owner's dead; how many widows remember it's their duty to turn hubby's passport in once he's planted?

I nodded. 'And after that, what?'

'Once you're on the boat you're on your own. Use your own passport—you've got it haven't you?—to get off at Dunkirk. No problem.'

'And nobody cares that I've gone AWOL from the tour?'

'It's no crime, even if anybody noticed. Same thing for the passport control over there: they get twenty-four passports, they count twenty-four heads. Just don't wiggle your hips at any rich widows in the coach: they might start asking what happened to the nice man with the military manner.'

'I'll try and remember, Dave.'

'Fine. This Sunday work knocks hell out of me. Care for a quick one?'

Before I could answer he'd lifted the bottle out of the deep file drawer on the right of the desk—just like the classic private detective. So? So you get plenty of people behaving like the popular image of themselves, including judges and politicians as well as private eyes and sergeant-majors. It keeps their clients reassured.

It was a very pale single malt Scotch; good, maybe too good for me. I still prefer my whisky soaked in soda. There had to be a good reason why the Cards left Scotland.

We toasted each other. Outside in the main office the phone rang and got answered, the typewriter clattered, a drawer in a filing cabinet screeched.

Tanner said: 'There's just the sordid business of money, Major.'

'Of course.' I took out my wallet and dealt him a double flush in fivers. He collected them slowly and stacked them on one side by the desk intercom, and asked: 'You're sure you don't mind about it being France?'

'I'll survive.'

'I expect so. Did you have time to get some protection into your luggage, or d'you want to borrow something? Hire it, I mean.'

I smiled a little bleakly. 'No thanks, Dave. I'm all right.' At any rate I wasn't going to land in France carrying an extra, and unfamiliar, pistol. The derringer on my arm was risk enough.

'Okay. You heading anywhere in particular?'

'Norway.'

'Again?' But he didn't press it. 'Had you thought of hiring us to try and clear things up for you so's you can come back?'

'Not yet. I think things'll just blow over.'

'You ought to know.'

'That's what I keep telling myself.'

We had one more drink and it got to be after half past four. He stood up. 'The wife's got people coming in, and you'd better not be late, neither.' I gulped the last of my Scotch and then waited while he locked and double-locked the office door behind us. Every serious private detective has files he doesn't want his employees to see, and maybe particularly the employees junior enough to land the Sunday evening switchboard watch. There's more than one way to the top in private detection.

I picked up my suitcase from near the door and followed him downstairs. We shook hands before we left—separately, just in case. I had to walk right down to Theobald's Road before I caught a taxi.

THIRTY-FOUR

VICTORIA COACH STATION late on a winter Sunday was a draughty parade ground with a sketchy pretence at a glass roof. A few dark buses stood around like abandoned hulks, and little clumps of shivering passengers huddled against the walls below posters for sunny Italy or the Devon coast, waiting for the overnight to Scunthorpe.

One of the two lit buses had *Denniston's* in big flowing script down the side, yellow on green. It already looked crowded and most of the windows were solidly steamed up.

A busy little man in a quilted anorak pounced on me. 'Are you Mr Evans?'

Was I? Christ, yes. 'That's me.' The driver appeared, snatched my case and hurried it round to the back. I heard the hatch slam.

'You're the last,' the courier said, ticking me off on a typed list. 'Got your passport?'

I handed it over. He skimmed it quickly, nodded, and shoved it into a sort of satchel slung from his shoulders. 'If anybody in the coach asks you, I should say you belong to the firm. Just hitching a ride to Dunkirk. That'll help explain it when you scarper.'

'Good idea.' I climbed aboard and he followed.

A few seconds later and we were on our way.

We had the road pretty much to ourselves and made as good a time as I've ever done to Dover. The seats were good—high-backed, airliner-style—but so they'd ruddy well better be; the other poor sods were going to sit in them for forty-five hours out of the next eighty.

The bloke next to me was a widower in his fifties, as quiet and dull as I'd hoped when I chose to sit by him. I asked if he'd been to Belgium or Holland or Germany before and he said: 'Yes, the hard way.' It turned out he'd been a gunlayer in a Cromwell in 3rd Armoured Division from late 1944, so we talked about tanks most of the way.

At Dover docks the immigration boys came aboard, did a quick head count and a shuffle through the stack of passports, and we were allowed out for twenty minutes drinking and leaking, no more, dinner to be served aboard the boat itself.

I stuck to my gunner in the terminal bar, although it cost me a double Scotch. He was useful cover—two men look far less conspicuous than one solitary drinker. We were all back

211

in the bus in a bit over twenty-five minutes, and it drove on board soon after.

The courier gave us a little lecture about getting back into the bus before we docked and turned us loose—for nearly four hours on that crossing. I made sure I was last off.

'Nice to have had you with us—Mr Evans,' he said insincerely. Or maybe not—he'd be earning more from me than anybody else on that tour, and probably only for the cost of typing up a second set of papers.

'What about my case?'

'Oh God, of course. Where's Harry?' But there wasn't any Harry with the luggage hatch key. 'Pick it up when we come back on, right?'

I didn't exactly have a choice. I nodded and found the stairs up to the main decks.

I tried to shake off my co-tourists immediately, though it wasn't too easy since the boat was anything but crowded; over half the vehicles below were loaded trucks or brand-new cars going for export. In the end I simply skipped dinner and then roosted in the bar; they weren't likely to be expense-account drinkers if they were going on this sort of holiday.

Halfway across there was the usual announcement about passengers *not* with cars or suchlike going to the passport office to pick up a landing ticket. So now I went back to being James Card again, although I didn't like it, not going into France. But hell—I wasn't that important; Arras could never have got a permanent lookout set up for me, even if they'd thought I might be stupid enough to come back so soon.

I had no trouble at the office, anyhow.

We docked about a quarter of an hour late, just on midnight. I was one of the first down to the bus and this time Harry the driver was around with his key. My case had been last in, so there wasn't any problem to hauling it out. I carted it back up to the deck where the mere pedestrians were waiting.

In the cold blue lights at the bottom of the gangway there were four gendarmes and two other officials. One had a sub-machine gun. Just slung from his shoulder, but still not the normal way to greet innocent ski-parties and coach tourists who don't want to see more than five capitals in four days, if that much.

A bunch of schoolboys went down first and were let through —but their master was stopped and his passport checked. A couple of women went through without any trouble. And that was enough for me. I broke some sort of record back down two flights of stairs and up to Denniston's Tours' bus; Harry was just starting the engine.

The courier gave me a look of genuine home-cooked fright and held out a hand to stop me swinging back on board.

I said: 'I'm coming off with you, after all.'

'You can't!'

'We can but try. Get my case out of sight.'

He reached and pushed it away behind him, in a sort of cubby-hole behind the driver's seat. Then he started to protest again.

I soothed him. 'You've still got the Evans passport. Use it. You're not risking any more than I am.'

That really got through to him. 'I'm not risking *anything*!'

'Yes you are, chum. If anybody asks, I did this deal directly with you. No Dave Tanner, no middlemen at all. Swing, swing together—is that how the Eton Boating Song goes? I wasn't ever there anyway—were you?'

Harry the driver, who must have overheard at least some of this, growled: 'For Chrissake—do *something*; I've got to move.'

The bus lurched forward a few feet, waved on by a sailor controlling the unloading.

The courier flapped his hand in small circles and squeaked: 'But what can we do? If they're looking for you, they'll see you.'

'Then I'll stand up here beside you and you explain I'm learning the trade. They won't mistrust your nice honest face.' But I pulled off my sheepskin and slung it into the rack along with all the plastic bags of duty-free booze and cigarette cartons; *that* had been in my Arras description. The bus moved forward in whining jerks.

Behind me, most of the interior lights were out and most

213

of the passengers dozing; it was after midnight and they weren't going to sleep anywhere else tonight. We followed a short queue of cars up the ramp and out across the cold neon-lit concrete towards the passport control.

Suddenly, sooner than I'd expected, a gendarme swung up on to the step and sang out: 'Les passeports, s'il vous plâit, et les noms des passagers.'

Silently, the courier gave him the stack of passports and a typed list—the right one, I hoped. Then he nodded nervously to me and said: 'Je vous presente Monsieur Evans. Il est en train d'apprendre le métier.'

The cop shook hands without really bothering to look at me, and went on shuffling passports. I asked: 'Cherchez-vous quelqu'un en particulier?'

'Un Monsieur Card.' Then, to the courier: 'Est-ce-que quelqu'un d'autre est monté dans le car depuis l'embarquement?'

'Non, non. Personne.'

The cop nodded briskly, handed over the paper and passports and hopped off.

'There, you see?' I said. 'It wasn't so bad, was it?'

He looked back at me with a sick expression. Half an hour later, we were in Belgium.

They dumped me off outside the Gare Central in Brussels at half past five, with a bloodshot dawn breaking behind the Palais de la Nation and a nagging cold wind scouring the empty streets. The courier didn't even bother to wave, and Harry nearly made the bus stand on its hind legs getting away from me. I knew I must have BO by now but I didn't think it was *that* bad.

I had a few coffees in the station itself and when I came out, the Aerogare opposite was open, so I booked on the eight-fifteen Sabena flight for Copenhagen and then a Dan-air connection to Bergen. Out at the airport I found a chemist shop open and bought a razor and blades, and spent most of the flight standing straddle-legged in the toilet of a Caravelle, balancing against the air pockets and trying to shave a face roughly smeared with perfumed airline soap.

At Copenhagen I got my case back just long enough to snatch a fresh shirt out of it and hand it back for the Bergen flight. And to find out that while it had been supposedly shut up in the back of the Denniston's Tours' bus, somebody had worked open the locks and taken the log of the *Skadi*.

THIRTY-FIVE

I CLIMBED on to the plane in a daze, my jaw waggling loosely as I nodded back to the stewardess's 'Good morning, sir.' I'd've nodded just as willingly if she'd asked 'Are you smuggling a .38 Special copy of the Remington .41 derringer up your left sleeve, sir?'

But after a time, the numbness wore off. I'd still got the photo-copies; I'd still got Willie as witness to its existence and what it said. And I *wasn't* in Arras jail, was I? And it hadn't been BO but guilty conscience that made Denniston's Tours leave me at such speed. Which reminded me, so I went back to the toilet and changed my shirt.

Beside the washbasin there was a small bottle of lime-green after-shave lotion and for a moment I wondered what it tasted like and, if so, I might fill my KGB flask with it. Which must prove something about how I still felt. But at least I was thinking Nygaard. It might help me find him.

The Friendship whistled down into Bergen at a quarter to one, just five minutes behind time—and guess what?—it was raining. I tried to ring Kari, couldn't get her, and left a message to say I'd be lunching at the Norge. So then I caught the airport bus and got myself hauled to the terminal in the hotel itself.

She was there to meet me, and even offered to carry my case, so maybe I looked as bad as I felt. But I decided to leave it at the terminal; I didn't yet know where I'd be for the night anyway.

'Any news?' I asked it just for the record, though her face was as long as an Arctic night.

She shook her head.

'You've tried the hospitals and police stations?'

'Ja, ja.' So it wasn't so likely that he was dead under a bush somewhere, unless he'd gone right out of Bergen—and why should he?'

'You asked Mrs Smith-Bang?'

'She is very worried also.'

'I'll bet. Just when did he go missing?'

'He left the Home on Saturday morning, before midday.'

'Forty-eight hours by now. Well . . .' It wasn't too long for a practising alcoholic. Amnesia's a normal part of the game at this stage, so he could still be under somebody's table thinking that Saturday was taking a long time to go past. 'Well,' I said again, 'I've got to eat or die. D'you want to lunch here?'

The short answer was No, though she spun it out a bit. I don't know if she really didn't want that size of lunch, whether she was scared of the flossy great dining-dancing room with its thirty-two Japanese lanterns, or whether she thought I was suggesting she paid for it herself.

Any how, she obviously preferred to go out for a coffee and a sandwich, so I made a date for a quarter past two and gave her a cable to send off to Willie, reassuring him that I wasn't in jail—yet. No mention of the *Skadi*'s log, though.

After lunch I had time to ask at the desk about Maggie Mackwood—but she'd left for London two days before.

Kari's Volkswagen hadn't gone to its Great Reward yet—not quite—so we started down at the Home itself. After a fair bit of ringing and knocking the door was opened by a character who'd sailed as cabin boy on the first Ark. He thought young Herr Ruud was out, and as for Nygaard—who?

I don't think he was hiding anything; it was just that his mind hadn't touched harbour for ten years and Nygaard had only been around for the last four months.

Still, it reminded me to ask Kari: 'Did you try asking any of the other sailors here?'

'Oh, ja. But they did not know where he had gone. He went in the morning and they do not get up so early always.'

'Had Nygaard said he was going away?'

'No.' She seemed pretty definite about that. 'What can we do now?' She just stood there in the rain, wearing her dark blue anorak again, only with its hood up, and looking expectantly at me.

'Well,' I said feebly, 'I suppose we could go and see Mrs Smith-Bang. And come back here later.'

I was surprised how easily she took the idea. Maybe she really thought I knew what I was doing.

The house was high on a suburban hill north-east of the town and—on that day—barely below cloud level. It was a rambling modern split-level affair in what looked like creosoted wood, backing into a gully of spindly pines. A pale green Volvo 145 station wagon was parked in front; Kari put the Volkswagen in behind it.

An elderly bloke in a grey apron opened the door and listened gravely to Kari's fast spiel. It didn't seem to be doing us any good until a voice yelled: 'Who's there? Jim Card, is it? Come on in, son.'

I leered politely at the butler or whatever and we passed on in. Kari seemed to know the way.

It was a big room, a female room, but not a feminine one. All cheery blues and yellows and knotty pine and fluffy bright rugs and colourful plates and vases. I could imagine the cold polite look on Lois Fenwick's face if I'd led her in. Then I shivered and remembered why I was here.

Mrs Smith-Bang was shaking Kari's hand, then mine. 'Howdy, son. Nice to see you again so soon. Glad to see you know young Kari here. Great girl, she's being doing great things for old Nygaard. I guess you heard about him, huh?'

I nodded. 'That's more or less why——'

'You wouldn't have a certain book for me, would you?'

'It's safe in London. I had to leave in a sort of a rush. Sorry.' I wasn't in a truth-telling mood right then. 'Anyway, the bloody thing's no use without Nygaard to swear to it, is it?'

217

She looked at me rather seriously. 'I guess. So—sit down, sit down. It's about him, huh? I was getting pretty worried myself. It's two days now, isn't it?'

Kari nodded.

'I guess he could still have gone on a real dinosaur of a toot and he's still shacked up in some bar. Hell, my second husband climbed aboard a bottle one night in Tampico and it was *ten days* before they——'

Kari said: 'Fru Smith-Bang: you forget it was Saturday. The bars and the Vinmonopolet are closed for Saturday and Sunday. On Saturday he could not have gone out to drink; for that he must have stayed in at home.'

I'd forgotten it myself, since I'd only met it in the guide-book. So he wasn't in the back room of some bar. But also he probably wasn't frozen stiff under some bush.

Mrs Smith-Bang said: 'Hell, yes. You're right, girlie. Don't do much bar-crawling myself nowadays, so I forgot. . . . Well, what do we do now?'

Kari said: 'We could tell the police.'

Mrs Smith-Bang and I both sighed in chorus, glanced at each other and grinned ruefully. She said: 'You say it, Jim.'

'Well, I'm not an expert on Norwegian law, but in most of the world it's no offence to be missing. Not even if you've a wife and ten starving kids complaining, the cops have got no case to hunt a man down. Not until he's done something really serious like not paying a parking fine. Then he's a criminal and they can haul him back from the hot end of hell at public expense. Mind you—' I looked at Mrs Smith-Bang '—you might invent something along those lines. Can't you create a legal hearing and get a subpoena on him or something?'

She nodded her long bony head. 'It's an idea, son. But, God damn it, I don't want to antagonize the old bar-sponge. What-ever happens, *he's* not vulnerable. A chief engineer can't be blamed for a collision. But, like you say, I need his evidence to tie down that logbook.'

I nodded. Kari looked at me curiously; I'd forgotten she hadn't even heard of the book—unless Nygaard himself had mentioned it, which didn't seem likely.

'Okay,' I said. 'But there's still private detective agencies. International's got a bureau here, and there's others.'

'I thought you were one of them yourself,' she said calmly. I felt Kari's sudden hot glance without looking into the glare of it.

'Tell you what I'll do, Jim,' Mrs Smith-Bang said. 'You look around, ask questions, check in with me. If you're not happy at the end of the day, I'll farm it out—right?'

'Well, maybe. . . .'

'D'you want any advance expenses?'

'Je-sus.' As if I didn't have enough employers already. I waved a hand weakly and avoided Kari's icy-hot eyes. 'No advances. And let's see at the end of the day—okay?'

I stood up and tried to look more decisive than I felt. But that's what military training's mostly about. 'Come on, love,' to Kari, and I went out without catching her eye. But she followed.

The chap in the grey apron materialized from nowhere and opened the front door for us. Outside, the cloud had dropped a couple of hundred feet and we were in solid fog. That was going to be fun.

Mrs Smith-Bang poked her long nose out and cackled. 'Great weather, ain't it, Jim? Like the Newfoundland Banks upside down and without Spencer Tracy. Give me a ring, son.'

She held out her hand and I shook it and headed for the Volkswagen.

Kari muttered something that sounded polite and hurried after me. The engine wound up to its normal nagging whine and we hippedy-hopped out on to the hillside road and plunged into the mist.

She asked: 'Are you really a detective?'—as if I'd fed her young sister on aphrodisiacs.

'No. But I've worked for one or two. Watch the *road*!'

The car levitated itself back on to flat ground. She shook her head and the long fair tresses swished impatiently. 'Then what are you?'

'Most of the time I'm a security adviser.' She obviously didn't understand what that was, and I didn't rush to explain.

'But we're both after the same thing, right now: finding Nygaard. Agreed?'

She nodded; then, thank God, we ran out of the fog and there was Bergen spread out below, the headlands like fingers of a hand reaching away from us out into the grey sea. She asked: 'What do we do now?'

'Try for Ruud again, I suppose. How did you tackle him before?—what sort of questions did you ask?'

'Oh, just . . . where was Engineer Nygaard, when did he go. . . . I think that is all.'

And they say women are inquisitive.

'All right. Now we'll try it my way. I won't get rough, but just stay calm, whatever I say, and agree with me.'

There was a trace of suspicion in her face, but that wasn't exactly surprising; I was a foreigner to her country and an outsider to her relationship with Nygaard. But she nodded again.

THIRTY-SIX

RUUD HIMSELF opened the door this time. His eyes flicked from her face to mine, puzzled to see us together.

I leant a casual hand against the door, just to save further ringings and knockings, and said as formally as I could: 'I understand that this is no longer the address of Herr Nygaard?'

The eyes flickered again, the face made mumbling movements. Then: 'Ja. He is gone away.'

'Good. Now, all I need for my office is your statement to that effect, all right? May we come in?'

Sheer bewilderment had rotted the defiance he'd been prepared to throw at me. He just let go the door and it creaked open. I said: 'After you.'

His own room was on the ground floor at the back, overlooking a small concrete courtyard with some straggly plants in wooden tubs. The room itself was small, dark and jammed with furniture and pictures and vases; Ruud was obviously the type who couldn't bring himself to sling anything out. But it was all fairly clean and very neat.

He weaved expertly through it all, his tin leg just missing a chair, a table, a standing lamp, as it always would in his own careful setting. Then he sat in a high-backed chair like a throne, the leg stuck straight out in front. I found myself at a small Victorian table with a heavy tasselled cloth; I put down a handful of papers, took out my pen and got stuck in before he could object.

'Herr Nygaard first came here when?'

'In . . . before Christmas.'

'December? You don't remember the exact date?'

'No-o.'

Kari was still standing up, hardly daring to move for fear of knocking something over. I asked her: 'Do you confirm that he came in December?'

She nodded. 'Ja.'

'Good.' I wrote it down. 'And he left when?'

Ruud frowned, coughed and muttered: 'On Saturday.'

'Do you remember if it was morning or afternoon?'

He gave me a resentful glance. 'Morning.'

'Good.' I wrote that down, too. 'Was he alone?'

'What is this about?' A spat of the old anger—maybe of the old concern.

'Only a statement. But you don't know if he went alone or not?—it doesn't much matter.'

There was a long thick silence. Then Kari sat gently on the arm of a green velvet sofa and it creaked like a jungle bird. Ruud growled: 'I think there was an auto.'

'Taxi?'

'I do not know.' Getting stubborn, now.

So, very politely and uninterestedly, I asked: 'Did he carry his own luggage?'

After another pause, he said: 'I do not know.' I heard Kari give a prim little gasp at the obvious lie.

But I played satisfied; actually, I was—so far. 'Fine,' I said briskly, and held up the paper and read from it: ' "Herr Nygaard came to the Gulbrandsens Seamen's Home last

December. He left last Saturday morning. I did not see him go. I do not know where he has gone." Is that correct?'

'I did not say about where he has gone.'

'Well, *do* you know?'

A low reluctant growl: 'No.'

'Then this is correct. Will you sign, please?'

I gave him the paper and pen. He took them, peered at the paper and then back at me. 'Why should I sign?'

'Isn't it true?'

'Ja, but . . .'

'We're all going to sign. We're witnesses.'

'Witness? Of what?' The eyes were really hunted, now, flickering from one to the other of us and finding no hiding place.

'The truth, you said.'

He crunched the paper, hurled it into a corner and said something.

Kari stiffened, so it must have been quite an interesting something. But it didn't gain him any sympathy.

I stood up. 'It doesn't matter. We both agree on what he said, I think?' The girl nodded; I went on: 'Good. That's all, then, Herr Ruud. Thank you very much. You'll probably hear something before the end of today.' And I moved towards the door.

Ruud said: 'Wait. I . . .'

I turned back slowly. 'Well?'

'I think he went with a doctor.'

'Oh yes? Where to?'

'The home for . . . for drinking, you understand?'

'Alcoholics' home, you mean? Where?'

'On Saevarstad.'

'Never heard of it.'

Kari said: 'It is a small island near Stavanger.'

'Good.' I sat down again and got out another piece of paper.

As we drove away, Kari asked: 'But why did you write it all down again and make him sign?'

'Just to impress him. Now he can never say it wasn't him

told us. And that might stop him telling somebody that we've found out. If that matters.'

'I see.' She thought this over. 'You are a bit cruel.'

'Are you glad we know, or not?'

When she didn't answer, I asked: 'How do you get to Stavanger from here?'

'You are going? There is a hydrofoil—but I think it is too late, now. There is an aeroplane.'

'Good. Back to the terminal, then, please.'

She said thoughtfully: 'I think I will come, too. I have an aunt who lives near there.'

'Fine.' I was surprised, though. 'But what about the university?'

'The term ends tomorrow. And I can say my aunt is ill. She is, often. But can you lend me the money for the ticket?'

'I owe it you, after all this driving around.' But of course she wasn't taking *that*. Anyway, we caught the six thirty-five plane.

Stavanger is another port, smaller than Bergen, just a hundred airline miles south. And since it was dark by the time we got into the town itself, that was about all I knew or could see. But Kari knew her way around; we took a taxi out to the ferry quayside and found there was one ferry still to go out to Saevarstad—but not another coming back. If we went now, we were stuck for the night on an island that couldn't be two miles long, and not even a youth hostel. I wanted more room for manœuvre than that.

So I booked in at the Victoria Hotel, right down on the waterfront, and Kari rang her aunt, then caught a local train to spend the night at Sandnes—another small town about ten miles up the fjord. She'd pick me up at nine in the morning.

With her gone, I could take a serious drink in comfort, so I did that while the hotel put through a call to Willie.

The Victoria suited its name: old-fashioned, comfortable, ceilings as high as its principles and polite with it. They said how terribly sorry they were they couldn't find Mr Winslow, but it was promised he'd ring back.

He rang when I was in the middle of a bath.

'Hello—Mr Card? James? Is it you, old boy? You got to Norway all right, then, but what are you doing in Stavanger?'

'Various complications, chum. Nygaard's down near here. I hope to find him tomorrow.'

'I see. Good, what? But the log's all right, is it?'

I must have stayed silent too long, because he said: 'I say, it *is* all right, isn't it?'

'Let's say I know who's got it.'

'Oh, crikey.' A humming pause. 'It sounds as if I'd better pop across, what?'

'You're welcome. I'm at the Victoria.'

'I'll be there by lunchtime or so.'

I thought of going back to my bath, but then put in a call to my London answering service—just in case. There was the usual amount of communicational fluff, but also a message from Draper: he'd heard that Pat Kavanagh was last heard of working for Dave Tanner.

Now he tells me.

THIRTY-SEVEN

IT WAS A GLITTERING BLUE MORNING; the sun warm but not yet the air. I finished breakfast early and got out for a quick stroll along the quayside before Kari arrived. Past the old wooden warehouses, the red-tiled chandlers' shops, through the bright umbrellas of the flower and vegetable market and into the sudden aroma of the fish market. But it wasn't until then that I'd realized the weird thing: there'd been no salt sea smell in the air. That was taking the Scandinavian passion for cleanliness a bit far.

Kari was there just before nine and we walked out around the quay to the north side, where the ferries started. The place was like Piccadilly Circus on water, with every size of ferry loading cars and trucks for trips half a mile across the bay or fifty miles up the coast.

'It is how we travel in Norway,' she said. 'Do you know how long it would take me to drive to Bergen? Three days, and even that would need one ferry crossing, and I cannot do it now anyway because the roads are blocked with snow.'

Just beside us, a scruffy little trawler-shaped boat was unloading a whole family, furniture, potted plants and cat. A removal van. Why not?

We walked aboard our own boat, one of the smaller jobs, fitted to carry about six cars and maybe forty passengers. It did a regular round tour of the smaller islands up to about ten miles away; we sat down on a wooden bench and bought tickets off the conductor. The romance of the Viking country.

Saevarstad, according to the tourist map I'd nicked from the hotel, was about five miles away, a kidney-shaped blob marked for a church and a circuit road that couldn't have been more than four miles in all. We weaved towards it, never seeing a real horizon, never more than half a mile from some other island and stopping briefly at two of them. After three-quarters of an hour, we were there.

It looked like a neat little wooden village with the quay itself as the village square. There were a few parked cars and trucks, a storage shed, a heap of crates and oil drums and two shops. One was half hardware, half ship's chandler for the dozen or so motorboats moored at the quayside, the other the post office and everything else. It was the only one open, so we started there.

A middle-aged spinsterish-looking bird told us that the sanatorium was a couple of kilometres out along the coast road southwards. Big yellow house. And she was sorry the island taxi wasn't around—would we like her to phone hither and yon to try and find it?

I said: 'Never mind. But if it comes, send it on after us.'

'I will. Does Doctor Rasmussen know you are coming, or shall I ring to him?'

'He knows,' I said quickly. And we started walking.

The road was narrow—barely wider than a car—but properly made up. And around us, the land was lush and green and neat and, in a small way, prosperous. Once we were clear of the village it became a series of smallholdings, some with rows of well-kept greenhouses, others with a couple of cows or a small flock of sheep. How they could scratch even a living out of plots that size I couldn't guess, but every house was in good repair and freshly painted.

Kari explained: 'They are all also fishermen, in winter. For prawns and lobsters as well.' Well, maybe that told me something. Certainly we passed three or four tiny landing-places, with or without a small fishing-boat moored alongside.

It took about half an hour to the sanatorium itself, a three-storey-and-semi-basement wooden house with a steeply pitched tile roof built, at a guess, by a rich Victorian family. It was painted primrose yellow, with the carved bits under the eaves and the balustrades of the roofed porch that ran the width of the front picked out in white.

There was a Volkswagen Microbus painted up as an ambulance standing in the gravel drive, a Saab 99 parked around the side of the house.

We walked up the half-dozen wooden steps on to the porch and I rang the bell. There were a couple of weatherworn old rocking-chairs out there where maybe you sat on a summer evening and dreamed of the dry martinis and whisky sours gone by, for ever. Or maybe not; when you got close to the house you could see that every window, right to the top was barred.

The door opened with a complicated clicking and clacking of locks and a matronly woman in crisp white uniform stared woodenly out at us.

Kari said something quick in Norwegian, then introduced me. No handshake, just a crisp starched nod. Then we switched to English.

'We would like to visit Engineer Nygaard,' the girl explained. 'We are friends.'

'We do not have visitors in the morning.'

'We have come from Bergen,' Kari explained.

'If you had telephoned you would have been told. You should have telephoned.'

I chipped in my piece: 'Sorry, that's my fault. I've come

from London in a bit of a hurry. Can I have a word with Doctor Rasmussen?'

Somewhere inside the house somebody screamed. Not just in pain; a long wavering sobbing howl of simple terror that practically tore off my scalp.

But not with matron. She cocked her head and listened thoughtfully, like somebody trying to identify a tricky bird-call. Feet clattered on the stairs and a door slammed.

She sighed briefly. 'I will see if the doctor can speak with you. But he is very busy. Please to come in and wait.'

We waited in a big, bright, well-furnished room that still had that impersonal look you get in even the best of doctor's waiting-rooms. The pile of magazines, the chairs arranged so you didn't have to chat to anybody else waiting there, the carefully placed ashtrays.

We waited. Kari said in a carefully hushed voice: 'Perhaps we should have telephoned.'

'I doubt it. They'd just have told us not to come at any time yet.'

It was another five minutes before Doctor Rasmussen came in. He must have been about fifty, but very fit with it: deep-chested and solid-shouldered, with a bouncy gait and a rich tan on his knobbly face. He wore a short-sleeved white coat showing thick forearms covered with fine blond hairs, though the top of his head was a careful arrangement of thin grey.

This time we shook hands. He said: 'I am sorry you have come all this way for nothing. If you had rung up, I could have told you.'

'I wouldn't say it was for nothing, Doctor. At least we've established that Engineer Nygaard is still alive. I suppose he still is?'

He looked briefly startled, then laughed jovially. 'Of course. Did you really come all this way to prove that?'

'Maybe. When an elderly man in not very good health suddenly vanished without telling somebody who's been help-ing look after him—' I waved a hand at Kari '—or his ex-employer who's paying his pension, the least anybody can do is get a bit worried. There's an obvious chance that he's fallen into the harbour or frozen to death sleeping it off under a bush in the park.'

'I understand. Naturally a man in his state is rather careless about leaving messages. I must see that he writes letters to everybody who is concerned with him.'

'It runs to quite a number by now. You did know he was a star witness in a big court case?'

Kari was looking at me with a slightly schoolmarmish frown.

Rasmussen just nodded. 'He did tell me something. One does not know what to believe with such cases.' He turned to Kari. 'You were very clever to find him here, Froken Skagen. Or did he remember enough to leave a message with somebody?'

I said quickly: 'We were very clever. Can we have just a quick word with him so that I can tell my superiors in London that he *is* still alive and . . . as well as can be expected?'

The grin was gone, now. 'We allow no visitors in the morning, Herr Card. And for Herr Nygaard, at his stage of treatment, we allow no visitors at all. You must understand that.'

'What stage is he at by now?'

'I cannot discuss a patient's symptoms, of course.'

'Good for you, Doctor. But I've also got the shreds of professional ethics. You don't discuss a patient. I don't tell anybody he's still alive unless I've seen him.'

I started buttoning my coat.

His big, muscular face was twitching with indecision. Finally he said: 'Wait, please,' did an about-turn and strode out.

Kari whispered: 'What is happening?'

I shrugged, but I unbuttoned my coat again and sat down.

After a few minutes Rasmussen came back. He looked calm but serious. 'You may see him for a moment only. To reassure yourself. After that I hope you will leave me to complete the cure in peace.'

We followed him out into the hall, up a flight of broad, shallow stairs, with a big window at the turn. Even that was covered with a heavy wire mesh.

'Do many of them try to jump?' I asked cheerfully.

'Not from here. That comes later,' he said soberly. 'It is still about seven per cent that succeed.'

Kari was looking puzzled. 'Seven per cent? Of what?'

Rasmussen said: 'Cured male alcoholics who commit suicide—who *succeed*, not just who try. We can—often—take away the drinking. We cannot put back what he has drunk away. A marriage, a family, a fortune, sometimes.'

Kari frowned. Rasmussen added: 'But of course, some say an alcoholic is trying to commit suicide, subconsciously, by his drinking. So perhaps I meet only those who have suicidal tendencies already.'

I said: 'Perhaps you're saving ninety-three per cent rather than losing seven, you mean? Pretty good, that.'

He gave me a disapproving glance. 'You are forgetting those who fail to be cured.'

'Ah yes.'

The corridor was broad and well-lit and empty of furniture except for a couple of the metal tea trolleys that you see carrying drugs and stuff around in hospitals. And the doors weren't the original ones. These were painted in nice bright colours, but it didn't hide their blank solidity, the heavy lock, the central porthole at eye level.

Rasmussen peered in through one, then motioned me up to take a look.

Nygaard was lying in the bed, on his back with his mouth open, apparently asleep. Around him was a room such as you'd expect in a private sanatorium: walls freshly painted a gloss primrose, a heavy wooden wardrobe and cupboard, soft chair for visitors, a water-bottle, mug and flower vase all in plastic. No glass for Doctor Rasmussen's patients. No seven per cent while in his care.

I nodded, and let Kari take a look. While she was doing so, I leaned inconspicuously on the doorhandle. It moved, all right.

Rasmussen asked: 'Are you satisfied now?'

Kari looked at me. 'It is him.'

I nodded. 'I agree. Thank you, Doctor.' He looked momentarily surprised, then led the way back to the stairs.

Then somebody screamed again—the same long, shaking screech that went through your head like a file across your teeth.

Rasmussen stopped, listened briefly and shouted: 'Trond!'

Big feet clattered on the hallway below and a vast man in a short-sleeved white jacket came around the bottom of the stairs and pounded up towards us. He was built like Hermann Göring, with much the same bloated frog face, but he was fast on his feet and barely puffing when he reached the top. Mind, he was only in his middle thirties, I'd guess, so maybe most of his shape was hereditary.

The scream reached out again and Rasmussen raised his voice to cut through it. Trond got his orders, nodded and charged off down the corridor without giving Kari or me a glance.

The doctor looked at me and smiled wanly. 'What do they see?—we can never know. Hell is a private place.'

Kari was looking startled and bewildered.

Rasmussen said: 'The symptoms of withdrawal, that is the most likely time for the delirium tremens. Then they start to meet the terrors. We try to soften it with drugs, but . . . each body is different, we cannot always make it the perfect dose.'

He started downstairs. Behind us, the scream started, wavered and drifted into a muffled gulping sound.

'Often,' Rasmussen said, 'it is just somebody to touch them, like Trond to make them know the world is still around them.

'Trond must be a great comfort to you,' I said.

He looked at me sharply, then bent his head in agreement. 'A good boy. And very strong. For a few, very few, we need that.'

'Who committed Nygaard to you, Doctor?'

He stopped and frowned. 'There was no "committing"—this is not prison or insanity.'

'Sorry, Doctor. I'd just read something about a Sobriety Board that can commit alcoholics for a cure. If they're given the right evidence.'

He shrugged and started down again. 'It happens for perhaps one per cent of cases.'

230

'Ah. I wonder how he came to hear of you, though?'

'Alcoholism is not rare with sailors. The cheap drink, the long boredom. . . . He is not the first seaman officer in this house.'

'I'll bet.' We reached the hall and the doctor kept going towards the front door. Nothing we could do but follow.

There was a new car in the drive—a tattered old Ford Cortina with a youngish driver leaning across the bonnet breathing cigarette smoke at the sky.

Kari said: 'The taxi. We asked for it.'

Of course. Well, anything's better than exercise. I turned to Rasmussen. 'Thank you for letting us barge in like this, Doctor. But try and get him to write those letters soon, huh?'

He nodded stiffly, not much liking somebody else telling him what to do, but having to take it this time. We shook hands—a firm, dry hand—and I paused at the top of the porch steps and looked around. Off to both sides, beyond the flower beds with the first daffodils, and the driveway, there were thick clumps of laurel and rhododendron and conifer bushes.

'Must be nice in summer,' I commented. 'I hope your patients appreciate their luck, Doctor. Thanks again.'

I walked across to the taxi.

Kari had been chatting up the driver. 'The next boat is not until an hour, but he will drive us around the island if you like. He does not speak English.'

The face was young, bony, friendly, and somehow it was nice to meet a Norwegian who didn't give a damn about *my* language. 'Okay, let's drive around the island.'

'He says there is a very interesting church of the twelfth century.'

'If you want to see, go ahead.'

'I would like to.' She took the front seat.

The island itself went on being just as it had in the distance we'd walked: small bright houses and rich grass—but just the occasional raw rock poking through. Driving round it took twenty minutes and exactly nine kilometres on the clock, and we were almost back at the sanatorium when we came to the church.

To me it was just a whitewashed stone barn with narrow arched windows, even if it had been built by Eric the Red, so I wandered outside while she went in. Even at that time of year the grass in the churchyard was thick and wet around my ankles, and the stone wall was the same slate grey as the church roof and the gently restless sea a couple of hundred yards down the slope and past the road. Did they call it the Norwegian Sea up here? It didn't matter; it was really the same grey Atlantic, and the same stone church just beyond its reach that you see a hundred times on the west coast of Scotland and Ireland and wherever else the fishermen come home to be buried—some of them.

Inside, the tablets would say 'Lost at sea'; here outside were the ones that would translate 'drowned', the ones the sea gave back—but maybe after a month or two of quiet revenge from the cod and the hungry gulls. The ones identified from a bracelet or a gold tooth, the ones you'd like to turn away again, but never can. Any fishing village—or island—writes its history on stones like these.

Then the taxi driver gave an exaggerated cough and, when I looked up, glanced conspicuously at his watch. I nodded and walked slowly among the tombstones towards him; Kari came out as I reached the gate.

We'd been back in the taxi heading for the harbour for five minutes before she said: 'Inside that church, I saw names on the . . . the stones.'

'Me too, outside.'

'Ah, Bang?'

'Bang. Probably she inherited a part of this island as well as the shipping line. She could own the sanatorium.'

'Then—she must know Engineer Nygaard is here, no?'

'She must have put him here.'

Kari thought about that all the way down to the dock. Our ferry was just coming in around the corner of the island, hooting gloomily.

As we walked aboard, she asked: 'But then she is . . . hiding him while he becomes cured, ja?'

'She's certainly hiding him. But he's no more taking the cure than I am.'

THIRTY-EIGHT

WE MET WILLIE in the Victoria—he'd just signed in, and sat down around a pot of coffee in the lounge beside the dining-room. I introduced Kari and gave him the quick word about Nygaard, but he wasn't really interested.

When I gave him space, he said: 'All fine, old boy, but what about the logbook?'

'I've got photostats of the last four pages.'

He just looked at me.

I said: 'I made a mistake trusting a private detective in London. He arranged my getaway but he tipped off the French police *and* had my luggage gone over. I'm sorry.'

'Aren't we all?' he said heavily. Then: 'Well, you found it, so I suppose you've a right to lose it again—what? But who's got it?'

'The people Dave Tanner was working for—I don't know who, but the same people he was working for in Arras.'

'Are you sure about that?'

'Close enough.'

He frowned. 'But now—what's Mrs Smith-Bang playing at, hiding away her witness like that?' And he looked at Kari as well as me.

What he got back was a solemn wide-eyed stare. Whether he knew it or not, he'd rung the bell with her, with his curly fair hair, neat grey suit, club tie, glittering shoes—the perfect Englishman and all very *clean*; you couldn't imagine a smudge on Willie any more than you could dust on the Crown Jewels.

I shrugged. 'She's just hiding him.'

'From us?'

'Since she lied to us, yes, she's hiding him from us, but not necessarily *only* us.'

233

He absorbed this. 'But how did she get him to go there?'

'She's got some sort of hold on him.' I glanced at Kari, but she was looking elsewhere. 'And there's only one thing that Nygaard cares about, so my guess is she's been paying for his booze all along. Now she's moved the bottle and he had to follow.'

'Damned if I see the logic of that,' he said—and then apologized to Kari. She blushed prettily. He went on: 'I mean, why keep your chief witness permanently stewed as a prune? He's not going to make a frightfully good impression on a court, what? Make more sense if he *did* take the cure, you know?'

I shrugged. '*I* don't pretend to understand it, Willie.'

Kari asked: 'But what can we do, then?'

'If I could sit down with Nygaard and just ask him questions, we'd find out everything.'

'The trained interrogator, eh?' Willie murmured. 'How do we get him, though?'

'Go and take him.'

Just then, David Fenwick walked in.

'My God, what are *you* doing here?'

'Hello, sir.' We shook hands, and he grinned cheerily. 'Oh, when I heard Mr Winslow was coming over I asked if I could come, too, and Mummy said I could, if it was with him, so . . . here we are. It was all a bit of a rush; school only broke up today and I had to catch the plane still in uniform. I've just been changing.'

Now he was wearing khaki denim trousers, a blue-and-green flowered shirt and a light mackintosh zip jacket. I introduced him to Kari and he bowed politely.

Then I said to Willie: 'You might have told me.'

'Sorry, old boy; forgot you didn't know. All fixed up in a bit of a hurry last night, after you'd rung.' But he wasn't really concentrating.

David asked: 'What have we decided, now?'

'Your employee here,' Willie said heavily, 'is just introducing us to the kidnapping business.'

'Oh?' David sounded interested.

234

'Rescue, he means,' I said hastily, keeping a watch on Kari. She was the one that mattered.

She frowned slightly. 'You mean to take him away from Saevarstad?'

'That's right. What chance has he got to make his own decisions where he's only got a whisky bottle for company? Every time he wakes up they offer him another drink—and he takes it. But get him away and let him sober up a bit and maybe he'll have a chance to make up his own mind.'

'But Doctor Rasmussen . . .' Kari said doubtfully.

'He said he'd got no power to keep Nygaard there. If he calls the police in—okay. We explain our mistake. But if he doesn't call the police then he shows he's been acting illegally.'

After a time, she said: 'How do we do this, then?'

Willie gave a long, sad sigh.

I suppose, if I'd sat down and thought about it, I'd've realized that kidnapping—I mean rescuing—is a complicated, professional business. First, you need transport, and that included a boat. But Kari knew one: a diesel-engined fishing-boat belonging to an old boy who took her out to do the hard work whenever she visited Stavanger. And yes, she could borrow it to visit some imaginary friend on a small island.

You also need a hideout, and not the Victoria Hotel, Stavanger, no matter what else it's good at. But Kari knew that, too: her aunt owned a 'summer hut' on the Hunnedalen, which—from the map—was a valley road running up to the hills fifty miles from Stavanger, and most of which was marked 'closed in winter'. But she thought the closed bits would be further uphill from the hut. If she was wrong, it was going to be a damn crowded car stuck in a snowdrift overnight.

The car itself was easy: I just sent Willie out to hire one, and by the way, buy a couple of sleeping bags on the way back; Kari had some camping gear stored with her aunt. Rather late, I remembered to send *her* out to organize some food.

By sundown, we were ready. By nine o'clock, we were on our way.

*　　　*　　　*

The night was clear, starry and cold—and you never remember how cold it becomes the instant you get in a boat. This boat particularly.

It was a wooden job, broad and shallow and smelling like the cat's supper. Maybe a bit over twenty feet long, with the front third decked over to give a cabin that was honestly no more than three feet high but had a Calor gas stove, two bunks, a cupboard, a wood-burning stove in the bows sticking its chimney up like a flagpole through the deck, and a row of dangling pans that clattered in tune with the chug of the diesel.

Behind us, the lights of Stavanger didn't fade away, they just ruddy stayed there.

'How fast are we going?' I called to Kari.

'Five knots, I think.' She was just a bulky shape against the stars, hands in anorak pockets, woolly ski-cap on top, riding the tiller and steering it with her thighs.

'How fast *could* we go?'

'Seven, perhaps eight. Shall I show you?'

Willie said: 'No thank you.' He and David and the engine itself were in the middle of the boat, them studying it by thin torchlight. I was hunched on the deck, in among a clutter of rusty chains, ends of rope and plastic buckets.

'What the hell do you know or care about diesels, Willie?' I asked grumpily. The cold was beginning to bite.

He said evenly: 'They occasionally cropped up in my end of the Army, old boy.'

'Sorry. I'd forgotten the cavalry hadn't invented the high-compression horse.'

'You wouldn't say that if you'd ever been rolled on by one.'

I grinned unwillingly in the darkness. And around us, the busy evening went on, down, maybe, but busy enough: ferries that were just bright strips of light, fishing-boats that were patterns of colour, motorboats that sparkled white and roared and changed direction every five seconds; still Piccadilly Circus on water. Kari just chugged us through it, confident of a small tricoloured light slung to our stumpy mast and steering by occasional glances at a small tourist map of the bay and fjords; not even a compass. You find more charts, books, depth-sounders and stuff on a weekender's dinghy than you ever do in a serious fishing-boat.

Willie stuck the cover back on the engine, lit a cigarette and came and crouched beside me on the deck. He was wearing a thick, double-breasted fawn overcoat—like the old Army 'British Warm'—and the first thing he said was: 'Doesn't feel quite like D-Day must have done.'

'What d'you want? Couple of airborne divisions and battle-ship bombardment?'

'Something more than that little two-shot peashooter of yours, anyway, what? Seems to me it's just big enough to be illegal and nothing more.'

'It was never meant to be a first gun. But I don't expect any rough stuff.'

'How are we going to tackle it, then?'

'David stays in the boat. The rest of us just tag along, knock on the door, see what happens next.'

He grunted. 'Must say I'd rather we were doing it in a more military way.'

'If we're doing it the military way, we start with you standing up straight and calling me sir—lieutenant.'

For a moment I think he was really offended. Then he chuckled.

'In the Lancers we never called anybody "sir" except our wine merchants.'

THIRTY-NINE

IT TOOK US just over an hour, including a dog-leg around another small island, so probably Kari was right about that five knots. As we came up to Saevarstad itself, she asked: 'Where do we land, now?'

'There's a small harbour just south of the house itself. Quieten the engine and go for that.'

'You chose this place already, then?'

'Let's say it had crossed my mind. Will Rasmussen or the sanatorium own a boat?'

'They are sure to, yes. It is like a car for those on an island.'

That's what I'd thought.

The sanatorium was easy enough to identify; it was the only three-storey house in sight and the only one I remembered seeing on the island anyway. But a hundred yards out from the land, the little inlet still hadn't showed itself clear. And there were sharp black rocks showing against the starlight glitter of the water.

Kari said doubtfully: 'I do not think I can——'

'We need a light,' Willie snapped.

David said: 'There's a big signalling lamp in the cabin.'

'Get it, please.'

He dived inside and came out again with an aged Aldis lamp on a long tarry flex. Willie took it, looked at the plug, said: 'God knows what this does to the batteries, but . . .' He plugged it into a socket on the little instrument board beside the engine, and pulled the trigger.

A solid beam of light snapped out across the water and splashed silently on a small concrete quay dead ahead.

Kari kicked the throttle forward and we surged in, Willie standing up by the mast and fanning the light gently from side to side to show up any rocks.

David whispered: 'D'you think they'll see the light, sir?'

'Why should they be looking?' The big house was almost out of sight behind a hump of land. 'And why are you whispering?'

In the glow of reflected light, I caught his sudden grin and nod.

There were a couple of other boats tied up there, but one was a fishing-boat and the other just an open lifeboat with an engine stuck in the middle and smelling of fertilizer. Nothing to belong to a posh boozing-home; they'd keep their boat down at the main harbour, as I'd hoped.

David objected at being left with the boat—and out of what he hoped would be action—until Willie gave him a genuine military snarl, and he sat down abruptly on the cabin top.

The three of us walked up a short wide path to the coast road, and the sanatorium was about two hundred yards ahead.

Kari asked: 'What are you going to do, now?'

'Ask a few questions, maybe tell a few little lies. Be careful how you get in front of me, as well.'

'There is another car, now.'

A white old-model Cortina stood alongside the Saab and the Microbus ambulance. I tried the door and it opened, but the key wasn't in. House rule, I expect, about not leaving keys in cars, just in case somebody tried to break for it. I looked up at the house, but nobody had heard us yet, and the ground-floor rooms were all heavily curtained.

I bent and unscrewed one of the tyre valves. 'You fix the Saab,' I said to Willie.

He nodded and didn't ask why. Probably he'd been a soldier.

We walked quietly up on to the porch and rang the bell.

After a while there was the same clicking and clacking of locks and bolts and a light directly overhead flared on just as the door opened and Rasmussen himself frowned out at us.

No white coat this time, just a natty dove-grey suit stretched tight across his barrel chest, white shirt and club tie. Or medical society.

'You?' he asked incredulously.

'Us,' I agreed and held up a hand against his tendency to push the door shut in our faces. 'Couple of things I didn't quite get clear. You did say that you'd started treatment on Herr Nygaard?'

'Two days since. Now——'

'But you didn't say whether he'd signed an agreement to treatment.'

He frowned heavily, but the bright brown eyes weren't quite steady beneath it. 'I told you there was no commitment——'

'No, so there has to be an agreement giving you the right to keep him here for up to a year. The State doesn't want patients changing their minds and going back on the sauce halfway through. And every admission has to be registered with the National Director for Treatment of Alcoholics.'

'You have been reading a book again,' he said contemptuously.

'No, I just asked a good doctor. You could always do the same if you're in any doubt.'

He flushed, glanced quickly at the girl and Willie. 'Well, what do you want?'

'I want to see the paperwork that proves Nygaard's here legally—or Nygaard himself.'

'Tonight it is impossible.'

'Now, Doctor, now.' And I leant against the door harder.

'I will call the police.'

'Fine, we'll wait for them. Either he's properly signed in or he isn't. And if you got him to sign something when he was smashed, then we'll get Doctor Moe up from the village to run a blood or urine test. If he's been dry for two days he shouldn't show any alcohol. If he's registering four hundred, as I expect, then you can use your licence to light your next cigar. The paper or the patient, Doctor. There's no third way.'

But he tried one. He threw the door wide and yelled: 'Trond!'

I looked at Kari. 'Are you convinced?'

I didn't need the nod; her wide cold eyes and set Viking expression were enough.

'Then go and get him.' I stepped into the house behind them.

They'd just reached the stairs when big Trond galloped out from some passage behind them. He was still wearing the short-sleeved white coat and a hopeful expression.

I took the derringer out and aimed it loosely. 'Keep the Reichsmarschall out of this or you'll be treating a different sort of liver trouble.'

Rasmussen glanced down at the little gun.

I said: 'They're .38 Special wadcutters but you don't have to believe that, either. Just ask him afterwards.'

He said something quickly and Trond stopped near the foot of the stairs, slow disappointment spreading across his face. Kari had just about reached Nygaard's room, now, almost out of sight unless I kept well back towards the door. Willie just behind her.

Rasmussen said something else and Trond smiled and turned away.

I snapped the gun around at the doctor himself. 'Stop him. Keep him here!' He looked down the two stubby barrels, shrugged very slightly and called again. Trond stopped.

Rasmussen said: 'You will have much trouble with the police, I think.'

'There's trouble all over, Doctor. I think it's something going around. How did Mrs Smith-Bang swing you into taking up this ploy?'

The name jolted him. Not much, but enough to keep him busy for a moment. And moments were what I wanted. I just hoped Willie and Kari weren't playing dressing-up-dolls games with Nygaard.

I chattered on: 'I wonder if you know how much all this involves, Doctor? Did you hear of a man called Martin Fenwick?—shot dead in Arras two weeks ago. Steen, Jonas Steen?—murdered in Bergen, last week. Henrik Lie, fake suicide, same place. Did you know all about them, Doctor? And a man called Pat Kavanagh?'

By Christ, he *had* heard of Kavanagh. But just then, Kari and Willie hauled Nygaard out of his room and started for the stairs. He had an old uniform greatcoat on, with three stripes at the epaulets, and I couldn't see what else. But Willie was carrying a bunch of clothing.

The girl was carrying a bottle. 'They left this in his room, even!' she called, and threw it over the banisters. It exploded in a silver and brown spray and Trond shied away.

I said conversationally: 'New form of treatment, eh, Doctor? If they can't stand the cure they can go back to the disease without waking you up.'

'You should know it is dangerous to treat a man of that age. The withdrawal symptoms can kill as quickly as the drinking.'

'I'm not questioning your professional knowledge, Doctor, just your financial ethics.'

They were at the bottom of the stairs, now, and I could see

Nygaard had got some shoes on. I stepped further into the house, pushing Rasmussen ahead of me, to let them pass behind.

I said: 'Keep him going.' As they reached the door, Nygaard lifted his flabby, sweat-stained face, focused near me, and half smiled. Then they were gone.

The doctor said: 'You were very stupid. How can you escape with him?'

I said: 'If you've got any sense, you'll forget him and us both. Because if we get caught, we talk. You spend your time doing over his room and don't forget to scrub it down for fingerprints, and then you've never heard of him. Make your own peace with Mrs Smith-Bang somehow.'

They'd be on the road by now. If I could give them a minute more, I'd reach the boat at the same time.

Then Kavanagh stepped quietly from behind the stairs and said: 'Hallo there, Card. You get around, don't you?' Without the stocking mask, I didn't recognize the square face with strong cheek bones, thin lips and a sharp widow's peak of very black hair. But the voice, the bandaged right hand—and the big automatic in the left . . .

Rasmussen had a tight little smile on his face and was edging back out of the line. Trond was grinning broadly.

Was he any good with his left hand? But it hardly mattered, not at less than ten yards. He had at least seven shots to scatter at me and no professional could miss as badly as I needed him to.

I fired both barrels at him and stepped out of the front door. I didn't think I'd hit him, but I'd surprised the hell out of him. He shied instinctively, throwing up the gun hand across his face, and his one shot went somewhere up the stairwell.

The door slammed behind me, shaking the whole porch. I bounced off a rocking-chair, ran to the end and vaulted down into the doctor's best daffodils. Then across the drive and into the bushes. And there I could stop and reload.

Behind me, the garden reached another twenty yards, all nice thick cover. But beyond that there was a dry-stone wall and

242

then open pasture stretching down to the road one way and up the hillside the other. Using the wall, which stood about hip-high, I could reach the road in complete cover from fire. . . . By breakfast time, maybe.

The lights on the porch and in the hall suddenly went out. I lifted the derringer—then changed my mind. They'd come out cautiously enough anyway; why tell them where I was? I backed off as quietly as I could, weaving among the bushes to the wall; climbed it without knocking anything down—and then went diagonally across the pasture like a frightened rabbit. I was practically at the road when I heard the first car start behind me—but it didn't seem to be making much ground.

When I reached the quay, Kari was already down in the boat making urging noises at Nygaard; he was sitting on the edge looking cold, apprehensive and rather permanent.

Willie was just standing by. 'What was the shooting?'

'An old friend cropped up unexpectedly. Nobody got hurt. Get him *in*,' I panted.

Kari said: 'I am trying . . .'

I said: 'Oh hell,' and grabbed Nygaard by the shoulder of his greatcoat and heaved. He weighed the world, but he shifted. There was a startled squawk and he tumbled down almost on top of David. Willie jerked one rope loose, I took the other, and we swung aboard. Behind us, I heard a second car start—then it was wiped out by the clattering roar of our diesel.

Kari put the tiller hard over and pointed us at the starlit water beyond the dark rocks.

I said: 'Now try for those eight bloody knots.'

FORTY

WHEN WE WERE CLEAR of the harbour I told her to swing south and keep following the shoreline—trying to keep us out of sight of the house and the road between it and the main harbour. About then, I remembered to switch off the navigation lights, and that bothered her more than anything else that evening. A bit of kidnapping, a few gunshots, yes, but driving a boat without lights . . . !

The lights stayed off until we were a good mile from the island and ready to swing round on a new course. This ran about directly south-east into the mouth of the Hogsfjorden and then fifteen miles or more up it to where the car was parked at a small quay where they loaded gravel from a quarry. Nothing else happened there, so past midnight there wouldn't be anybody to ask what we were doing, humping Nygaard ashore.

And it looked as if we *were* going to be humping him. He'd spent the first busy five minutes lolling about on the deck beside the engine, more than half asleep again already. Then Willie and I had forced him into a pair of socks and put a sweater on under his overcoat—they'd got his trousers on over his pyjamas, back at the sanatorium—and suggested he try the bunk in the cabin. Me, I'd've rather lain down in a bucket of fish heads, which was what it smelt like, but he took it calmly enough. Just patted the diesel's wooden box, grunted: 'Not very good,' and crawled away out of sight.

About then, we turned south-east, lit our lights again and slowed down. They caught us just before eleven.

We had a little time to prepare for it. Probably there wasn't anything else they could do but rush about the bay in a big motor-cruiser, coming to a grinding halt beside each small boat still around and shining a small searchlight on it, but it didn't exactly make them invisible.

Willie said: 'What do we do now, then?'

Kari said hopefully: 'Shall we put out the lights again?'

'Christ, no. They'll have seen us already; that'd be as good as a signpost.' They were investigating a lobster boat about a quarter of a mile back. 'No, we just keep going. And let David steer; they've seen all the rest of us.'

Willie said: 'For God's sake, old boy——'

'That or surrender.'

David said: 'I could steer this boat, all right.'

'But you can't answer questions in Norwegian,' Willie pointed out.

I said: 'Let Kari prompt him. They won't expect us to have a boy his age along, anyway, and they won't hear much of his accent above the engines.'

Willie raked a hand anxiously through his hair. 'But, I say——'

'We don't really have a choice. There's some rough boys out in that boat and they won't observe the Geneva Convention if we *do* surrender. Now let's get organized.'

He went into the cabin first, me next because I had a gun. Kari stayed at the half-open door with a bit of engine tarpaulin draped artistically over her. David was sitting across the tiller in the proper negligently-professional style and—a last bright idea of his own—chewing a sandwich from our provisions. He reckoned it would help his Harrow accent along a bit and he was probably right.

We waited in the darkness that was as thick as fish soup, with Nygaard snoring and bubbling louder than the diesel, and Willie said: 'I really don't see why that doctor's chasing us at all—if all you said about his breaking the rules was true.'

'Not his decision any more. He sold out long ago.'

'To Mrs Smith-Bang?'

'Must be—God knows why. Maybe she owns his mortgage, maybe she caught him pushing drugs on the side—or maybe he just likes the crooked life. But he's got it now, anyway.'

The cracks in the bulkhead suddenly glowed with light. David called: 'They're coming.'

There were a couple of thick, dirty portholes but angled forwards, and I couldn't hear the cruiser's engines over the racket of our own. But past Kari's shoulder I could see the searchlight's glow getting brighter and brighter, silhouetting David's slim figure. He turned and waved his sandwich angrily —a nice touch.

Then the light sparkled direct into my eyes and I yanked my head back. Through a crack in the bulkhead I could just see the white shape slide up alongside on our right and match speeds a few feet away.

The light raked the open deck of our boat and settled back on David. A voice yelled: 'Hvilket skip?'

Kari's voice was half-whisper, half-shout: 'Stavanger Smaragd.'

'Stavanger Smaragd!' David's shout was nicely scrambled by sandwich.

'Hvor skal De?'

'Idsal,' Kari called.

'Idsal!'

So far—I guessed—we'd had the name of the boat and where we were supposed to be heading. But now they called something Kari didn't catch. She hesitated. I pulled the derringer back to full cock—and then David took over. He simply held his sandwich up in an ear-cupping gesture, leant towards them and yelled a completely international 'Ay?'

'HVOR ER FAREN DEN?' the voice bellowed. Trond, I think.

'Han sover,' Kari answered.

'Han sover!'

Then she added: 'Dra til helvete.'

'Dra til helvete!'

After that, nothing. I rammed my ear against the bulkhead —and got it filled with diesel vibrations. Had we missed something?

Then the light died, the big white boat swung away. From the porthole I could see the white wake suddenly thicken in the starlight as she piled on speed.

After a few moments, I asked Kari: 'What did they say at the end?'

'They asked where is his father.'

'And you said?'

'He sleeps.' She paused and said hesitantly: 'And also—Go to hell. I thought a fisherman's boy might say that, but do you think I should tell David what I made him say?'

Willie's warm chuckle of relief flowed over my right ear.

I said: 'I think maybe he's old enough to know.' I slipped the derringer's hammer off cock and put it back in the arm clip. Behind us, Nygaard snored on.

* * *

The lights of the towns and villages vanished behind us, switched off or blanked out by islands and headlands. Ahead the land rose up above us, closed in around and finally behind us.

We were a beetle of noise crawling along between silent black cliffs, the dim path of water ahead matching the narrow path of sky above. Maybe we threw an echo, or maybe it was the loneliness that made us sound so loud and feel so bright. When Willie snapped his lighter beside me, it was like a gunshot.

'What does this tell us about Ellie Smith-Bang?' he asked carefully.

'After you'd left the sanatorium, the bloke I shot at back there—and missed—is Pat Kavanagh. He killed Steen in Bergen; he's been working for Dave Tanner, the private detective in London who got the log off me. Between them, Kavanagh and Tanner sound like the two boys in Arras.'

Willie turned quickly, making a hushing sound. But David was still back in the stern, still steering, but with Kari crouched beside him sipping coffee from a Thermos top.

'Sorry, old boy,' Willie said. Then softly: 'So which one killed Martin?'

'In law, both of them are equally guilty.'

'Can you prove it against either of them?'

'I hadn't much thought about that, not yet.'

He breathed smoke and it whipped away ahead of him—though we were leaning on the cabin roof facing forwards. The wind was behind us, and coming down the funnel of the fjord it worked itself up into a real cold temper.

Willie said: 'So you mean, if it was Tanner and Kavanagh from the beginning, it was Smith-Bang from the beginning. She'd hired them to handle the blackmail and all—what?'

'Something like that.'

'If they killed Steen—just so he couldn't talk to you,' he said carefully, 'then why did they wait so long?'

'I'd guess——' Did the engine miss a beat, there? I glanced at Willie and he seemed to have sensed something, too. But now it was running smoothly enough. I went on: 'I'd guess

247

because Smith-Bang didn't know he was involved, that *he'd* found the log, until after Martin was dead. Somebody burgled the London flat, you know, soon after Arras.'

'How do *you* know?'

'I burgled it myself—or rather, David lent me a key.'

'Did you, by God?' A little more shocked than I'd expected. 'I don't suppose you reported that to the police, either? The amount you *don't* tell the police forces of various countries would fill a whole book of reports, what? You were saying . . . ?'

'Again I'm guessing, but the logbook must have had a covering letter, and Fenwick probably filed it in his flat. It wasn't there when I looked. So they'd know Steen was the middleman—but it would still take time to arrange his death. You don't buy a killing off a stall in the Portobello Road–or the Bergen fish-market.

'Anyway, Smith-Bang already had killers on hire in London, so it was the economical thing to bring one of them over. By then I was going as well—dammit, I even *told* Tanner that I was going—so they worked it to blackmail me as a bonus.'

This time the diesel definitely stuttered. Willie said: 'I hope that damn thing isn't going to . . .' and he went on glaring at it—through a layer of tarpaulin, a layer of wood and in midnight darkness anyhow.

Then: 'I still can't accept the idea of Ellie Smith-Bang hiring killers to . . . to . . .'

'To save the ADP Line and keep herself out of the poor-house? For a half-million insurance claim? People put their wives through the meat-mincer just for having a quick poke from the milkman which didn't cost them a penny. Probably got them cheap milk, if they'd sat down to work out the economics of it.'

He glowered at the cabin top. 'Well, perhaps you're right . . . so now we're sure it's a business between her and . . . and *us*, at *Lloyd's*?' There was shock in his voice.

I said: 'She was blackmailing her own insurer. Not the Sahara Line or anybody.'

'But what about what? Something in that log?'

'That's what I'm asking Nygaard tomorrow. That's why we've got him, whatever we told Kari.'

The diesel stopped.

The black blank cliffs echoed back tut-tut-tut, beats of a heart that had died already. The water slapped gently against us as we slowed, each tiny sound getting louder and louder in the vast dark silence that seemed to expand around us.

David creaked the tiller, coughed politely, and whispered: 'I haven't touched the throttle.'

Beside him, Kari stood up. 'We have enough fuel, I know.' Her torch came on and she waggled it over the instrument board. 'But yes.'

David said: 'Was it anything I did?'

'God, no,' Willie said. 'Diesels either go or don't, what? Now all we have to do is find out why not.' He pulled off the tarpaulin and then the wooden lid, and flashed the torch down inside.

Over his shoulder, all I could see was a dark, crusted green-brown engine with a lot of thin metal pipes poking into it. Willie poked the starter button and there was a chuffle-chuffle-chuffle but nothing more.

'What d'you think it is?' David asked.

Willie grunted: 'Probably fuel trouble. It usually is.' Chuffle-chuffle-chuffle on the starter.

'Injector pump?' I suggested, remembering the *Skadi*'s log.

He looked up quickly. 'My God, I hope not. If it is . . .' Chuffle-chuffle-chuffle. Only not quite as strong now.

I said: 'Should we switch off the light to save the batteries?'

Willie said: 'Oh, I don't think we need——'

The cabin door banged open and Nygaard crawled out like a bear from hibernation. 'Why engine stop?'

Five minutes later, the three of them were deep in the open engine, talking in grunts and mumbles, their faces shining in the light from a torch propped on the cabin top. Kari and I sat back beside the useless tiller, finishing off the sandwiches, and talking in whispers.

'Why did he wake up?' she asked.

'The engine stopping, I suppose. He's so used to being on a ship with the engines turning that the silence automatically wakes him.' And when I thought about it, a man who'd gone to sea at sixteen and retired at sixty could have spent more than half of his whole life sleeping to the sound of engines.

I glanced over the side at the black water. 'Are we going to run aground?'

'I think not yet.' We were about two hundred yards from the nearest cliff.

'We couldn't put down an anchor?'

'It is perhaps two hundred metres deep, here.'

I instinctively pulled back into the boat, with the sudden vertigo of a man sitting atop a black glass column. A quick shudder went from my shoulders to my knees. 'I see what you mean.'

The longest piece of rope or chain in the boat wasn't over fifty feet.

She said softly: 'He is a good boy, David. He tells me about his father being killed. I did not know about that. I see why you must ask Herr Nygaard questions, but . . .'

'I'll be as gentle as I can.' Or make sure she was out of the way first.

Then Nygaard stood upright with a grunt of triumph, holding up something like the Devil's heart: spongy, black and dripping. He dumped it overside and crawled into the cabin again.

'What on earth was that?' I asked Willie.

'The paper fuel filter. Blocked solid. He's seeing if there's a spare. If not . . .' He looked up and down the fjord.

Not a light showed anywhere, not the dim scratch of a road or the outline of a building. We could be a thousand miles or a million years from anything else man-made. 'If not, it'll be a long cold night.'

Then Nygaard crawled out again, waving something pale, so maybe it wouldn't be so long and cold—though it hadn't been short or warm so far. A few minutes afterwards, the filter was back in place, and he motioned Willie to press on the

250

starter. The chuffle-chuffle-chuffle was definitely slow and reluctant.

Nygaard called: 'Stop!' and bent to go on reassembling the engine. Just pulling fuel through the pipe up to the filter itself, I suppose. But it was only a few more minutes when he stood up and wiped his hands with a definite There-you-are motion. Willie set the throttle.

Chuffle-chuffle . . . chuffle . . .

Now it was the sound of the king breathing his last in one of those television epics.

Chuff . . . le . . . chufff. . . . The king is dead, long live the king.

'Stop!' Nygaard ordered.

'Anybody for a long cold night?' I muttered. 'Told you we should have switched off that damn light.'

Nygaard was asking Willie something; Kari went forward to help out. I caught the word 'ether', I think, and definitely 'whisky'. Oh hell; the old boy's asking for his reward, now. I stood up and joined in.

Kari explained, sounding puzzled: 'He wants some whisky for the engine—but we must do it. He does not want to see.'

Willie and I stared at each other, then David. I said: 'Okay. Try anything. Get out the whisky, Willie.'

He unwrapped the carefully hidden bottle and Nygaard crawled away into the cabin. Kari hauled the Primus stove out on to the deck, lit it, and started heating a cupful of whisky in a pan.

David asked quietly: 'Why doesn't he want to see?'

'He's scared stiff of naked flame—since the *Skadi* burned.'

The whisky hissed and bubbled. Willie took off the big round air filter, Kari sloshed hot Scotch into the inlet manifold, and Willie snapped his lighter at it. Blue-yellow flames flared up.

Willie said: 'God damn!' in a slightly charred tone, and stabbed the starter.

Chuff . . . Chuffff—the flames were sucked inside and the engine blasted to life.

Kari took the tiller while Willie and David put the engine

covers back on again. When Willie turned around, he was still shaking his head. 'I thought I knew something about diesels, but that . . . I suppose a chief engineer *ought* to know his stuff, still . . .' He stuck his burnt hand into his mouth and sucked.

David said wonderingly: 'But do you really think he was drunk while he was doing all that?'

'He seemed normal enough, didn't he?'

'Well, yes. That's what I mean.'

'So he must be drunk. If I had as much alcohol in me as he has, I'd be unconscious. You'd be dead.'

After a few moments, he said: 'But you think of drunks as being, well, happy and wild, or just sick.'

'They're amateurs. He's the real pro.'

After another few minutes, he said: 'There was one funny thing. He hasn't asked what he's doing on this boat at all, has he? He just sort of . . . accepted it.'

'He's ashamed to ask; he assumes he's already been told and he's forgotten. That happens, too.'

He made a small shivery noise that wasn't entirely from the cold.

FORTY-ONE

I'D TOLD WILLIE to hire a Volkswagen as being nice and inconspicuous, but things aren't that easy with him; I should have guessed from that dolled-up Mini. This was the Volks 1600 fastback version, and a nice bright orange to contrast with the pale pastel cars the rest of Norway drives. But at least nobody had stolen it.

The drive itself took just under an hour and we had the road all to ourselves—not that there was much room for a second car most of the time. Beyond the head of the fjord it ran fast and straight for about five miles of scattered farms and houses, then suddenly into a narrow gorge and a hundred yards of tunnel through the rock that leaked water like a thunderstorm. The clatter on the roof almost woke the back seat brigade: Kari, David and Nygaard all jammed together and all asleep after the first mile.

Beyond that, we reached the snow line. First just patches of it on the slope beside us, glowing briefly in the headlights, the places where we were driving between small walls of it, and finally, beyond the last crossroads and a handful of houses that felt important enough to call itself Byrkjedal, the road itself was rutted snow and ice, weaving uphill beside a slope that was solid white except where it was too steep for the snow to cling.

The other side was a river except where it broadened into narrow black lakes, with an eighteen-inch wall doing its best to keep us on the road. The ragged gaps every few hundred yards gave me the idea its best wasn't always good enough.

Willie asked: 'How far to go now?'

I flashed a torch on the map. 'Ten kilometres, about. I'll wake Kari in a minute.'

'No rush. Light me another cigarette, would you?'

I took his packet, lit one, passed it over. He was driving with solid concentration, mostly third gear work but never letting the engine get away from him.

'You never smoked yourself?' he asked.

'Tried it as a boy, of course. But once I was in I Corps it didn't seem a good thing. An interrogator shouldn't have habits that give away his own mental state. He should try, anyway.'

He gave me a snap glance and smiled. 'The complete professional, what?' And then, more thoughtfully: 'But how did you get into this bodyguarding business, what?'

'When I was with NATO Intelligence, they asked me to form a small section. I was already interested in pistols and stuff then, so . . .'

'Did the Russians really try assassinations, then?'

'Russians be damned, the worst times we had was when some clever German general wanted to go and revisit the scene of his 1940 triumphs in France or Holland. In uniform, of course. Those lads really needed protection.'

He chuckled gently to himself, and after a time said: 'I thought the old boy did rather well in the boat, tonight.'

'Was it difficult, that stuff with the engine?'

'No, not really. But how quickly he decided it was the filter, the way he took it down and put it together, you know. Then that trick with the whisky. . . .'

'I'm glad he knows two tricks with whisky.'

'Ye-es. . . . But I never realized he was quite that scared of fire.'

'I suppose it's natural—if you've seen your ship and most of its crew burnt up. And he's not kidding; he nearly went through the ceiling when he thought *I* was going to light a cigarette, once.'

'God, I must remember that.' He looked anxiously in the mirror.

'Don't worry, he's asleep.'

'The smell doesn't bother him?'

'Doesn't seem to. But even your cigarettes don't smell like methane and burnt flesh.'

'Thanks, old boy. Better wake Kari now, if you can.'

It wasn't a village: the cabins were too standardized, too scattered, for that. More like a formalized gold-rush camp, each cabin standing on its own little claim across the shallow bowl in the hillside. Between them, the snowy ground was broken with boulders and small gulleys, bridged with single planks. Not a light showed anywhere.

Willie pulled carefully off the road, skidded through a small snowdrift and stopped just before a gulley. In the abrupt silence, you could hear the distant whispering roar of a waterfall that fell almost vertically down the slope across the river, glowing to itself in the starlight.

'Which cabin?' Willie asked.

She pointed to one about thirty yards up the slope, solidly roofed with snow and nicely decorated with icicles. A thick pile of snowed-up logs sat by the steps up to the door.

The three of us got out and started organizing, leaving David and Nygaard asleep for the moment. We certainly weren't the first up there this year: the snow was rutted and flattened in places, and some of the snow on the roofs was melted around the chimney pots.

'They come at the weekend to ski,' Kari explained.

'Ski?' Willie said, shocked. 'Here?'

I knew what he meant, although I didn't know anything else about ski-ing. The place looked like a piece of the moon: any slope less than vertical was spotted with boulders the size of tables.

'This is not Switzerland,' Kari said coldly. 'To ski we do not need a mountain four thousand metres high and a cocktail bar at the top.'

Willie grinned and started unpacking the car.

The cabin itself was a bit over twenty feet long by maybe fifteen wide, split in two crossways and then one half split again; you ended up with one big room—well, say eleven by fifteen—and two small bedrooms. The furniture was a table, some wooden chairs and benches, a few cupboards and a big old stove slap in the middle, backing on to the dividing wall so that the bedrooms might get a bit of heat as well. Might. Right now, the place was as cold as a penguin's tombstone.

'Welcome to the Arctic Hilton,' Willie said, and dumped an armful of sleeping bags and blankets on a bench. Kari lit a hurricane lamp, then started working on the stove.

Five minutes later, by the time we'd hauled the rest of everything and everybody inside, the stove was crackling and spitting from the ice melting down inside the chimney, the hurricane lamp was hissing gently to itself, and the place was smelling of wood-smoke, paraffin—and even warmth. Nygaard had gone slap off to sleep on the bench, not noticing the stove.

Kari dragged a Primus from under the table and asked unhopefully: 'Do you want a hot drink, now?'

'No thanks,' Willie said quickly. 'I'll have whisky—now I've stopped driving.' The Norwegian law on that had come as a bit of a shock to him; I wondered if he yet knew he wasn't supposed to smoke while driving through towns. Well, that couldn't be *too* serious.

255

Kari looked at David, but he just smiled sleepily and shook his head. So she pushed the Primus back again. 'I think if we stay, we will use the other rooms also. But perhaps tonight, for warmth, we should all sleep here?' She glanced anxiously at Willie, to see if she'd offended the Code of the Winslows.

He smiled and said: 'Fine, fine,' and poured me a Scotch in an enamel mug. 'Well, cheers.'

'Cheers. You'd better hide that stuff before tomorrow.'

'Oh Lord, yes. Outside, I suppose? Whisky isn't supposed to freeze, is it?' He looked at Nygaard. 'I suppose we'd better get him to bed, too.'

It took three of us five minutes to get his shoes and overcoat off, and cram him into the sleeping-bag and zip it up. By then, David was in his own bag and asleep again. The girl went outside, presumably for a private leak.

Willie looked thoughtfully down at Nygaard and whispered: 'It *is* going to be cosy in here, what? I mean, he does rather smell like a dead horse.'

'Shut your nose and think of England. And if the cabin burns down, don't wake me till it's too late.' I wrapped myself firmly in three blankets, spread my sheepskin over my feet and shut my eyes tight. A few minutes later, the lamp went out.

FORTY-TWO

IT WAS NINE O'CLOCK in the morning when I finally decided to admit I was awake and sit up. I wasn't too sure I'd ever been to sleep, except that I'd remembered waking up twice before: once when Kari got up to fill the stove again, and once when Nygaard's snoring almost unwrapped me from my blankets. And I remembered the stove glowing a dusky red and thinking of that first winter in the Army up at Catterick. . . .

Kari, Willie and David were already sitting at the table sipping coffee; Nygaard still down and out. I unwound myself, stood up, stretched and took the cup Kari poured for me. Nobody said anything, though for a moment David looked as if he was about to.

256

The room had two small, dirty windows, and the day beyond them was thick and cloudy, the mountainside opposite fading into cloud a couple of hundred feet higher.

Kari said: 'It may snow, I think.'

Well, that would probably be warmer than a clear sky.

David asked brightly: 'D'you think we'll be snowed up here, then?'

Willie looked at him sourly, and lit a cigarette.

Kari said: 'They will clear the road right through up to Sinnes in a day or two. For the Easter skiers. Would you like some eggs?'

Willie said: 'Of course he'd like some eggs. What's a little frying to an atmosphere like this?'

'Stub out that mentholated bird-shit special and say that again. No thank you, but I'll take a bit of bread and cheese.'

David's quiet dark eyes flicked from one to the other of us, an oddly wondering expression on his face.

Kari said sharply: 'You men must behave, please. Now: what happens?'

I said: 'Willie runs you down to pick up the boat and give it back. That's what you said, wasn't it?'

She nodded. 'Ja. The boat must be back for midday.'

Willie sighed and stood up. 'Well, I suppose it'll be a change of air, anyway. Are you coming, David?'

David looked at me. I said: 'There's nothing happening here. You may as well take the ride.'

Kari was looking down at Nygaard. He wriggled restlessly in the sleeping-bag. 'Shall I—should I wake him, now?'

'Go ahead,' I said. 'I'll walk Willie down to his carriage.'

Willie looked at me suspiciously, but he put on his coat and led the way out.

And it *was* a change of air. Even the damp dull day smelled as fresh as tomorrow's daisies after that cabin.

When we reached the car, he turned and said: 'Well?'

'I'm glad I'm not married to you at this time in the morning.'

He glared, then grinned. 'Sorry, old boy. Getting soft, I suppose. Used to be able to get a dreamless eight hours under an armoured car in the rain, but now . . . What was it you wanted?'

'A short comprehensive lecture on marine diesel engines.'

Kari came down to the car a quarter of an hour later, glancing nervously over her shoulder. And not at David, who was just behind.

'He asked for a drink,' she said anxiously.

'It'll pass,' I soothed her. Which might even be true, for an hour or two.

'You won't let him have one?'

'I promise.' And that was certainly true.

I watched them off down the road now turning sludgy as the temperature crawled above freezing, then turned back slowly—almost reluctantly—for the cabin.

Nygaard was huddled at the table, a blanket slung around his shoulders, both hands locked on a mug of coffee that still trembled and slopped whenever he moved it. He watched me with eyes like small bullet wounds as I made myself a fresh cup, then sat down opposite him.

I said: 'My name's James Card.'

'I remember.' Probably that was true, though you hate to admit anybody could forget you anyway. But I just nodded, sipped, and waited.

We stayed there, quiet as two London clubmen, for a good fifteen minutes. Then he put down his mug, almost empty. I said: 'More?' and poured him some. We went on waiting. His hands actually were steadying up a bit.

Then I said: 'You did a good job on that diesel last night.'

He looked up vacantly but nodded, pretending he remembered.

I said: 'What's the best diesels you've handled?'

'Almost only the Burmeister and Wain. Most ships in Norway have them.'

'Two-stroke?'

'Ja, now. No more four-stroke, not much.'

'Single or double-acting?'

258

'For me, the single only.'

'You mean in the *Skadi*?'

'Ja, there. Two Burmeister and Wains.' The ship's name had gone past without a tremor.

'Good ones?'

'Very old, you understand? The engineer before, he had ground the—valves, so much . . .' he shrugged.

'You had a lot of trouble?'

'With everything, ja. With always the injector valves—and the cooling pumps, and the fuel filter also.'

I nodded sympathetically. 'What happened the last time? Cooling pump? Injectors?'

He got a look of cunning suspicion on his flabby face. 'Why you ask?'

'Sorry.' I sipped my coffee and didn't look at him.

More time went past.

Then he said: 'We had much trouble, then.'

'Like what?'

'The engine stop.'

'Why?'

He put his coffee mug down, though he still kept his hands on it. 'For beginning, we think perhaps an exhaust valve, it is with a broken spring.'

'Would that stop an engine?'

'At very slow, ja. Or very fast, it jam all the engine, crack-bang.'

'But it wasn't an exhaust valve?'

'No, we find no. So we think the fuel filter.'

'De Laval type?—centrifugal?'

'Ja, ja.' He looked a little worried.

'Was it that?'

'No. So maybe we think the . . . the injector pump.'

'And was it?'

'Ja, but very difficult. You understand?—the pump gives the fuel to each injector, just so much, like the . . . the . . .' he made a move like a hypodermic in his arm. I nodded. He went on: 'To each cylinder, in turn. But it must be just so much fuel, just right, like the . . .' the hypodermic syringe gesture again.

259

Now he was really talking, and I sat back and listened. Some I didn't understand, some I got just because of what Willie had told me, but broadly I got a picture of a high-pressure pump that was a lot of hypodermic syringes squirted in succession by a camshaft, putting exactly the right amount of juice into each cylinder at exactly the right time. . . . And the camshaft bearings had gone wonky so the pressure on the syringes varied so the cylinders got variable and unequal amounts of juice. . . .

I asked: 'Was this repairable?'

He looked blank for a moment. Then: 'Oh, ja, ja. We were working on it.'

'How far had you got at the time of the collision?'

Now he looked cautious. 'Perhaps almost finished. . . .'

'You'd had nearly forty-eight hours.'

'Ja, but . . .'

'Like some more coffee?' I tried to defuse him.

'Thank you, no.' He licked his lips, then rubbed them with the great stiff scar that was the back of his hand. 'It is time for another drink—ja?'

How such a face could look so plaintively hopeful.

I pretended surprise, looking at my watch. 'Not just yet, surely?'

'Ja, ja, sorry.' He acquiesced immediately. Of *course* he didn't want a drink, he'd only been suggesting it because he thought maybe I wanted one and had been too shy to suggest it. . . .

You bastard, Card.

'How did you get rescued from the *Skadi*?' I asked casually.

'Why do you want to know?'

'Sorry.' I poured myself the last of the coffee and didn't look at him as I drank it.

He said: 'On the . . . the Carley float. Raft.' He'd know the name from the war days, of course.

'Who cut it loose. You?'

'No, the other sailors I think. I . . . my hands . . .' He held up his crumpled claws. 'I just jump in the sea and swim and on to raft.'

'Alone on it?'

'Oh, ja.'

'Did you paddle it?'

'No, My hands.'

'Sorry. So what happened?'

He heaved his shoulders. 'I am picked up.'

'And that's all you remember?'

'Ja.'

'Why is that all you remember?'

He shivered his flabby face. 'I don't know. . . .'

'Drunk all the time, were you?'

'No,' he said. 'No. No. *No!*' Then he threw the coffee-pot at me.

'It wasn't so bright of me to let him get to that state,' I told Willie, 'though you can't really measure what any addict's feeling.'

'I thought getting him into a state was part of what you were up to,' he said coolly.

They'd got back about half past one. Now Kari and David were working up some lunch while Willie and I strolled the road and threw stones into the galloping black-and-white river below the crumbled parapet. For the moment, it was fairly warm. The road itself was turning sticky, and some patches of spongy grass were appearing among the snowdrifts.

'Have you concluded anything yet?' Willie went on.

'Maybe. His description of the engine breakdown was pretty detailed, but he doesn't really remember anything of the rescue at all. Now, according to the log——'

'Which we don't have any more,' he reminded me, just missing the river with a grenade-sized stone.

'Thank you. But according to it and the clever work you did with the atlas and so forth, that engine must have been out of action until *nearly* the collision even if it actually was working again when they hit—right?'

'Er, yes. That's right.'

'For the moment it doesn't matter if they ever got it fixed or not. The point is that thing was out of action for about *forty*

261

hours, while he mucks about thinking first it's the exhaust valve and then the fuel filter and finally the injector pump camshaft. We saw him in action last night; what took him so long aboard the *Skadi* with an engine he knew far better?'

He heaved a rock and got a weird brownish splash; maybe the river was full of gold dust. 'What do you suggest?' he asked.

'Look at who survived. Nobody else from the engine room, nobody who was on the bridge. Just three sailors who were off watch and probably asleep in cabins—and Nygaard.'

'So you think . . . ?'

'I think all the stuff he gave me about the breakdown comes from some other time; he doesn't remember the last one at all any more than he remembers the rescue. He was blind paralytic drunk the entire time, stretched out on his bunk. That's why it was taking them so long to fix the engine. And why they died and he survived. And what does a boozed-up chief engineer do to a Lloyd's insurance policy?'

'Nothing, I'm afraid,' he said sadly, and threw another stone.

'*Nothing?*'

'Afraid not, old boy. I mean, it wouldn't matter if the *captain* was smashed out of his mind. I dare say it would make a difference to who was held to blame and all that, but it wouldn't invalidate the insurance. You've got to remember that one of the biggest things an owner's insuring against is the damn stupidity of the crew—you know? "Negligence of Master Officers Crew or Pilots", that's how the Lloyd's policy puts it. Suppose it goes back to the days when you recruited your crew out of the dockside pubs half an hour before sailing. But as long as they're on board, they don't have to be sober or even awake.'

Then he added politely: 'You seem to have had a lot of trouble for nothing, what?'

'Damn it.' I slung a stone across the river and it crunched into a deep, crusted snowbank. 'Damn it, there's got to be *something*.'

'I thought Kari said Nygaard hadn't really started drinking until *after* the accident. Rather because of it, you know?'

'She didn't know him, before. And you don't get to his stage in months; he's been boozing at top speed for years. Maybe since his wife died,' I said, thinking of it suddenly.

For a while we just threw stones silently. Then Willie said: 'I say—how did Paul Mockby get involved in all this?'

'I think because he was scared that the Sahara Line *might* have been behind it all. If the other directors had started the blackmailing and all, they wouldn't have told him anyway, would they?—conflict of interests. He just wanted to get hold of that log to see what it *did* prove; then he'd know where he stood—he hoped.'

'So you still think he was lying to us, that night?'

'Yes. Fenwick didn't tell him anything about what the log proved.'

'Ah.' He sounded relieved. 'Didn't sound like Martin to tell just one of us, you know.'

'But just because a man tells you lies, you shouldn't jump to the conclusion that he knows the truth. Useful rule of interrogation.'

'Ah yes. Are you going to . . . go on interrogating?'

'Yes. I want you to take the girl out shopping this afternoon. Just down to the crossroads to buy a tin of beans or something, but out. He's going to get worse.'

He frowned thoughtfully. 'It's not going to bring Martin back to life . . . and Nygaard's a . . . a person, as well.'

'Dammit, I know. But he knows *something* about the collision. Something he told Steen or Steen guessed, from him and that log.'

'But I'm not sure it matters, does it, old boy? As Paul said, it's only forty thousand against us, a small piece of the year's business. He was telling the truth there.'

I stared at him. 'Hell's teeth, Willie, we've come so far——'

'Speaking as Light Cavalry, that always struck me as a jolly good reason to turn back.'

IT WAS A QUIET LUNCH, and without Nygaard; he'd wrapped himself in the sleeping-bag and retired to a bedroom. Not hungry. The rest of us ate tinned fish soup and scrambled eggs and biscuits and cheese, and I hurt Willie's feelings by taking a shot of his whisky. He was getting pretty tired of his job as a teetotal chauffeur.

'I mean, just *one* whisky,' he grumbled. 'In Britain that wouldn't make the slightest difference, I could drive all over the country, through any traffic. And that road out there isn't exactly liable to be swarming with police, is it?'

Then he caught the horrified expression on Kari's face. 'Do you really feel you *must* have a drink?'

His turn to look horrified. 'Good God, no. It's just that, about lunch time, well, it's my habit to have one, you know?'

'The habit is how it begins.' And she gave me a brisk, cool look.

I shrugged. 'I just hope I live long enough to die of drink.'

She started clearing away with a fair amount of unnecessary clattering.

I went outside to see them off; David had decided to stay with me. As he climbed into the car, Willie looked back at the cabin and asked: 'D'you think anybody'll be looking for us?'

I looked back for myself. I suppose if you knew, for sure, we were in one cabin, you could pick out which: there was a slight bare patch in the snow around the chimney pipe, and an occasional whisp of smoke from the top. But not much more; the ground was too rough, the snow too old and trampled already for our footprints to show any patterns.

I said: 'I hope they'll think it's hopeless. We could be anywhere in Stavanger—or anywhere out of it, by now. And we didn't tell the hotel where we'd be.'

'We didn't book out, either,' Willie reminded me.

'No.' We'd need the rooms again—and anyway, we had to have somewhere to leave most of our luggage. The Volkswagen couldn't have taken all that and the sleeping-bags and all.

'Well,' Willie said firmly, 'we'll be finished by this evening.

We'll go down the hill then.' He caught my eye and stared unblinking. And that was that.

I shrugged. Well, I'd got a few hours left. The Volkswagen crawled on to the road and buzzed off down it.

I'd just turned back to the cabin when David burst out of it. 'Mr Card! Mr Card!'

I ran. He pointed inside, white-faced, and I jumped the steps and crashed through the door.

Nygaard was standing at the table, holding the paraffin lamp in one shaking hand and a mug in the other. . . .

I ripped the lamp away and the mug scattered the fuel across the room. 'For Christ's sake! You can't drink that stuff!'

Couldn't he, though. The little eyes were hot coals of hatred. The mug fell from one twisted claw and then he rammed both hands on the table to try to stop the shaking that was rattling his whole body like a bumpy road.

'I want a drink,' he pleaded.

'Let's get back in there.' I could feel David behind us, guess at his sick, horrified expression. I took Nygaard's arm and led him through into the tiny bedroom. He slumped on the edge of the folding metal bed.

'I want to go home to Gulbrandsens,' he moaned.

'Not Rasmussen's?'

'Who is Rasmussen?' His body suddenly clenched with a shuddering spasm.

'Do you know where you are?'

'By Bergen, of course.'

And Mrs Smith-Bang was going into court with *his* memory to help prove that logbook?

Gradually the spasm passed; his shoulders sagged wearily and he panted heavily. Watching him carefully, I opened the door again and called to David: 'Can you make us some coffee or something?'

He could. I came back and leaned against the wall by the window. 'Where was the engine-room in the *Skadi*? Right aft? —or amidships?'

'Amidships.' Between shivering teeth.

'How did you get in and out? Stairs or a ladder?'

'There is both The stairs to inside—where the cabins are. The ladder to the hatch on the deck.'

'Which did you usually use?'

'The stairs. But in summer, the good weather, we open the hatch also.'

'Where was the hatch? Ahead of the bridge or aft of it?'

'In front.'

I didn't have to ask how the other engineers had died. Fire flooding—just that—in from the bows, sweeping the deck, cracking the hatch, sucked down inside into the lungs of the ship by that hungry-breathing diesel. Or diesels.

I didn't *have* to ask how they died, down there. But I asked anyway.

He looked up quickly, shook his head, gave another brief shudder.

'What happened?' I said again.

'Just—the fire.' He flapped his crumpled hands in a downwards motion.

'When did your hands get burned?'

He stared at the floor. 'On the ladder . . . I reach up . . . ah!'

'On the *ladder*?'

'No, I mean the stair. I open the door at the top . . .'

'You'd better remember which when it comes to court.' But I already knew he'd been in his cabin at the time, anyway.

Then David knocked, and came in carrying two mugs of coffee. He looked pale and tense.

'Thanks.' I took both, put one on the floor beside Nygaard's feet.

David said: 'I think, sir . . . I think I'd like to go for a walk.'

I didn't blame him. 'Okay. But keep off the road and if you hear a car, any car, get under cover. All right?'

'Yes, sir.' He gave me one quick glance, and went out.

After a minute or two, Nygaard bent down with a grunt, picked up the mug, slopped a lot of it out, but drank the rest.

I said: 'Did you know we'd found the log, the deck log?'

266

'Ja?' Question or answer?—or a man who can't remember whether he remembers or not.

I took the copies from my jacket pocket. 'Do you remember when Steen came to see you? Man called Jonas Steen?'

He looked up with a flabby sneer, then leaned over and patted his backside. 'You call him man? I think in England you say fairy mostly.'

I frowned. Nygaard went on leering. 'You like him?'

'Shut up.' So how could I tell?—I'd only met him dead. Women say to you: 'But I thought men could *always* tell,' just like I can always tell they're not cheating on me and who's going to win the Third World War.

Wait a moment. 'How do *you* know?' Steen might have been Tinkerbell Mark One, but he'd never have waggled at this broken-down old barrel.

'Everybody know.' He threw the question away with a flap of his right claw.

'And hadn't Mrs Smith-Bang asked if I'd met this man alive?—before she'd had him killed.

So now I knew what was in Henrik Lie's suicide note. A 'personal affair,' wasn't it? That's what that bastard Inspector (First Class) Vik had been hiding; an unrequited-love story. Had Lie really been homosexual as well, or had Kavanagh invented it for the occasion?

Never mind. I said: 'It doesn't matter what Steen was. But who's H and Thornton.'

'I do not——'

'Oh yes you do, mate. Who are they?'

'No.'

I took a box of Kari's matches out of my pocket and shook it once and laid it down. He stared at it as if it was a tarantula. Probably he'd have preferred the spider.

I said: 'Well?'

'Hucks and Thornton,' he said hoarsely.

'Good. And who are *they*?'

'I . . . they . . .' his eyes were still on the matchbox. I picked it up, slowly, very slowly, and pressed it gently open . . . and he watched all the time. Sweat flooded his face.

Then I said: 'Oh bugger it. No.' And I pulled open the door and threw the matchbox the length of the main room.

A car rushed past. Not a Volkswagen, but I was too late at the window to catch it on the only piece of road I could see. But going uphill, fairly fast.

Wasn't the road blocked, above here?

By the time I was out of the door and with a view of the full stretch of road, it was out of sight. I ran back and emptied half a bucket of water into the stove—and nearly blew the cabin down. For a moment, smoke and steam filled the room and the hot metal fizzed like a snakepit. But it faded quickly. There'd be no sign of life when the car came back.

But it didn't come back. Not right away and then not just after that and . . .

. . . and David?

I'd told him to stay off the road and out of sight. He could hear a car as well as I could; I'd just be giving away my own position by stepping out and yelling at him.

I moved from one window to another and to the front door, open a crack and bleeding cold air in on us. Behind me, Nygaard said: 'Please shut the door.' I didn't.

Then a figure moved across a gap between two cabins, up the road. A figure like—no, I didn't know what it was like. Not just on one glimpse. But the next time it moved, it was Trond. You can't make a mistake about that frog shape, not twice.

Nygaard said: 'What is happening? It smells burning.'

'I doused the fire. Now shut *up*.'

Trond was moving from cabin to cabin, checking each one and pretending he was an infantryman under fire but forgetting an infantryman has a firm sense of direction. Wrong, maybe, but firm.

Trond was hiding from our direction for one moment, then running up and planting his backside to me, peek-a-booing around a corner back the way he'd come.

When he was within thirty yards, I took out the derringer and cocked it. He checked one last cabin and started for our one. I let him come to fifteen yards . . . ten—and he stopped. He'd seen the door wasn't quite closed.

I opened it and stepped out, holding the gun pointed. I wasn't going to shoot at that range, but I wanted him to decide whether he came any closer.

'Hello, Trond.'

The wide fleshy face creased into a grin and he stepped forward. Then two shots sounded, back up the valley, and he stopped, head cocked. A distant voice shouted: 'Trond!'

Then he scuttled away around a cabin and out of sight. I waited. Nothing. I dropped down the steps, derringer in hand —and the car rushed past down the road. A white Cortina, old model, that could be the one we'd seen in Rasmussen's drive, or maybe not.

I shouted: 'David?' The far slope bounced back a sloppy echo. But I was still prowling and shouting when Willie and Kari got back, half an hour afterwards.

FORTY-FOUR

HE BOUNCED OUT of the Volkswagen almost before it had stopped, screaming: 'You bloody idiot! They've got David!'

I just nodded. By then I was sitting perched on the parapet at the side of the road and feeling rather tired, plus other things.

'How do you know?' I asked dully.

'They stopped us on the road!' Kari was out now, staring white-faced at me.

Willie went on: 'I *saw* him!'

'And who else?'

'What does that . . . ? Well, there were three of them, men. Two British, I think. The other was Trond.'

'One of them with a bandage on his hand?'

'I didn't see. They said——'

'White Cortina, was it?'

'Yes. Do you want to know what they said?'

'I can guess, but go on.'

'They'll swap him for Nygaard.'

Kari said: 'We cannot do this.'

I said: 'I guessed that, too. Why not?'

'He is a person! Not a slave! You do not give him away—even for a English schoolboy.'

I looked at Willie. 'Did they say when and where?'

'At the crossroads at Byrkjedal, at four.' He looked at his watch. 'Fifty minutes.'

'So there's no rush.' I looked at Kari. 'Nygaard's not in any danger, you know. He's still a key witness in a big case. Once we're down the hill, we can report him to the police and have them pick him up as an alcoholic. Get him properly committed to somewhere. We can do that, too, under Norwegian law. No problem. Now start packing him up.'

I led the way confidently towards the cabin. That's what Majors are for, isn't it?—to show confidence?

Ten minutes later we were all packed—well, the Volkswagen was—and three of us standing around sipping a last cup of coffee while Nygaard sat in his uniform greatcoat on the bench and shivered at other things beside the cold.

Willie murmured: 'Did you solve the mystery of the *Marie Celeste*?'

'No. I missed it. But it's there. In him and in the log.'

'What'll they—I mean Ellie Smith-Bang—what will she do to him?'

'Why anything? She seems happy with him as he is.'

Nygaard got slowly to his feet, so slowly I didn't notice until he was nearly upright, his eyes fixed on the door. He let out a low, horrified moan.

My coffee mug spun away and the derringer was aimed—but not at the devils he could see. . .38 Specials aren't enough for them. I slipped the gun back into its clip.

He was still watching the door—or whatever had walked through it. He began a gentle, gradual, horrible scream. . . .

Now I'd got him. Now he'd tell me any damn thing he knew, or could fake or could remember—and I'd know the difference.

He'd put his naked soul on the counter and I could buy it for a half glass of whisky—as long as I didn't pay.

I looked at Willie. Then Kari. 'Give him a drink.'

'But no!' She was horrified.

'Why not? He'll get worse from now on—and it's the first thing *they'll* give him, down the hill.'

She said pitifully: 'But weren't you curing him?'

'No. Just starving him. So that he'd tell me something. It doesn't matter now—does it?' I looked back at Willie. 'Only forty thousand, that and three men's lives so far.' Back to Kari. 'A real cure is something else. And it'll only work if he wants it to, if he's got a reason for it to. Find that and you'll find the cure. Maybe. But meantime give him a drink.'

She said: 'You are very cruel, I think.' But she went outside to dig up the whisky and brought it back and slammed it into my hands.

He hadn't noticed any of it.

I sloshed some into a mug and gave it to him. He took a gulp, choked and splattered, gasped and gulped again. The second shot went down easier. In half a minute he took on nearly a quarter bottle and was sitting happily at the table sipping the next quarter as politely as any Paris boulevardier.

I said to Willie: 'That's it, then. Come outside, I want to talk to you.'

He frowned, but came.

The sky still began a bare two hundred feet higher, and now a few grains of snow were toppling down in the wind. Instinctively, we began a parade-ground circuit of the cabin.

I said: 'Simple yes-or-no answer: was Martin Fenwick a homosexual?'

'Oh really, old boy. . . .' All the woolly speech mannerisms were suddenly back.

'And Jonas Steen was his steady boyfriend. That was why he gave Steen the surveying jobs—and why Steen gave him the log of the *Skadi*, even sent it to his flat in London. It was probably why he *had* the flat, why his whole life pattern— Jesus, the things I didn't notice!'

271

Willie cleared his throat and wriggled a bit and said: 'Well, you know, he obviously wasn't *entirely*, if you see what I mean. . . .'

'You mean David?' There was no question but he *was* Fenwick's son, not with the amount he'd done for him. 'Christ, why do these people have to be dynastic, as well?'

But hadn't Lois used almost that word at me—when she was trying to convince me how great a lover our Martin had been and he probably hadn't touched her in years? Keeping up the image her father had seen through? Building that over-masculine study at Kingscutt? Taking me to bed?

Willie said gently: 'You can never be sure, you know. I mean, some women marry them because they're sure they can change them—you know?'

I just nodded and kicked at a snowdrop that had been stupid enough to bloom in a patch of bare turf in my path. Its head ripped off and spun into a gulley.

'And Maggie Mackwood,' I said. 'She wasn't having an affair with him any more than with the Cat in the Hat.'

'I don't think that was entirely her fault,' he said dryly.

'Maybe—but he wasn't being blackmailed about her, then. Just about his queerness. Would that have buggered him up at Lloyd's—if you'll pardon the expression?'

'Well . . . Lloyd's is pretty old-fashioned and everything rather depends on what brokers think of an underwriter. . . . Yes,' he admitted finally. 'It would have finished him.'

'But Mockby must have known?'

'Oh yes, and a few of Martin's closest friends. But you know Paul: he judges a man by his profitability, that's all. And it wasn't as if Martin dressed up and chased the young clerks— they aren't all like that, you know.'

'Of course I know; I was in the Army.'

'Yes, but in your shop you'd probably just think of him as a security risk.'

'Well, in the end he was, wasn't he? He laid the syndicate open to blackmail. Every few months you'd club together and send him off for a nice discreet dirty weekend in Bergen and write it off as "Keeping in touch with Norwegian shipping developments".' I shook my head slowly. 'Good Christ.'

He stopped and his jaw jutted. If I said the wrong thing now I was going to need a face transplant.

'You were saying?'

I shrugged. 'The same that everybody's always saying: I make a lousy detective. I've been working on Fenwick, backtracking him, trying to see what made him tick . . . and all the time it was somebody else's arse.'

He threw a right-hander, but I'd known he would before he did himself. I stepped aside and he went on one knee.

'Try that again, Willie,' I said, 'and I'll break you in places you didn't know you'd got. I haven't fought a clean fight in my life and I'm too old to start now.'

He straightened up slowly; his voice sounded a bit breathless, but fairly controlled. 'I shouldn't have expected sympathy from you, I suppose.'

'Sympathy for what? I don't understand homosexuals. Neither do you. Fenwick just seemed a nice enough bloke, and I'd guess he had a pretty good life while it lasted—thanks to certain people. Anyway, he managed without my sympathy while he was alive, so . . .' I shrugged again. 'Only—Willie— *why* didn't you tell me?'

He wiped his knee. 'Why should I have?'

'Willie, this was at the heart and guts of why he was killed. The moment you knew he'd been blackmailed you knew what about. You knew who Steen was. *Why didn't you tell me?*'

'Well, old boy,' he drawled, 'you have been rather the fearless seeker after truth—what?—but not doing much with it when you got it. I mean, you seem sort of happy enough just knowing what's happened without actually doing anything about it. All the things you don't tell the various police forces, you know. . . . Well, maybe it's the Intelligence Corps training: just finding out, not having to act on it.'

I felt cold, far colder than the wind. Somehow, we'd started walking again; we did half a circuit of the cabin in silence. Then I nodded. 'All right, but it was all over when he died. You still could have——'

'What about David?'

273

The thickening snowflakes stung my eyes. 'Of course. He wouldn't know. That's who you're protecting now.'

He nodded.

'And that means Mrs Smith-Bang can blackmail Fenwick beyond the grave. If we let her.'

He nodded again and just looked at me expressionlessly.

I said: 'David hired me to find out what happened to his father. And why.'

'I'll pay you more.'

'People like Mockby and Smith-Bang say things like that.'

He frowned thoughtfully, finally said: 'Sorry.'

I said: 'I'm not promising. Best be getting down the hill.'

As we turned, he said: 'One thing, you know—we know Ellie Smith-Bang didn't find out through Steen that Martin had the log—but how did she find out?'

Should I say? But when he thought about it, he'd probably come up with the same guess that I had. 'When did Maggie Mackwood join the syndicate's office?'

'Six months ago. About.'

'Just time. To fall for the boss, to get turned down because he doesn't go for girls, to act the Woman Spurned and tell Smith-Bang—anonymously—that he'd got hold of the log.'

'Well, I'm damned,' he said softly.

'But she couldn't have guessed what might happen. She must have gone through hell since. . . . That's why she was spending money on private detectives, trying to protect Fenwick's name, atone somehow. . . . I'd forget her, Willie.'

In an odd way, it was a cheerful ride. The whisky bottle was empty and Nygaard was full, for the moment, and telling Kari a few things she'd rather not have known about the night life in Pernambuco. But I spent most of my time studying the road map.

And outside, the snow thickened in the air swirling all about us.

The Byrkjedal crossroads wasn't exactly quite that; more a couple of road forks, with the few houses in between. The last fork gave us a choice of last night's route back into

Stavanger, or a half-made road around various lakes that fed on to the main road to Sardnes and Stavanger.

'You've never taken the left fork at Byrkjedal, have you?' I asked Willie.

'What?—no.' He was barely listening.

'Apart from Trond and the bloke whose right hand you *didn't* notice, did the other chap have a boxer's face?'

He flipped me a quick glance. 'You might say, yes.'

'Or like a military policeman?'

'Something like it.'

FORTY-FIVE

WE REACHED BYRKJEDAL just before the hour, with the snow swirling with real confidence and visibility down to about a hundred yards. We passed the first fork, a handful of houses, coming up to the second fork—and two cars parked on the right.

'Stop *behind* them!' I snapped. Willie pulled in about ten yards back.

Closest was the white Cortina, beyond that the Saab 99. Two men climbed out of the Cortina and stood carefully spaced across the road. Tanner and Kavanagh, of course.

Willie said: 'Were you expecting a second car, then?'

'More or less.' I pushed open my door and got out into the whirling snow, but keeping the door in front of me, and the derringer in my hand below its window level. Ahead of me, neither Tanner nor Kavanagh was showing a gun, but they weren't showing any hands, either. Just dark figures against a white kaleidoscope of snow.

Tanner called: 'Afternoon, Major. Things seem to have got a bit complicated.'

'All in the day's work,' I called back. 'By the way—was there really a security job for me if I'd stayed around in London?'

'Of course, Major. All fixed. You should have taken it.'

'I'm beginning to agree with you.'

'So no hard feelings?' he called—but not getting any closer. 'The lady just wants her witness back, and that's that, okay?'

'Fine. He's all yours. How do we do it—like the agents across the border bit?'

I could hear his laugh at that distance and through the snow. 'We're both been on those ones, eh, Major? Okay, get him started.'

I turned to the car. 'Get Nygaard out. Willie, stay there.' Without looking away, I reached back and pulled the seat-back forwards.

Nygaard oozed uncertainly out behind me.

And Kari followed. 'I am going with him.'

Willie blew up. 'You're *not*!'

'I came with him, I go with him.'

I said: 'She can try. They won't take her.'

She looked at me curiously, then started to help Nygaard across the patch of swirling whiteness towards the other cars. He seemed suddenly subdued inside his greatcoat with its glistening epaulets.

Tanner raised a hand and David got out of the Saab.

He moved uncertainly towards us, a topheavy figure in his thick parka jacket and passed Nygaard and Kari about midway between us, glancing at them, and then coming on.

Tanner and Kavanagh shifted out sideways to cover us . . .

. . . give me a gun, a real gun like both of them have got in their pockets, not some two-shot popgun that couldn't win a prize at a village fairground, and things would be different . . .

Nygaard and Kari passed the Cortina and went on to the Saab. As they reached it, Mrs Smith-Bang stepped out and waved at me. 'Hi, Jim.'

I raised my left hand. 'Everybody's bloody cheery about it all,' I muttered.

David came disconsolately past me, his parka hood down and the snow flecking his limp hair. 'I'm terribly sorry, sir—getting caught like that and messing things up.' And he honestly looked it, too.

'God, that doesn't matter. Did they hurt you?'

'Oh no. They didn't take much notice of me, really. But they know you.'

'Yes. Who's in which car?'

'When they caught me, it was that man Tanner and Trond —is that his name?—in the Cortina, and then we met Mrs Smith-Bang and the other man, Kavanagh, in the Saab. But now Trond's driving the Saab and the two British men are in the Cortina.'

Willie said impatiently: 'What the devil does that matter?'

'They spread the guns for the search, now they're grouping them. What do you think it matters? Get in, David.'

He climbed into the back. Nygaard was clambering painfully into the Saab—and Kari being turned away. It looked as if she was arguing it, but then Tanner took her firmly by the shoulder and pushed her towards us. She walked sadly back.

The Saab suddenly bloomed white exhaust smoke and rushed away down the hill. Tanner and Kavanagh closed slowly in on the Cortina, but in no hurry to get started.

'When we go, Willie,' I said quietly, 'take the *left* fork. But we don't move until after they do.'

Kari came up and I held the seat forward for her. 'Why did they not want me to go?'

'Get in.'

I gave Tanner a half-wave-half-salute and went on leaning on the Volkswagen's door. He waved back, then he and Kavanagh climbed into the Cortina. It crawled slowly off down the right fork, leaving a square black patch in the thin smooth snow.

When they were out of sight, I swung aboard and said: 'Now go, Willie. I mean *go*.'

He went, all right, but he argued. 'I don't see what's the hurry, now, for heaven's sake——'

'Because those two goons are going to ambush us.'

'Oh, *really*, old boy. I mean, they could have gone for us just now, if they wanted to.'

'Yes, but we'd've ended up with bullet holes in us. *And* some

277

of them. This way, we can just drive neatly over a cliff and no questions asked.'

David said: 'But haven't they got what they want, now?'

'The logbook and Nygaard? Yes, *and* four witnesses to the way they got them. They know perfectly well the police'll have Nygaard away from them five minutes after we get down the hill. If we get down.'

Kari said: 'So that is why they did not want me.' She sounded more cheerful about it.

'That's right, love. They'd only have to have killed you separately, and this way it's easier. Wind it up, Willie.'

But he'd wound it up just about as far as it would go; the trouble was the road. It was weaving through some sharp uphill bends, and whatever there was under the new snow and old frozen stuff, it wasn't tarmac. The car bounded from rut to rut the engine whining-like a penned animal.

'How much more of this?' Willie asked.

I looked at the map. 'About twenty miles, but it can't be all this bad.'

I was right, too. A few hundred yards later it got very much worse.

We came over a small rise and started downhill—and suddenly there was nothing on our right. Just nothing. A void of swirling snow and it could have been a lake or a city or just nothing below it. And on the left, a sheer cliff that sometimes roofed us in, with the road cut along it like a one-sided tunnel.

Willie dropped down a gear and his hands were white on the steering wheel. '*What* did you say about somebody pushing us off a cliff, old boy? There was nothing like this on the other road.'

'There's those two gunslingers.' I looked back, but they weren't behind us. Yet.

The windscreen wipers wish-washed back and forth, piling up snow at the corners of the screen. Ahead, the cliff faded out at maybe fifty yards, and if something was coming the other way, we were going to hit it solid; Willie was way over on the left-hand side—except it wasn't really wide enough to have two sides.

278

After a time, David said timidly: 'Did you find out what you wanted from Mr Nygaard?' And when nobody said anything, he added: 'Oh, sorry.'

'Hell, we should be apologizing to you.'

Willie said: 'But there just wasn't anything in that log. Except the breakdown.'

David asked: 'Did he really escape from the burning ship, then?'

'Yes, but not from the engine-room. He was lying boozed on his bunk.'

'In his overcoat?' he asked.

Willie threw a quick glance at me and nearly lost the car.

I said slowly: 'How many overcoats would a chief engineer need?'

'Barely one. He wouldn't stand a bridge watch. He'd only need it when he went ashore.'

I nodded. 'He wasn't aboard. Not since Tallinn. The cops picked him up drunk there and slung him in jail—no, in one of those drying-out centres the Russian cities have for drunks. You can't get bailed from them; they keep you twenty-four hours no matter what. And the captain rang Bergen and she said sail without him.

'And when he got out of the coop they'd fly him home to Norway—probably planned to put him back aboard at Kristiansand, they'd got plenty of time for that, and you'd never have known. Except *crunch*, the *Skadi*'s burnt out and they have to stage a fake rescue instead. But no bloody wonder she wanted to see that log and make sure it didn't mention him being missing. I bet *that* invalidates your policy.'

'If you can prove it.'

'There must be some record in Tallinn. It'll take time to spring it loose, but what are lawyers for? Oh—he gave me the full name of the firm or whatever. At least I got that, Hucks and Thornton.'

'No,' he said suddenly, remembering. 'Not H *and* Thornton, but H *versus* Thornton. A case back in 1815; it decided a Lloyd's policy only works if the ship's properly manned.'

Kari said icily: 'If he was not on the burning boat how did his hands become burnt?'

'Oh blast,' Willie said sadly. 'He *must* have been aboard, after all.'

I said: 'I can think of other ways of getting burns on a man's hands. Ways that'd be a sight more likely to give him a screaming fear of fire—if he'd half woken up while they were doing it to him.'

'No!' she shouted. 'They could not do that!'

'They can kill three men, shoot me full of drugs and try to kill us now. Don't tell me what they *can't* do.'

Willie said: 'But you can't just turn a—a blowtorch or something on a man, you might kill him, and then you'd need to give him medical attention . . .' His voice trailed off.

'Useful chap, Doctor Rasmussen,' I said. 'But I suppose he was wearing a surgical mask so Nygaard doesn't remember him.'

David said: 'I think there's a car behind us.'

FORTY-SIX

COMING OUT of the next bend, we were sure of it. Two headlights showing briefly, maybe seventy yards back.

'Wind it up, Willie.'

'What the devil d'you think I'm doing?' He was doing fine, really, hanging the car on the very edge of control and keeping it there. But a Volkswagen isn't a Jaguar. It isn't even a Cortina, and their one had been the GT with the wide radial tyres.

On the next straight it simply walked up behind us—and its lights went off. An honest car would have put its lights on at that point.

'How long does this sort of road go on?' Willie asked grimly.

I looked at Kari. 'I do not know it so well—but I think until we go down to the lake.'

'You aren't joking.' We were winding gently, very gently, downhill—but the void on our right could still have been a hole right through the world.

Willie slowed into a left-hand turn with the centrifugal force shoving us out, out, out. . . . And the Cortina nosed in to our left and *clang*.

The Volks twitched and slid and the void rushed in beneath us—and then we were sliding the other way and scraping along the cliff itself.

'Christ!' Willie fought the wheel steady. We straightened up.

The Cortina cruised around the bend fifteen yards behind us.

David was braced against the rear corner, white faced but tight-lipped. Kari's expression was sheer puzzlement. People like Tanner and Kavanagh just weren't in her book of rules.

Willie said: 'For God's sake, man, if you're ever going to use a gun, why not now?'

'Yes.' But I only had six rounds left—and damn little good they'd be to me falling down, down, down into that swirling emptiness a couple of feet to my right. I took the derringer from my sleeve, wound my window down. A cold hurricane rushed in.

Maybe they should institute a new class for pistol competition: offhand from a moving vehicle at another moving vehicle, to be shot on winding mountain roads in a snowstorm. And from a right-hand seat which means you have to twist your body right round and lay your arm out along the car. Probably it would be won by the actors who play in FBI movies. Certainly not by me.

I could only fire slightly right of straight backwards, so only on a right-hand curve—the inside bends where centrifugal force shoved us safely towards the rock wall on our left.

The moment I stretched out my arm, the Cortina checked and dropped back. Tanner—it had to be him driving—knew exactly what I was doing, and he had a pretty good idea what gun I was doing it with.

I fired one, but God knows where to.

Then we were slowing into another left-hander and the Cortina closing up and out of my line of fire. They touched us again, but this time Willie accelerated into the curve on a prayer that it wouldn't go on too long. It didn't. Just as the front wheels started to go, he could flip the wheel across. We rocked but straightened. The Cortina came around much slower and twenty yards back—but he could pick up those yards any time he wanted to.

A straight bit, then a gentle right-hander and I stretched my arm and fired again. But he was a good thirty yards behind. He didn't need to be close except on the left-hand bends where I couldn't shoot anyway.

'Oh hell,' I said. 'This is getting ridiculous. Drop me off around the next corner.'

'Do *what*?'

'Drop me off. We'll try a little justice instead of mere truth. But then go like buggerit.'

He gave a faint brief smile and nodded. 'All right, old boy. After the next left-hander.'

I reloaded the derringer and put it back in the arm clip. I might need both hands when I jumped.

Then we were coming through a reverse S, from a right-hand curve to a sharp left under an overhang of solid rock.

'Here?' Willie suggested.

'It'll do.'

'Of course,' he said thoughtfully, '*they* don't know this road any better than I do.'

He handled it beautifully. The Cortina closed up as we came into the straight between the two bends of the S.

Willie rammed on the brakes, far earlier than Tanner could have expected. If he'd been telepathic, he could have shunted us straight ahead—and straight over the edge of the corner. But he wasn't planning that for another ten yards; now he instinctively stamped the brakes. The Cortina's nose dug in, wiggled, hit us—but by then we were accelerating away in first and he was sliding to a stop in third.

We went around the corner with the engine screaming like a siren under Willie's foot. Then we were straight and he